EXTRAORDINARY ACCLAIM FOR
HUSH

"A well-crafted and sophisticated psychological thriller that captures in frightening detail the fevered inner life of a psychopath. Elegant and darkly powerful."
—Vincent Bugliosi, author of
Helter Skelter and *Outrage*

"A taut wire of a thriller."   —*Seattle Post-Intelligencer*

"A striking debut . . . Nykanen's writing style, skill at characterization and sense of irony make HUSH [a] first-rate story."   —*Portland Oregonian*

"The pace is pulsing and the terror of a woman fighting for her life is so real that it is impossible to put this book down . . . This well-written novel is highly recommended."
—*Library Journal*

"Chet Boyce is a terrific creation, a dangerously insane fellow who . . . is drawn with such precision that he seems not only real but chillingly familiar."   —*Booklist*

"Fans of deep-rooted psychological drama that digs into the essence of the mind and even deeper than that will find this the ideal book. HUSH is a unique, tremendous characterization study that dives into the guts of a psychopath and the fearful relationships he causes with the people he directly and indirectly affects."
—Harriet Klausner for *BookBrowser*

"Nykanen's first novel, HUSH, is a blood-drenched, compelling variation on Thomas Harris' *The Silence of the Lambs*."   —*New Times L.A.*

more . . .

P9-CFF-157

HUSH

MARK NYKANEN

St. Martin's Paperbacks

HUSH

Copyright © 1998 by Mark Nykanen.

Cover photograph by Herman Estevez.

Library of Congress Catalog Card Number: 97-37120

ISBN: 0-312-96852-3

Printed in the United States of America

St. Martin's Press hardcover edition / March 1998
St. Martin's Paperbacks edition / March 1999

10 9 8 7 6 5 4 3 2 1

FOR LUCINDA SUZANNE TAYLOR

ACKNOWLEDGMENTS

I thank Monique McClean, MAAT, ATR, who spent many hours sharing her expertise in art therapy; and Catherine Zangar, Dale Dauten, Mark Feldstein, and Lucinda Suzanne Taylor, who provided ongoing criticism and counsel.

I'm also grateful to the following readers for their thoughts: Deanna Foster-Joyer, John Joyer, Bud Murphy, Peggy Dills Kelter, Sally LaVenture, Eric Bucy, Steve Saylor, Kevin Donald, Aina Josefsson, and Deborah Phillips.

Special thanks to my agent, Theron Raines, and to my editor, Jennifer Weis.

Davy Boyce climbed on top of another gray stump and fired again. Each time he shot his imaginary pistol he used both hands, just like a real detective; and each time he pulled the trigger he said, "Pow-pow, you're dead," just like a little boy.

As he jumped down to the dusty ground, ready to shoot anything that moved, he heard his mother calling him.

"Davy, come here. Your daddy's going to be home in a few minutes."

"He's not my daddy," Davy muttered, but his mom couldn't hear him because she was folding laundry by the old silver trailer a good acre away.

Davy aimed toward the road and fired one more time. A moment later, "You're dead" unsettled the still air.

He headed back to his mom through a sea of stumps and the long shadows thrown by the setting sun. She waited for him with the laundry basket propped on her hip, a plain-faced woman as worn and faded as her washed-out dress. She smiled at him, then shaded her eyes as she peered down the dirt road at her new husband rolling along in his old pickup. A dark cloud rose in his wake. October had come but summer had never ended, and the drought-stricken land of Idaho appeared as parched and brown as sunburned leather.

Davy slouched by his mother's side and listened to the distant rumble of Chet's truck. He didn't look up. He didn't need to. He could always sense the comings and goings of his stepfather. One he greeted with terror, the other with relief.

"I want my real daddy."

His mother put the laundry basket on a folding chair and crouched beside him. She rested her hands on his bony shoulders.

"Davy, you know your daddy's in heaven and you're not going to get to see him for a long, long time. But he's watching over you, and he wants you to be happy with your new *daddy. He wants you to play with him and have fun.''*

She ran her hand over his crew cut as she stood back up. They could now hear the rattle of the chain saw that huddled in the bed of the pickup among the wood chips and bark, like some dirty animal that makes its nest wherever it can.

''I don't like to play with him. He hurts me.'' Davy spoke with his eyes still on the ground, the earth that would shake whenever Chet walked by.

''You just don't like to be tickled, that's all. I'll talk to him about that.''

''No, Mom, it's not the tickling. I told you and told you, he hurts me. He hurts me bad.''

He tugged on her dress to turn her away from the truck, which had started up the short stretch of logging road that ended at their trailer. Davy pointed to the front of his pants.

''He hurts me right here. Inside. He does. And also my—'' The boy froze when the pickup braked and the door flew open. Chet sauntered up.

His mother turned to him, and the skin around her eyes wrinkled, like the sun might have been too bright all of a sudden; but there was no sun in her eyes, just the shadow of her husband with his hard handsome features.

He smiled and gave them a big hello.

''Hey, how's my guy?''

He patted Davy's butt, and she pulled the boy aside.

''Wait a second.'' She put up her hand to stop him. ''He just told me that you've been hurting him. He pointed to the front of his pants. What's going on?''

''Don't be silly.'' Chet spoke gently and his smile never strayed as he patted Davy's rear again.

''No, please, stop that.'' She pushed his hand away. ''I'm not being silly. I want to know what's going on.''

Chet looked up at her slowly, and his words came out soft as dust.

''You do, do you?''

She nodded, and Davy clung to her dress.

''We'd better go inside and talk.'' He shook his head sadly, but when he spoke again his voice stiffened, like a steel spine now ran through every word: ''Yeah, you better get inside, both of you.''

She backed away, but he grabbed her elbow and rammed her through the door. He jerked Davy up the steps so fast the boy stumbled into the dim, narrow room. Chet pushed him onto the couch, and turned around slowly. Her furious voice filled the momentary hush that followed.

"Don't you dare treat my son like that!"

Chet never replied. He glanced down as he made a fist, and she lunged for the door handle; but as she reached for it he grabbed the back of her dress so hard the fabric tore. Davy heard the seams explode—pop-pop-pop-pop-pop—and the way she cried Chet's name, like that might make him stop. But it didn't.

He spun her around and gripped her shoulders tightly, and Davy thought maybe he was going to give her a good talking-to. But Chet hissed in her face, "It's all over, don't you see?" and jerked down the front of her dress. This time the boy didn't hear any popping sounds, just saw the blue-and-white fabric rushing away from her skin.

Chet turned from the sight of her breasts and fixed his eyes on Davy, who was hugging his knees on the battered couch. He warned him not to move. Davy couldn't move, not any-more. When Chet grabbed his mom and ripped her dress, the boy lost his breath. His daddy had told him that a man never hurts a woman. Never, he'd repeated. But Chet did. It left Davy all hollow inside, like a thing that can't eat, that gets eaten instead.

"Cover up!" Chet roared at her. "The boy, damn it."

She hesitated, and Davy thought, Hurry, hurry; but she didn't, and that's when Chet punched her head so hard it sank into the wall like she'd hit a cushion or a pillow. Davy saw her drop to her knees and pitch forward, and the hole in his belly grew as large as the world.

"Get up!" Chet yelled.

She raised her face off the floor, but when she looked down and saw the red drips on the linoleum, she paused.

"Up!" he screamed.

Again she hesitated, and once more Davy thought, Hurry, hurry; but she didn't, and that's when Chet grabbed her hair and dragged her to her feet.

She looked at her son as Chet forced her over to the sink,

and spoke to him in a strangled voice. "Davy, go on, get out of here."

Chet bellowed, *"Don't you move!"* as he dragged her over to the door and locked it with his free hand.

"He doesn't need to see this." It was a voice Davy had never heard before, like she was hurt and scared and angry all at the same time.

"Yeah, he does. He needs to see exactly what happens when he opens his big mouth."

Davy stared at the lock as he heard those words. There was no way out. Not for her, not for him. Not ever.

When he looked at his mom again, Chet had her back at the sink with a razor pressed against her neck. He whispered fiercely in her ear, like a man who doesn't want to be heard one moment but couldn't care less the next.

"I'm going to tell you a secret. It's the last one you'll ever hear. You listening? 'Cause it's a good one."

She nodded, as if to humor him and buy time; but each movement brushed her neck against the blade and left fine lines of blood on her pale skin.

As he started to speak Chet leaned even closer to her and his hips twitched back and forth, like his whole body was working up to something.

"I married you . . . for the boy." He looked over at Davy. *"You watching? You watching?"* His voice cracked with excitement as she struggled to break free. *"You're old and ugly, but he's smooth."* Chet tried to draw out that last syllable— s-m-o-o-t-h—but his voice betrayed him and trembled, and his body continued to quake.

He tightened his grip and steadied himself. *"I've had a whole string of you and Davys. What do you think of that?"*

She started to say something, then stopped. Frantically, and for the last time, Davy thought, Hurry, hurry; but she didn't say anything at all, and that's when the razor finally moved.

"No!" Davy screamed, *"no, no, no!"* He screamed it over and over, until his words fell to whispers and his whispers to silence and his hands clasped his mouth and he heard only her body dropping heavily to the trailer floor.

Davy's hands collapsed to his legs. His lips still moved—

no, no, no—but their sounds had slipped away.

Chet's head swung slowly toward him, and he locked his dark eyes on the boy. Right then Davy knew Chet would always be there watching him, never letting go.

1

Celia took off her smock and draped it over a chair, happy to shed the extra layer. The heat was starting to get to her, and she knew she'd better quit. Her Sunday-morning session at her easel had ended. As she walked out of her studio she glanced at the wall to her left, which was covered with children's art, and smiled at her growing collection.

Jack was no longer in the living room where she'd left him with the newspaper, what, two hours ago? That long, really? She wandered out the front door and found it just as stifling outside as it was in the house, then walked around the corner of the deck to the bathroom window. Last weekend he'd painted the inside trim, but hadn't taken the time to scrape the splatters off the glass. He said he'd clean them up today, and it looked as if he'd finished the job, but where was he? She had trouble seeing in because of the sunlight on the screen.

"Jack?"

She heard him quickly fold up the paper. "Yeah?"

"We better get moving on this. I'm going to go on down to the tank."

"Okay, I'll be right there."

They had put off the fire drill for months, and she wanted to inspect the equipment and check the water supply before the temperature topped one hundred. The sun already burned directly overhead, and the trees offered little shade. The day was turning into a real scorcher. Smoky, too. Half of Oregon seemed to be in flames. Nothing but forest fires and drought from one end of the state to the other. Land as dry as a biscuit.

Celia and Jack Griswold lived on an exposed ridge twenty minutes from Bentman, far outside the reach of the town's modest fire department. But they thought the inconveniences—even the dangers—were worth the solitude and the view. The Bentman River Valley spread out almost two thousand feet below them, and wherever they looked they saw irrigated orchards, mountains, streams, and rivers.

But they could also see thousands of acres of clear-cuts—more of them every year—and even on a hazy day big brown gaping holes appeared in the green fabric of the land, dead spaces, like abandoned buildings, where nothing much lived.

Celia walked down their well-rutted driveway, lined on her right by brittle grass and growths of scraggly scrub oak, and on her left by a row of young firs that looked like neatly trimmed Christmas trees. But when she stopped and rubbed the needles, they crumbled in her hand.

She looked up at the gray pall that hung over the valley.

"Where there's smoke, there's fire." Jack caught up to her. "That's from the big forest fire near Portland. Seven thousand acres so far."

Celia nodded. "Seems like half the state is burning. Let's make sure everything is still working."

They brushed past the branches of one of the young firs and made their way around bushes and trees to a large wooden cover that seemed to hover inches above the dry grass. It capped a round tank that had been sunk deep into the ground. The tank measured eight feet across and could store enough water to fight a serious blaze. A short weathered wooden shelter stood nearby. It housed a motor about twice the size of a lawn mower's, and a long thick hose that looked exactly like the cream-colored ones Celia had seen stacked neatly on the backs of fire trucks. Only, Jack and Celia's hose wasn't stacked neatly; it had been tossed onto the motor like a tangled net, and Celia had a pretty good idea why.

"Jack, when was the last time you checked this?"

He shrugged. "I don't know. I guess it's been a while. I'll take care of it."

"I can help," Celia said cheerfully. She really didn't mind. She knew she needed a certain amount of physical activity, especially on weekends. It was such a welcome escape from the emotional demands of the work-week. Yesterday, for instance, when Jack went into his insurance agency to catch up on some claims, she hiked up Mount Bentman—a good five-hour effort—and later today, when it cooled off a bit, she might hit the trails near their house.

But now they had to deal with the hose. She and Jack hauled all of it out of the housing, then carefully laid it back in place.

As she bent over to check the gas can, she heard Jack lift up the cover of the tank and swear.

"Come over here and get a load of this."

He pointed to more than a dozen dead rats floating on the surface of the water, which had receded a good six or seven feet.

"God, that's disgusting. They're huge. I've never seen rats that big."

"They're just bloated from the water. You would be too if you'd been down there that long."

"That's a horrible thought."

"What's that?"

"Being stuck down there. How long do you think they've been there?"

"Who knows?" Jack stared at the rotting rats. "I guess they drowned."

"That's a safe assumption." She laughed and squeezed her husband's shoulder affectionately before looking back into the tank. "There sure has been a lot of evaporation. The water level has gone way down."

"My guess is the drought forced them to try and get something to drink, but once they fell in they couldn't get out." He nodded at the slick black plastic walls. "Now, Christ, I guess we've got to do it for them."

"How about a shovel? We could scoop them out." She thought it might work but Jack threw her a skeptical look.

"What about a crab net? Do we have one of those?" Celia knew that would be perfect. She had used one as a little girl to catch crabs all along the docks of her hometown. They were crafty little red-and-yellow creatures with dark beady eyes that stared up at you through the oil-streaked water. They had quick stubby legs and could scramble under the pilings so fast that if you didn't scoop them up on the first pass, they disappeared.

Even so, she'd caught quite a few of them and dumped

their struggling bodies into a bucket. Sometimes they hung on to the net as if they were holding on for dear life, and she'd had to take a rock or a stick and beat them till they let go. As the pail started to fill, they'd fight and tear off one another's legs. That would really get to her, the way they'd hold up their pincers as if they were showing off their bloody prize. Then they'd start fighting all over again—when there was fresh meat to steal.

"A crab net? Sure, Cel, it's right over there by the shrimp boat." Jack laughed with good humor, much as his wife had moments ago.

"Okay, okay, but we've got to get them out or they might get sucked up into the line." She nodded at the black intake line running down the far side of the tank.

"No, they won't." He rubbed drops of perspiration off his upper lip. "There's a wire cage over the end of that thing."

"Still . . ." Her voice faltered as she placed her hands on her hips. With short brown hair and pretty features, Celia could have been the girl next door, if there had been a next door.

"Yes, I know," he sighed.

"I've got it!" She clapped her hands once, startling Jack. "We can fill up the tank, and then we can drag them out with the rake and shovel."

"Yeah, that ought to do it," he agreed without much enthusiasm.

They linked together two fifty-foot lengths of green garden hose and turned on the faucet. Celia could hear faint splashing sounds as they went inside to get a drink.

Their house was attractive—single-level cedar—and had three bedrooms, the smallest of which she used as her studio. Her favorite haunt for just hanging out was the living room. It had a cathedral ceiling with massive beams and a blue-enameled woodstove. The color matched the tile in the adjoining kitchen, which easily accommodated a full-sized antique oak table and chairs. Jack propped himself on one of them and yawned as Celia rooted in the refrigerator.

"Would you grab me a beer?" He sat down.

"Sure."

She handed him a tall-necked bottle and poured herself

some mineral water, which she doused with a splash of cranberry juice. The dark liquid blossomed into a pink cloud as it drifted to the bottom of the glass.

Celia took a deep, satisfying drink, and almost spilled the bubbly concoction on her cotton top. She quickly wiped away a dribble running down her chin, and tried mightily to put aside any thoughts of the rats because more than anything she wanted to make love. She'd been thinking about it all weekend. She was pretty sure she was ovulating, and if they were ever going to have children they'd have to make the most of these moments.

"How long do you think we should let those hoses go?"

"I think an hour ought to do it." Jack sipped his beer and looked dreamily out the window.

Celia sat down and slid her hand across the table and toyed with his wedding band. "That ought to be enough time, don't you think?"

She imagined his warm damp lips on her neck and ears and felt the first flush of arousal. It was true Jack had put on some weight over the years, but his blond hair remained rich and full and his smile still unsettled her in a pleasing way. Besides, she wanted to be held and hugged, and she wanted the rougher edges too.

He glanced at her. "What do you mean?"

She wondered why he was proving so difficult, but carried on despite her misgivings.

"I got a special-mail order, and I thought you might like to open the package and see what's inside."

He looked around the room, as though he might find a parcel suddenly appearing amid their well-ordered surroundings.

"Where is it?"

She took a deep breath and stood up.

"It's right under here." She lifted her top just high enough to give him a glimpse of the pink lace. "And here." Her hands slipped inside the waistband of her shorts and slid them down slowly, seductively, until the sheer front panel of her panties appeared, bold and revealing in the sunlight. "From your favorite catalog, Victoria's Secret."

Jack groaned, and her heart sank.

"I'm sorry, Cel, but Victoria's going to have to keep her secrets to herself today. I'm too hot and tired to move."

She sat back down and stared at her glass. When she looked up, her inviting smile was gone.

"Look, we haven't made love in weeks, and once again it's that time of the month when all systems are on go. If we don't go for it today, we'll probably miss another month." Her arms crossed her chest, as if she were cold all of a sudden. "It's always one thing or another with you lately. Do you want kids or don't you?"

He looked away as he talked. "Yes, I want kids very much, but I don't find looking at a bunch of rats very romantic—"

"No, I can understand that, but—"

"And I'm hot and tired and it's been nothing but chores all day long. I need a break."

"Wait a minute, did you just say chores?" This stunned Celia, that making love to her should fall so casually into such a dreary category. "Thanks a lot."

"That's not—"

"I love being grouped along with scraping paint off the windows and cleaning up a bunch of dead rats." Her eyebrows, dark brown like her hair, rose and fell with her words.

Jack shook his head slowly. "I didn't say that. You're twisting it all around."

"No, I'm not. That's exactly what you said."

"Well, it's not what I meant."

She took a long swallow of her watered-down juice and tried to calm down. The thought of making love had made her nipples flutter to life like two little birds, but now they embarrassed her with their brazenness. She felt awkward sitting there as Jack once again stared out the window.

Another moment of uneasiness passed before he stood up and carried his beer into the living room. She watched him sink into the couch and pick his way through the remains of the paper. Her skin dampened from the heat of his humbling indifference and the flood of footlights she now trained on her every imagined flaw. The bathroom with its cool shower beckoned.

She saw the single-edge razor lying on the vanity, with

dried paint curled along its length, and stared at it for several seconds. Last weekend they'd painted the inside trim but hadn't bothered to scrape off the splatters. Jack had said he'd clean them up.

"Are you through with the window, because—"

"Yeah, I'm done," he shouted back; "you can put it away."

She brushed the shavings into the wastebasket, then noticed a paint drip left on the window and scraped it off. She dusted the razor once more and placed it in the cabinet below the sink.

As she stood back up she looked into the full-length mirror on the back of the door and stepped out of her shorts and top. She unhooked her bra and slipped out of her panties with far less fanfare than she had anticipated when she put them on. After laying aside her clothing, she scrutinized herself.

More than Jack's distance came into play here. Last month she had turned thirty-eight, and even though she considered it entirely unliberated she looked for the physical signs of decline that usually began to appear on the downhill side of the fourth decade. The sweaty humiliation that had beaded on her face and arms minutes ago now cooled, and she looked at herself candidly. She did not feel too abused by the experience.

Yes, I'm thirty-eight, and yes, I'm not quite what I used to be, but—her eyes moved up and down her body—things could be worse. A cheerfulness flickered, and an irrepressible good-naturedness soon smiled at the silliness of standing there. She thought of how she was approaching the autumn of her life, and consoled herself by quipping that at least the leaves hadn't started to fall. She did regard her breasts suspiciously, as if they might let her down if she placed too much confidence in them. They were small, but hardly absent, and her nipples—damn them!—were still erect as church spires. She considered herself fortunate to have been poorly endowed. She hadn't always felt so lucky. As a teenager she envied the larger cups of her classmates and had noticed the way the boys eyed them too, but after a period of almost ceaseless breast-building exercises ("We must, we must . . .'') she gave up and resigned herself to her diminutive status.

The braless seventies had been her first real hint that maybe small was indeed beautiful, and every year since had reinforced this opinion. She wore a bra to work for the sake of modesty, and she wore more suggestive styles at home for precisely the opposite reason. Not that it had done much good lately. She suffered her resentment of Jack briefly, and then her fingers threaded down through the dark hairs below her pale little belly.

She turned from the mirror to the tub with its promise of simple fulfillment. The window shade was up, and beyond the tile the tall pines stood. She leaned over and turned on the faucets for the bath; and now both of her hands were wet and warm, the one that touched herself and the one that tested the water.

She sat down and scooted close to the delightful pressure that spilled and puddled and warmed her bottom. She lay back, and as her heels climbed the cool ceramic wall she inched forward until her open legs welcomed the steady pulse that poured from the spout. She reached to turn up the hot water just a little and took a momentary pride in the neat tensioning of her stomach muscles. When she leaned back they relaxed, and the soothing flow soon warmed her entire body.

2

Filthy streams of sweat poured off of Chet's bare chest and pockmarked the dusty earth. He'd been digging for going on two hours, but the hole still looked only about half as deep as he knew it ought to be. The damn drought had leeched out every last drop of moisture and left the dirt as dry as adobe and as dense as concrete.

He straightened his aching back, grabbed the pickax, and tried to make himself work faster. He felt too damn exposed at the moment. Not that he expected any company out here—only six or seven people had drifted by all summer—but stranger things had happened and he wanted to finish that hole, finish with her, and get the hell out of Idaho.

Again he raised the pickax and drove it straight down, crumbling the earth. When he had broken up enough of it to make it worth his while, he put the shovel to work.

The kid was no goddamn help at all, just sitting on that stump and not saying a word. Hadn't said boo since last night, just sitting and stewing and staring. Chet had a mind to smash her face with the pickax just to get a rise out of him, but he had a lot of experience with young boys and knew they could be vindictive as hell. They could also be sweet, very sweet.

"What's the matter, cat still got your tongue?"

He chuckled as he leaned on the shovel, but the boy wouldn't even look at him. Time to take a breather. He had to, his back was killing him.

He hauled himself out of the hole. He figured he'd better get started on little Davy right now, bring him around, make him understand. You had to make them believe in you. One way or another, you had to do that.

"Hey, move over."

The boy didn't budge, so he shoved him with his hip until he'd made a space for both of them on the stump. Then he touched Davy's shoulder tenderly. The boy drew back but Chet tried not to take these things personally.

"Come on, Davy, you can talk to me. Are you angry 'cause of your mom?" Chet spoke softly and slowly. "You know I didn't want to have to do that but you made me do it. Remember how I said that if you ever tell your mommy what we do she's going to die, and then you went ahead and told her anyway and now she's dead." Chet pointed to the body lying under a blue tarp a few feet from the hole. He got up and walked over to it and drew back the cover. "Look at her, Davy. Come on, take a *good* look. See, she's dead." He left her uncovered body baking in the sun and returned to the boy's side. "I know it's sad but you killed your mom by telling her those secrets. That's what happened, just as sure as you're sitting here with me. You killed her, not me. Now, come on, shake it off. I could use the help of a big strong boy like you."

But Davy wouldn't move. Chet knew it would be a struggle to make him work, and he sure had his hands full at the moment. He stared at the unfinished hole and felt sorry for himself. Then his eyes settled on her, and he clapped Davy on the back because it occurred to him that every cloud really did have a silver lining.

"Maybe it's just as well that you're not talking." He started back to the hole. " 'Cause if you ever do talk about your mom, Davy, you'll end up dead too, and that's a promise. And you know," he added cheerfully as he jumped into the hole, "that I'm a man of my word."

The boy still wouldn't look at him, even after he'd given him five minutes of his time, and that drained Chet's good humor in a matter of seconds and made him want to smash that pickax right into her face, just like he'd been thinking about doing before. Get even with the kid.

But he knew that restraint counted for something in this life so he didn't hit her with the pickax. No, he didn't do that. Instead, he pitched a shovelful of earth up into the air, high as he could. Then he watched those dirt clods rain down and explode into little dust bombs all over her bloody face and chest.

Davy flinched. Chet smiled. He was feeling good all over again.

3

Celia and Jack stared at the black water in the tank. The level had risen but still remained about three feet from the top.

"Good enough," he declared.

Celia shook her wet hair and held up her hand.

"Wait a second, Jack. Where are they?"

"What?"

"What do you mean, 'what?' The rats, the rats, what else?" She pointed to the smooth surface. "They're gone. Did you get them out while I was showering?"

"No, you saw, I was inside reading the paper. Maybe they sank from the pressure of all the water we put in."

But Celia didn't buy that. "I don't think so. We didn't even put that much in."

Jack wiped his brow. "It's going to be pretty tough to fish them out if we can't even see them."

"Now I wish we really did have a crab net."

He shook his head. "It's pretty deep down there, Cel. You'd have to have a really long handle."

"So what are we going to do, just leave them in there?"

Jack shrugged and pulled out the hose. "I don't know. We'll think of something. Let's bag it for now, I've had enough."

Later that night, as Celia lay in bed, she thought of the rats and the fire drill they never ran. But as soon as she brought it up Jack patted her on the hip and spoke in a sleepy voice.

"Forget about it, hon. I promise you the house is not going to burn down."

"Wait a second. Lots of houses burn down. If they didn't

burn down, you'd never sell any fire insurance. This one could too, and you know it.''

"The odds against it are tremendous, Cel, okay? So just relax.''

Jack rolled over and bunched the pillow up under his head. Celia glanced at his back, then stared at the window right above the bed. The night sky was coming to life. She saw the sliver of moon, the stars too, and the vast empty spaces that filled the world with darkness.

4

Davy woke to the static on the radio. His stepfather was playing with the silver dial as he drove. The trailer also made a racket every time they bounced over another tarry seam in the old cement.

"We're on the back roads, Davy boy." Chet had seen the kid grab the door handle to steady himself. "Let me see if I can't find a station." His fingers worked the dial until he pulled in a clear signal.

A man's deep voice boomed, ". . . to KLOG Country, Bentman, Oregon, where every day is Earth Day. Timberrrrr."

Davy listened to a tree falling. It sounded so real he sat up and looked out the window before realizing it was just the radio.

"Fooled you, didn't they?" Chet laughed.

They drove down into a wide valley. The boy could just make out houses scattered here and there in the woods, old places that didn't look cared for. That's what his real daddy used to say. "They don't care. If they did, they wouldn't live like that." Davy wondered what he'd say about Chet's trailer.

He spotted the sign for Bentman on the shoulder of the road. Green with white letters: "Pop 2,493 Founded 1896 Elevation 180 feet."

"Bentman, I like the sound of that." Chet's words competed with a tire commercial. "And hey, it looks like they've got lots of trees around here." His eyes roved over the walls of the Bentman River Valley, which resembled a patchwork quilt of clear-cuts. "And it looks like they left some for me."

Davy tried not to listen. Chet made his head buzz with all kinds of noise, like the static on the radio. Nothing made sense.

A pickup roared past them, and Davy glimpsed a bumper sticker. "I like Spotted Owls . . . fried." He wondered what they tasted like. He'd never eaten owl. Maybe like chicken. That's what people were always saying about weird kinds of food, tastes . . . like . . . chicken. But everything couldn't taste like chicken. Except maybe owls really did.

Chet slapped the steering wheel when he saw that bumper sticker. "Yeah, I think I'm going to like it here. What do you say we find a place to set up the trailer? Somewhere without a lot of people around?"

They drove through downtown Bentman, past a gas station, an insurance agency, a bank, two clothing stores, a pharmacy, and a couple of gun shops. Davy knew Chet would be stopping there sooner or later. And a True Value Hardware with chain saws in the window. There too.

But Chet didn't do any shopping in Bentman today. He stayed on the road as it curved south of town along a narrow rock-lined river. Davy hoped they'd never find a campsite. He just wanted to ride on and on until he was home again.

He saw himself holding his mother's and father's hands and heard them singing, "One-two-three!" as they swung him into the air. He could feel his legs pumping as he flew higher and higher. But then his daddy died, and now his mom was gone too. He'd already forgotten how that happened. Just that she was gone. His memory was like a blotter that could soak up all the blood and make it go away.

But not the hunger for home. No, never that.

5

Celia was shuffling over to the automatic coffee-maker when something alive and furry brushed against her bare leg. She gasped and jumped away so quickly that her hip hit the kitchen counter and her heart thumped madly. But it was just Pluto, her ancient one-eyed cat.

"Jesus, you scared me!" She put her hand on her chest to calm herself.

But she knew it wasn't Pluto that had scared her so, it was the rat dreams she'd had all night long—rats in the tank, rats in the house, rats all over her bed, rats all over *her*. What a night.

She picked up her cat and nuzzled his neck as she murmured to him. "You'll keep those rats away, won't you?" She felt his motor start right up. "Who said black cats are bad luck? We've been plenty lucky since you showed up."

"I'd say he's the lucky one, finding you." Jack trudged into the kitchen in his bathrobe and made his way over to the coffeepot. "You want some?" He held up a cup.

"Sure, thanks."

Pluto purred some more as Celia stroked the back of his head and let him out the door. They'd found him the day they moved into their new home on the ridge. What a sight he'd been: ears scarred and crusted with blood from fighting, a patch of fur missing from one of his flanks, and an infected right eye that was sealed shut and oozed pus.

"Christ, what is it?" Jack had sputtered when the black cat tottered toward them. "I hope to God it's not some kind of omen."

Pluto heard Jack's voice and moved in his direction.

"Holy shit, get that thing away from me." Jack jumped up onto the newly stained deck, visibly disturbed by the disfigured cat; but Celia's heart had gone out to Pluto, and she'd taken him to a vet. The eyeball had to be removed—it was wormy and smelled—but vitamins had taken care of his bald spot and castrating him had turned Pluto into a peaceful, and at times even playful, cat. If the spirit moved him he would chase a string or bat a ball around, and his hunting instincts had kept the house mostly free of pests, an achievement Celia hadn't fully appreciated until she'd seen all those rats.

She poured herself a bowl of cereal as Jack headed back to the bathroom, but just as she opened the utensil drawer she heard Pluto hissing loudly and a dog barking. A dog?

She hurried back to the door and spotted a Border collie looking up at her cat, whose back was arched and whose tail had turned into a Christmas tree, as he stood on the woodpile.

But Celia didn't think the black-and-white dog appeared very threatening. If he really wanted to give chase he could have climbed up after Pluto, but instead contented himself with an occasional bark accompanied by a wagging tail, as if he hadn't the heart really to hassle a cat.

She opened the door and called him over to her. She also alerted her husband.

"Jack, take a look at this; we've got another visitor."

She crouched down and turned her attention back to the dog, patting her thigh and urging the funny-looking animal to come to her. He did have a most peculiar face. It was split right down the middle by his two-tone coloring, and he had a noticeable overbite, as if he'd been inbred. But he looked so sweet. Surely he wouldn't bite. Celia talked softly to him and patted her thigh. "Come on, come on. What are you doing out here all by yourself?"

Jack walked back in the kitchen. "Begging for a bone, a home, and the easy life. Christ, sometimes I wish I was a pet."

Celia ignored him because the dog was now approaching her slowly, perhaps a little wary but with its tail still wagging.

"That's it, come on." When he stood inches away she commanded him to sit, and he did. His tail continued to swish back and forth, dusting the deck.

"Good boy!" As she said this the animal reached up with

his paw, and she delighted in slapping it with her palm. "High five, okay!"

She looked over her shoulder at Jack. "What should we name him?"

He bent over and made a show of studying the dog's unusual face. "How about . . . Bucky, in honor of those *handsome* choppers?"

Before she could respond, Jack shook his head, as if waking up. "What am I saying? Forget it. No way. I'm dropping him off at the pound on my way to work, which is just what the jerk who dropped him off up here should've done in the first place."

Celia's hand froze on the dog's head, and she looked at her husband with alarm.

"No, you can't do that. They kill them. And besides, look how friendly he is."

Indeed, the dog was now cuddling right up to Celia and resting his chin on her thigh.

"Come on, Cel, you've got to train them."

"Don't be silly, he's already trained."

"And clean up their shit—"

"We've got lots of space."

"And I'll bet he comes loaded with lots of land mines."

"*I'll* bet he has great personal habits."

"Listen to me, Cel, I don't want a dog. You've got a cat, and besides, I'm allergic to them. Their fur makes me itchy as hell."

"Wait a second." Celia looked at him closely. "Since when are you allergic to dogs? I've known you for almost ten years and I've never heard you say that."

"Trust me, dogs make me itchy. Hell, they make themselves itchy. Haven't you ever noticed how most of the time they're either licking their balls or scratching themselves?"

Jack panted and scratched himself like a dog, and Celia couldn't help but laugh.

"Come on, you're being silly again."

"All right, but now I'm being serious. I don't want a dog, really."

"We could use one, living alone up here, especially with you starting to travel so much."

Jack sighed, which Celia took as a possible sign of surrender, and turned to leave.

"Let's give it a try," she said in a raised voice as he exited the kitchen, but Jack gave no indication that he'd heard her.

She glanced over at Pluto, still standing rigidly on top of the woodpile, and realized that a dog could be tough on him. But maybe they'll learn to get along.

Pluto might have had his doubts. He appeared haunted, as if the intruder was nothing but bad news. He never took his eye off the strange-looking canine, and it was the only eye he had.

6

Celia drove her old Honda wagon past thousands of stumps. The road down to the valley could be treacherous, and she negotiated it carefully on her way to work. Last fall a deer hunter had skidded off the gravel into a steep ravine, and it took the rescue squad more than four hours to free him from his mangled pickup. She'd heard that the hunter wasn't seriously hurt, just a few minor cuts and bruises; but what had really piqued her curiosity was whether he was the same man she'd once caught poaching on their land.

When they bought their fifteen acres six years ago, they didn't know that some of the locals favored the ridge during deer season, which officially ran for most of October.

Fine, Celia and Jack agreed when they saw the hunters arriving and heard gunshots booming in the forest near their home. We'll live with it. It's just one month out of the year. How bad can it be?

Back then they thought their land, at least, would remain a safe haven; and they put out a big salt lick to attract the deer. But the salt lick also attracted the hunters with the promise of easy prey, and on her frequent hikes Celia started seeing coyote tracks around the gutted remains of deer that had been poached, dressed, and dragged off to the road.

Jack tried to console Celia by reminding her that deer season would soon be over. "It's only a month," he kept repeating, "only a month."

But a month turned into two, and two turned into three, and the killing went on well into their first winter.

Finally, on a sunny Saturday morning in early January, an hour or so after Jack had left for work, Celia heard a gunshot that sounded as if it came from right outside their kitchen window. It was so loud and so close that she stiffened and couldn't move for a couple of seconds. When she did step out onto the deck she saw a man driving down the long sloping meadow in front of their house in a shiny new Jeep. He rolled right over the reedy stalks of wildflowers and didn't stop until he pulled up by his kill in one of the few remaining patches of snow.

"You son of a bitch!" She reached in the door and grabbed a jacket and started down the meadow. Sure enough, the deer had been shot right beside the salt lick. As she approached the hunter he turned the animal on its back, pulled out a huge knife and, to her considerable horror, plunged it into the deer's anus and sawed it open. It took her breath away to see the blood drooling onto the snow, and she had to force herself forward.

He was busy trying to crack open the pelvic bone with the tip of his knife when Celia stormed up to him with her arms folded across her chest.

"You're trespassing," she said, "and you're poaching." Her voice was too high, and she sternly ordered herself to calm down.

She wished Jack had been home. The hunter—middle-aged, balding—was looking her up and down. He made her feel as if *she* were a piece of meat.

"Is that so?" He sounded like some kind of backwoods cracker, except he had that new Jeep and must make money somehow. A logger, she thought, or a pot farmer. It was hard to tell one from the other anymore.

He used a rock to pound the butt of his knife, and the pelvis split apart with a nauseating sound—sharp and dull at the same time, truly sickening. Then he split the deer's underbelly, and what looked like a bucket of blood spilled out. Celia thought she might vomit. She had to turn away but she could still hear him working hard. His breath came in loud puffs, and she also heard the gristly sounds when he cut open the hide.

"Yes, that's so," she said fiercely. She tried not to show any fear, and she made herself look at the hunter and his prey. He'd shot a yearling. Its antlers were little more than mossy stumps, barely legal during hunting season, and hunting season ended months ago.

"You wouldn't deny a man the privilege of getting himself a deer, now would you?" he said as he yanked open the flaps of gray fur. Then he pulled up the sleeve of his camouflage jacket and stuck his arm up inside the animal to pull out its guts. But he did this for only a second or two—long enough to bloody himself up to his elbow—before he rolled the yearling onto its side facing downhill. He reached back in and with the aid of gravity started pulling out the lumpy mass. Celia saw it stream onto the snow like the earth's own lava, red and angry-looking, steaming in the cool air.

He put his knife back to work, slicing this and that. Snip-snip-snip. She heard this too.

"Yes, I would."

"You would, huh?" he snorted. "This your land?"

"Yes," Celia almost shouted.

"Well, don't be getting so uppity about it. Some of us been hunting around here a helluva long time. You just don't come in here and have things your way. Who the hell you think you are?" He made eye contact with her for the first time. "Big mistake, lady."

"My name is not lady, it's Mrs. Griswold to you, and mister, let me tell you you're the one making the big mistake."

"Think so, huh?" He chuckled and looked back down. "Guess we'll see about that. Me? I'm taking this deer home, so you can squawk all you want. Don't make any difference to me."

He finished field-dressing the deer and dragged it over to his jeep, the open kind with a roll bar. He left behind a bloody smear in the snow, a disturbing depression that led back to the entrails still steaming in the bright sun, resting on a wide oval of red slush now soaking into the spongy earth.

He dumped the deer in the back of the Jeep. Celia heard a metallic sound as the animal's body fell on some tools, its head hanging over the side. Sunlight flared on one of its smooth dark eyes. She made a note of the license plate.

"I'm reporting you."

"Hey, you do what you want, *girlie*." He smiled when he said that. Then he slammed the Jeep door—the only evidence of his anger—and drove up past their house, leaving dark tire tracks in the untouched meadow.

She marched back inside and called Charlie Vates, the game warden. He came over and took her statement that very morning. When she mentioned the new Jeep, he paused.

"You know who that is, Mrs. Griswold?" he asked as if he didn't expect an answer, and he certainly didn't wait for one. "That's Bill Keiter's brother, Hal. You know Keiter, the fire chief?"

"I know of him."

Vates put his pen down on the table, and she realized he was trying to tell her something without saying anything at all. She looked him right in the eye.

"I don't care if he's the President's brother. I'm pressing charges."

Vates nodded thoughtfully and picked his pen back up. He made a few more notes before asking her a final question.

"You in the fire district up here?"

She shook her head no, and Vates smiled.

"Good thing."

A month later Vates called to say that Keiter had been fined a hundred dollars.

She nodded as she hung up the phone. The son of a bitch had trespassed, poached, and hunted out of season to bag maybe fifty pounds of meat. A hundred bucks? Two bucks a pound. It wasn't much but she thought it was a lot better than nothing.

As it turned out, the hunter who plunged into the ravine last fall wasn't Hal Keiter. If it had been, Celia might have wished him a lot more than a few cuts and bruises.

She continued on her way to work, leaving behind the stumps and enjoying the way the narrow road snaked through the trees; but as she whipped around a familiar bend she spotted a new logging road gouged out of the forest, a brown smear with skinny roots sticking up at odd angles.

She had to slow down to pass a large yellow bulldozer parked by the side of the road. About twenty feet away two men worked their chain saws, spilling a steady steam of sawdust in the air. As Celia drew closer, the noise of their engines turned into a shriek. A third man smoked a cigarette by a head-high stack of neatly trimmed conifers.

Before moving to the Northwest, Celia held a rather storied view of loggers: rugged individualists who used their wits and brawn to brave the forest and help build the nation. After living here a few years, she decided loggers were no more romantic than cattlemen once you'd seen a slaughterhouse.

The man smoking smiled and waved, and even though their presence made her uneasy, she waved back.

Up ahead she could see the biggest, prettiest meadow on the ridge, and as she drove toward it she spotted patches of bright-orange poppies, like the one she tried to paint yesterday morning. They always appeared in abundance at this time of year. Perfect, she thought, for the Halloween season just around the corner.

She smiled as she sped past the meadow. At least they can't spoil this.

She pulled into the driveway that ran alongside the Bentman Children's Center and mumbled, O-G-I-M, short for "Oh God It's Monday." She figured if Friday had an acronym all its own, Monday certainly deserved one, though she did enjoy her work as an art therapist. She used her talents as an artist and her training in psychology to decipher the secrets that most children hid in their artwork.

The Center sat on the outskirts of town, directly in front of a large hill that had been logged during summer vacation. The barren face of that rise loomed over the entire area, and even from a distance Celia could see the stumps and the sickly tint of sawdust. The father of one of the boys at the Center had worked this clear-cut, a point of considerable pride for the seven-year-old, who boasted about it continually:

"My daddy done that. He cut down every one of them trees," to which Celia or one of the other staffers would reply gently,

"Eddy, it's not correct to say, 'My daddy *done* that.' It's 'My daddy *did* that.' And it's not 'Every one of *them* trees,' it's 'Every one of *those* trees.' "

"Did too, did too. He done that."

Patience, Celia would counsel herself, patience.

The Center consisted of two buildings: a single-level structure in the back that housed the classroom; and the two-story main house, which was built in 1920 and renovated before the Center opened fifteen years ago. Celia and the two child therapists had their offices on the main floor, along with the clerical staff. As she made her way from the parking area she heard someone laughing. It sounded like Ethan, although dark humor was common among most of the men and women who worked here, and in this respect they differed little from cops, reporters, ER doctors and nurses, or anyone else who deals with the grimmer aspects of human nature.

At the moment eleven children were enrolled at the Center, which served all of the region's schools. Originally it had been part of a pilot project for "special needs" students, but the state started providing ongoing funding and opened other children's centers around Oregon—after it became apparent that dysfunctional kids were turning into a growth industry. Some of the children attending the Bentman Center lived in towns twenty miles away. All of them had been classified as "severely emotionally disturbed," and a few, including an eleven-year-old schizophrenic, were in much worse shape.

Passive-aggressive behavior was commonplace, and it was not unusual for children to defecate or urinate on themselves. Not surprisingly, the rules required parents to make sure their offspring always kept an extra set of fresh clothes at the Center.

As difficult and as objectionable as the children could be, Celia found it gratifying to work with them. Whenever she got depressed about a child's behavior she made herself remember the children who had established control over their impulses, caught up on their academic work, and returned to their neighborhood schools.

She hiked up the steps of the main house. It was a large white rambling structure with canary-yellow trim around the windows and doors, which she had found a bit garish until she'd learned that the color had been selected by a vote of the Center's first clients.

A large porch welcomed guests, and a vestibule the size of a studio apartment received them. There were hooks for coats, a hip-high Japanese ceramic pot for umbrellas, and a six-foot perforated rack that had been placed above the metal grate of a hot-air duct. Most years it rained a lot, and they used this system to dry their soggy boots.

Celia walked into the living room, which served as the reception area. The imperious Barbara Kneese presided over it, she of the bifocals, rigid posture, and severe manner of a Prussian. Only Barbara's wild hair humbled her dignified older presence. Her frizzy curls sprang from her scalp and raced like white water down over her shoulders. For years Celia had watched Barbara war against it with straighteners, scissors, and sprays, never fully surrendering to its shameless spontaneity.

"Morning, Barbara." Never Barb.

"Good morning, Cecilia." Never Celia, much less Cel. The receptionist paused to swipe at a wiry hair hanging in her face. It bounced around teasingly before settling right back where it had been. Barbara grimaced. "And how are you today?" After more than two decades in the States, her German accent remained as flatulent as ever.

"Okay. Is there coffee?"

"Indeed there is. Dr. Weston made it, but there was no milk today. It went sour over the weekend, and *plop-plop* I had lumps in my coffee this morning. Lumps!"

"That's a drag," Celia sympathized as she swept into the Center's kitchen. The smell of fresh coffee greeted her warmly.

She fished around on a shelf above the sink until she came up with the mug a child had molded for her last year in a ceramics class. She poured herself a cup and was just taking her first sip when Ethan Tantry walked in and gave her a huge smile. Ethan was one of the child therapists, and often volunteered to take the toughest cases. Yet he was a slight man with a receding hairline, wire-rim glasses, and such an exaggerated effeminate manner that Celia had been genuinely surprised to learn that he was married *and* straight.

"Morning, Miss G."

"Morning, Mr. T."

Their exchange was as familiar to them as their faces.

"And how is Mr. G. these days? Counting on disasters? Making money off of other people's fears, pray tell?"

Celia laughed. Ethan's mockery of Jack and the insurance business never ceased, but it was all an act. Like most of the town, he bought his homeowner's, car, and life insurance from The Griswold Agency.

"He's fine, no complaints."

"Fancy that, no complaints. That's a first around here. And do tell, how *is* that visually challenged kitty of yours?"

"Pluto is fine, thank you." Celia performed a half-curtsy with her free hand. "But we did have an unexpected visitor this morning."

"Don't tell me; one of his mountain-lion cousins dropped by for a meal."

"No, no, nothing that dramatic. A dog. A Border collie showed up at the door."

"Oh, my, my, a new member of the household."

"We'll see. Jack's not too keen on the idea."

"Well, if you don't keep him, Fido's gonna fry. Did I ever tell you about the time Holly's little Pomeranian slept on my jeans?"

Celia shook her head. "No, I don't think so." She knew it would have been hopeless to try to discourage him.

"This was back when we first started dating, when life was *so* simple. Anyway, it was the first time I'd ever spent the night there and Flibbitts—that was her name, can you believe it?—curls up on my jeans and falls asleep. I'm thinking, Oh, this is really sweet. Everything's going to work out just fine." Ethan shook his head. "No, the little bitch was in heat but did moi know? Of course not. The next day I started across campus and these dogs came out of nowhere and started trying to hump me. I mean, it's like they're *stapled* to me. They're on my legs, my knees, there was even this little guy trying to hump my foot. He looked like a Brillo pad with a carrot stuck to it."

"I think you're putting me on," Celia said with a smile.

"No, as God is my judge, that's exactly what happened." Ethan crossed his heart.

"Sure."

"Okay, okay, maybe I embroidered just a little." He gave Celia an impish grin and pointed to the coffeepot. "Pour me a cup, would you? I *love* to watch." Ethan made this remark sound positively lascivious.

Celia favored him with an act of her own, lifting the pot a foot or so above his mug and aiming with the supreme confidence and flourish of a flamboyant waitress, which she had been for more years than she cared to recall. Ethan sounded pleased to be so honored.

"Look at that, look at that," he exclaimed as she lowered the lip of the coffeepot to his cup. "Are we stylish this morning, or what? I'm so impressed, Miss G, really. You do it with such flair, such"—he paused to roll his eyes dramatically—"panache, and it's so lacking around here. See what I mean? Look, he's here, the big lug himself."

Dr. Tony Weston, the Center's new director, didn't seem to know just how to handle Ethan's gibes. In the three weeks since his arrival Tony had been crisp with the staff and had not allowed himself to settle into their relaxed rhythms. Celia wondered if his size had always made him feel separate from others. Tony stood six and a half feet tall, and even though he was well into his fifties he carried a solid athletic frame. In appearance and temperament, he was quite the opposite of Ethan.

"Any left?" Tony tried to look around Celia, who realized she blocked his view of the coffeemaker.

"Oops, sorry. I think there's—"

Ethan interrupted her with a French accent: "For you, Tony? Why, but of course. Here, let Cecilia do it. She's in such a sporting mood this morning."

"No, that's okay," Tony replied in his starchy manner.

Ethan put his hands on his hips and eyed Tony's feet. Even before he said anything, Celia knew he was about to goad him some more. She didn't think this was very wise. He was, after all, Ethan's new boss. Hers too. But once Ethan got going, he rarely stopped, and this morning proved no exception.

"Say, are those new Nikes, or did you just rent a couple of barges for the day?"

Celia tried to stifle a laugh, but couldn't. Tony, in fact, was wearing a new pair of athletic shoes—white, which made his feet look enormous, even larger than they were; and they were huge, something like a size fifteen or sixteen. They had been a source of some raillery almost from the day he walked in the door.

Ethan would not let up: "I'll tell you, if I were an otter and I saw you coming, baby, I'd book. I'd get out on the first thing smoking."

Tony granted Ethan a tense smile. He tolerated him, that was clear to Celia. Maybe me too, she thought. He certainly didn't think much of art therapy. He'd been clear enough about that. Tony was very much the behaviorist. He appeared to care only about fast results. He glanced at both of them.

"Sorry I can't hang around for more of the fun," he said, without sounding as if he'd had any fun at all, "but I've got some case reviews to attend to."

As he turned to leave, Ethan piped up one more time: "See you, Sasquatch."

Tony ignored him.

"Me too," Celia said, checking her watch. "I'd better book."

"Bye, chile." Ethan gave her a beauty-queen wave.

"Toodles."

What a silly word, Celia thought as she walked down the hall. Why'd I say that? She wasn't even sure there was such a word. But Ethan made her laugh and feel playful enough to say things like that. She liked him. She worried that she was starting to like him too much.

7

Jack shook the hand of young Larry Thorston and wished him a very good day. He'd certainly gotten Jack's day off to a fine start. Monday mornings usually brought in only claims—Saturday-night car wrecks and Sunday-morning fender benders—but Jack had just sold the recently wedded Mr. Thorston a two-hundred-fifty-thousand-dollar life-insurance policy. Not nearly as flush as Jack's own, or the one he'd taken out on Celia's life, but still not bad considering the guy barely earned twenty thousand dollars a year at the only mill still operating in Bentman. But the kid had a teenage bride even younger than himself and the good-natured giddiness of a small-town boy delighting in his first regular hump. In short, young Larry was pliable, suggestible, a nearly ideal client.

Ah yes, the pleasures of owning an insurance agency in a burg like Bentman. It sure beat the slash-and-burn tactics he'd had to put up with in Chicago. For starters, he didn't have any competition here. That counted for a lot. Folks either dealt with him or they drove the twenty miles to North Fork. Usually, like young Mr. Thorston, they dealt with Jack. And why not? He did his best to keep them happy. You just couldn't take anything for granted, not even a monopoly, and by no means a marriage. He could have told little Larry a thing or two about that, but then he might not have been so pliable . . . suggestible . . . ideal. Besides, Jack believed that marital cynicism was the province of older males. Someday Larry Thorston would know this, but by then he'd have at least one unhappy wife and several unruly children, and more insurance than he'd ever need. Most of Jack's customers did.

But in truth, Jack envied the young man his unbridled innocence and undivided love. Jack possessed neither, and for the tenth or eleventh time—he'd honestly lost count—he found himself right smack in the middle of a raging affair.

Back around the Fourth of July he had advertised for someone to fill a clerical position. With the timber industry in such rapid decline, jobs had become scarce. Even so he'd been shocked when thirty-two people stopped by to fill out applications. After two full days of interviewing he was exhausted, but when Helen Atkins walked in the door he sat up and took notice. Her full figure had commanded his attention first. Then, when she sat down, her snug miniskirt rose half-way up her substantial, though shapely, thighs. She volunteered that she was twenty-six, loved to make work a "fun place," and despite the rings on her finger never once mentioned her husband. Jack was smitten, and decided then and there that if she could type, she could have the job. She could type. Could she ever!

They'd flirted for more than two months before ending up on the carpet in the walk-in vault where he kept the most critical documents. She'd turned out to be an aggressive, athletic lover, much different from Celia, who displayed her affections softly, both in word and deed. Helen was a big woman, and he had quickly come to see that her lust matched her royal stature. In just two hours on Friday night she left him drained for the entire weekend. At forty-five he was slowing down, but Helen had almost twenty years of youth on her side and was almost always raring to go.

He saw her rise from her desk and straighten out her skirt. The fabric rubbed against her buns and revealed their full, firm shape. She turned toward him, and his pulse quickened. The very sound of her hose-covered thighs brushing against each other—*swish, swish*—made him want to fall to his knees and pleasure her instantly.

She tapped playfully on the glass partition that separated Jack from the rest of the office.

"May I come in?" she asked demurely.

He loved that silky voice coming from a woman so robust, so Rubenesque, so . . . *rapacious.*

"Of course, of course, you're welcome in my little space anytime. Here, have a seat." He patted the chair next to his desk and wished that for the next few minutes he could be nothing more than the cushion on which she was about to perch.

She stepped into his cubicle—*swish, swish, swish*—and eased past him. He smelled her perfume and resisted the urge to bite her behind. He also tried mightily not to steal a glimpse up her legs as she sat down. He failed. She noticed, but proved to be a generous spirit and allowed him quite an eyeful as she arranged her skirt. Neither of them commented on her pert performance.

He forced himself to glance at Ruth, his only other employee, and was relieved to see her busy with a customer. He thought of her as an older woman, though she was much closer to Jack's age than Helen was.

"I have a problem," Helen said with great seriousness.

Jack coughed. "A problem?" He coughed again. His mouth suddenly felt dry, and as he picked up his coffee cup he desperately tried to calculate whether it was even possible for Helen to be pregnant yet. As he swallowed he reached a conclusion so dreadful that he almost gagged.

"Well"—he recovered as smoothly as he could—"I'll be glad to help you out in any way I can." He was thinking abortion, of course, and wishing like hell he'd been generous enough to include health in his employee-benefits package.

"I don't know how to put this," she said in those same grave tones that most of us reserve for the most direct of circumstances, "but my problem is you."

"Me?" His voice came out as a squeak.

Helen nodded and dropped her eyes to the hem of her skirt, which had settled a distracting distance above her knees. Jack shared the view as he made every effort to sound more confident.

"I hate to think that I'm causing you any problems because, as you know"—he shot a glance at Ruth, then lowered his voice along with his eyes—"I have nothing but the warmest feelings for you."

"I *know*," Helen said with sudden urgency. She raised her head to look at Jack, and he felt compelled to leave behind the vision of those lovely legs. "But that's the problem. For a month now all I can think about is you. I mean, I'm a married woman. I shouldn't be thinking about doing all those things to you, but I do—all day long!''

"I know *exactly* what you mean.'' He reached out to pat her knee but stopped short when he spotted Ruth looking at them. His hand fell lamely to his desk, which he then drummed pointlessly. "I'm married too, you know.'' He thought it important to remind her of this. "But when I look at you out there working away, I just want to reach out and squeeze your cheeks and—''

"I know. *Me* too. All I think about is what we do and how much I like doing it. A lot more than with Ralph,'' she added with what sounded like true remorse.

Jack felt guilty at the mention of Ralph's name. Last year he lost his job when one of the timber companies folded, and Helen had recently confided that he'd run out of unemployment benefits and spent his days watching "Oprah'' and "Geraldo.'' But just as Jack was feeling the virtue of his guilt, Helen crossed her legs and her thighs issued that sweet *swishing* sound, and he promptly forgot all about What's-his-name.

He realized that he'd been leaning closer and closer to her as she talked, and wondered if his tongue had been hanging out too. He made himself sit up straight. No sense making Ruth suspicious, if she wasn't already, which in his more sober moments he knew she had to be.

Though he'd assumed a more businesslike posture, Jack kept his voice warm and intimate.

"Helen, I don't have a lot of experience with these things, of course, but I do think that when they happen we have to listen to our heart and do what it tells us to do.''

She nodded as if she'd just heard the wisdom of the ages. "I think you're so right. That's what I love about you, Jack, you're so . . . mature.''

"Maybe we ought to go to lunch and talk about it some more.''

"Maybe we should.'' She smiled as she replied, and Jack knew they wouldn't be breaking bread anytime soon.

8

A chubby eleven-year-old boy burst through the front door of the Bentman Children's Center and tossed his balogna sandwich into the air. Slices of pink meat and white bread fell as he scrambled down the steps. No more than a second later Celia dodged the debris and called out to him.

"Harold, time-out. Harold, time-out this instant!"

She nimbly took the stairs three at a time and was just about to nab him when Dr. Tony Weston walked around the corner of the building and neatly lifted the boy up off the ground.

Harold Matley's legs pumped spastically in the air, as if his body were still trying to catch up with his mind, but when Tony put him back down the boy crumpled to the ground and his tears began to flow.

Celia kneeled beside him, placed her arm around his shoulders, and wiped away his tears. Tony watched from his considerable height.

"Harold," she said softly, "what's bothering you today?"

He shook his head, as if he didn't want to talk. But Celia had a pretty good idea why the boy had fled the Center.

"Are you seeing those things again?"

Now he buried his face in his hands and moved his head up and down.

"Do you think you're ready to draw them for me?" She stroked his dark curly hair. "I'll bet Dr. Weston lets you skip group if you'll draw for me."

She glanced up at Tony and saw his pained expression. But the director quickly relented.

"Yes, I suppose I could do that."

Harold nodded into his hands one more time, and Celia whispered to him,

"You're a brave boy. You really are."

Children's art covered all the walls of Celia's office, a dizzying array of pencil and crayon drawings, along with finger paintings and watercolors. It was an even larger collection than the one she'd hung in her studio, but a more important distinction lay in the presentation: in her office every picture had black electrician's tape over the young artist's name, which was the anonymity she granted each of her clients.

At her desk she studied a painting of a tree by a ten-year-old girl as Harold worked with his colored pencils. When he looked up his eyes were still moist, and his voice still trembled.

"I'm done."

He held out his drawing at arm's length, as if he found it distasteful and wanted to get rid of it as soon as possible.

She walked over to the worktable and took it from him. What she saw was alarming, but hardly surprising. He had written the word "Mad," and drawn the letters *a* and *d* inside the jagged yellow lines of the *M*, which also contained two burning red eyes. Red beetles swarmed over the letters.

Celia felt deeply for Harold. It was unusual for a child his age to be diagnosed with schizophrenia, even more so for an eleven-year-old to suffer hallucinations. They appeared without warning, as they had this morning, and the very fact that he knew they weren't real made the monsters he saw on the walls and ceilings and in the air that much more painful to him: *If the giant red beetles aren't real, and I know they aren't real, then why do I see them, and why do they scare me so?*

Celia had formulated his confusion and fear into simple language, but schizophrenia didn't yield to words the way less serious mental disorders often did. She could not discuss, cure, and ease the pain. No one could. Harold had been dragged across a genetic land mine, and bits of his brain chemistry had been scattered forever. He would never heal or be whole. He would know a lifetime of deeply disturbed days.

She had tried to understand the grimly disruptive world in

which he lived, and had studied the disease extensively; but the more she read about it the more she realized how little was actually known about schizophrenia. A few weeks ago she ran across an article in a book review that said all the major symptoms of the disease seemed to be matched by countersymptoms, what the author had chillingly described as an "antiworld where everything appears in reverse." An *antiworld*. The word haunted Celia, for it captured the quiet eeriness of everyday life.

It gave her a cold feeling to contemplate this antiworld, not unlike the discomfort she'd known when she tried to imagine Harold's fears. Shortly after he was referred to the Center last year, she learned that she would have to define the extent of her empathy clearly.

On his second day he experienced some of his worst hallucinations, and she'd seen just how quickly terror could grip the boy. He shook terribly as he tried to fight off the unseen demons; and at times he squeezed his eyes shut, wrinkling his entire face in a frantic effort to block out the sights that scared him so. His fear had been so great—and Celia's sense of it had become so real—that she'd felt his pain sharply.

When his eyes had suddenly opened and he'd pointed wildly and screamed, "See, they're coming, they're coming to get me, they're coming to get me," she had not been able to look for fear that she, too, might see what could not be seen. Instead, she had kept her eyes on Harold and pleaded with him to listen to her even as he pleaded with the monster to leave him alone.

"Go away!" he'd screamed over and over. "Go away," he finally begged; but they hadn't gone away, and another half hour of panic passed before they vanished. Celia had held him and quietly—so quietly he hadn't noticed—cried for him as well as for herself. She had felt his terror to her very core, and it had scared her as nothing had for many years, for Celia had suffered similar pain all of her life, those silent threats to sanity that insinuated themselves into her psyche and crawled like dark insects along the back corridors of her mind. She had always feared that the full force of this nightmare would unveil itself at a vulnerable moment, and that when it did she would blank out, not to nothingness but to horror, to the crushing meltdown of consciousness. She feared this still.

She sat on a child-sized chair next to Harold and placed his picture on the table before them.

"You really worked hard on that. Can you tell me about your drawing?"

The boy forced himself to glance down, then pointed to the beetles. "It's like them. I see them on the walls and, and"—he began to cry again—"sometimes in the air, like they're flying and they're coming to get me and I can't get away."

Celia saw the fright in Harold's eyes, in the way his fingers had frozen to the edge of the table. Then she looked at his picture and saw it there too, in those three simple letters— *Mad*—that spelled out his complex fate.

"Harold, why don't you draw a picture and lock up those scary beetles?"

He nodded, but he didn't pick up any of the colored pencils.

"Do you think you could do that?"

"I could, but . . ."

"But what?" she prodded.

"But," and now he spoke so softly she could barely hear him, "I think they'll escape."

9

Davy sat in the back row and stared at the teacher. He didn't like her one bit. Every day this week she'd asked him questions and made nasty faces when he wouldn't answer them. She had done it on Monday, Tuesday, yesterday, and she did it again today. And then the kids laughed at him, every time. She'd be sorry. He'd make her so sorry she'd never forget. Never. Same for the kid next to him. He'd poked Davy with a pencil three times so far today. One more time and he was going to get it. Davy knew just what he'd do to him, and when he did it he'd never let go. Never.

He hated this new school. He wanted to go back to his old school, the one his real daddy had taken him to. That was last year, a long time ago. Then his real daddy died and went to heaven and his mom met Chet and they moved to that trailer. And then she went away and they moved here. To Oregon. He hated Oregon. He hated that trailer even more. Every time he went inside he could see the dark cracks in the floor. Stains, that's what they were, dark stains that wouldn't wash away. He knew 'cause Chet made him clean them with Comet. "Keep scrubbing," he'd say, "it's your mom's mess, clean it up." My mom's mess? But why? He couldn't remember, but he knew he hated those stains more than anything in the whole world.

Davy had scrubbed them till his hands got sore and red, but he couldn't scrub them away no matter how hard he tried. They were buried in the cracks. He couldn't forget them neither. He'd think about them in the middle of the day when he was thinking about nothing. They'd just be there all of a sudden and he'd see them like he did when he scrubbed them, and he'd get this awful feeling in his stomach that wouldn't go away nohow, not even when he rubbed his belly or sat on the toilet and tried real hard to go.

Dark stains inside him, under his skin, like the stains on the floor.

The kid got that pencil out again, looking at it like he wasn't thinking about anything at all, then looking at Davy, smiling, but not at him, at the other kids·watching.

They giggled, and the teacher turned around fast. She was angry, but not at them. No, she liked them. On Davy's first day she had told him, "I've got a good class, and I want it to stay that way."

She had let the other kids go to lunch, and then made him stand there while she talked some more. "We do not have any problems this year, so learn to cooperate."

She smiled at him but Davy could tell that being nice was hard work for her, and she'd said that last word real slow— *co-op-er-ate*—like he was stupid and she had to sound it out for him. "Do you know what that means?"

Davy stared at the floor and felt his stomach growling. He was plenty hungry and all he wanted to do was eat.

"It means you try, Davy. Your stepfather says you used to talk, so we know you can do it. Even if you don't know the answer, you try just the same."

Now she had another question. He could tell by the way she looked at him. He didn't like her eyes. They were as small and dull as dirty old dimes.

"Do you think"—her voice reached an uncomfortably high note and cracked—"do you think that you could spell the world 'man'?"

Davy glanced at the kid with the pencil. He was giving the teacher all of his attention, just the way she liked.

"I'm *waiting,* Davy."

As soon as she turned to pick up a piece of chalk, the kid whispered,

"Betcha if I stab you hard, you'll say something."

His lips hardly moved but Davy heard him and got ready. The kid wasn't going to get away with it again. Davy scowled at him as the teacher wheeled around.

"Davy, please do not pester your neighbors. If you're not going to answer my questions, at least behave properly."

She shuffled the chalk from hand to hand. "I'm going to give you another chance. It's the last time this week that I'm going to do this. If you don't cooperate I'm afraid I'll have to speak to your stepfather. Do you hear me?"

The teacher nodded, not like she was happy, though, more like she was letting off steam, the way the lid on an old kettle bobs up and down when the water starts to boil.

"Okay, how do you spell 'girl'?"

She turned back to the board, holding up the chalk as if she really expected him to answer.

"Davy, I'm *waiting*."

She had to say it like that, like she was no more patient than a hungry cat.

This time the kid with the pencil caught him on a soft spot right below a rib. Davy moved quickly. He grabbed the boy's arm and bit his hand so hard the kid lunged out of his seat and screamed. Davy heard the teacher yelling too, and rushing toward him, but didn't care. He had what he wanted, the kid crying and yanking and getting nowhere.

Davy saw her bony hands flashing by his face, and felt her fingers digging into his jaw, like a vet pilling a pup. When he couldn't stand it anymore he opened his mouth, and the kid's arm snapped back like a spooked snake. Then he grabbed the teacher's wrist and bit her arm just as hard as he could.

Red spray shot up, like mist from an orange peel, and then it was gone, as if he'd blinked it away. The moment hung too, a speck in time before she slammed the side of his head. His ear rang, his face burned, and his teeth ached from the force of her blow, like they'd tear right out of his gums if she did it again. And she did, over and over, but the harder she hit him the more he knew that he was hurting her more than she was hurting him.

10

Celia leaned back in the chaise longue and took in the pine smells that drifted up from the mill. Each time one of the big saws ripped into a log it released more of that sweet odor, and even a slight breeze could stir the scent all the way up to the ridge.

Gray haze rose from the giant drying shed where the freshly planed lumber lay in tall blond stacks, and farther west the last of the sun tinted the sky pink and purple; but it was her sense of smell, not sight, that filled Celia with pleasure this evening.

The Border collie she'd been feeding since Monday disturbed her idyll with its high-pitched bark. Must be Jack with the drinks. She heard him close the door as the dog issued another shrill warning that carried with piercing clarity around the corner of the deck. Then she listened to the quick shuffling of Jack's shoes. Celia figured he was jabbing at the dog with his foot again. She didn't consider this the greatest training technique, but Jack had made it clear that he didn't want any pointers on how to deal with the dog.

"Go *away*," he snapped.

The dog barked again, as if bearding Jack. It had been barking at her husband all week. It was as if the critter were allergic to *him*. Perhaps it sensed Jack's dislike. Whatever the reason, Celia could tell they weren't exactly bonding.

Jack wheeled around the house, glancing back at the disgruntled cur.

"Christ, that thing's a pain in the ass."

He handed Celia her glass of zinfandel and sat down. She thanked him, and watched the animal settle quietly on the far end of the deck. She decided not to comment on the latest skirmish. They were both males. Maybe it was some kind of turf thing.

When Jack opened his beer she continued telling him about Harold.

"He's really a great kid, very bright."

"What's that?"

She frowned at him. "Harold, the schizophrenic boy who's been drawing for me. I was just telling you about—"

"That's right. Sorry. I got a little distracted with the hound from hell."

Celia waved away his forgetfulness. "That's okay. Like I said, he's a bright kid but he comes from a really bad background. Both parents are substance abusers and just don't give a damn about him. I'll tell you, we have to work so hard just to build up trust with these kids. That's the biggest issue so far. Most of them don't trust anyone anymore, and who can blame them?"

She tasted the wine, letting the liquid swirl over her tongue, as she watched the dark outline of a hawk floating almost motionlessly on an updraft. She studied the elegant hooked beak—the distinctive predator's profile—and made a mental note to incorporate the lines in a future painting.

"Anyway," she added, "that's what it always seems to come down to—trust and family. That's what's really important. At least I've got that with you."

Jack nodded slowly, and she reached over and tenderly touched his hand. It felt cold and damp from the bottle and gave her a chill.

"The fact that Harold started letting me see into his world was a real breakthrough, but then to see the horrors that poor kid sees every day. That was kind of hard to take. Of course, Tony"—she shook her head—"still seems to think that art therapy is some kind of voodoo."

She looked at Jack again, closely this time, and saw that his eyes were far away. She resisted the urge to shout at him, and continued in the same casual voice as before.

"So at lunch I pulled Tony into my office and went down on him, and now he thinks art therapy is the greatest. He smiles every time I bring it up."

Jack continued to nod listlessly, and Celia rested her wineglass on the small redwood table that separated them.

"Jack," she snapped, "you haven't heard a single word I've said."

He looked at her, clearly startled.

"Yes, I have," he insisted, "you were talking about the Center."

"Good guess. I just told you that I went down on our new director."

"You did what!" Jack jumped forward in his seat.

"No, of course not. I just wanted to see if you were listening."

He sat back, clearly relieved. "I'm sorry, Cel, I've been a little preoccupied with work lately."

"I guess."

"And now"—he spoke with visible disgust—"I've got to go up to Trout River next weekend and look over a front loader that George Reeples is buying. He wants me to ball-park liability, loss, the whole shebang."

"That's going to take all weekend? Why don't you do it during the week? Ruth and that new girl, what's her name, can take—"

"Helen." He raised his beer to take a drink.

"Right, Helen, they can take care of things for a couple of days, can't they?"

He started shaking his head even as he pulled the bottle away from his lips. "That's what you think," he sputtered, "but that's because you don't have to work with them all day. I have to check everything they do to make sure it's done right." He wiped his mouth with the back of his wrist. "Come on, why don't you go with me? I think it would be good for us to get away for a couple of days. It's beautiful up there this time of year."

"I can't go, Jack, you know that. It's marked on the calendar. That's my weekend to be on call."

"Oh, that's right," he said, his voice heavy with regret. "Sorry. Forgot all about that. Well, it'll only be one night, and then I'll be back on Sunday."

The news didn't please Celia at all, but she knew he had to cover a fairly wide territory if the agency was to remain profitable. Not all the business walked in the door.

So instead of complaining she took a deep breath and smelled the pine once again. Then she remembered the huge whirling saws at the mill, and tried to forget that it was the odor of death that delighted her so.

11

Chet slammed the door shut and fumbled around with the keys hanging from the ignition. He had to get his pickup all loaded with firewood and drive over to that guy Marshall's place before the afternoon wasted away. He'd met him downtown at Andy's Market. Chet had no sooner stuck the sign to the side of his door when the old guy limped up on his cane and said he needed some. Cutting scrap and poaching a pine here and there was no kind of living, but Chet would get $110 for a cord of that crap; and if this old asshole was ready to pay that kind of price, why, Chet felt duty-bound to find it for him. Hell, this was Oregon. You could always find wood somewhere.

Just as he cranked the ignition he glanced in his rearview mirror and spotted Davy dragging ass up the road. Sorriest-looking kid he'd seen in a long time. But then he reminded himself that they were always like this right after their mamas died, moping around. It's like they'd been born to a whole new world, and they had blood all over them, just like the first time when they came crawling out of those lower parts. Chet knew about boys, had made a real study of them, and sometimes it took months for them to get used to the way things were meant to be. No different with Davy.

The kid inched up to the truck like the goddamn thing might explode. He had his knapsack over his shoulder and was holding a sheet of paper. Chet figured it might be a class project of some kind. "Drew our hands today and colored them. See, don't it look just like a turkey?" He remembered one of the boys saying that. Couldn't remember which one, though. They were all gone, dead and buried and mostly lost to him now, even their memory.

"What are you worried about? Think I'm going to bite you or something? Jesus!"

Be *nice,* he warned himself. You'll scare him worse than he's scared already. Little dick doesn't even talk. Chet softened his tone.

"Okay, what's up, Davy boy? I got to get moving here. Got to put together a load and take it to town."

Davy held out the paper and Chet saw that it was some kind of note. He eyed it suspiciously. It looked official, and nothing official ever turned out good. A fact of life. Never once.

"Report cards out already?"

The kid didn't so much as smile, and the only sound Chet heard was his own forced laughter, strangled by the silence.

He sat in the cab and unfolded the note, saw the school letterhead. Damn right, bad news. Kid's been acting up. He glanced at Davy and opened the truck door.

"Says you're a very bad boy." He sat on the rusty running board so he could look Davy in the eye, except the kid never looked back. Always had his head down, like he'd rather be on the ground than be with you. He will be soon enough if he keeps this up.

"It says you bit some kid, bit him pretty bad. Now why'd you want to go and do something mean like that? That's a really mean thing to do, biting somebody."

Davy just kept looking down, and Chet had to tug his arm. Gently, though. *Gently.*

"Big boys don't bite, Davy. Hey, that's what girls do. That's no way to fight."

He made a fist and tapped Davy on the chin. The boy's head snapped back as if he'd been hit much harder.

"Someone gives you trouble—pow—you let them have it right on the old kisser." He cocked his fist again, but this time spared the boy. He could see he was scared. "Punch them, punch them hard as you can. Break their damn jaw, that's what I do. But don't go around biting."

A boy needs this kind of advice, Chet thought. This is nothing a mother could do. He turned back to the note. There was more. Oh Jesus!

"Your teacher too! Oh, no." He shook his head. This was

different. "They're throwing you out. They want to put you in a special school, 'cause you're biting and not talking." Chet did not like this at all. "I'm supposed to go in there and meet a Mrs. Griswold." He looked back at the note. "But that's not till Monday." His eyes rose from the paper. "Guess you got yourself a three-day weekend. But you know what this means, don't you? It means I got to take time off to take you there."

He grabbed Davy's shoulder and slowly began to squeeze harder and harder.

"I don't like to take time off, Davy. I don't like that one bit."

Davy dipped down to try to get away, but Chet held him tightly. He could see pain in the kid's face. That's okay, do him some good.

"But I guess you're worth it."

Chet eased his grip as slowly as he'd applied it.

"Sure you are." He smiled at him. "Now go on in and wait for me. Watch that video if you want, but don't go anywhere. I'll be home soon enough. Now go on."

As Davy turned to walk away, Chet gave him a pat on the butt. It felt so good, he had a mind to follow him right on in.

12

*O*h God, it *is* Monday.

Celia locked up her car but didn't bother pocketing her keys. When she pulled up to the Center she realized she was the first one in and would have to open up and make the morning coffee, duties she rarely had to perform since Tony came on board. He usually arrived first and left last, and reminded the staff of this whenever it proved convenient. But Celia had awakened early after a bad night's sleep and decided to get a jump on the new workweek.

She'd gone hiking on Saturday afternoon. She would have enjoyed taking along the Border collie for company but after she left for work on Friday Jack had lured the dog into his pickup with some fresh meat, leashed it to the bed, and drove it to the pound. No doubt to its imminent doom as well. Celia knew she could have made a huge stink over it but Jack had been so determined to get rid of the dog that keeping it would have become a constant struggle. So now that cute little black-and-white dog would be killed. It saddened Celia when she recalled how he'd warmed right up to her. It was Jack the creature couldn't stand. That turned out to be a fatal mistake. And she couldn't help wondering about his so-called allergies; exposure to the dog sure hadn't slowed him down any. He was still working overtime at the office. A full day Saturday. With all the hours he was putting in, you'd think that earthquakes and floods were pummeling the region. When he got home around six she dragged him into bed and they made love for the first time in a month, but their time apart had hardly increased his ardor. In fact, he almost lost his erection twice, and she'd become quite sore before he finally came. She'd heard this could happen with much older men, but Jack was only forty-five.

Then on Sunday morning she spent a few frustrating hours working on the painting of the poppy. The color had been the problem. She considered it closer to the orange worn by hunters than anything else she could think of, but she just hadn't been able to come up with the right hue. After her exacting eyes rejected every one of her efforts she abandoned the project to brood about their marriage, which she had been doing anyway and which probably explained the pitiful state of the painting. She'd even begun to worry that she and Jack were not going to make it, and she found this extremely disturbing.

She had almost ten years invested in Jack—she couldn't help thinking of it this way, as an *investment,* the most important one of her life—and at thirty-eight she desperately wanted children. She knew that under the best of circumstances she had only a few dependable years left to get pregnant. If her marriage fell apart she doubted that she'd ever have the time or the emotional resources to pull herself back together, find a new partner, and have a family.

When they first met, their lives had been very different. Jack had been the manager of a large insurance agency in the Chicago Loop, and Celia had been completing her last semester of graduate school. A burglar had stolen everything of value from her apartment and, like so many other victims, she had decided to buy her first insurance policy "after the horse was out of the barn."

Those were among the first words Jack ever said to her. Their eyes had met across the office, and he had hurried to help her. He was so obvious about his intentions that they both laughed when he'd tripped over a chair en route.

Three months after they met he proposed, and a week later a Justice of the Peace pronounced them man and wife. Great sex had prompted both his offer and Celia's acceptance. Back then her whole body would shiver from the sheer excitement of terrific lovemaking.

Almost a decade had slipped away, and the shivers had taken leave along with the passion. Not that she thought they had a bad marriage, not yet anyway, but they just didn't have a great one. And that's what Celia wanted, if not the wild romance of their first evening together, then at least the sweet intimacy of the morning after. But now, when she needed

Jack most of all, when he'd finally agreed that yes, it was time to have a family, he'd become withdrawn. Making love to her was a "chore." She cringed all over again when she remembered how just last weekend he'd grouped their love-making right next to duties like cleaning out the rats from the tank. If that's how he thought about it, no wonder their sex life was on such a slide. Once a month? Forget it. Christ, at the rate they were going she'd never get pregnant. She wished they hadn't been so damn careful about birth control during all those years when they'd christened every corner of the house with sex. Couldn't they have made just one mistake? Weren't couples always smiling and saying that little so-and-so had been a mistake? She wished she had a little mistake running around the house. Two, even. But no, she had been so damn conscientious about the pill, condoms, the IUD, her cycle—when she was safe and when she wasn't—and for what? To prevent what she now wanted most of all. The irony pained her deeply. But she'd done it for Jack. He was the one who wanted to "plan" a family, and she had agreed. So they'd planned this and they'd planned that—*planned planned planned!*—and the years had passed and now Celia was starting to feel like planned obsolescence.

As she unbolted the front door, Tony rolled up in his new Toyota. She waved, threw on the lights, and headed back to her office. She hung up her jacket and plopped her briefcase onto her messy desk, then cruised into the kitchen and threw together a pot of coffee. She had just turned to leave when Tony walked in with a file tucked under his arm.

"I trust you had a good weekend."

"Not bad." She wasn't about to share her anxieties about her marriage with him. "The drought may be killing the plants, but it's great to have Indian summer."

"You mean it's not always like this in Oregon?"

"You *are* kidding?"

Tony smiled. "I am." He handed her the file. "But there's nothing even remotely funny about this case. He's supposed to be here at nine-thirty with his stepfather."

Celia eyed the wall clock. Not quite eight.

He took down a cup and saucer from the shelf right above

the sink. "I had to pick it up at the district office on my way in. They called me at home this morning. That's why I'm a little late. Evidently, somebody was supposed to get this over to us on Friday and forgot." He held up the cup. "You need one?"

"No, thanks, one of the kids made me one last year." She retrieved a brown mug and showed it to him. Her name was misspelled on the front: Seala. "He wasn't the greatest student."

"It's the thought that counts." Tony lifted the pot to pour her some coffee, and she found herself softening toward her new boss.

"Anyway, that"—he glanced at the file she now held—"is something you'll want to look over before the boy gets here. He's a handful, from what I hear, and the district office thinks you might be able to help him. Who knows?"—he shrugged—"maybe you can."

"Thanks for the vote of confidence." The softening ceased.

"Well, don't take it the wrong way, but this will really be a test of your art therapy."

She placed the file on the table and leafed through it. "What do—"

"He doesn't talk. He appears to be an elective mute. When he was enrolled, his stepfather said he was talking just fine until his mother died. I gather that was sometime last year. Anyway, he didn't say 'boo' all last week. He's new, they just moved here."

Tony sat down and looked up at her. "But here's the clincher." He paused to sip his coffee.

"The clincher?"

"Yes, the clincher. The boy"—Tony paused one more time—"is a *biter*." He finished on an overly dramatic note that Celia didn't find at all becoming.

"A biter, really." She made herself sound more relaxed than she actually felt. "How bad?"

"Bad enough that he sent one of his classmates to the emergency room for six stitches on his hand."

"Ouch."

"Bad enough that he also bit his teacher when she tried

to drag him off the kid. She ended up with four stitches.''

"Maybe he's Hannibal the Cannibal's kid." Bad joke, she immediately told herself, but Tony didn't seem to mind. She even detected a slight smile as she slid into a chair across the table from him.

"So let's see"—she positioned the file in front of her—"we have a seven-year-old boy who's stopped talking for some reason, but uses his mouth to communicate his anger very well.''

Tony lowered his cup and didn't even attempt to conceal his surprise: "Celia, that's very well put, and that about sums it up. You tell me what a kid who doesn't talk is actually saying with his artwork, and you might make a believer out of me yet.''

She shook her head as she stood back up. Tony saw but she couldn't have cared less. She was starting to appreciate Ethan's bold approach to their new boss.

As she exited the kitchen, Tony called after her,

"By the way, Davy Boyce, that's his name.''

"And biting's his game," she mumbled.

She rubbed her arms protectively as she walked down the hallway to her office. If she had been told about this on Friday, she would have worn long sleeves. Any kind of covering helped when you worked with a biter. She supposed she could put her jacket back on but the day was already warming up, and it was likely to get a lot hotter.

The Center had come alive with activity, and she ducked into her office without running into Ethan. So much the better. She wanted to review the Boyce file and didn't need any distractions, especially that kind.

She put her briefcase on the floor and pushed aside a stack of drawings. There wasn't much material on Davy Boyce, just those few pages. "Seven years old . . ."—right; ". . . motherless''—I'll have to ask about that; ". . . registered for school a week ago . . ."—okay, he's new, as Tony said. "Elective mute." She stopped reading and scrunched up her lips to the side of her mouth, an unflattering expression that she indulged only in private. She reminded herself that boys might not talk until they were four, unlike girls, who almost invariably started earlier, but for any child to stop talking entirely, and suddenly, was highly unusual.

She turned the page and saw the teacher's report. She had written that Boyce's ". . . savage assault on his classmate, one of my best pupils, I might add, and a popular boy, had been completely unprovoked." She said she'd had a difficult time pulling Boyce off the boy "because he attacked like a pit bull." Celia considered that descriptive flourish both uncharitable to the child and completely unnecessary. The teacher then offered a detailed account of how Boyce bit her when "I pried his jaw off poor William's hand." She concluded her comments by saying that she found Boyce to be a "thoroughly objectionable boy who is not welcome back in my classroom under any circumstances."

Celia had never been bitten but knew this was an unsteady claim, not unlike that of the dog trainer who talks uneasily about his own unscarred record; it's significant only because it's not expected to stand. She'd learned to keep her hair short to prevent angry children from grabbing a fistful of it when they tried to tear off her head, and she long ago stopped wearing earrings to work because of the dangers they posed, unless they were the clip-on variety; but biters were just so damn unpredictable.

She'd seen pictures of bite victims in a class on aberrant behavior, and had learned that the human bite was far more gruesome than she'd ever imagined. It could be absolutely devastating, and her fear of being bitten had been born in that class. Of course, seeing *The Silence of the Lambs* hadn't helped.

She tried to remember a maneuver she'd been taught to get out of a bite. It had been demonstrated at a two-day training session in self-defense for child care workers that she'd taken a couple of years ago. She was supposed to have practiced the move at home, but never had. She remembered the instructor really well: Renata. Tall, blond, smart and funny, the perfect qualities for someone teaching that kind of course. Renata had demonstrated a simple method for freeing themselves from biters but Celia could not remember it. She did recall that she'd had to bite herself lightly as part of the training. She lifted up her left arm and did it again. God, does this feel stupid. Now what did we do next? She was sitting there trying to remind herself of the answer when Ethan poked his head in the door.

"Really, Celia, most of us start with our nails."

She dropped her arm down and turned bright red. "No, listen, I was trying—"

"Hey, you don't have to explain anything to me—I work here too. But it's *only* Monday."

"No," she protested. "Remember the training we took on how to deal with biters?"

"Oh that. What do you want to know?"

"I'm trying to remember how to get out of a bite."

"Why, you planning on counseling Lassie? Here girl, here's the paint, here's the paper, now take your paw and do your thing."

Celia laughed and her blush faded. "Please, come on. There's a way to get out of a bite, some kind of thing you do, but for the life of me I can't remember what it is."

"Move in, roll down."

She snapped her fingers. "That's it. Thanks."

"Anytime. Anything else?"

"Nope, that's it. Why, what did you want?"

Ethan looked over his shoulder to make sure they were alone.

"I've got a new one for you."

Celia knew it was time for another round of "Name that Child Charades," a game mostly of Ethan's doing. Every time they played it she felt guilty. Talk about dark humor.

He looked down the hall once more, then lay down on the large children's worktable by the window and started wiggling, with his arms pressed tightly to his sides. He moved spastically all over the surface before pausing to look up and smile.

"Got it?"

"I got it," Celia said, still feeling guilty.

"Okay, who?"

"You know who. Stop it." He'd mimicked Mary, a nine-year-old hyperactive. Last month the Center's consulting psychiatrist had put her on Ritalin as part of a double blind study. But the staff always knew when she had taken the placebo because Mary started jiggling, jumping around and, as Ethan had just demonstrated, wiggling all over the tables and floors. "You always make me feel guilty."

"I do?" He grinned broadly.

"Yes. You're bad, Ethan." But Celia was also smiling.

"You think so?"

"Yes, I do."

"And how about you, are you bad?" he asked suggestively.

"Sometimes," she responded coyly, "but right now I've *got* to get through this file."

"Okay, I can take a hint. Ciao."

Ethan, now making his exit, wiggled once more as Celia watched him depart. She couldn't help herself—he had the cutest cheeks—and she turned red all over again.

Move in, roll down. That's right, that's what Renata had said. She had warned them against trying to muscle their way out of a bite, especially by exerting pressure upward. She explained that the top part of the jaw was very strong, and that even a child could use it to apply tremendous force. She had been very insistent about this.

"And never"—Celia remembered her repeating this point a couple of times—"never try and pull away from a bite. If you do, you'll leave something behind."

"Like what?" a man had asked.

"Like"—Renata had stopped to smile at them, as if she'd been asked this question before and took particular delight in giving them the answer—"an ear, a nose, a finger, a joint, or . . . your genitals." This had caused the class to offer a genuine groan. "Just about anything they can sink their teeth into. If it swings, sways, or sticks out, it's fair game."

"Oh," she added with a mischievous grin, "and breasts. We have lots of little boob biters out there too." There were more groans.

"Now it's real important," she had gone on to say, "to figure out if you're a fight or flight person. I'm sure you all remember from Psych 101 that the body releases adrenaline when you're scared. What I want you to do is try and think about what you've done when you've been in a scary situation. Is there a pattern there? Did you stand and fight, or did you run away? This is important to know. You don't have to tell us, so be honest with yourself.''

Celia sat there in her office with Davy Boyce's file in her hands and wondered about this again. She had never really been sure what she was: a flight person, or a fighter? She'd stood up to the poacher, even though she'd been scared. But when she thought about her childhood, she decided she might really be a flight person. It was easy enough for her to understand why: if you grow up scared, it's hard to change. And she'd been plenty scared as a child. She knew she'd matured in many ways, but the frightened little girl she'd been thirty years ago still hung around inside, flinching before her mother's angry face. It could crop up without warning: those furious eyes, cheeks red with rage, lips curled and tight like snakes ready to strike.

"Around and around we go, where we stop nobody knows."

Her mother had sung and smiled and enjoyed the cruel tease, with eyes as alive as light sockets. Celia was five years old. She stood in the kitchen and stared up at that angry face.

"Around and around we go, where we stop nobody knows . . . right, Cel?"

Celia turned away.

"Put out your hands," her mother said.

Celia *couldn't* move her arms; fear soldered them to her sides.

"Put . . . them . . . out . . . and . . . look . . . at . . . me." Her mother's voice sounded strained and low, like the rumbling of a dump truck as its bed is raised inch by inch, until the whole dirty load starts to slide.

Celia's hands shook, and she extended them slowly as she raised her eyes to her mother. She felt tight and cold—all of her—like something that freezes in the night.

"Scared? Are you scared?" Her mother's face was as tense as iron.

"Yes, Mommie," Celia cried.

"But you weren't scared before, were you?" Her voice sounded tortured, anger like a well that falls into darkness forever.

"No, Mommie." Celia's sisters watched, eager and scared

too; and glad they had been spared . . . for now. Their mother had taught them the basics of the jungle: that while she preyed on you she couldn't prey on them; playing them off one against the other, dividing and conquering the kingdom of childhood.

"Well . . . you . . . should . . . have . . . been." And then she took the big wooden spoon and smashed its hard oval face across Celia's knuckles. The pain made her scream, and she pulled her hands to her chest.

"What . . . did . . . I . . . say?" That voice again. "I . . . said . . . put . . . them . . . out. And don't you dare scream."

"Mommie," Celia pleaded with her eyes closed, her whole body shaking.

"Don't stamp your feet or I'll crack them too. How would you like that?"

Celia tried to still her body.

"Are you listening?"

"Yes, Mommie."

"I . . . don't . . . see . . . them."

"What, Mommie?"

"Don'tplaygameswithme." She spit those words out in a fury. "Youknowwhat." And then the spoon struck Celia's cheek and jaw, and her eyes blinked open as betrayal clawed another hole in the cheesecloth of her childhood.

"Your . . . hands."

Celia looked up. Her mother was a big woman, bigger than her youngest daughter would ever be, and she held that spoon like a club. Celia could feel a burning pain as her tears washed the cut that had just appeared on her cheek.

"You want me to do that again? Do you?"

"No, Mommie." Celia shook her head back and forth frantically.

"Then . . . put . . . your . . . hands . . . out."

And Celia had tried, as a child does, to figure out which was worse—the hands or the face. Slowly, she lifted her red hands, which had already begun to swell, and closed her eyes.

"Around and around we go, where we stop, nobody knows."

She had only a dusty memory of her father, and she had never been certain whether it was real or borrowed from an old photograph. He was a broad man leaning against a scrawny tree with a fedora tilted rakishly over his forehead, and he'd had a big smile, the kind that creases an entire face. But she concluded long ago that he must have been terribly unhappy because he walked out on his family two weeks before Celia's third birthday and they never heard from him again. Her mother said he was a vicious alcoholic who had beaten her repeatedly before finally leaving. Looking back, Celia thought violence had moved through her family like the flu, targeting the weak, leaving them weaker.

The fatherless family moved from house to house until they settled in a suburb on the south shore of Long Island. But this home proved no happier than the others, and by the time Celia entered high school she had already made plans to leave as soon as she turned eighteen. You have to be hard enough to survive, she told herself back then, and soft enough to make it worth your while. It was more wisdom than some people acquired in a lifetime.

On the very morning of her eighteenth birthday she fled with a suitcase and a knapsack. It was all she could carry; it was all she wanted of her life till then. She left behind her rosary and holy medals and the memory of saints' days and observances. She took a train to Chicago, a city large enough to hide in, and far enough away to make even a casual contact unlikely. For six years she did not communicate with her mother. She came to understand the cruelty of this and wrote her a brief note saying she was alive and well. Celia did not intend for it to start a correspondence or lead to a reunion, and it did neither.

Her mother died three years ago. Jack persuaded Celia to visit her after she entered the hospital for the last time. Her colon cancer had advanced to its final stages. She was days away from death, and looked weary of life. Her shrunken head sank heavily into a white pillow. Celia saddened when she saw her from the doorway, and she filled with feeling for her mother, but no reconciliation took place. Her mother's old anger hadn't died: it had just grown older and angrier.

"*Saint* Cecilia," she summoned the energy to announce when Celia walked in the room. A second bed was empty, and the television droned on: a game show, a low hum that remained faithful in the background—occasional laughter, moans, voices, clanging bells.

Saint Cecilia. The same scornful voice that Celia had heard throughout her childhood, the one that haunted her still. When she heard those words she knew the anger could not be far behind.

"You're so nice to everyone, aren't you? But your family? No, we're not good enough for you. We're not worth your precious time, are we, dearie? I guess we don't pay you enough, like those kids."

Celia could have fainted. All that hate, all those years. Even now. Her belly washed with blood, the way it did in moments of great fear. Her two sisters—older, married, mothers themselves—stood looking down silently. This had been too much even for them, family loyalists till the end.

"Oh, you're a cold fish, and don't think I didn't know it from the get-go."

Hate dribbled from her deathbed lips, and Celia slipped out of the room after her mother turned away. She had always needed someone to hate, and Celia had always been that someone.

But why me? She had asked herself that question so many times, and at the hospital she finally wondered if she'd been the result of rape: her father forcing his way in, bringing his seed to life with a drunk's bludgeoning indifference.

Marion, her oldest sister, had followed Celia down the hallway.

"I'm so sorry, Cel." Marion's eyes had teared.

"That's okay. I really didn't expect much. I mean, people don't change, right? They just become more of whatever they are."

But Marion stiffened, because Marion's mother was different from Celia's: same blood, but a different woman. They'd had two mothers: one kind enough to instill Marion's loyalty, and one cruel enough to have driven Celia away.

"Look, I've got to get out of here. It's killing me." She started crying then, and Marion had put her arms around her little sister and held her.

Their mother's death came two days later. At the funeral Mass Celia found that the stained-glass saints still separated the sunlight into beams of color, and the pungent odor of frankincense still filled the air; but the service itself had changed, infused with a warmth she did not remember from childhood.

The priest's voice echoed in the mostly empty church. Her mother had had no friends. Marion, her husband, Jim, and their children, Beth and Steven, occupied the first row. Sharon joined them. She was the tallest of the three sisters and had always been less tolerant of Celia's deviations. Celia sat behind them in a pew by herself.

The priest referred to her mother as a loving parent, and as a child of God called home. Later Celia watched the casket being lowered into the earth, and then Marion and Jim had taken her back to the airport.

No, Celia didn't think she was a fighter. She had fled the quiet crime of her childhood.

So I guess I'm into flight, she decided once again. It was the same verdict she'd reached during the training session. But as she sat at her desk waiting for Davy Boyce and his stepfather, she thought for the first time that maybe running away wasn't cowardly. What else could you have done? It's stupid to think you were a coward. It's more of that macho crap everyone grows up with, boys and girls all believing there's a moment of truth that defines us; the guys thinking they've got to be John Wayne, and all of us girls believing they have to be too, and now pretty much believing it for ourselves—another hand-me-down myth from men.

Moment of truth. Celia shook her head derisively. As if a single moment could define us. That's so ridiculous.

She laid the Boyce file on her desk and noticed the first page was damp from where her fingers had been squeezing it. She checked her watch. A little after nine. Father and son would be here soon enough. Renata's voice nibbled at the crust of her consciousness one more time.

"But no matter what you are—a fighter, or someone who runs away—the blood will come rushing from your brain to your organs, and your reasoning power will be at its lowest. So you want to know long before a client attacks you, What am I going to do? How am I going to react? You have to have a personal plan. That's very important."

All right, Celia asked herself. What'll I do if he bites me? You know, when the blood starts running out of my brain into his mouth. She shook her head—she'd have to think about it some more—and skimmed the rest of the three-page file, but there wasn't much to know beyond the fact that the boy was an elective mute and a biter.

She went over to her shelf of art supplies and picked up a box of felt-tipped markers and brought them over to the worktable. From a higher shelf she pulled down blank sheets of paper and grabbed a lead pencil. She studied the sharp point before deciding against giving him a potential weapon.

She reminded herself to keep her tone neutral during the evaluation. No matter what happened, she knew she had to maintain a calm demeanor when she had him do the drawings. And who knew, maybe everything would go just fine.

And if he bites you? The question returned, as persistent as rust or rot or anything that refused to relent.

She looked at her bare arms. Move in, roll down. The teeth, after all, came with the turf.

13

Chet loaded his chain saw into the bed of his pickup, back with the bark dust and dirt. He figured he'd need it sometime today. First he had to go in with Davy, meet this Mrs. Griswold, and find out what they were up to. He didn't like having to take him to that place for fucked-up kids, but he couldn't just up and leave. Money was too goddamn tight. How far could he go? He'd spent what he had to get here. So he'd take him in, play the game. The kid wouldn't say anything. This was one boy he didn't have to worry about. And when he was through with them and their questions—they always had questions, nosy motherfuckers—he'd put his chain saw to work. He kept it back there pretty much most of the time. You had to strike when the iron was hot—he knew this to be a fact—and it seemed like every time he got lazy and left his saw behind, he'd run across a whole bunch of windfall just waiting to be taken. It was true in Idaho, probably was here too. Wood was getting up there, and you could always find somebody to buy it. Look at that old man Marshall, paid $110 for a cord, and not even a full one at at that. Old fool couldn't tell.

Hell, when the timber companies cut, they'd leave behind a whole field of stumps, some of them three, four feet high. That was a hell of a lot of wood waiting to be taken, just like the fruit hanging from those trees all over the valley, though wood didn't pay nearly as good as fruit, and Chet knew this to be another one of those goddamn facts that hurt like a sore toe. Those orchard guys made out okay. They must. More tax breaks than an oil well. He'd heard that the other day and had no reason to doubt it, not with the way they drove around in those fancy fucking trucks.

Doing a lot better than the loggers. No jobs with the timber companies. From the sound of it things had got so bad, some of the owners were back out felling trees themselves. If they didn't need you and there wasn't much work to go around, they had two strikes against you before you ever got to take a swing at a tree.

But Chet knew he'd make out okay. He had his trailer. He even had a woodstove rigged up. Did that last year, opened the side of it. Just like peeling off the top of a tin can. One minute the silver wall was just shiny and saying "No, don't touch me," and the next it was hanging open and he could see the insides, the carpet and the bottom of a cabinet, the one with his tools. It made him think about things. It did.

But that stove was hell to haul around, and he never did get it to vent right. It got smoky every time he used it. Smoke drifted out so slow you couldn't even see it, just smell it, like someone was spraying acid up your nose. Chet knew he'd have to get that stove figured out soon. This weather wouldn't keep.

He looked around for Davy. Called him five minutes ago and told him to get moving. He hated to run late, hated it. Made him feel . . . *inferior*. And it was ten after nine. Shit, where the hell . . . there he is. Already in the damn cab. Doesn't talk and moves like an Indian. Kid will be a good hunter when I teach him to shoot. But not now. Later, when he's older. If he's good. They got to earn your respect.

He climbed in and shook the boy's shoulder. "When we get there, don't go popping off about your mom. Remember, I *keep* my promises."

The kid wouldn't even look at him. What else is new? But he'd heard, Chet could tell. Nothing wrong with those ears. Nothing wrong with the rest of him either. Chet smiled. Hell, it couldn't have worked out better if he'd taken a pair of pruning sheers and cut his damn tongue right out of his head.

He liked having a son again. He never went without one for long. A son was good for a man. As he started driving into town, Davy was good for hearing him out. Sometimes Chet had a lot to say, had to unload his every concern. This was one of those times. They were passing a roadside park with picnic tables and tall trees.

"You see that? They got as many trees as ants in that

place. And that's just a goddamn waste. Those trees are like fruit. That's right, just like pears and apples. If you don't pick them, the worms get them. Trees are no damn different. You go in the forest and see a tree dying by itself, that's a crime. There are all kinds of things feeding away at it, like worms and bugs, but not people. See, if I took down those trees back there, we'd eat for a year. Easy. And no one would miss them. It's for the tourists, and they can't miss them if they don't know they're not there. They can't. Like there.'' They were driving by a broad clear-cut that extended all the way up the side of the valley. ''That fed a lot of people. That park back there, that's not doing a damn thing. Not for you, not for me. No one even there. Whole country's full of parks, big parks, and no one's there and they keep us out. It's just worms and bugs feeding in places like that. But that'll change when people get hungry enough. You'll see. Then we'll all get to feed.''

Davy gazed at the stumps and broken branches, all gray and bleached by the sun. Bark? he wondered. He didn't see any. He knew it protected trees, his real daddy had told him so, but the bark was gone. Why?

He also saw the weeds, some as tall as he was. They looked like they had stickers on them, like nothing he'd want to touch. And dead ferns lay beside the road like fossils in the dust, like maybe there were dinosaurs around here that did this, big scary things with huge teeth. He'd seen dinosaur movies and once had a dinosaur book, but he couldn't remember much about them now. He could never remember stuff, and his head felt like it was filled with ants or some other kind of itchy things that crawled around inside and wanted to get out.

Davy looked at the stumps again. Hundreds of them. All the way to town. Trees all cut down. The bark still bothered him a lot.

14

Without looking away from Harold Matley's self-portrait, Celia hit the intercom button on her phone and thanked Barbara.

"Tell them I'll be right there."

She hurriedly put aside the latest drawing by the schizophrenic boy and arranged the papers on her desk, producing a semblance of order in a matter of seconds.

In the reception area Barbara, with her half-moon glasses nesting in her cloud of white hair, suggested the Boyces take a seat while they waited. Chet looked over at the couch by the window but didn't move, so neither did Davy; and when Celia stepped from the hallway she thought they looked as rigid as fence posts.

"Hi, I'm Mrs. Griswold, and you must be Mr. Boyce?" She let her voice rise when she said his name, like the smile that some people can place at the end of a greeting without sounding affected.

"Yeah, that's me." Chet offered her a firm, eager handshake, which Celia took as a positive sign. A lot of parents showed up full of resentment because they thought their children's problems reflected poorly on them. Often they were right. The staff typically fought their biggest battles with the mothers and fathers or guardians. They were generally the most disturbed members of their families and getting them to change their behavior usually proved more difficult than working with their offspring. When the staff did manage to make progress with a child, it almost always happened *despite* the parents. In her more charitable moments Celia reminded herself that rotten family trees have deep roots, and that the parents themselves probably had been abused; but she found it hard to be so generous, especially after she'd made small gains with a child only to see the boy or girl battered into a stunned submission by another beating—or worse—at home.

But Celia considered it a mark of her professionalism to remain nonjudgmental when she met a parent. You had to give them the benefit of the doubt. If you didn't, you'd become suspicious of everyone and never make significant progress with the families. And some parents honestly concerned themselves with the plight of their children. She could only hope this was true with Mr. Boyce. He did appear pleased to be here. That was a start.

"And this is my stepson, Davy."

She found this impressive too, that he took the initiative with the introduction. A lot of parents lacked all social skills and became belligerent with the staff right in front of their children. It didn't make working with the kids any easier when the parents signaled their disapproval so obviously.

"Hi, Davy, I'm glad to meet you." She stuck out her hand, but the child refused to acknowledge it. Mr. Boyce nudged his stepson, then bent over and murmured, "Do it." But even with this stern prodding the boy kept his eyes fixed on the floor.

I'll bet he *is* a handful, thought Celia.

"Remember my promise. Now shake Mrs. Griswold's hand."

She wondered what Mr. Boyce had promised his stepson. Candy? Money? She hoped not: bribery worked only in the short run.

Whatever it was, it did prompt Davy to offer Celia his limp hand to go along with his downcast eyes and empty expression. Some children are instantly likable. She realized the Boyce boy was not among them, then reminded herself that her cool reaction to him might be little more than a mirror reflecting Davy's reaction to the world. If he found it cold, or even cruel, he would no doubt withdraw from every encounter and produce the same response in the people he met.

"Davy, why don't you and your stepfather come back to my office and I'll explain to you what we'll be doing here?"

Chet shook his head. You and *your* stepfather. Explain to *you*. Not even talking to me.

"Mr. Boyce." Celia saw that he looked unhappy. "Is that okay with you?"

"Sure, sure." He recovered quickly. "It's just no use talking to him. Most times he doesn't listen. Might as well just talk to me."

"How about if I talk to both of you?" she suggested cheerily.

Chet nodded. "Might work." But as he followed her down the hall he clenched his jaw and locked his eyes on her bottom, all snugged up in those tight-ass jeans, and he realized that she looked just like a . . . *boy.* Short body, short hair, tiny butt, nothing on top. Nothing like a woman. That sickened him, truly sickened him, seeing her parading around like this, like a boy. Just who the hell does she think she is? Chet hated that more than anything, when women weren't women. He couldn't take that kind of misbehavior, not one little bit. Wasn't meant to be, but here she was ordering him around— "Here, how about this seat, Mr. Boyce? And Davy over there, that's right"—and he couldn't do a damn thing about it. Not a damn thing except sit there while she walked around her big desk, sit there while she made you look at her tiny goddamn ass, sit there while every goddamn thought ate away at him till his whole goddamn mind fried in an acid bath of anger.

When Celia worked with children she often sat in front of her desk to eliminate as many barriers as possible, but during their evaluation she preferred to keep some distance to avoid unduly influencing their responses. Her initial posture with the children dovetailed nicely with the need to establish professional authority with the parents, though Mr. Boyce did not appear troublesome.

But the more she talked, the more Chet could feel his rage building. She was drawing the fury right out of him. Hell, if she wasn't. That sweet smile, those smooth words, they always had those *smooth* words. Always.

"Now, Davy, I understand—"

There she goes again, ignoring me. He could not take this . . . this undermining him in front of his boy, making him sit there and take it. And take it. And take it.

". . . you've been having some problems in school, so that's why we're meeting today to see if we can find solutions. I also understand you're also having difficulty expressing yourself, so when we get started here I'm going to have you draw pictures. Do you like to—"

Pictures? PICTURES? They take him out of second grade and make me bring him here so he can draw some goddamn pictures? Chet spoke up. He had to, but in a soft voice that belied the seething inside.

"Draw pictures? Why? Davy doesn't even talk. How's that going to help him? Is this why you pulled him out of school, to draw pictures?"

Celia saw the honest confusion on Mr. Boyce's face. She'd run into it before with other parents who considered art frivolous, not a real school activity.

"Mr. Boyce, this is Davy's school now. This is where he's going to have to come every morning, and where he'll have to stay until we can figure out how to get him talking again."

"And how are you going to do that with picture drawing?" This worried Chet, but for reasons he could not yet explain.

"Because I'm an art therapist, that's what I do, and sometimes I can be especially helpful with children like Davy who don't speak."

Celia noticed that Mr. Boyce, unlike most of the parents she worked with, paid close attention to her, so she continued,

"You see, a lot of children don't talk because they're not comfortable with themselves. But if we can get them to draw, we can help them. Instead of saying how they feel with words, they say it with pictures."

Enough of that, Celia told herself, you're probably boring him to death. But much to her surprise Mr. Boyce sat forward, as if to ask another question. Imagine that, she thought, a parent who's really interested.

"No kidding. So you're really kind of like a . . . a detective." Chet almost winced when he realized what he'd said.

"A detective? I never thought of it like that. What do you mean?" But even as she replied she knew he was right. Art therapy was detective work. She used lines and colors, shapes and forms instead of fingerprints, blood analysis, bullets and ballistics.

"You're looking for clues in what they draw, right?" Chet knew he'd made a mistake suggesting she was a detective, but he couldn't turn back now.

"Yes, I suppose you could put it that way, but I'd prefer to think of myself as someone just trying to help."

She really didn't want to encourage this art therapy as detective business. Too much of that could make a parent feel persecuted. If you could get them on your side or keep them there, as Mr. Boyce appeared to be, you could make progress with their children much more quickly.

"So what do you look for?" Chet had a familiar feeling in his stomach, the way it acted up when things weren't just right in his world. It wasn't a good feeling at all.

"That varies from child to child."

"But you've done this before?"

"Oh, many times. I've worked with lots of children like Davy who don't talk." Celia had stretched the truth, she had actually worked with only two other elective mutes, but she considered it important to build confidence in the boy and his stepfather.

Lots of children. Chet found those words chilling. Maybe the kid wasn't so unusual. Maybe this art therapy really did work. Maybe the very first thing Davy would say was . . . But no, he wouldn't let that happen. He'd never let it happen before. You stop them. You stop them dead in their tracks if you have to. But you keep up a smooth front . . . like their smooth words.

"But it's not like he's *really* talking, is it?"

"No, you're right, Mr. Boyce. It's not like he's talking like you and I are talking, but you'd be amazed at how clearly some children say things with their drawings. Sometimes it takes a while to get them going, but sometimes it happens quickly."

"That's really something. That's great." Chet put his arm around Davy's shoulders and hugged him. "Isn't that great, Davy? They're going to be able to help you. Finally, someone who can help." He smiled at Celia. "Is it just you that does

this or do the others"—he gestured vaguely at the Center—
"do they do it too?"

"No, it's just me. I'm the art therapist. There aren't that
many of us in the country, not like psychologists, but we're
having a lot of success . . ."

So it *is* just her.

". . . I won't be the only one working with him, though.
Our entire staff will be involved. We all work together."

"But you're the one"—Chet pointed playfully to her—
"that we're pinning our hopes on."

"No, not really." Celia smiled modestly. "I can't do it all
by myself." She looked directly at Davy, who had remained
stone-faced throughout the meeting. "I'm going to need your
help, Davy, but I bet you'll like the drawing we do." She
raised her eyes to Chet, a handsome man, she thought. "And
of course if there's anything you can tell us that might help
Davy, we'd like to hear about that too. I understand you'll
be talking to our director, Dr. Tony Weston. You should feel
free to bring up anything with him. With all of us working
together, we might see some very quick developments."

"I'll do everything I can," Chet vowed. "It's been a tough
time for us, ever since the boy's mom died."

She heard his voice crack when he said this.

"I'm so sorry. When was that?"

Chet blinked a tear loose and felt its warm trail run all the
way down his cheek. Whenever he pulled this act he really
did feel sad, and it was easy to sound all torn up inside. Fun,
too.

"Last year. That's when Davy stopped talking." He laid
a protective hand on the boy's shoulder.

Celia fought the lump forming in her throat. They really
were a sad pair, a widower and a motherless boy. One so
traumatized he couldn't talk at all, and the other barely able
to speak of his grief. She must have been a remarkable
woman. I wonder how she died. But Celia knew it would be
bad form to ask.

"Thank you for telling me that, Mr. Boyce. That's exactly
the kind of helpful information we need." She already knew
about the deceased mother from the file, but wanted to encourage Mr. Boyce's openness as much as possible. "Is there

anything else we should know about, or that we should talk
about by ourselves?''

By ourselves. He liked the sound of that. Some of them
want it long before they know it. They speak in codes and
give you clues. Her too. He wiped away a tear and shook his
head mournfully, still feeling the sadness, still having great
fun.

''Then I guess we should get started. If you want to come
back at noon Davy will be ready for you then. Our school
normally goes from ten to two-thirty, but we keep their first
day short.''

''How about if I just stay? I'd love to see how you do this
art therapy.''

''I'm afraid you won't be able to, Mr. Boyce, but you're
more than welcome to wait in the reception room.'' As she
spoke, Celia rose and walked out from behind her desk. She
gently took Mr. Boyce's arm and guided him out the door.
''You see, Davy and I need to work together in privacy. After
the evaluation is complete I'll be glad to review all of this
with you if you'd like. It's wonderful when parents take the
kind of interest in their children that you do, Mr. Boyce, but
Davy and I will need this time to ourselves.''

Chet wasn't even sure how she did it but she'd left him
in the hallway before he knew what had happened. And then
she shut the door. But he was certain of one thing, had absolutely no doubt about it: she touched him first.

15

Davy looked up nervously. Now that they were alone his eyes darted around Celia's office, and she figured her biggest challenge would be to focus his fidgety energy.

"Davy, I'm really happy you're here today." She paused to smile, but all he did was glance at her warily. "What I'd like to do is have you draw some pictures."

He turned away, and his eyes continued to jump around.

"We'll start by having you come over here." She'd have to prod his every move, she could see that already. And she'd have to watch him carefully. She did not want to be bitten. "Come on."

He didn't budge. She thought he looked extremely tense. She put her hand on his shoulder to coax him along and detected a trembling under his shirt. The boy was scared. Of her? The Center? Probably both, she decided.

Davy stood up under her gentle guidance, much as his stepfather had before him, and moved over to the table.

She laid a single sheet of white paper in front of him, picked up a black felt-tip pen and placed it in his hand. He held it for barely a second before dropping it and leaving a dark smudge on the blank sheet.

Hmmm. Celia studied him but he no longer returned her gaze, not even for a jittery second or two, for now his eyes moved past her to the shelves full of supplies. She turned and saw the sharp tip of the lead pencil, the one she had decided against giving him because it was a potential weapon. She looked back and, yes, that's what he was staring at.

"Do you want the pencil?"

He didn't answer, not exactly. He just kept his eyes pinned to the pencil point, which stuck out about an inch from the edge of the shelf.

Okay, she conceded uneasily, if that's what you want. But even as she considered the pencil's menacing possibilities she knew it was even more important to appear fearless. Once a child learned he could intimidate you, he was likely to turn therapy into a war of nerves. She could not let that happen under any circumstances, so she handed him the pencil.

Davy received it with both hands and examined the yellow barrel, turning it round and round before testing the tip with his index finger.

"Now, Davy, I want you to draw a picture of a person."

She watched her words register in his eyes, which no longer remained on the pencil point but rose to meet hers. She knew he was not supposed to have any difficulty understanding speech.

"You may start now, Davy."

But he didn't start. He looked at her, and though Celia was tempted to encourage him, she held back. She knew that children also conveyed a great deal when they refused to draw: their defiance, insecurity, or fear of their innermost feelings. But she'd found that most of the kids who wouldn't cooperate were older than Davy. She'd encountered a number of reluctant adolescents when she worked at the Illinois Psychiatric Clinic in Chicago. They had been sophisticated enough to understand that art therapy could reveal their secrets, and fearful enough of the past to want to keep it hidden. When a child Davy's age refused to draw, the reason could be simpler, and a lot sadder: art was play, but some kids didn't know how to play because their childhoods had been stolen from them.

Davy tapped the pencil point against the paper but kept looking at Celia, as if seeing her for the first time. Then he propped open his mouth with the eraser the way children sometimes do. His top teeth stuck out at an unpleasant angle, and she felt bad for him. He definitely needed orthodontic work, but would probably never receive it. The Boyces did not appear to have those kinds of resources. Davy's top two front teeth were also crossed at the bottom and brought to mind swordsmen touching their weapons before a match. The words *en garde* rang hollowly from the memory of a college boyfriend who had taken up fencing, and who had once scared her almost senseless by jumping out of a closet wearing only his wire-mesh mask.

Davy's canines also protruded and looked very much like the fangs for which they had been named. His teeth gave his face a threatening appearance it did not deserve. His lips, for instance, were perfectly formed and sweet, and did his face the favor of covering up its principal flaw. As a young girl Celia also had had terribly formed teeth, but braces had been out of the question until she'd left home and could pay for them herself. Throughout her childhood she'd tried to keep her mouth closed, concealing her teeth much as she'd learned to hide her thoughts and fears from her mother. Celia figured Davy might be doing this already. By not talking he was clearly hiding his feelings, and the tortured arrangement of his teeth might be the perfect metaphor for the jumble of thoughts he kept hidden inside.

She saw that he could turn out to be a handsome man, if his teeth were fixed and he grew into his nose. It looked a bit large for his face, though hardly so pronounced as to command more than fleeting attention. And that crew cut, that has got to go. She knew crew cuts were back in style, but she had never cared for them and thought Davy's did little for his appearance.

He looked down, as though to begin, and when he actually put the pencil to the paper and started to draw, Celia wanted to applaud. She was genuinely happy to see this and not at all discouraged by the undersized nature of his effort. A lot of adults were also self-conscious when they worked on their first picture, and many of them likewise drew small figures, as though to minimize the mistakes they imagined they were making.

His lines were hard and dark, and he drew slowly and with concentration. Remarkably, he drew well, not with the blessed instincts of an artist—not yet, anyway—but with a steady focus and a basic appreciation of form. The line quality was sure and he lacked the certain crudeness of many seven-year-olds, and not a few adults. He even used shading, which would make Celia's job easier: it almost always revealed what a client worked hardest to cover up. Shading was one of the paradoxes of art therapy that fascinated her.

She couldn't be sure just yet but it appeared that Davy was drawing a woman. If that turned out to be the case, she'd have to give a lot of thought to this highly unusual decision. But she tried mightily not to interpret his work right now because she believed that at some instinctive or intuitive level he would feel judged and therefore inhibited. Much of art therapy was predicated on the power of the unconscious mind. The behavior therapists dominated psychotherapy in the United States, and cared little for this notion. Tony, their new director, clearly belonged to this straitlaced school, which typically disparaged art therapists as a largely useless lot of women who had succeeded neither as artists nor as therapists.

Women did dominate the field, and Celia was convinced this was the real reason for the strong bias against art therapy. She wasn't without her own passions and prejudices, and had little patience for behavior therapy and all its hard-nosed devotees produced in droves in North American universities. She attributed their preeminence to the society's emphasis on product as opposed to process. These were the same fools— and that's precisely how she thought of them—who had taught parents to tell their children, "I love you but I don't like what you're doing," as though the behavior and the child could be separated from each other in such a tidy fashion. Celia found this approach consistent with a system that preferred to deal only in surface qualities, that devalued women when their looks faded, and older people when their productivity faltered.

At times like these Celia wished she could be relieved of every last vestige of vanity so she would never again stand before a mirror in judgment of herself, for it played right into the hands of all the men and women who promoted surface qualities at the expense of the larger, wilder world that existed under things. That's what counts, she thought, all the messages hidden in the lines that Davy draws, the story behind the story.

Her faith in art therapy had grown slowly, for she'd possessed an ample store of skepticism when she was introduced to it. Like most of her colleagues, she did have a strong background in art. She had majored in it at the University of Illinois and minored in psych. Art therapy was a natural for

Celia, but her exposure to behavior therapy during her undergrad days had been so successful that it took some time for the magical means of the unconscious to wave its marvelous wand.

Intellectual curiosity had driven her to take a weekend seminar offered by one of the field's pioneers, an elderly gentleman from Seattle who sat by a slide projector and narrated one case history after another. He pointed out what would later become obvious to the fledgling Celia: that people revealed themselves through their art; whether they intended to was completely irrelevant. They did it with what they chose to draw, how they chose to draw it, their line quality, shading, color, and the way they handled facial features and rendered bodies. In short, the entire universe of inclusions and exclusions.

Celia began to study her own paintings and saw that this was true. The inner world of her fears, anxieties, hopes, and dreams came to life in her brush strokes, once she'd learned to look beyond the seductive surface of simple forms.

She grew increasingly enamored of the field, and while she would have preferred simply to paint for a living, no one had shown a great inclination actually to buy her artwork, mostly flowers and trees that filled her canvases with voluptuous folds. She was well aware of the O'Keeffe influence, but didn't care. She was driven to paint these swirling sensuous objects, so that's what she did.

Her only other career option had been commercial art, but that had seemed a sure way to deaden whatever talent she possessed. Art therapy, with its appeal to her intellect, her sense of aesthetics, and her altruistic inclinations, came along at the right time. She enrolled; she excelled; and she even landed a job in Bentman, which seemed the greatest feat of all.

She checked on Davy, saw him working away, then moved over to the window and spotted Jimmy and Ira on the swings in the play area. The van must have just arrived. She checked her watch and saw that it was almost ten o'clock, which marked the beginning of the "children's day," the term the staff used for the hours from ten to two-thirty when their clients were present. During this time the children attended

school in the small building behind the Center, received counseling from the therapists, ate lunch, played during recess, and
met as a group twice—at the start of the day to set goals, and
at the end of the day to talk about whether they'd achieved
them. Then they boarded the van for their return trip home.

It was just a four-and-a-half-hour day for the children, but
all of them suffered from short attention spans, and keeping
them in class any longer had always proved self-defeating.

On a typical day, one or two of them would whirl out of
control and have to be restrained. Celia disliked doing this
because it meant that the various peaceful means of working
with the child had failed and the Center was resorting to muscle to operate in a timely manner.

The staff rarely hurt a child during a restraint, and when
they did it was usually a minor bruise and was always—to
Celia's knowledge—an accident. More often it was the adults
who were were injured during these confrontations. They had
to take hold of a rampaging child, carry him or her downstairs
to containment—a small room with padded walls, floors, ceiling, and one-way glass—and wrap their arms and legs around
the boy or girl to immobilize what was most often a thrashing
body. That's when it could get really tough on Celia and her
co-workers: lips were split, genitals were kicked or squeezed,
muscles wrenched, and eyes blackened, as one of hers had
once been. In general, when an angry child had to be restrained, the therapists could undergo a wide range of physical
abuse.

Celia prided herself on holding her own during these
rough-and-tumble sessions. Although short, she was strong,
with clearly defined arm muscles, and legs that had been
firmed up from all the hiking she enjoyed up on the ridge.
Only the children who had used their teeth to attack had made
her hesitate; but never for long, and never enough to get in
the way of her work. Now another biter was on board, though
Davy's behavior so far had been much better than she'd expected.

She found his cooperation encouraging, and in sharp contrast to the boy who initially had refused even to shake her
hand.

When he finished he pushed the paper to the side and looked at her.

Ordinarily, she asked children about their art: What's going on here? Can you tell me a story about this picture? But she had to admit that Tony was right when he said that she wouldn't get any help from Davy. There would be none of the verbal give-and-take that characterized her sessions with other clients.

She picked up his drawing and thanked him. They had about forty-five minutes before his stepfather was due to return, so she decided to give Davy his tour of the Center. He might also be hungry, so she would offer him a snack when they reached the kitchen. It pleased her when he walked along without hesitation, and she soon forgot that he was the ferocious little biter depicted in the file.

16

Chet watched the waitress fill his cup. Ugly old bitch. Just looking at her made him sick, and he had plenty to be sick about without her.

PICTURES! He was still shaking his head over that one. You get a kid that doesn't talk, hell, that's as good as it gets, and then she turns around and says she's going to have him draw some pictures so he can *communicate*. Her and her *smooth* words.

I'm sorry, Mr. Boyce, but Davy and me need this time for us.

Or whatever the hell she said.

Chet felt his mood grow as dark as his coffee. He stirred in three packets of sugar and took a sip. Tasted like syrup. Good. He drank some more, then picked up his fork and played with his cinnamon roll, what was left of it. Not much more than a piece of crust. He couldn't finish it. A raisin had lost its sticky grip and fallen off. That spoiled everything. It lay on his plate like a ball of fucking rat shit. Goddamn, he hated rats. He wanted to take that raisin and mash it, smear it across his plate, stab it with his fucking fork.

But there were people around, so he just played with the fucker. He rolled it back and forth. It couldn't do shit. He was waiting for the right moment. It would come. It always did. He'd know it too, just when to stab it. Back and forth, back and forth, looking at how black it was, and wrinkled like that old bitch, like it would just as soon be dead. Be better off dead, wouldn't she? Well, *wouldn't* she?

He angled his fork carefully. An outer tine rested on the raisin. This was it. He started pressing down real slowly. He saw the way the skin sagged, but there's a point—it's a fact, like the sun going down—when it just can't sag anymore and has to give. He watched the skin break and the tine cut right in. The raisin's belly juices oozed up along the metal, and that's when the fucker died, when he had it on the tip of his fork, stuck there like some shriveled-up old thing. Like her with the coffeepot. He wanted to dump it on her. Scald her *good!*

She smiled and topped off his coffee.

"Can I get you anything else?"

He shook his head.

"Well, you have yourself a nice day, you hear?"

She put the check down.

Chet watched her walk away. He saw the fork sticking out from the side of her neck. He blinked, and it was gone. But the blood, he could still see the blood. Red holes running.

17

Celia quickly gathered up several file folders and checked her watch. She didn't want to be late for Dr. Punctual. Tony had asked to see her at three to find out what she'd learned, "if anything," about Davy.

"Plenty," she'd replied impulsively during their brief hallway conversation. But now she wished she'd been more reserved because Davy's artwork was actually quite puzzling.

As she walked upstairs she noticed how quiet the Center had become since the van departed with the children half an hour ago.

Mr. Boyce had picked up Davy promptly at noon. She had spoken to him just long enough to let him know that his stepson had cooperated with the first phase of the evaluation, but that it was still likely to take at least a week. She'd wanted to explain that you just couldn't rush these things, but had refrained because he'd seemed so withdrawn, maybe even sullen. She'd found that surprising after the energy and enthusiasm he'd displayed that morning. Quite the mood swing. Perhaps he was just tired or having a bad day.

She tapped on Tony's door, and he waved her in without looking up from the note he was writing.

He'd arranged his office with the kind of precision that she could only admire. Unlike her home, Celia's work space always ended up a complete mishmash. Captain Chaos, that's what Jack called her. Like he should talk. But Tony had placed everything—pens, files, books, journals, staff assignments, reports—neatly in place; and nothing appeared the least bit ruffled from use, which Celia also regarded as amazing. In her own office every pad, book, and folder seemed to sprout dog-ears after a few days of occupancy, and coffee stains sprang up like mushrooms overnight.

Tony finished his note and folded it crisply before inserting it into a file, which he placed in the cabinet beside his desk.

Only after swiveling back around did he offer Celia his attention, and then only with a "Well?"

Well what? she wanted to reply, which is how she thought Ethan would have handled it; but Celia stifled this response because she wanted to establish a positive mood with Tony. She had an unusual request for a man as rigid as he appeared to be, and she wanted him to be as receptive as possible.

"Well, we got off to a good-enough start." She handed him the drawing, which he looked at for no more than two seconds.

"Okay, so it looks like he drew a picture of a woman. At least I can see what it is. Most of these kids, you can't tell what they're drawing."

"Sure you can," Celia said with as much encouragement as she could muster, "you just have to look closely. Now this one"—she pointed to Davy's drawing—"I find interesting. Ninety-nine kids out of a hundred, you ask them to draw a picture of a person, they draw themselves."

"Really?" Tony glanced back at the picture. "So what does an art therapist make of this?"

"I'm not sure exactly, except that in and of itself it's . . . well . . . peculiar."

Tony picked up the picture and studied it. "Maybe the boy misses his mother. During my talk with Mr. Boyce he mentioned that business about the boy no longer talking after she passed away."

"I know, he's told all of us about that, the school too. But I think Davy wants to talk."

Tony pushed away from his desk, leaned back in his chair, and smiled.

"That's putting a positive spin on it. The young man has been in school for over a week and hasn't said word one to anybody."

"But when I gave him a pencil and asked him to draw, he did give us this, even if it is a little . . . perplexing."

"I thought you said that he'd given you 'plenty.' "

"In a lot of ways he did," Celia insisted gamely. She

walked around his desk so she could point out details in Davy's work. "Look at the nose."

Tony rolled back up and studied the drawing again.

"What nose?"

"Exactly," she said softly. "Davy didn't even bother with one. Just like those Japanese children who come from perfectly controlled families that never show emotion, those kids never draw noses either. Here"—she reached for the files she'd brought with her—"I want you to take a look at some other pictures so you can see what I mean."

She spread out five drawings.

"Look at these and find me a single American kid who draws a picture without a nose, and these aren't unusual, not a bit. And you know why? American families show emotion. Look at this one." She pointed to an oversized drawing of a woman. "She's snorting like a bull, breathing hard just like people really do when they're angry and emotional. And let's face it, the kids who drew these pictures are not the products of the healthiest homes—they're *our* clients. But with Davy it's like he doesn't want to let go of any emotion at all."

Celia ran her fingers over the neck of the woman Davy had drawn.

"See how the lines don't even connect? There's a definite separation between the mind and body."

"You're sure you're not stretching this a bit?" Tony covered his mouth as he yawned.

"No, not at all. You say it could be his mom, right?"

"That seems likely enough to me."

"But a child who's lost a parent generally draws them with little feet, or no feet at all, and that's because they've taken flight. This woman has huge feet, exactly what a person draws when they feel tied down and can't escape."

Celia tapped the mouth of the woman. "And look at that, a single line, sealed up like a bank vault."

"That is interesting, given his mutism. I'll grant you that much."

"It makes me wonder if this is a self-portrait, and if it is, what are those clues saying—"

"Clues?" Tony interrupted. "Are you the Inspector Clouseau of the paint-and-crayon set?" He smiled when he said this and she wasn't sure if he was being pleasant and playful, or sarcastic. Celia decided that he'd made a weak stab at humor and let it pass.

"The question"—she began to pace—"is why would he see himself as a woman? None of it adds up."

She stopped to peer out the window at the empty play area. "Davy seems to have a good-enough stepfather. Mr. Boyce is a breath of fresh air compared to some of the parents we get in here. At least he's interested. He sure asks a lot of questions."

"But I didn't find him terribly open"—Tony pulled on his lower lip—"other than saying that Davy's mom died, which he'd already told the school."

"But that's not all that unusual, is it?" Celia turned away from the window. "I mean, it was the first time you talked to him, and you weren't with him that long. How open could he be?"

"No, that's true."

Celia quickly straddled a chair with the back facing forward.

"I don't exactly have Davy talking either, and I never will working with him just twice a week." She paused, wondering how to make her plea, then decided to just go for it: "How about if I get him for an hour a day? It's not like you or anyone else around here can spend time interviewing him."

"No, but I've already got him scheduled for other types of therapy, and—"

"An hour, Tony! Please, just an hour a day with him. This is a kid who doesn't even talk. It'll be his best chance every day to say something, maybe something important."

Tony frowned at the drawings spread out in front of him. Celia couldn't tell if he was irritated over her request or the fact that his desk now resembled her own. But when he looked up he agreed.

"All right, you can have an hour a day. I'll rework the schedule, but I want to remind you that I see this as a real acid test of your technique. You're not going to get any short-cuts with this kid. He's not going to be able to tell you about his drawings. It's just going to be you, the kid, and the cray-ons."

"I know," Celia said as she stuffed the pictures back in the folders, "you said something like that earlier."

"Yes, and you shook your head when I said it."

He looked at her intently, though she wasn't sure if it was with anger or understanding.

"Sorry, it's just that—"

"Forget about it," he said abruptly, "just think about wearing long sleeves when you work with him. The thicker, the better."

18

Jack waved good-bye to Ruth and locked the front door behind her. It was five o'clock, and he was glad to see her go. She often joked that she'd been "born and bred in Bentman with a bottom as big as a barge." All of which was true. Jack liked her outgoing nature and thought she worked well with people; but what had started to bother him was her suspicious nature, a quality he'd always admired when she dealt with insurance claims but found less endearing now that he was trying to carry on an affair right under her nose. And if Ruth knew, then the whole town knew, and if there was one thing Jack knew it was that he didn't want Celia to know. He'd met any number of women who could make him violate his vows, but none who had seriously tempted him to leave his wife. Helen was no exception. He expected her back any minute. This had become their routine of late: Helen would leave. Ruth would leave. Helen would return.

And there she was, tapping on the rear door. When he unlocked it, she reached out and kissed him before he could even swing it shut. His eyes frantically searched the alley for anyone passing by as her tongue sought out his weak spots and made them come alive. She spoke with that soft voice of hers, and he felt her breath warm and moist against his neck.

"I can't stand it, being so close to you all day long and not touching you."

Not that Helen ever really let those working hours go to waste. No, not hardly. Even with Ruth no more than ten feet away and with customers at the front counter she would swing her chair around and let Jack have a good long look up her legs. Sometimes she wore the sheerest panties, and sometimes she didn't wear anything at all. At first he reveled in her bold

playfulness, but the spectacle had proved less pleasing as his
fear of discovery had grown.

He laid his hands on her shoulders and backed away a half
step.

"We need to talk."

"What do you mean? You told her, didn't you?"

"Yes, I told her." He remembered sitting on the deck,
casually mentioning the Trout River trip to Celia, asking her
to come along for the weekend, when he knew she was on
call. It had been a cheap ploy that still made him feel guilty.
He was tired of deceiving her, especially now that they were
actually planning to have children. It felt . . . unseemly. And,
well, to be honest, Jack had to admit that there was another
reason he was having second thoughts about this affair,
maybe even the most important one: his libido just wasn't
what it used to be, and since he'd started up with Helen he'd
had trouble getting it up with Celia.

He caressed her youthful shoulders and tried to put aside
how much he liked the feel of her silk blouse.

"But I'm really not . . . comfortable . . . with what's been
going on."

Helen nibbled his neck and ran her hands down his body
until her fingertips brushed lightly against the front of his
pants. Up and down. Up . . .

"What are you talking about, sweetie?" . . . and down. "I
told Ralph I was going to my sister's, and you've set it up
with Celia. Come on, don't go losing your nerve now."

"It's not that, it's just that maybe we ought to slow down
a little."

"Okay, Jack," she whispered, "we can slow down, *after*
this weekend." Her fingers fled to his chest, brushed aside
his tie. "But not before."

He thought he'd heard the slightest hint of anger, but
couldn't be sure because she pulled his face close to hers,
stared intently into his eyes, and kissed him. The front of his
pants came even more fully to life, and his hands turned
greedy for the profits of touch. As he put his arms around her
and lifted her skirt, he moved her gracefully to the side until
he caught her near-naked reflection in the mirror by the bathroom door. She wore sheer gray pantyhose that rose like a

veil to her waist and revealed all the sweet dark shadings of sex.

She opened his zipper slowly. Jack could feel the tug and tease of the silver teeth separating, and her fingers inching down the length of him.

"Until then I'm going to wear you out, mister, or die trying."

She reached inside, and he delighted in those first few movements. Then she bent over just long enough to kiss the moist tip. "Okay, Buster Brown, hand it over."

Buster Brown. Jack couldn't figure this. Women always had nicknames for him. Why was that? He'd been called Moon, Bear, Jigs, and now Buster Brown. Only Celia had refrained from giving him a pet name.

He let go of Helen's skirt, and with great regret watched the hem fall to her thighs. She stepped away and waited, and he stood there feeling foolish with his private parts so publicly displayed. But she was smiling at him and he realized once again that she had the most amazingly full lips he had ever kissed, and she kept them quite red. He had never known a woman who applied lipstick as often as she did. At the most appropriate moments too. She said she did it to "accent the act." Indeed.

Hand it over. It didn't feel right to him, a betrayal that cut deep; but even the first time, when they'd made love in the walk-in vault and their breath had echoed loudly in that closed space, she had paused to ask for it. No woman had ever made such a request, and there had been more than a few. He'd even thought of saying no, but hadn't wanted to destroy the mood, so he'd taken off his wedding ring and handed it to her.

He took it off once more.

19

Despite the unseasonably high temperatures, Celia did start wearing long sleeves to work. Not that they proved necessary. On Tuesday Davy remained quiet, kept to himself, and never tried to bite her or anyone else. He actually behaved better than the other children. They had been riled up by his arrival, which wasn't at all unusual: as soon as the kids saw the pecking order up for grabs, they started jockeying for position. But Davy appeared as oblivious to them as he was to the adults who now studied his behavior. Celia would have been more concerned about his unresponsiveness if he hadn't applied himself so diligently during their afternoon session.

After he left her office, it occurred to Celia that he might benefit from homework. She gathered up some supplies and planned to talk to him after the children met with Tony and the teacher at the end of the day.

A half hour later she joined Ethan, who had pulled "van duty," and watched for Davy as the children poured down the front steps and fled to the parking area where the driver waited for them. She spotted Davy slogging along at the back of the pack, head down, knapsack dragging on the ground, and called to him softly. He continued trudging along and didn't stop until she tapped him on the shoulder.

"Davy, would you step aside for a minute?"

He looked up slowly.

"I thought you might like these. Just for fun."

She handed him a sketchbook and a box of colored pencils, both of which he immediately clutched to his chest.

"Draw anything you want, you're good at it, Davy."

His eyes fell to the ground shyly, which expressed more emotion than he'd shown all day, and he hurried away, his knapsack still bumping along the path.

Ethan turned to Celia. "Is he really good?"

"Actually, he is." She watched the van until the driver shut the door behind Davy. "He's got a pretty good sense of composition, and so far he's been willing to draw anything I ask. I mean, he's no Picasso, but he could be a good little artist with the right direction."

Ethan cocked his head and smiled. "Which Mrs. G., no doubt, could provide?"

"I think so." Celia saw the van pull away and started back to the building. "I wish someone had worked with me when I was that age. All I did were pencil drawings and doodles and a little bit of painting before I got to college. Then an instructor finally pulled me aside and told me I was good at it."

"Like you did with Davy?"

"Right. And it made all the difference in the world." Celia stopped at the steps. "But art's a tough field, and the other art majors had a real jump on me."

Ethan paused alongside her. "I don't know, from what I've seen you're a pretty good artist. And don't forget Grandma Moses. She didn't start painting until her dotage."

Celia frowned. "Have you ever actually seen her work?"

"No."

"Well, when you do you may find that as dotage art it really excels."

"Oh."

Celia scooted up the front steps feeling nimble and naughty, girlish and faintly flirtatious because she was all too aware that she was giving Ethan plenty of time to scope out her butt. She turned around when she reached the top.

"But thanks for the encouragement anyway. If I'm lucky maybe someone will discover me in my dotage."

Ethan locked eyes with her and smiled.

"Maybe somebody already has."

20

The kid's got that new pad, those new pencils too. No bite marks. She must think he's something, giving him stuff like that.

But he's still watching that *Batman* video, the one *I* gave him. Always got that on, no matter what, morning to night if I let him. Except now he's drawing too. What the hell is he drawing?

As the minutes passed, Chet's curiosity grew. It was like a snake curling around his brain, choking off every thought but what that kid was up to. He had to see, had to. It might be me. He might be drawing *me*.

He stood over Davy and looked down, and right then could've laughed. He's even drawing Batman. The kid's got Batman on the brain. Chet could make out the mask, the cape, and those big gloves. But he stopped smiling almost as soon as he began because it occurred to him that there might be other things in the picture that he couldn't see. Dead give-away kinds of things.

He kneeled down and stared at it closely and tried to see it like she would. But he'd be damned to hell and back if he could see anything but Batman. But that didn't make him feel a whole lot better because you can't see fingerprints either. You walk in a room, you see the body, you see the blood, but you don't see those secret things that detectives see. Maybe it's the same thing with her. Like I told her yesterday, *You're a detective,* and she said no, tried to play it down, but she could be, and Davy could be putting all kinds of things down on that paper for her, stuff that only she can see.

He had a mind to take the pad away. Stick it in a fire and burn it up. The whole thing made him sick. He just wanted to be left alone with the boy. And then she came along. But if he burned it up she'd just give him a new one. He knew the type. They had a never-ending supply of pads and pencils and smiles and *Good Mornings,* and they just kept throwing them at the world. The only thing you could do with her type was take care of the smile, and that would take care of all the other stuff. You get a woman like that to stop smiling and you had them beat. Give her a good scare, the kind she'd never forget. He tapped his pocket, the one with the razor sitting right over his heart. That'll stop her smiling.

He leaned a little closer to Davy's picture and shook his head. It's not that good. It's even got a hole in it. Look at that, will you? A tiny one right there, right in the middle. Kid's got a filthy mind.

21

The following morning at recess Celia spotted Davy at the picnic table under the old oak. He was drawing in his sketchbook, apparently oblivious to the taunts the other children tossed at one another during a game of kickball.

"That's Batman, isn't it?"

She sat beside him, and when he looked up he might have smiled. The movement of his lips was subtle and ended too soon for her to be sure.

"The way you've drawn him it looks like he could fly if he wanted to." She pointed to Batman's cape. "Like I bet you could talk to me if you really wanted to."

Davy's eyes never lifted from the page, and his pencil idled in his hand.

Celia's finger lingered on Batman's cape before she ran it down over the rest of his body. As she passed over Batman's crotch she felt the tear in the page. She hadn't been sure it was there because of the blotchy mix of sunlight and shadows, but she'd found it, a hole right in the blackest part.

"Do you mind?" Celia flipped through more than a dozen pages of Batman pictures, each with a darkly shaded crotch, each with that perplexing hole.

"May I have one of these? They're really good."

Davy nodded, and she took quiet delight in his first obvious response to her.

She carefully tore out the page and made a point of admiring it again, though most of her attention was drawn to the black hole.

She pointed to a rosebush in the flower bed that bordered the Center.

"Do you see those pretty flowers over there?"

Davy looked up from his pad; he'd already begun to work on another Batman.

"I'd like you to play a pretend game with me, okay? I'd like you to draw a rosebush for me, but I want you to pretend that you are the rosebush. You have to really think about this one and decide if you're a tall rosebush, or a short one, if you have flowers and what color they are, because rosebushes come in all kinds of colors. And think about whether you have thorns and roots. Are they long and straight or do they twist around? And where are you if you're a rosebush? Do you live in a park or at the seashore, or a home? You decide, Davy. That's what's so much fun about this game, you can be any kind of rosebush you want to be."

He stared at the roses, yellow, like the trim on the Center, then started on his drawing. In black.

She felt great driving home. Okay, so she didn't have Davy talking yet, but he was drawing, and he'd taken her every suggestion. He'd worked on the rosebush all during their afternoon session, and then made a point of closing his sketchbook when she came up to him at the end of the hour.

If he didn't want her to see it just yet, that was fine with Celia. Honor the child's feelings and sooner or later he'd honor yours. It worked in therapy, in the classroom, and at home, though Celia's knowledge of healthy family relationships was strictly abstract. Her own feelings had rarely been honored by her mother.

But she brimmed with pleasure over Davy's progress, and found herself smiling until she passed a gun shop with a huge sign in the window announcing, "Wanted: Rifles, Pistols, Shotguns." Her spirits dimmed but as soon as she cleared the town limits she brightened back up again. Hump day, that's what she called Wednesday. Once you're over it, you're on your way to the weekend. No matter how gratifying her workday had been, she liked her free time too.

She was glad they lived out in the country. At least she had some open space to go home to. She regarded their house as a retreat, a place in the forest where she could experience a little solitude every afternoon. The drought had sapped some of the life from the land, but it hadn't affected her enthusiasm.

And she wanted to enjoy the late afternoon while she still could; daylight saving time would end this weekend. She always remembered because it came right before Halloween, guaranteeing an extra hour of darkness for all of Bentman's witches, goblins, and monsters.

She finished up a candy bar as she headed south. When she came to Broken Creek Road she made a left and started up the ridge. She passed a big gravel pit where the county work crews had loaded up the golf ball-sized rocks they'd spilled all over the dirt road, an expenditure of taxpayer funds wholly for the benefit of the timber industry with its huge logging trucks.

She could have done without the "improvements," preferring the ruts and dirt to the gravel they'd put down. The sharp rocks tore up her tires—three flats so far this year—and were slowly beating the underside of her car to death. It scared her to think about breaking down so far from help.

The town receded steadily behind her as she gained the almost two thousand feet of elevation to the top of the ridge. Wherever she looked she saw stumps and slash, the mean remains of the timber industry. She guessed the loggers had chain-sawed at least three hundred trees in the past few days alone. Each of their trunks had been sprayed with an ugly blotch of red paint to designate that it was to be cut. It made her think of Mercurochrome, but there would be no healing of these wounds, not in this life.

She turned on the tape player, Sinead O'Connor, and cranked up the volume. The road wound through a beautiful stand of tall pines. She had delighted in them since moving up to the ridge and was pleased to see they had been spared the chain saws. So far. She knew they could be gone tomorrow with nothing but red blotches on their trunks.

A fully loaded logging truck approached, forcing her to edge over so far that she feared the Honda would slip off the road. Branches scraped the passenger side until she crawled past an abandoned logging road that converged on the right. There were dozens of these two-tracks all over the ridge, mostly overgrown and overlooked, but not by everybody.

Chet stood with his chain saw about a hundred feet down the old logging road, barely visible through the tangle of unruly growth. But he could just make out the two vehicles, and he watched them passing each other with intense interest. Davy sat in the pickup, sleepy from sun and boredom. His stepfather walked up to the cab and leaned against the door. The boy never looked up.

"What do you know about that! Mrs. Griswold lives around here somewhere. Can't be too far off. There's not a whole lot around here."

And to think he'd taken her for a town woman. There's just no fixing people nowadays. He'd tried to find her address in the telephone book but all he'd come up with was the insurance agency. He figured they were one of those secretive types, don't want their address out there.

Chet stared at the dust rising from the road, dearly thankful to Mrs. Griswold for this . . . this *gift*. He'd figured on having to spend at least another day or two finding her place, maybe even tailing her home. Now he wouldn't have to. He'd just follow the road. He'd find her. Hell, he always found them. Always. And he already knew most of these old logging roads like he'd been born here. He took a lot of pride in learning terrain quickly, and he was sure he could outsmart a pack of bloodhounds if he had to, especially during the rainy season when there would be streams to cut his trail.

He'd been born a century too late. He knew for a fact that he would've been better off when they were first exploring the West. He could have been a trapper, a hunter, killing all there was to kill and not having to worry about any goddamn game laws or season for this or season for that. Open season all the time on everything. Having . . . dominion—that was the word—over every goddamn thing. He wanted . . . DOMIN-ION . . . he didn't want to have to answer to those assholes at the school, especially Mrs. Griswold with her smooth words sitting around looking at those pictures and maybe figuring out what Davy's got stored away in that head of his. Just what the hell is he saying? It's like the two of them were playing some goddamn game and he was the only one who didn't know the rules. That just wasn't fair. So he'd make new ones. That's what he'd do. Scare the shit out of her. *Done it before, I'll do it again.*

He couldn't hear the Honda or the logging truck anymore.

He'd watched them closely and never saw the driver or Mrs. Griswold look his way. Too worried about inching by each other. Good thing, too. He sure didn't want to get caught poaching wood around here. Not with the plans he had in mind.

Up ahead Celia spotted the meadow with the orange poppies, but strangely most of those bright patches of color had disappeared. She navigated the curve right before the meadow, but had to stop short to let a flock of sheep cross the road:

"What the hell is this?"

She turned down the stereo, as if to concentrate more fully on the spectacle parading past her. Then she smelled the sheep, a hellishly sour odor that startled her and left a foul taste on her tongue. She quickly rolled up the window and covered her nose and mouth with her hand and tried to understand why they smelled so god-awful bad. That's when she saw the filth, the muck smeared all over their fleece, a sordid and besmirched color. The wool looked like it was rotting on their backs, as if they'd been penned tightly together for long nights of sickness and defecation. Several suffered from open wounds, dark gaping holes on their sides and backs that appeared putrescent and hideously painful.

As the flock crossed to the meadow they began to eat the few remaining wildflowers, munching on the orange blossoms, green stems, even the plants and roots themselves. There must have been a hundred or more sheep trodding along, grinding to dust the tender stalks that had managed to survive the drought.

Celia waited patiently with her hand over her nose, trying to smell the chocolate bar she'd eaten on the drive home. But the stench overwhelmed such a weak defense.

"How you doing?"

She jumped in her seat, frightened by the sudden appearance of a wild-looking young man. He stood by her window, which she reluctantly rolled down.

"I'm doing fine. What's going on?" She dropped her hand to speak, and a deeply-instilled sense of politeness kept it on her lap. But she paid a stiff price for her good manners because as soon as he leaned toward the open window another wave of vile odors assaulted her, rancid smells that seemed to ooze from all of his openings. She thought it must have been weeks since he washed. Her nostrils felt raped.

"Got here about a week ago from California. Drought chased us north. Trucked 'em here and been grazing 'em all through these hills. Paid the timber company good money for the right."

He spoke slowly, deliberately, like the developmentally disabled. This softened Celia, but only a mite. He still stank, and behind him his sheep were casually ravaging the prettiest meadow on the ridge.

"You've come to the wrong place, because the drought here—"

"Thought Oregon's wet."

She sniffed her nose, as if she had a cold, and ran her hand under it, finding blessed relief in the faintest hint of chocolate.

"Wrong time of year and the wrong year," she replied, using as little air as possible. She tried breathing through her mouth.

The shepherd leaned closer and picked at his straggly blond beard. Flakes of dried-up food or dead skin—she wasn't sure what it was—fell onto her shoulder and arm. She shivered with disgust.

"Wrong as wrong can be, I guess, and now my dog's gone. You see him? Black-and-white feller? Lost him soon as we got here. Name's Bucky 'cause he's all buck-toothed, but he can herd like no one can."

"Bucky?" Celia said feebly. She looked away. Oh shit.

"Yeah, that's what I call him, Bucky. Friendliest dog you ever seen. I'm hard up without him. Can't hardly keep them sheep straight with him gone. Keeps them cougars away too. Them cats hate them dogs, and with him gone my sheep been taking a beating. Lost two lambs already. Cats drug 'em off like they was nothing. They been tearing hell out of the herd." The shepherd looked at his flock, then turned back to Celia. "You seen him?"

She winced when he asked that question, she couldn't help herself. And he noticed. She could tell by the way he tilted his head and stared as if he was studying her.

God, his breath stank too. It filled the driver's side of the car. She could see the tartar caked on his teeth, and a greenish gel that covered his gums. She shifted to her right to try to get a whiff of untainted air, but as she did the shepherd leaned in until almost all of his shaggy head hovered over the steering wheel.

"No," Celia finally found the courage to lie, "I haven't seen your dog. I didn't even know you were up here till just now."

"We been here, that's for sure. Me and Bucky."

With her body scrunched over to the right, she started to ease the car forward; but this didn't discourage the shepherd, who remained inches from her face, nor the sheep still straggling past her car.

"He's a good dog, and I need him bad."

Celia nodded and tapped her horn softly, but the sheep didn't move. Neither did the shepherd, who appeared unaware of her efforts.

"To tell ya', I think someone stole my dog. See, old Bucky, he wouldn't get lost. He's too smart for that."

And you, Celia thought uncharitably, would be *such* a good judge of that.

"I'd sure like to get my hands on the son of a bitch that took him, too."

His eyes grew as large as hens' eggs, and Celia noticed the dirty hands he wanted to use on her husband.

"Have you checked the—"

"Checked? Checked the what?"

She swallowed and paused. The shepherd pushed in even closer. His ghastly breath and body odor pummeled her once more.

"The . . . the pound."

As soon as she said this, she wished she hadn't. What if they've already killed the dog? What if they say some guy up on the ridge brought him in last week? Oh shit.

"The pound? They got them a pound here?"

"Never mind, I don't—"

"Why'd he be at the pound?"

"Well, if he got picked up."

"Why'd he get picked up?"

"I'm sure I don't know. Perhaps someone thought he was

doing your little Bucky a favor and took him there.'' You're
such a lousy liar, she screamed at herself.

"Who's that?"

"What?"

"Who's doing me a favor?"

"I'm sure I don't know that either."

"Is that right?"

The shepherd hardly looked convinced, and Celia honestly
feared that at any moment he'd take his filthy hands and shake
the truth right out of her. Why the hell didn't Jack just let
her keep the damn dog?

"Look, I'm truly sorry about your little Bucky, but I don't
know anything about him."

She eased out the clutch and the car slowly rolled forward.
She hit the horn aggressively, and when the sheep finally
moved out of the way she quietly cursed herself for not doing
this sooner. But even as she started to gain speed the shepherd
ran beside her, his head never more than a foot from her own,
his slow dull voice asking the same haunting question over
and over again: "You sure? You sure? You sure?"

22

Chet and Davy bounced along the short, rugged stretch of logging road until they came to the T-intersection where Chet'd spotted Mrs. Griswold edging past the truck. He turned right and began to climb the last one hundred yards to the ridge. The steepness forced him into first, but that was okay because he didn't want to overtake Mrs. Griswold, just find her.

Once he topped the ridge he followed the county road south. The sun was sinking but there was still lots of daylight, which he needed. A series of gentle curves carried him past a stand of pines that looked ripe for poaching. Then the road leveled and he started to move faster, easing the old pickup through the forgiving terrain until the meadow opened up to his left. A second later he saw the sheep and felt his hunger. Meat, he said softly to himself. *Meat.* His tongue swam in saliva, and he swallowed without thinking. He slowed and stared at the young ones, and his memory tasted their roasted flesh. He knew he could butcher one of them with his chain saw and be out of there in minutes. He saw the blood, the torn fleece, the two legs of lamb safely in hand. *Here, Davy, take them.* But then he caught sight of the mad-looking man with a heavy stick walking beside the flock, and he choked the steering wheel and swore to himself. His hands had grown itchy for action but there would be no lamb to butcher today, no leg to drip fat from a spit, to turn crisp and sweet in the night air.

As he drove past the shepherd he looked him over carefully, and tugged Davy's arm.

"Now *that's* a creepy son of a bitch. Don't ever let me catch you near the likes of him."

Chet turned away, disgusted by the shepherd's appearance,

and drove another two miles before a house appeared up ahead on his right, barely visible through the tall firs that rose just beyond the road. A row of much younger trees lined the long driveway, but at the end of it he spotted an old tan car and knew he'd found Mrs. Griswold.

He immediately braked and looked for a place to pull off. He figured if he drove any farther he'd risk exposing himself to her. He saw another overgrown logging road by an ancient pine off to his right, but the two-track quickly disappeared into dense growth. Though he knew it was risky, he plunged into the thicket and bounced hard off a fallen log. Branches and bushes raked the cab, and a long limb from a deciduous tree brushed across his windshield and blunted his view. But he drove ahead slowly, steadily, until the branch sprang back and showered the pickup with dead leaves.

He found himself on an open stretch of logging road bordered on both sides by walls of fir and pine. This is where he stopped. When he looked back he saw that the trees and bushes had once again closed around the path. He couldn't have asked for a better place to hide. No one passing on the county road would ever see his faded green truck. He told himself he should explore the road he'd just discovered and see where it went. But not today. He had other plans.

He turned to Davy but the boy looked sleepy, like he wasn't paying attention, so he poked him. Not even hard, but the kid shrank back against the door. Chet thought he looked all shriveled up all of a sudden, like his finger had stuck a hole in his goddamn chest and the air had come rushing out.

"What the hell are you afraid of? I haven't hurt you yet, have I?"

Davy kept his eyes on him, wary as any creature caught in a corner. Chet saw his fear and wiped his own face roughly with his hand. He could have kicked himself for losing his temper. He knew that you can break a boy that way, and once they break they're broke for good.

"Davy, I'm sorry." He waited to see the effect of his apology. None, goddamn it. He tried another approach, putting his hand on Davy's knee, but the boy grew even more rigid, and Chet retreated. He wasn't making any headway with this kid. Usually after a week or two they'd at least start to see things his way. Buy them treats and toys, be a good guy. Hell, he'd done all that, but this kid was turning out to be a hard case. He decided to give up on all this pleading bullshit for now. He could feel his anger and it didn't feel good.

"Now listen up. You remember what I said about touching things in my truck, right? You never touch these keys"—he pointed to the ignition—"and you never *ever* touch these." He reached under the seat and pulled out a pistol. The handle caught on a second gun that slid out just far enough for Davy to see the end of the dark barrel. Chet held up the pistol as he spoke.

"You ever touch these, I'll break your neck." Though his words were harsh, his voice remained gentle, easygoing, and his smile sincere.

He rested the pistol on his lap and reached out the window. He snapped off a thin branch, turned back to Davy, and casually broke it. "Just like that, I'll bust you in two."

He tossed it back out and picked up the gun, shifting it from palm to palm, feeling its weight, running a thumb over the chamber.

"These are nice. Very nice," he added approvingly, "but nothing," and now his words filled with feeling, "and I mean *nothing* beats a blade."

He lowered the pistol once more and unsnapped the pearl button on his shirt. With his index and middle fingers he tweezed out the single-edge razor that he'd used on Davy's mom. The boy turned away, his eyes fixed on the windshield. But he saw only glass, nothing of the world beyond—the trees, the leaves, or the living bark.

Chet watched him and smiled even more broadly than before. He held the razor up before his eyes and admired it, then rubbed the sharp edge against his face and a soft scraping sound violated the cab.

"It's all in how you use it," he whispered, his voice almost gone now, a lover's sound instead. "See, like this, it cuts my beard. But if I take it like this"—he held the edge perpendicular to his neck—"it cuts me deep."

He could see that Davy wasn't watching, but didn't care anymore. He let himself stare at the blade, tranquilized by its sheen, the steady pulse of its threat, and remembered how sweetly it sank into skin.

His hands longed for that motion, like sex longs for touch, communion, sweet and strain. He felt the urge sudden and strong, as he had with the boy's mother, the way she'd brought it right out of him, like they'd both been born to that moment and would forevermore. He opened his mouth and placed the blade on his tongue, sharp edge forward, and lowered it to his teeth. Then he bit down slowly and the blade disappeared. He looked in the rearview mirror and saw the way his lips stuck out, flattened around the steel wafer. He peeled them back and stared at the two sharp corners sticking out from between his teeth.

He held fast to the clean taste of steel before opening his mouth and lifting the blade up with his tongue. He tucked the razor back in his shirt.

"I think they're overrated," his voice returned as he shoved the guns back under the seat. "They're too damn loud, but it's good to know how to use them, and I'll teach you when I can trust you. Know when that'll be?"

Davy remained lost in the glass, the windshield that froze his vision and held his every thought.

"When you talk to me, that's when. To *me*. When I hear you say even one word, then I'll know I can trust you and that's when I'll teach you how to use a gun. Every boy should know how to use a gun, right, Davy?"

Chet shook his head. Even his amiability now sounded strained. "I guess it'll be a while before you're ready to learn. That's fine, but I'll tell you one thing you're going to do. You're going to sit there till I get back. I don't care how long, you just sit there and don't move. I've got something I've got to take care of."

Be nice, he reminded himself. Be nice.

23

Celia unlocked the door and found Pluto in his preferred position right in front of her on the mud-room floor.
She fulfilled her part of the routine by scratching his ears, but
she did this only briefly because she really did want to hike
for at least an hour.

She hurried through the kitchen, noticed the red light
blinking on the answering machine, and punched the ''play''
button. Jack's voice reached her as she flew down the hallway
to the bedroom.

''Hon, it's me. I'm running late. Something's come up and
I'll be a bit. Go ahead and start dinner without me. I'll just
pop mine in the microwave.''

''You and your damn dinner,'' she mumbled. She shed her
athletic shoes and searched under the bed for her hiking boots.
As she laced them up she reminded herself to grab her bright-
orange vest out of the mud-room closet. She did not want to
end up impersonating a deer in some hunter's hair-trigger
imagination.

She heard Pluto meow in the mud room and wondered
what had set him off. Normally, he wasn't the most vocal cat.
He certainly had lost his explorer's spirit. Sometimes he'd
accompany her to the country road, but never any farther. He
seemed to have had his fill of the wider world before he ever
moved in with them. Jack put it differently. He maintained
that based on Pluto's battered appearance—one eye, scars all
over his head, chewed-up ears—the cat had used up eight and
a half of its lives and was taking no chances with the little it
had left.

When Celia marched into the mud room to grab her vest
she saw that the outside door was ajar. This puzzled her, but
not for long. She'd been in such a rush, after all.

The closet door, which also had been closed, hung open a fraction of an inch as well, but she didn't notice this, or that Chet was peering out at her through the crack. As she tried to remember why she'd come in here—the outside door distracted her momentarily—Chet tensed. He did not want to be discovered, he wanted to do the discovering. He'd slipped in the house and hid in here so he could spy on her, see how she lived, the furniture, hallways, and hiding places. Guns, too. Under the pillow or under the bed? But most of all he wanted to steal a little piece of her, the scent of her clothes, the sound of her toilet, the way the silver handle flushed and the cabinet door squeaked open, the magazines and sex toys she kept hidden away. Who was she? He'd listen in, look around, he'd find out. Buy clues with his time like she was buying them from the boy. Tit for tat, now how about that, Mrs. Griswold?

Celia finally remembered the vest but as soon as she weighted her foot and reached for the closet door, Pluto let loose with an unearthly howl.

Chet froze, his concentration rattled by her sudden move toward him—*what's she doing!*—and the feline scream. Celia also stood rock-still, startled and unthinking, then looked down and saw that she'd stepped on Pluto's paw. She hopped aside and tried to scoop him up, but he bolted away so fast his feet slipped on the smooth surface and his body bounced off the closet door, slamming it shut and leaving Chet in darkness.

He heard Celia's pathetic apologies as she chased the cat, but mostly his thoughts raced as he tried to regroup. She was leaving, great, but she wanted something in here first. What the hell does she need in here? It's too goddamn hot for a jacket. He looked around but couldn't see anything in the dark. If she did open the door he'd be forced to do something, and he didn't want to do *that,* not without some more planning, though he smiled when he remembered a woman who actually fainted on him, just collapsed like a column of sand when she reached in for her coat and found him staring right back at her. But he'd brought her around. You bet he did.

He heard her moving back toward the mud room and touched his breast pocket, felt the razor and fished it out. He would do what had to be done. And if she doesn't open the door? He brushed the razor against his jeans as if to strop the blade. Well, then the afternoon would take another twist, one more to his liking, especially if she was going for a walk in the woods.

As she approached he closed his eyes and silently commanded, No, no, no, concentrating so hard that she'd have to hear him, *obey* him. Then he listened and heard *her* words, the sickening way she spoke to her cat, baby talk, and he imagined her cradling the beast in her arms. For the briefest moment he reached for the handle, felt its cool welcome, and wanted to end all this uneasiness . . . by . . . smashing the door into her. Take them both down. But he checked himself and closed his eyes, and concentrated once more. Go now, *go!* He believed he could make her leave, even as he believed in his other powers, the ones that made him God.

Suddenly he smelled her, the soap she lavished on her skin or the shampoo that bubbled in her hair. He inhaled deeply, delighted by the first discovery of the day. The scent she gave off now belonged to him, and forever and ever it would be his to relish and remember. She could never take it way. He *owned* it. Each of these moments promised a gain, but as he started to inhale again he stopped because he heard his breath and feared that she did too. There was, in fact, a troubling silence on the other side of the door. He braced himself but the handle that turned wasn't the one in his hand. It was the one for the outside door, and she stepped past him. Just as quickly, it closed.

He cracked the closet door and watched her walk away, then turned to the interior of the house, the broad wooden beams above and the blue ceramic tile below, and felt a tingle in his stomach, like a spark of static electricity had lived and died there in the space of a second.

Her house. And now mine too. He would take away pieces of her before he was through, secret parts she wouldn't miss. Not now. Not ever.

He looked out the kitchen window and saw her turn down the driveway. That's when he lost her to the trees. But not for long. He was a tracker from way back. He'd find her, and then he'd find a way to wipe that smile right off her face, set her thinking straight.

Celia cuddled Pluto and drifted halfway down the driveway before remembering her vest. She stopped and turned around. She promised herself years ago that she would never hike without it, not with all the hunters stalking the land. It was such a simple and effective precaution. Why not go get it, girl? It could save your life.

Okay, okay. She walked up the driveway and stepped up onto the deck, glad that she'd made the effort to go back. If she hadn't she would have felt vulnerable the whole time she was out. It definitely felt safer to wear the eye-catching orange.

She put Pluto down on the deck and walked into the house. She barely glanced at the closet door on her way into the kitchen to get a drink of water. She turned on the faucet to let it run cold. As she took a glass down from a cabinet she noticed an unusual odor, piny, yes, but something else too, something . . . sour.

She filled her glass and drank it halfway down before realizing that she was smelling sweat, pine and sweat.

She lifted her arms and sniffed herself self-consciously. She shrugged and finished her drink. She walked into the mud room and moved a boot back under a shelf, most likely jarred loose during Pluto's wild scramble. Through the window in the door she saw him sitting there looking back at her with his one eye.

She swung open the closet door, grabbed her vest, threw it on, and went back outside. She hugged her cat and nuzzled his neck. "Okay, sweetie, we can go now."

Chet stood in the hallway just off the living room listening to her every move. When she returned to the closet he had abandoned only minutes before, he flooded with victory, for he'd outsmarted her silly efforts to find him. He'd willed her away when he'd stood behind the door, and had slipped from her grasp when she returned. She would live . . . for now . . . because she had *obeyed* him. He'd given her life with those few powerful words—Go now, *go!*—and that life was the most precious gift she'd ever receive. She had only him to thank, not the God above but the God right here in this house, the God who had stood just a few feet away and let her suck the air right into her lungs and swallow water and know the elements a little while longer. Yes, He had given her life, and if He wanted to He could take it away. The power was in His hands, and He had used it well. Sometimes he gave them death, and this he willed too. He looked back at the kitchen tile and mud-room floor and saw the aftermath as he had seen it before, the *limpness* of their bodies, when the only part that moves is the part that tries to run away, the cooling blood that rolls across the floor.

He took a satisfying breath and knew the God within, fully, deeply, richly. He felt the same glorious power when he murdered a boy and felt the young muscles surrender, and the bones turn still as stone.

The God above might as well be dead.

When he was eight he'd pressed all of his wiry weight against a gray pigeon. The wild beating heart had hammered insanely in his hands, like the pulse belonged more to his palms than to the bird itself, and then he had felt it stop, a burp so soft he'd almost missed the sacred moment; and that's when he'd learned the most important secret of the universe: that when they died they were yours, and through all eternity nothing would ever have the power to change that. Nothing. Chet had the only power that mattered anymore.

Murder made him immortal. Death made him God.

He returned to the mud-room closet and pulled out one of Jack's coats, holding it up as if taking the measure of the man.

He executed a fast search of the kitchen, throwing open drawers and cabinets and finding no surprises. He hurried into the living room and gave it the once-over before moving back to Celia's studio. He threw open the door and paused when he saw her paintings, large and luminous, and the dozens of smaller ones by children. He wondered if any of these were Davy's. He didn't see any Batman pictures. Otherwise there was no telling. He stepped to the easel and looked at the flower she'd been working on. He didn't know what it was called but he'd seen bunches of them by the side of the road.

They grew like weeds. Orange, like those chickenshit hunters wore, on their caps, jackets, and dogs. But she'd made it big. A flower bigger than a man's head and shoulders. He liked this, getting a chance to figure out what she was all about by looking at *her* pictures. Even up the score. He stared at it and stared at it, eyes unblinking, and then he saw how she'd made the flower look just like their privates, their bottom parts. She was a dirty one, all right. She was. The painting offended him and made him turn away.

He closed the door, glad to be done with that roomful of filth, and walked into the guest bedroom, where he rummaged through two bureaus with nothing but sheets and towels. He noticed the dust, another disgusting flower painting above the bed, then checked the closets and left.

He found her room, the one she shared with Mr. Griswold Agency. He rifled Jack's armoire and Celia's big bureau until he found her underwear. He picked up a pair of pale panties and studied its sheeny surface in the afternoon light. Then he looked at the lacy front, the discreet leafy pattern that tried to hide what could never be hidden, not from Him. He turned it inside out and held it close to his open mouth, exhaling slowly, deliberately, until he was certain he'd fogged the narrow panel. He ran his thumb over the moist strip before returning it to the drawer.

He picked up a second pair and tensed them, pleased at the stretch. He tensed it some more and a seam screamed as it tore apart, a deafening sound that rolled like thunder and made him dizzy. But he let the pressure in his hands grow until he heard another seam explode. And another. He watched the pink lace blow apart in slow motion, bursts that ripped open the braided surface of the thread and left it limp and cratered. Tiny bits of fabric swam up into the air and hung like motes, twirling in the cold nothingness.

What had been smooth and silky now hung from his hands in pieces. But he had touched her here in this room as surely as she had touched him in her office at the Center. He had great power over her. He felt it in his hands and in his heart. Even the appearance of the physical world had come under his command, for he had frozen the arc of light and prized decibels from silence. A foolish doctor had once called them hallucinations and tried to give him pills, but Chet knew better. You hallucinated what you could not see, but he saw the world for what it was. There was no question of this, for his eyes had the clarity of a lens ground too fine ever to be fooled. And she would know this too.

He stuffed the remains in his pocket and ignored a gold watch that lay on the bureau. He closed her underwear drawer and checked under the pillows and mattress of the unmade bed before deciding that they did not have any guns. Imagine that, living out here without them. They must think they're on Mars.

A creaking snapped the silence, and he looked toward the window by the head of the bed. He did not like surprises. He listened closely as he crept over to it and scanned the property. Nothing. He noticed the unlocked window and nodded. From long experience he knew that people who live in the country rarely checked them. If they're not locked today, they won't be locked tomorrow.

Celia put Pluto down by the entrance to their property. She watched him walk around, pleased that he didn't favor the foot she'd stepped on. From the sound of his screech she could have sworn she'd broken at least two of his legs, but he was back to his affectionate self, rubbing up against her jeans and shedding a considerable amount of his coat.

She dallied by the entrance for another minute or two, stroking Pluto and trying to lure him along; but he would have none of it and paced by the fence post with the small sign that said "Griswold."

"Okay, Pluto, God of the Underworld, do what you want but you're missing out on all the fun stuff if you stay home all the time."

She crossed the county road to a deer and elk trail, one of dozens that meandered through the forest; but she'd taken no more than a few steps on the single track when she heard a crackling back in the dense vegetation that stood between the driveway and the house.

The sound stopped as suddenly as it had started. She wondered if an animal was caught in the brush, but had her doubts. Most animals are as silent as air. Then she remembered that the scrub oak had started to fall. They'd seen a lot of that since the drought set in. When the shallow root systems dried up, the trees, never more than ten or fifteen feet tall, toppled easily. She wondered how many would survive. The strong ones, she told herself, the strong ones would make it through the dry spell.

She started down the trail, delighted by the smell of the earth, the pine sap, the special fragrance of the forest itself.

Chet picked himself up and hastily brushed off the dirt and dry grass clinging to his pants. He was surprised that he'd tripped and angry that he'd made so much noise.

Now as he began to stalk Celia again, he moved as stealthily as any animal that calls the forest home. Each foot settled squarely in front of the other. He would not fall again.

Celia entered a densely canopied section of huge firs and pines shading a thick carpet of ferns, and quickly came across the rotting tree that had blocked the trail since a fierce windstorm blew it over three years ago. Like countless deer and elk before her, she edged onto a new path that wove around the upended trunk. She passed the dark root system, which rose high above her like the claws of a giant crustacean. This was the first time she saw the resemblance, and she found herself studying the unusual shape, wondering if it would make a good subject for a painting. She pulled out a pocket sketch pad and started to take a few notes. When she looked back up she noticed one of the roots slithering down through the rotting mass. It glided silently and swiftly onto the ground. With a start she understood that she'd been staring at a snake, and began to back up blindly as the creature slipped through the grass and ferns.

She stumbled backward and fell into the thick undergrowth, saw the snake still moving toward her and rolled blindly to the side in a surging panic. She clambered to her feet, but even these brisk movements could not keep pace with her racing heart. She sprinted up the trail, glancing back at least as often as she looked ahead; and as she neared the road ran straight into Chet's arms. Shocked, she tried to move away, but he held her firmly.

"Whoa, Mrs. Griswold, what's the matter? You're in some kind of rush, aren't you?"

Chet spoke in a light-hearted manner, but his hands maintained their strong grip on her upper arms. Celia became acutely aware of this as she breathlessly tried to explain her fright.

"A snake," she gasped, "I just saw a snake." Even as she blurted this out she knew how foolish she sounded, and now that she'd run away from the snake she wondered why she'd been so alarmed.

"A snake?" He let go of one of her arms, much to her relief. "What kind of snake? I know all about them. They're nasty things."

"A dark snake," she said calmly, now fully embarrassed by her behavior. But as her fear subsided she became uncomfortably aware that Chet still held her left arm. Subtly, she tried to move away from him. He did not appear to notice her efforts.

"What are you doing here?" she said in a strong voice.

He shrugged, a movement she felt in her own body, then replied, "Me? I'm looking for downed timber. Doing some salvage work."

"Forget it, this is all timber company or county land." She knew that Mr. Boyce and his stepson had arrived in Bentman only recently, but surely he must be familiar with cutting permits.

"That's okay, I take it where I can find it. Now let's take a look at that snake."

When he tried to lead Celia back into the thick of the forest she made an obvious, though unsuccessful attempt to pull away from him. He ignored her, and for the first time she feared him.

"Let me go!" she demanded.

As she tried to twist her arm free she heard a logging truck and started waving frantically toward the road before she could even see it. When the truck appeared a moment later the driver waved back and tooted his air horn. That's when Chet released her. She took three quick steps up the trail before he spoke again, his voice as gentle as before.

"Okay, Mrs. Griswold, if you don't want to go you don't

have to, but I'll be glad to fix that snake that scared you.''

"It's gone." She moved a few more steps away. "It crawled into the brush."

"You think so?" He smiled and shook his head wisely. "You might not see it but that snake didn't go far. Snakes are sneaky that way, always just hanging around waiting for something to eat."

Celia shuddered noticeably. "Look, I'm out of here."

She ran the last thirty feet or so to the county road where she finally felt comfortable enough to bend over, catch her breath, and try to collect her thoughts. As she straightened up she checked her back pocket and found her notebook missing. She realized she must have dropped it when she ran from the snake. But she wasn't about to go back and search for it, not with Mr. Boyce around.

She started to walk over to the entrance to their property, heard rapid footsteps, and spun around. Mr. Boyce held a snake. It was struggling to break free of his grip, as she had been just minutes ago. The creature looked weak and helpless, and she wished he'd let it go.

Instead, he walked right up to her, so close that the snake's cold tail whipped against her bare arm. She backed right into the rusty barbed-wire fence that bordered the road.

Chet appeared oblivious to her fear and moved even closer.

"Get that thing away from me."

"Is this maybe the snake that scared you? There's a whole nest of them back there. Nothing but old wood snakes. See, it can't bite you as long as you got it like this."

To her considerable disgust, Mr. Boyce held the snake out to her with one hand wrapped tightly below its head. The creature's body snapped around, and once more its tail smacked Celia. She pulled back her arms so quickly she caught a barb on her shoulder blade.

"I don't want it," she insisted in a scared voice.

"That way," Chet continued as if nothing out of the ordinary were taking place, "it can't get you. Like I say, they got a whole nest of them back there, Mrs. Griswold, just as many as you like."

She slowly tried to move sideways, careful not to press against the fence, but fearful that at any moment the snake would be thrust in her face. Finally, to her great relief, Mr. Boyce seemed to notice her fear and pulled it away.

"Hey, if this thing scares you so much I'll take care of it, Mrs. Griswold. I don't have much patience for things that scare me. Never have, never will."

He fished his razor out of his shirt pocket and matter-of-factly started to cut off the snake's head. Its long body thrashed madly as Celia shouted,

"Stop it! Jesus! What are you doing! Just leave it alone!"

Chet looked puzzled over her outburst.

"I'm sorry. Sure, I'll stop, if that's what you want."

He tossed the snake on the ground, where its half-severed head flopped around in the dust and gravel.

"Christ, look what you've done."

"Look what I've done?" He shook his head in apparent disbelief. "It's just some old wood snake."

She stared at the dark twisting form. "But look at it," she pleaded. "You almost cut off its head. Put that poor thing out of its misery!"

She turned away, fighting tears, refusing to give in to them.

Chet kicked his boot tip into the ground, spraying dirt and gravel on the snake. "First, you tell me not to do anything. Then you tell me to kill it. Please make up your mind, Mrs. Griswold. I can't take this back-and-forth business. A thing's either up and alive, or it's down and dead. There's no in-between. You're an art therapist, didn't they teach you that?" He stared at the snake, then looked at her. "So what's it going to be? You want it dead"—he kicked the dirt and gravel again—"or alive? I'll do whatever you want."

Celia had no answer. Her eyes returned to the tortured snake, and that's where they remained as he spoke his final words:

"I guess I can't help you then. You do what you want."

He walked away with a smile she could not see, deeply pleased with himself, with all the fun he'd just had. He'd scared her, scared her plenty. She sure wasn't smiling anymore. Probably starting to think things out. He'd give her a few days, see if it took. Right now he'd just keep walking down the road, no looking back. She'd have to decide. Bet she ends up killing it. Taking a life. But she won't know the God inside. She won't *feel* it forever and ever. The only thing she'll feel is bad, and that'll make her think she's better than him. They all thought they were better than him. He could tell by the way they talked and looked at him, and she was just like the others, her with her *smooth* words. Mr. Boyce this and Mr. Boyce that. Now there's no more Mr. Boyce, so what are you doing to do, Mrs. Griswold? Let it die real slow? *Kill* it?

Things were starting to go his way. He could see it in her eyes when he cut the snake, the look she gave him. Usually they only looked like that when he started in on them. If she kept pushing him he'd see that look again real soon. Her choice. He'd just do what had to be done. And if he did he'd make sure he could see her eyes, see if she cares as much for herself as she does for some old snake.

Celia watched in horror as the creature twitched and squirmed around and stirred up a small cloud of dust. She actually considered calling after Mr. Boyce, but shook her head. No, not him. She couldn't. She wiped away the tears that had finally spilled down her cheeks and saw a rock by the barbed-wire fence. Doing something felt better than doing nothing, so she struggled with it. She knew even as she lugged it over to the snake that dropping it would take more strength than picking it up. More strength than she had. The thought of beating it to death sickened Celia, and her stomach began to turn. She heaved the rock aside and started to cry again. But in the midst of her anguish she heard the creature's rustling and glanced down at its pathetic struggle for life. She saw that Mr. Boyce had disappeared, and in a powerful rage picked the rock back up and smashed it down on the bloody head of the snake. She felt the rock rebound dully, as if she'd hit solid rubber, and saw the serpent's spastic movements as it fought even more furiously for the life she was taking away. Again she raised the rock, and again she brought it down, weeping loudly now, her tears splashing on the hard, uneven surface. Again and again she crashed the rock down, until the snake no longer moved.

The rock peeled from her hands, fell heavily to the earth, and rolled over, revealing the dark stains on its underside. She vomited repeatedly, coughing and gagging on the stomach acids that filled her mouth and scorched her throat.

24

Jack roared up the county road determined to make up for lost time. Actually, he quipped to himself, you didn't lose it at all; you spent it on Helen, and all in all it was a mighty fine investment.

He tried to enjoy the warm afterglow of his intimate afternoon because he knew that as soon as he saw Celia his guilt would start making the rounds of his conscience like the village constable of yore, peering down every one of his dark alleys and finding all the shop doors he'd left unlocked. But—*oh crap*—even thinking about guilt made it real. He could already feel it creeping up on him, and in a forlorn voice he reminded himself to take a shower before Celia could sniff out his sins.

He pressed on as the forest—what was left of it—whizzed by. He reasoned that if he hadn't tried so hard to be monogamous for the first three years of his marriage he wouldn't be feeling so guilty now. Not that he considered his infidelities all that unusual. Hardly. An important part of his private compact with his gender was the implicit understanding that men everywhere agreed with him, and that together they were engaged in a vast impersonal conspiracy to dupe the women in their lives. He was amazed at how well they had succeeded. But even with all the support he imagined himself having he still felt small, stingy, and guilt-stricken when he cheated on Celia. He never got a break. Never. His conscience was a radar gun that nailed him every time he cruised the fast lane.

As he pulled up to the house he saw her sitting on the deck crying. Lord, not just crying, but *sobbing,* for Christ's sakes. How'd she find out? Had she stopped by the office and heard Helen howling? That woman could shatter crystal when she came.

Oh, sweet Jesus, he prayed, help me and I'll never do it in the office again.

As he opened the cab he glanced in the rearview mirror and spotted lipstick on his neck. He wiped it away in a white panic and stepped gingerly out of the truck, as if walking lightly might somehow appease Celia.

When she looked up, her eyes were red as flares, and her face was flushed of all color.

"Sweetheart," he croaked, "what's the matter?"

She just sat there crying and shaking her head. That really worried him. He settled beside her and placed his hand stiffly on her shoulder. .

"Hon, are you all right?"

"Do I look all right?" she sniffed. "And where have you been?"

When she said that, he could have danced, he could have sung, he could have praised the sky above and the deep dark earth below because if she had to ask, well, then she didn't know. Once more he'd crawled through the eye of the marital needle. *De*lightful.

"Could you please get me a glass of water?" Speaking made her throat burn, and she wanted to rinse out her mouth.

"Sure, sure." Jack hustled inside, happy to walk off some of his nervous energy. He returned with the water quickly.

"Thanks." She swished it around and spit it out, then swallowed a mouthful and relished its soothing effects on her raw throat. She drank the rest without stopping.

"You really are thirsty."

"Jack, I'm really scared," she said softly. "And where were you?"

"I left a message for you, hon. I had to work late. I had some claims come in at the last minute."

"I wish you'd been here." She clutched the empty glass tightly as she described what Mr. Boyce had done to the snake and how she knew him from the Center. "Jack," she said, as she started crying again, "I had to beat that snake to death with a rock."

"Oh, Cel." He hugged her before realizing what he was doing. He broke the clinch quickly, fearful that Helen's scent would prove as powerful as her sex drive. "Let's call the sheriff. We don't need a weirdo around here.''

Celia dried her eyes on her sleeve. ''Speaking of weirdos, did you see the shepherd in the big meadow?''

''Shepherd? No, I missed that.'' But it wasn't exactly unusual to see dogs around here. Big ones, like shepherds, smaller ones, like that ugly hound he'd gotten rid of last week. All kinds.

''But I'll bet you remember the dog you took to the pound?''

''You mean the one that needed braces?'' Jack laughed.

''Please don't do that.'' After the horrors of her afternoon she couldn't bear her husband's cheerfulness. ''It belonged to a really strange guy who's got about a hundred sheep grazing down in that meadow. He says he lost his dog right after he got here last week, a black-and-white dog with buck teeth. Sound familiar? But he thinks it was stolen and he says he can't wait to get his hands on the guy that took him.''

''Wait a second, you mean a shepherd like with sheep, not a—''

''Yes, of course; what did—''

''I thought you meant the kind with big ears and big teeth. Did he really say that he can't wait to get his hands on the guy that took his crummy little dog?''

''Jack, it was a nice dog, and if you'd just—''

''That's it.'' He raked his hair with his fingers. ''I'm calling the sheriff. The last time I checked we weren't living on the set of *Deliverance*.''

She looked at him with raised eyebrows. ''I'm beginning to wonder. But look, I screwed up. I told the guy to check the pound.''

''Oh no.'' He rolled his head to the side. ''Why'd you do that? They probably nuked that mutt already.''

''Because I screwed up, okay? Because he's leaning in my car, he's filthy dirty, his face is right on top of me, and he's asking me one question after another. I never do well under that kind of pressure. So if he does check the pound—''

''They might tell him about me.''

''Right.''

Jack stood up and his hand traveled slowly to his chin. ''You say he's kind of strange?''

"Actually, he strikes me as kind of stupid." She saw his hairy face, the bits of food or skin falling from his beard, those awful rotting nubs of teeth.

"Then maybe he won't put two and two together."

"I don't know if he's *that* stupid. But listen, if you're going to call the sheriff about the shepherd, forget about Davy's stepfather."

"Davy who?"

"The new boy at the Center. Don't you ever listen?"

"I got it. I got it. You don't want me to mention him?"

"That's right, don't. I'm trying to work with the boy and it's a delicate situation. If we bring in the sheriff, it's only going to complicate things." She couldn't imagine Bentman's hick sheriff giving a hoot about some snake anyway.

Jack looked toward the county road, which he could barely make out through the trees.

"Oh, screw that sheepherder too. I can already hear them saying they can't do anything until the creep actually does something. We're probably better off just ignoring these assholes."

"I doubt we can do that." Celia was working with Davy every day now, so she could not avoid his stepfather. No avoiding the meadow either; she had to drive past it to get to and from work. "But if I were you I sure wouldn't slow down if I saw the shepherd."

25

Davy sat in the back of the classroom with his chin on his chest and his hands resting on his desk. Celia couldn't tell if he was scared, or just tired. She felt a bit of both. She stood no more than five feet away, watching him from behind a large one-way mirror. Her encounter with Davy's stepfather had given her a fitful night's sleep and left her shaky this morning. Tony had joined her just a few minutes ago. This was the first class of the day, and as soon as she had a few unencumbered moments she wanted to tell him about Mr. Boyce. It chilled her to even think about the way he'd just appeared out there in the woods. She rubbed her hand over her left arm, as if she could erase the memory of his rough grip; and then a terrifying possibility struck her: he hadn't just appeared out there at all, he'd been *stalking* her.

She glanced around the small observation room, as if the mere thought of the man could make his fleshly presence real.

But why would he be stalking you? Isn't that a bit much? A little melodramatic? That's what her mother used to accuse her of: *Stop being so melodramatic, Celia.* Stalking did make her think of bad movies in which women acted as the perfect foils for homicidal maniacs, but it also forced her to remember the horrifyingly true stories of women hunted and killed by the crazies of the world. There were lots of real-life horror stories, though some of them taunted memory more painfully than others. The grisly photographs of Nicole Brown Simpson's body came quickly to mind, and Celia shuddered once again over the lesson some men had learned from that case.

Then she recalled the weird remark Mr. Boyce made when he held the snake, just before he tried to cut off its head, about not having any patience for the things that scared him. Was that a coincidence too?

She rubbed her arm again and forced herself to focus on Davy. The boy looked up as Mrs. Tucker's aide, Allison, started handing out supplies. The teacher's voice melted into the observation room.

"Now, I want each of you to either write about your family or draw a picture of them," the teacher said. "You can do either—write or draw—but I want you to do it about your family."

Davy's eyes followed Allison hungrily until she gave him his paper and pencil. Celia recalled how as a child she'd also been greedy for her own materials whenever a new project had been announced.

"This ought to be interesting," she whispered.

"He looks like he might cooperate." As Tony spoke he pulled on his bottom lip, a nervous gesture that Celia had taken note of only recently.

"Actually, he's been drawing well all week. Today I'll have him do the House, Tree, Person Drawing."

This news did not rouse any response from Tony, but Celia tried not to let it bother her.

"I haven't really had a chance to review his work yet. Tomorrow I'll have him do the Family Drawing, and I'll look them over this weekend. By then I think we should have all we need for a comprehensive evaluation."

"We've got you on call, right?"

"You do, but Jack's taking off for Trout River for two days, so I'll probably have some time to work. Frankly, each of Davy's pictures gets creepier and creepier."

"Creepier?" Tony repeated superciliously. "Now that's a professional term."

She refused to respond. She wasn't going to let him get to her, not this morning. "By the way, I need to talk to you about something that happened yesterday."

But Tony already was reading his beeper and opening the door, pausing long enough only to say, "It's the district office," before disappearing.

She turned back to Davy, who was gazing at a child's picture hanging on the wall just a few feet from his desk. Tears began to roll down his cheeks. She took a second look at the picture and saw a roughly drawn woman holding a little boy's hand.

Mrs. Tucker walked over to Davy and spoke softly to him, too softly to penetrate the one-way mirror.

As the teacher studied the picture, Davy slowly lowered his eyes to his desk. His every move appeared to require some effort until he focused on his pencil. Then, in a sudden flurry of motion, he gripped the yellow barrel and raised his arm. Celia pounded the glass to warn Mrs. Tucker, but it was too late.

Davy stabbed at his teacher, who surprised Celia—and no doubt the boy as well—by swiftly deflecting his attack and pinning his wrist to the desk.

Celia exhaled with such relief that she felt empty. She certainly hadn't expected the stout Mrs. Tucker to react that quickly. But neither Celia nor the teacher was prepared for what came next.

Davy lunged forward and savagely sunk his teeth into her arm. Even behind the glass Celia could hear his ferocious grunts as he chewed on the ample flesh just below Mrs. Tucker's elbow. The teacher gasped and released Davy's wrist, but that only enabled him to use both hands to hang on to her as he ground his teeth deeper into her arm.

Celia rushed into the classroom as Mrs. Tucker made desperate and wholly ineffective attempts to wrench herself free. Celia took hold of her arm and forced it in the opposite direction—right into Davy's face—which clearly angered the injured woman.

"What are you doing?" she shouted.

Celia didn't even consider responding because Davy's mouth had begun to open under pressure, and she saw how she could break his bite. Using both hands, she jerked Mrs. Tucker's arm down toward his chest, which finally freed her. Davy turned away, as if in shame.

Mrs. Tucker stepped back and stared at her bloody wound as Celia gripped the boy firmly by his shoulders.

"Davy, I think we need to go to containment right now."

Curiously, she did not fear Davy at all, not even when he clearly eyed her left hand. She simply did not believe he would try to bite her after her show of force. She was wrong.

"Do you hear me?" She raised her voice and shook him gently. She wanted him to look at her. He wouldn't.

She glanced at Mrs. Tucker. "Please have Allison get one of the child therapists, and you better get yourself some medical attention."

Davy's teeth had left a clear impression on the teacher's skin, like a cookie cutter with scalloped edges. He'd drawn a lot of blood, and before Celia turned back to the boy she saw a stream run down Mrs. Tucker's arm and drip off her wrist.

Davy did not appear at all agitated by the panic and commotion he'd caused. He sat unmoving, with his head still turned to the side, as Allison rushed out the door and Mrs. Tucker moved hastily to the front of the class.

"Davy." Celia stepped around his desk to try to make eye contact with him. "Are you going to walk out of here on your own or do you want some help?"

He looked at her with a stony expression, hate or fear or something else, Celia couldn't tell. Out of the corner of her eye she saw Ethan hurry into the room with Allison, and she heard Mrs. Tucker telling the students in a remarkably collected voice that she had to leave to see a doctor.

"Allison," the teacher added, "will take over for me."

"Ethan," Celia addressed him without taking her eyes off Davy, "we need to go to containment right now. We're going to see if Davy will take my hand and walk out with us."

She released her hold on his shoulders but the boy would not take her hand. She then tried to guide him out of his seat, but this proved no more productive.

"Ethan," she said in the same authoritative voice she'd been using all along, "would you help me take Davy to containment?"

Ethan moved swiftly to the other side of the boy's desk, and the two of them shifted his chair all the way back to the wall with the one-way glass. As they did this Davy locked his hands on the plastic seat. They quickly unpried his fingers and picked him up. Ethan held Davy's legs, and Celia stood behind him and wrestled her arms around his upper body. He chose that moment to strike a second time, baring his teeth so suddenly that Celia had to thrust his body to the side and pin his arms tightly behind his back to avoid being bitten.

But this time he did not make any noise, no groans, moans or utterances of any kind; and when she foiled his attack he ran out of steam and hung between them like a clothesline.

They carried him out of the classroom as the other students and Allison looked on quietly. They negotiated the cement walkway back to the main building, where they carefully descended the stairs to the containment room.

Celia freed her hand to open the door, and the awkward threesome entered the room. They lowered Davy to the dark sponge mat that covered the floor. Every surface of the eight-foot-square room had a cushioned covering.

The boy tensed as they laid him down between them, but made no attempt to break free. They continued to hold him as they began to breathe together audibly. After about a minute Davy started to relax. Celia watched Ethan as he looked intently at the boy, and wondered what kind of a father he'd make. A good one, she decided. Despite his dark humor, he was kind to kids.

She spoke in a soothing voice:

"Davy, everything is okay. We're going to keep you safe. This is a safe place where you can't hurt yourself or anyone else."

She stroked his head as she talked, and when her eyes indicated to Ethan that he could leave, he mouthed, "Are you sure?" She nodded.

He released Davy's feet, and the boy immediately drew them up to his body in a protective posture. He lay still as Ethan walked out of the room.

Celia let her arms go limp, though they remained draped around Davy's chest.

"Davy, let's try breathing together, okay? I'm going to take a deep breath, and you see if you can do it too. Then we'll blow it out slowly, okay? One-two-three."

She drew in her breath in a deep, exaggerated fashion and exhaled in the same manner. Then she did it again. A second or so later he joined her.

"That's good. Now let's do it together. One-two-three."

She felt the boy breathing with her, and after a few moments he rested his head against her chest. She craned her neck around his head and saw for the first time that he ap-

peared calm. She leaned back against the padded wall, and a
smile spread across her face.

Davy let her take his hand as they left the containment room,
and he held on to her all the way upstairs to her office.

"Go ahead, grab a seat," she said cheerily.

He settled in the child's chair by the big table where he'd
been drawing all week long. He looked at her openly and
expectantly, and when she spoke he watched her keenly. For
the first time since meeting Davy she sensed that he wanted
to be at the Center, and maybe even with her. She was surprised by how much this pleased her.

She handed him a pencil knowing this was a calculated
risk after his attack on Mrs. Tucker, but she wanted to rebuild
trust with him as soon as possible. Besides, he'd made his
preference for pencils clear during every drawing session. As
she handed him a sheet of blank paper she told him to think
about the place where he felt safest.

"Whenever you're scared, like you were in that classroom,
or whenever someone's mean to you, I want you to think
about the one place that you'd like to go because it feels safe.
Got that?"

Davy didn't reply, of course, but she talked on as if he
had.

"Good. Now I want you to draw that place, Davy. It's
important."

He moved his head up and down. She thought he might
have been nodding, but couldn't be sure. Then he leaned over
and went to work.

26

Chet heard the chain saws and knew that if he started cutting, the loggers would hear him too. Too bad. A whole string of stumps all lined up by the side of the road waiting for him. Just waiting. And he couldn't cut them. Look at that one, all fat and round and standing there saying, Cut me, cut me, like some dumb-ass hitchhiker with sweat meat stacked up all over her body. *Come on, get in. You need a ride? Yeah, sure, I'm going that way.* He'd picked them up . . . and dropped them off. One, two. Maybe more. You lose track. Once they're gone, they're gone. No use to remember.

He'd have to move on, get away from the sound of those saws. He thought he should do that with Davy, too. Leave Bentman. Get the hell out. Every goddamn day he's drawing pictures—of what? What's he saying? It's like he's talking Russian all of a sudden. They don't mean shit to me but they could be saying anything to her. Everything, even. There's no telling with that kind of talking.

But it doesn't matter, he told himself. Doesn't matter one bit, not if she's not listening. And if she straightened out her thinking, she won't be listening. And if she didn't? Hell, then she won't be listening either. He'd given her life. It was His to take away.

The dirt and gravel road curved to the west, and when he spotted the long driveway to his left he smiled without knowing it. He realized with a start that he'd driven up the county road the back way and hadn't even known where he was. He sure as hell did now. The name on the fence post saying to all the world "Griswold," like she didn't have a thing to be afraid of.

He pulled on the parking brake and let the truck idle. He

walked up the drive till he could see the house. He had time for a good long look. Nice. He'd burn it down if he had to. He could see the flames licking the walls, cedar turning black as night, crumbling and falling on top of her, a huge smoking mess, the flesh roasted right off her bones. All the evidence burned away, her blood bubbled to ash. Go ahead, find the cuts. Like finding the white when the snow melts.

His smile spread till he felt it all the way down to his crotch, rich and thick with joy.

He turned away and started back to the truck. He stopped at the fence post to look at the sign. It had been there awhile; he could tell by the rusty nails holding it in place. He pulled and felt it start to give. Then he jerked it hard and split it right down the middle, right where those nails were. The only part still hanging was the ''Gris,'' and even the top of the *s* was missing. He liked the way it dangled there, like it might not last for long. A hard wind could rip it right down. It could. It could.

27

Stevie bulled his way through the kitchen door of the Center and headed straight for Davy. Stevie was ten years old with frizzy red hair and more than one hundred seventy pounds of weight burdening his young body. The poor boy's face was a buckshot of freckles, and except for this frenzy of orange he was as white as a sack of flour. He was obese, bossy, and terrorized the other children. Not surprisingly, he was also friendless, which he rued loudly and daily.

"Hey, you," he shouted as he shoved Davy, who was sitting at the table eating a sandwich while a crowd of children on either side of him scrambled to trade doughnuts for cupcakes, peanut-butter-and-jelly sandwiches for tuna, "shut up. Don't say a word." Stevie turned to his classmates. "See, he does what *I* tell him to!"

He shoved Davy again, hard enough to drive his chest into the table, "Hey, you're dumb. You know what dumb is? You! It means you can't talk, *dumb*bell."

Stevie thought this was hilarious, and so did pixie-headed Anna, who quickly concluded that it was open season on the new kid.

"Stay, boy, stay," she giggled as she held up both hands, "and *no* biting!"

She squealed with laughter, which enraged Stevie.

"Anna banana, shut up or I'll—"

The steadily rising noise level made Celia realize that something must be amiss down in the kitchen. She hurried from her office and found that the children had been left unsupervised in the most dangerous room in the Center—appliances, gas stove, knives. Allison was supposed to be here. Where the devil was she?

"Stevie, take your lunch and get over there." Celia knew

she had to assume command quickly and decisively. She figured the children were only one insult shy of a food fight, which could turn into a mini-riot with this crew. "I'm giving you a time-out."

She pointed to a smaller table in an alcove where children who misbehaved were banished for varying periods of time.

"Why me? I didn't do a f—a thing, I mean."

"Thank you for catching your tongue, Stevie, or you'd be catching more than a time-out. Now move."

Stevie slumped his shoulders and shuffled off to the Center's version of Siberia.

Davy was glaring at his tormentor, so Celia walked over and gave him a warning: "Don't get any ideas about getting even. We don't do that around here. Do you understand? Good."

She continued to ask Davy questions and speak to him as though he were not a mute because she wanted to create the expectation of conversation without pressuring him too much. Sooner or later he would probably talk. Almost all elective mutes did. She remembered an old joke a psych professor had told them about mutism. It was a late spring day and at least half the class were having a hard time staying awake, so he told them to perk up.

"Joke time," he announced, which surprised most of them because he'd never told a joke before. "Okay? Everybody awake? You'll be tested on this." The few remaining sets of droopy eyes snapped open. "All right, there's a boy, actually he's not a boy, really, he's twenty-one years old, and he's never said a word. His parents have taken him to all kinds of specialists—hearing doctors, throat doctors, witch doctors, you name it—but no one can find anything wrong with him. Well, one day they're all sitting around eating dinner and the young man looks up and says, 'This tastes like shit.' "

A few students laughed.

"His mother, she's so amazed she's not insulted. She says, 'Bobby, that's wonderful, you're talking. Oh, thank God, you can talk. Look, Harry, he's talking.' The father, he's sitting there dumbstruck, he says to the kid, 'Jesus, Bobby, what's up? How come you've been so quiet?' And Bobby just shrugs and says, 'Hey, everything's been fine up till now.' "

They had all laughed, some more dutifully than others. The point, her professor had said, is that you can make too much of mutism. Some children will talk when they're good and ready and not before.

"So let them be. Life's not always complicated." He'd smiled. "Lots of times it's very simple. Remember, even Freud said that sometimes a cigar is just a cigar."

Celia thought that might be true in some cases, but she worried about Davy. His stepfather linked the boy's refusal to speak to the death of his mother, yet thousands of children lost their parents each year and that didn't stop them from talking. She was beginning to wonder if Davy's silence said more about the parent who survived than the one who had died, especially after the picture he'd just drawn showing where he felt safest. Not to mention her encounter with Mr. Boyce out in the woods. That had left her with serious questions, as well as profoundly shaken. If he could be so casually brutal around her, how did he behave when he was alone with the boy? Celia also wondered how many other elective mutes had been ignored and forced to suffer, thanks to the glib opinions of professors and other so-called experts. Probably a bunch.

Besides, she thought, I hate cigars.

Allison rushed back into the noisy kitchen full of whispered apologies. "I'm so sorry, Mrs. Griswold, but my period started right after I got them seated, and I—"

"That's okay. It's really not your fault anyway. This is much too much work for one person. Either we get you some help or we cut out their allotment of white sugar."

Allison laughed quietly. "I'd go for that, the help, I mean."

Celia looked toward the doorway. "Where is everyone? I heard the racket all the way down the hallway."

"I just saw Ethan and Dr. Weston coming out of his office. Please don't mention this to him. He said the other day that—"

"Don't worry about it." Celia could see that Tony had the youngest member of the staff cowed. "Just let me bring you up to speed." She looked over at Stevie. "He's in a time-out. I'd give him another five minutes. Davy was giving him stink-eye, so I warned him, but you definitely want to keep an eye on him too. You'd want to anyway. The rest of them are no worse than usual." That included Harold Matley, who sat stone-still now that he'd finished eating, as if any movement at all might stir up his scary hallucinations.

Allison started thanking Celia but stopped short as Tony and Ethan walked in the kitchen.

"Celia." Tony stepped forward. "I understand we had a serious problem after I left this morning."

"Yes, Davy acted up. How's Mrs. Tucker doing?"

Tony held up his hand and spread his fingers. "Five stitches in her arm and a tetanus shot. I've had happier staff." He looked past her and frowned. "Do you really think it's safe to have him in here eating with the others?"

"I don't think it's a problem." She hoped that Davy would not choose this moment to cause a disruption.

Tony shook his head in obvious disagreement. "So what did you do with him after containment?"

Celia explained that she had him draw a picture of the place where he felt safest.

"You had him draw a picture after he *bit* Mrs. Tucker?" Tony said with mock amazement, which Celia found offensive. "Really," he went on, "I think we must come up with ways of disciplining him."

"Right," Ethan chimed in, "it's about time we started kicking some ass around here. Let's requisition a rack from the district office. I'll bet we can get that kid talking real fast. It's time we put our big foot down, right, Sasquatch?" Ethan made a show of staring at Tony's huge feet, while the director looked at him with open incredulity. He started to say something, but managed only to part his lips before stomping away.

"I guess I'm a real disappointment to him," Ethan said with a smile.

"Jesus, don't you worry about offending him?" Celia's hands had turned clammy as soon as he'd started in about the rack.

"Not in the least. Besides, I've about had it with him. He just made me sit in his office for fifteen minutes while he lectured me about respect, my lack of it for him, to be specific. Anyway, what's Sasquatch going to do, send me to Vietnam? Too late, buddy, I've already been there."

"I didn't know that." The news shocked Celia; she'd worked with Ethan for years.

"That's because I don't like to talk about it. It's a time I'd just as soon forget, okay?"

"Sure."

"Now, Miss G., on to more important things because inquiring minds want to know: Did Davy actually draw a picture of where he feels safest?"

She nodded. "He sure did. He drew—"

Stevie picked that moment to start pounding the table in the alcove, and Anna screeched "No!" at dark-haired Robby, who was sitting next to her. Robby sniffed loudly and flipped her Twinkie back onto the table. It broke in half, and she started to cry. Allison, trim and nimble, moved around the kitchen like a hot-footed waiter.

Celia turned to Ethan. "Does this place ever get to you?"

"Every day. I wasn't kidding about the rack."

"Yes, you were. Anyway, there's something about Davy's picture that really bothers me. You know how most kids draw a picture of where they live, no matter how bad things are at home? Not Davy. He drew a picture of this place, only he had it surrounded by a moat with sharks, and barbed wire, and he had guards in towers with big guns protecting him."

"A little concerned with personal security, are we?"

"Just a little. Then I ran into his charming stepfather yesterday"—she paused to nod portentously—"and I can understand why. I was hiking up by my place, and that asshole scared me half to death. He just showed up out of nowhere, and then almost cut the head off a snake while—"

"Wait a second, where'd the snake come from? Did he bring—"

"No, I was going down a trail and it came crawling out of an old dead tree trunk. I got spooked, I shouldn't have but I did, and I ran into Mr. Boyce, literally. I was looking back and ran right into him. He grabbed ahold of me and wouldn't let go, and then he started dragging me back to where the snake was. Thank God a logging truck came by, because he saw the driver and let me go, and I took off for the road. Now here's the creepy part." She reached out and touched Ethan's arm briefly, as if to steady herself. "I turned around and he had that snake—"

"The same snake?"

"Ethan," she said in a trying voice, "who knows? It's not like it had a bunch of tattoos and a nose ring. He said there was a nest of them. I don't know. All I know is he started to cut off its head with a razor blade. I freaked out, I was yelling at him to stop, so he did. He just dropped it on the ground and walked away, and I had to beat it to death with a rock so it wouldn't just lie there in pain. It was like it was being tortured."

"You? You beat a snake to death with a rock?"

"What else could I have done? I couldn't just leave it there."

"No, of course not. I—"

"You should have seen it. It was one of the most horrible things I've ever seen."

"I just didn't think you had it in you."

"Neither did I. Anyway, I can understand why Davy didn't draw a picture of home sweet home, not when he's got to live there with Attila the Hun."

"Watch your step."

"I am, but I'm not going to let him intimidate me. That kid deserves a lot better."

Their eyes met and lingered for a moment longer than Celia found comfortable. She looked away as Stevie, once again, began to beat the table with his fist.

28

Chet wiped his hands and tossed the oily rag onto the worktable he'd set up outside the trailer. He groaned as he lifted the chain saw. He'd been bending over for half an hour sharpening and cleaning it, and now his back burned with a familiar pain. He tried to stand up straight but that didn't do any good at all. It had been eating away at him for days and made every move a misery.

The video played in the trailer, and he knew the boy was sitting there staring at it like a zombie while he ate dinner. He was starting to hate that kid. No matter what he did for him, nothing. And when he took him to bed, nothing. He had to make him do everything and the little bastard did nothing. Give him a home and you get *nothing*.

He laid the chain saw in the back of the pickup and looked up at the sky. A sharp pain shot down his leg and he swore at the stars as if they were to blame. He started back to the trailer.

Davy sat hunched over his bowl of chocolate-flavored cereal and watched *Batman*. Black wings, black mask, black as night. Fly so good. And the Penguin. Somebody's got to die. Got to. His sketchbook and pencils lay on the floor beside him.

His stepfather threw open the door and the night rushed in, the darkness that crowded the world outside. Davy felt it harsh against his skin and wanted it to go away, for everything to disappear.

His stepfather edged around the kitchen table and moaned when he poured coffee into his cup. Davy saw him hold his back like he was pressing on an open wound. When he turned to him, the boy fixed his eyes on the video and clenched his spoon.

Chet inched back past the table, feeling the tightness of the trailer as he never had before. Everything about it felt tight, made for fucking midgets or something. Even the air felt close, pressing in on him like all those molecules were heating up right in his face. Sweat ran down his spine in a filthy itchy stream. It made him want to rub up against something hard and pointy. But when he moved he caught his jeans on the corner of the table. Some fucking finishing nail that hadn't been finished. He had no patience for this shit and yanked it free. The table shook violently. He took an angry, irritated step and pinned his knee to a goddamn corner of a goddamn open drawer.

He swore loudly and grabbed his leg like he could wring the pain right out of it. And the boy just watching the video, not caring, not even looking at him, no sympathy at all. His knee throbbed. He slammed the "off" button and the screen made a fizzing sound and went blank. Now the boy looked at him. Goddamn right he did.

You got to be nice to him. He'd told himself that a hundred times before, but he was tired of listening. Hadn't done a bit of good with this boy. Maybe the others, but not him. Maybe not being nice is what he needs; and for the second that lives inside of a second he wanted to punch him, smash him, knock him into the middle of next week. That's what his old man used to say, *I'll knock you into the middle of next week, Chester.* And he'd do it too. *Did you see stars, boy? Did you?* Standing over him, swaying back and forth, those fists hanging by his sides. Then he left and the beatings stopped. But not the memories. They never went away, or the scars. If he studied his face closely he could still see them, rough ridges that had finally started to blend in with his age lines, as if it had taken a lifetime for his body to absorb the beatings and make them go away. At least he didn't beat his boys. He knew he wasn't perfect but he never did that. He might want to, might have the *urge,* but he never did it. Not even come the end, when he wanted nothing more than a fresh start.

Chet squeezed next to Davy on the floor. The pain in his knee had eased and he was ready for the night's pleasure. He pushed aside the damned pad of paper, the pencils too. The hell with her. The boy stared straight ahead, a blank face for a blank screen. That's all he ever gives me, that blank look. Chet put his arm around him, but Davy tried to squirm away. Chet didn't care for this one bit; but he didn't bear a grudge, and when he pulled him close he played with him, rubbing his head, a crew cut just like when he himself was a boy. Soft bristles like those brushes she'd favored. He'd kept one of them. It was around here somewhere. He always kept a memento, and sometimes he would take them out and feel rich with memory. A charm from a bracelet, an earring that had caught his eye, a hair plucked from a private spot, Mrs. Griswold's little notebook, the one he'd found by the snake. And her panties, what was left of them, the shiny part and lace. Small things. Most of them could fit in his pocket. Sometimes they did. Sometimes he got them out and ran them over his skin—a hair, a brush, they all felt good. And those pages she'd touched, they felt better than all the rest, for they were the promise of what could come. He'd sat in his truck while she killed the snake, and opened the notebook and seen those first few pages with the flowers she'd drawn, like the ones in the house, those paintings that looked just like their lower parts, *dirty* flowers from her *fingers*. Later, in the dark, he'd fanned himself with the pages, their edges soft as feathers as he reached down his body and closed his eyes and felt his skin blossoming against each sheet.

A hair, a brush, the notebook, every one of them was a memory, and a woman too. He liked the way they could reach out to him even now, years later, and flood him with genuine joy. Their murders had made all things possible with their sons, and their sons had made him happy with his life. He thanked them for this, now and for—

Davy moved again, disturbing Chet's sweetest thoughts. He gripped the back of his neck firmly, and his smudged fingers pressed against the boy's milky skin. The smell of engine oil filled the space between them.

"Don't ever try and get away from me again. I don't like that one bit. When I tell you to stay, you stay. When I tell you to come, you come."

But as soon as he released him Davy tried to inch away,

and Chet knew the boy would never love him as he loved the boy.

He grabbed him again, picked up the bowl, and threw it in Davy's face. The boy sat paralyzed as milk dripped down and soaked his shirt. Bits of brown bloated cereal stuck to his cheeks, nose, and eyebrow. Chet thought it looked like dry dog food all spongy and swollen and puked up.

The boy remained absolutely motionless as those dirty fingers moved toward him. Chet hummed as he tenderly picked pieces of cereal off Davy's face and placed them in the bowl.

"Here, you better take off your clothes, they're all wet."

He hummed some more. The boy shook as his stepfather started to undress him.

"Hey, look at you, you're so cold you got the shivers. Come on, you need a shower. Let's warm you up."

He knelt in front of Davy and lifted his T-shirt over his head. When the boy's arms were up in the air and his face hidden, Chet leaned forward and kissed his pale chest, his pink nipple. He could feel the trembling beneath the skin, the place deep inside where the blood and bones come alive.

He would be good to the boy. He would. Just as long as he could.

29

Celia tensed as she turned out of their long driveway and headed down the county road. She used to enjoy the drive to work, but now worried about the shepherd whenever she neared the meadow. She'd spotted him twice this week off in the distance tending his flock. But that wasn't the worst of it. The stand of tall pines that had stood for more than two hundred years and given her so much joy had been marked with red paint and chain-sawed in just the past thirty-six hours. It seemed horribly unfair that those ancient trees should take so long to grow, and then should die so quickly in a disgraceful explosion of dust and broken branches. But at least the loggers were friendly, unlike Mr. Boyce. He called yesterday afternoon to say he wanted to see her later today. What a way to end the week. Given the increasingly grotesque nature of Davy's artwork, she didn't care if she ever saw him again. But that wouldn't be possible. You have to work with the families too, she reminded herself; and she knew the boy would never get better if she excluded Mr. Boyce. But then she asked herself if he'd ever get better living with him. Davy's most recent drawings were eerie enough to make her wonder.

The loggers were taking a break when she drove by. They waved and Celia returned the favor. She may have despised what they were doing, but they were pleasant enough. The shepherd made her positively queasy, and every day that passed without her seeing him made her all the more certain that he would loom beside the road on her next trip. She'd even begun to think about selling the house, leaving the ridge. The hunters had been bad enough, but now she found herself running into the likes of Mr. Boyce and the shepherd. They also had the fire dangers to contend with. Another huge blaze had started near Wilkinson, about forty miles to the north. Seventeen homes had been reduced to ash. You tell yourself it can't happen to you, but there are a lot of yous out there that it happens to.

Then there were the yellow jackets that had started finding their way into the house. At first she'd come across one or two of them clinging lazily to the inside of the screen. Now it wasn't unusual to see fifteen or twenty at a time. She'd taken to vacuuming them up, but quickly discovered that she had to use masking tape to seal the end of the long black tube. Otherwise they'd crawl right back out. She used to say that when you live in the forest, some of the forest lives with you, but her growing unease had made her wonder if the ridge was really worth it. She hadn't broached the idea of moving to Jack, mostly because she hadn't found him all that approachable these days; but she intended to have a serious discussion with him right after his Trout River trip this weekend.

As she drove she twisted her neck from side to side to try to work out the muscle tension. Thank God it was Friday. Work didn't exactly fill her with joy these days either. Since Tony's arrival the atmosphere had definitely become stuffier, as if the entire staff except for Ethan had become emotionally constipated. She promised herself that tomorrow she would take a good long hike. Maybe you can exorcise this . . . this *anxiety*.

She remained so lost in thought that when the shepherd stepped into the road it took her a full second to slam on the brakes. The car began to skid but the shepherd never flinched as it floated sideways toward him. She spun the steering wheel but with the brakes locked she couldn't get the Honda to straighten, and with the shepherd standing in the middle of the road she couldn't just ride it out. So she kept the pedal pinned to the floor and her hands frozen to the wheel, and fully expected at any moment to hear the dull thump of his body. When the careening car finally stopped it had stirred up so much dust that she couldn't see which way she was pointed, or where the shepherd lurked. As the dust drifted away it unveiled the meadow in front of her, and she understood that she sat on the road crossways. A moment later she spied the shepherd's fuzzy profile slowly coming into focus a few feet from her door.

"What the hell do you think you're doing!" she screamed as she rolled down the window without thinking. "You damn fool!"

The shepherd walked slowly up to her and never said a word before slamming his fist on the roof. He struck it so hard that Celia ducked in her seat, fearful that his fury would drive his hand all the way to her head. He leaned over and hissed in her face,

"Remember little Bucky?"

"What?"

"Little Bucky, my dog."

Oh shit. She stared straight ahead at the meadow. The sheep were chewing on the few remaining wildflowers.

"Yes," she finally said with considerable anger. "I remember you telling me about your dog."

"Good, I'm glad you remember."

She wished for just a second that she'd run him over. At least she'd be done with him. She noticed the bright indicator lights on the dash and immediately cranked the ignition. After a minor protest, it turned over.

"You better hear me out." The shepherd hadn't moved his filthy face, and the odors from his foul body and rotting teeth assaulted her.

"No," she volleyed in as strong a voice as she could muster. "I'm going to work." She found "reverse."

"Just so you know," the shepherd said in his slow voice, "I went to the pound like you said, but they killed little Bucky like he was nothin', like he was nothin' but dirt. I had me little Bucky for eight years, and now he's just dead. I didn't even get his body so I could bury him proper. They just take them dogs and throw 'em in the dump and leave 'em rot. That's where my little Bucky is, some dump."

"I'm sorry. I'm truly sorry." And she was. Her anger had turned to pity, guilt, sadness, too. For the dog, even for him. But mostly she wanted to leave.

"You know what they told me down at the pound?"

"What did they say?" She spoke slowly, deliberately, not

to be heard and understood, but to hide the shallow breath that would reveal her fear.

"They said some guy brought him in, some guy that lives up here brought my little Bucky to the pound. You know anything about that?"

Celia stared at the steering wheel. "No, I don't. I don't know anything about some guy and your dog."

The shepherd shook his head wearily. "I think you're lyin', lady. I think you're lyin' right through them teeth of yours, just sitting there lyin' and lyin' and lyin'."

That's *it,* she said to herself. She found the courage to back up, but had to move carefully because the last thing she wanted was to roll her rear tires into the ditch beside the road. As she looked back over her right shoulder the shepherd leaned in and spoke one more time. His horrible hot breath curdled in her ear.

"I think you better tell that guy that you don't know nothin' about that he's in a world of hurt when I get my hands on him. And if I don't get him I'll take what's his and make it mine!"

He smashed the roof even harder than before. Celia found "drive," then turned the wheel sharply and floored it. She felt her whole body shaking as the tires spun. She knew she should ease up, but her fear wouldn't let her. She fishtailed from side to side as she plowed ahead. When she gained speed she glanced in the rearview mirror but saw little of the man who had frightened her so. He was already disappearing into the dust cloud she'd left behind.

Ashes to ashes, dust to dust. Those words haunted her all the way to work. It was as if they captured the real nature of a shadowy world that she had only begun to glimpse.

30

Davy walked down to where the van picked him up for the Center. He was way early, but didn't care. He'd rather wait an hour down here than stay in the trailer. He kicked rocks into the brush, aiming carefully with the tips of his scuffed-up shoes, hard brown shoes with holes in the bottoms where the pebbles got in and hurt until he took them off and shook them out.

Chet had stuffed some paper and cardboard inside and told him he'd never know the difference, but that was a lie. The rocks still hurt his feet and the kids all knew about the holes and teased him bad. Davy wanted those soft shoes you could run in, like the basketball players wore. If he had a pair of those he'd run and run and never stop.

He'd woken up early that morning and slipped out of Chet's bed. He'd moved as quietly as he could because he hadn't wanted to disturb him. No telling what he'd do . . . or want.

Davy had gone to the bathroom and felt the soreness deep inside. Every day he felt the soreness. He tried and tried to get the pain out, but couldn't. He didn't flush 'cause of the noise, and headed back to his bed, scared the whole time Chet would wake up. He liked being alone in his own bed, though it wasn't safe either. He had plenty of reasons to know that, over-and-over-again reasons. But it was still safer than being with Chet, so he tiptoed over to it. As his feet pressed down on the cool linoleum he tried not to think about all the dark cracks touching his skin, the stains on the floor, Chet saying, "Your mama made them, you clean it up."

Your mama made them. What did she make that was so dark? Try as he might, he could not remember. Only that she was gone, left him just like his daddy. Except his daddy was up in heaven, and he didn't know where his mom was. He thought about this a lot, like he thought about those stumps by the side of the road, the ones that didn't have any bark, just sitting out there with nothing on. Just like him. Chet wouldn't ever let him put on pajamas.

You don't need them. Come on over here. I'll keep you warm.

But it wasn't warm with Chet. It was cold, like ice melt, and hurt. Never one time it didn't.

Davy had slipped into bed and pulled the covers up around his neck and felt his breath warm on his hands. It was Friday. After today he wouldn't get to draw with Mrs. Griswold till Monday. He liked to draw, especially when he was all alone with her. He liked it better than anything in the whole world, how there was nothing but paper and then his hand moved and he could make a picture. He had all these pictures in his head, thousands and thousands of them, like the pages in a big book, each one with a different story.

He had just picked up a stick to draw in the dust when Chet's truck rolled out of the woods. The chain saw clattered in the back. Chet had come to get him, he could tell. He wanted something from him, maybe more. Sometimes he did, sometimes in the morning even.

Davy tightened all over, like a chain that goes to rust. He stared at his shoes. He wished he had those soft ones that could run and run and never stop.

Chet pulled up with his arm hanging down over the door. He smacked it to get Davy's attention, but the boy just kept looking down.

"Hey, you okay? Out awful early today."

Davy's eyes never strayed from his ugly shoes.

"You want a ride to school?"

No, Davy thought, no! But he couldn't say it, and if he didn't say it Chet might open the door. He could hear him like he'd heard him before, *Get in, Davy. Get in* NOW. So he concentrated as hard as he could and made his head move from side to side.

"Hey, look at that, he's talking to me like a regular guy. Better than those pictures, right, Davy boy?"

Davy moved the stick in the dust, first one line, then another and another, all connected. After the letter *N* he drew a circle. It was a secret answer. Chet would never know.

"All right, catch you later, you little alligator."

He smacked the door, softer this time, and drove off. Davy took his foot and wiped away the letters. When he had it smooth as a chalkboard he began to draw.

31

Celia dried her hands and glanced in the mirror. She almost laughed when her reflection reminded her of how little she had to fuss with: short hair; no earrings, none today anyway; and a minimum of makeup, certainly nothing that needed touching up. Even so, she stepped back and looked herself over, and decided for the umpteenth time that she'd dressed appropriately: simple blue blouse, relaxed slacks; nothing snug or clingy, nothing provocative, though she knew a diseased mind could find provocation in a fingernail.

She had almost ten minutes before Mr. Boyce was due to arrive, and as she unlocked the bathroom door she searched for a pat response she could offer the man. These kinds of non-answers never came to her easily, and she'd found that they sometimes led to a verbal Bake-Off in which both parties turned up the heat and tried like hell to make whatever they concocted—usually lies—palatable. The alternative was to be wholly truthful, but she no longer trusted Mr. Boyce enough for that.

She hurried down the hallway to her office, poking her head into the reception area long enough to determine that he hadn't shown up yet. As she settled behind her desk she opened Davy's folder and studied the picture he'd drawn yesterday of where he felt safest, the barbed wire and guns, the obvious attempt to insulate himself from a world he perceived as teeming with danger. The boy's other drawings didn't exactly inspire confidence in his well-being either. Though she'd had no time to analyze them thoroughly, she had glimpsed disturbing elements in each of them; and the "creepiness" she'd mentioned to Tony had become even more pronounced when the boy drew his stepfather.

Just as she began to leaf through his file for one of those

drawings, Mr. Boyce himself strode into her office, startling her with his sudden appearance.

"Hi," she stammered. She looked at her watch. "You're a few minutes early." Mostly, she was thinking of how she hadn't expected him simply to appear. There was an order to these things: her intercom would buzz, and she'd come out to greet him. Then they'd walk back to her office and get started. But here he was already grabbing a chair roughly by the back and pushing it forward until he could comfortably prop his arms on her desk. And he peered so intensely at her that his eyes seemed to loom from only inches away.

"I hate to be late," Chet replied. He knew what really bothered her, the way he'd walked in, sailed right past where that German bitch with all the hair usually sat. You got to take command, let them know you can't be pushed around. If there's any pushing to be done, then—

Celia interrupted his thoughts: "I always try to be early too, but punctuality is turning into a lost art nowadays." She was talking just to talk, killing time until he told her why he'd called for an appointment, though she figured he wanted to know how the evaluation was going. When she first met him she would have been encouraged by this, but after seeing Davy's artwork, and going through that horrible business with the snake, Mr. Boyce's interest only made her uneasy. This was the first time she'd seen him since he'd frightened her half to death, and she could still feel a shadow of that fear as he leaned across her desk and reached for Davy's drawing of where he felt safest. For a second she almost stopped him, had felt an urgent need to hold the paper back from him, but his fingers slipped it away before she could react, and then it was in his hands, filling up those eyes as they moved over the drawing like a pair of dark sponges, soaking up the elements so intently that she wouldn't have been wholly surprised if the boy's pencil lines had disappeared entirely from the page by the time he was done.

"What is this?" His first question proved as abrupt as his arrival. She heard belligerence as well, and saw arrogance in his refusal to look at her when he spoke. And then he did, and she wished he hadn't. Those eyes again. So dark and nearly opaque they could have had a layer of skin growing over them, onion paper for the eyes that left only a palimpsest of pupil to study. What had he seen, what had registered there, and what had he blinked away?

She felt an urge to lie, to tell him that she'd asked Davy to draw a fort, but she also wanted to gauge his reaction to the truth. So she told him.

Chet looked up, and an increasingly uncomfortable physical presence seeped through the brief space that separated them.

"This is where he feels safest? Where is it?"

"Here. He drew the Center, or"—her hands danced above the desk for a moment—"his idea of it anyway."

"This place?" As Mr. Boyce spoke those two words he moved his head back and forth dismissively.

"Yes, it *is* a drawing of the Center." She would not let the unstated go unchallenged.

"How do you figure that?" Chet's eyes sank to the page.

Celia told him to look at how Davy had drawn the porch that wrapped around the Center, and the distinctively oval shape of the attic window, but Mr. Boyce ignored all this when he spoke again.

"I take good care of him." The belligerence was gone, and Celia heard those words as they might have come from an honest man, a man who goes to work each day and makes the best of a difficult life, which was precisely what Chet had wanted to convey. He'd learned long ago that simple expressions of fact worked for him, linked his appearance and his words in a compelling manner. The same, he'd come to understand, was true of simple lies.

"I'm sure you do."

But Chet knew she was lying too. They were both liars, sitting there like card players tossing chips to the center of the table, raising stakes with empty hands.

"What about the others?" He handed back the picture and reached for the folder, but Celia deftly put it aside as she thanked him for Davy's drawing. She didn't want him to see anything else just yet, especially the rosebush picture, which Davy had turned in yesterday.

"I haven't had a chance to go over them. I expect I will

this weekend, and then I'll be happy to talk to you about them.''

Chet's hand hung in the air between them, arrested by the withdrawal of the folder; and he felt a powerful impulse to keep going anyway, to grab her blouse and shake her till she understood that you don't *do* that to him. You don't deny him his desires.

"Mr. Boyce, how can I help you? You said you wanted to see me.''

He let his hand fall to the desk. It reached almost halfway to her. She looked at it lying there—big veins, dark nails, scraped-up knuckles and sun-stained skin—the kind of hand that wrings a living from its finely scarred flesh. A hand, she suddenly realized, that looked just like an animal as it began to crawl back to its owner.

He sat up as he answered. "I wanted to know how Davy's doing. It's been a week now. You learning anything?''

He slipped it in as an afterthought, *you learning anything?* Not with any emphasis, and she caught that, the way he'd tried to squirrel it past her nonchalantly.

"I think Davy's doing well, all things considered. He's drawing for me, following directions, and at this point I couldn't reasonably ask for much more.'' She had ignored his question, sidestepped it as neatly as he'd presented it. But no more effectively, for he saw right through this.

"Great, but when do you think you'll know something, you know, about the boy's problems?''

"I think I'll have the initial evaluation done by the first of the week. I know it might seem time-consuming, Mr. Boyce, but I have to go over these drawings carefully. There is one thing I wanted to ask you.'' She paused to weigh his reaction but met only those umbral eyes. "Has the boy been abused?''

Celia had carefully calculated the possible effects of her question before asking it. She wanted Mr. Boyce to know that she thought Davy had been abused. If her suspicion proved correct, and Mr. Boyce was the perpetrator, she hoped that signaling her concern so clearly would force him to back off, though her experience told her that any attempt at abstinence by an abuser would be brief at best. Better that than nothing; it would buy her time. Davy, too.

"Abused?" Chet fired back. "What do you mean?" he demanded.

"Physical abuse, possibly sexual abuse. As you might have noticed from the picture you just saw, personal safety is a major concern of Davy's."

All he'd seen were guns and a prison. But he guessed she was seeing a lot more, seeing things he couldn't see. And he guessed the boy was talking to her with these goddamn pictures after all. But there was no guessing about the most important thing: she hadn't straightened out her thinking, not one little bit. She might as well have said, Mr. Boyce, you fucking the kid? He smiled to himself and shrugged for her.

"I don't know what things were like for him before I came along. I know his mom hated his dad, said he was awful to the boy, didn't miss him when he left. But I figured he was just rough with him. Maybe he got to the boy. I don't know. I can't"—Chet shook his head and tried to look disgusted—"I just can't feature that kind of thing. Davy, no kid should have to put up with anything like that."

"Was that the end of the abuse, or could there still be abuse occurring?"

"No, that was it, whatever his dad did to him, as much as I can figure from what his mom told me." Chet's eyes strayed to the folder by Celia's side. "So he's talking to you with those pictures."

"Like I said, I haven't had a chance to go over them thoroughly yet."

"He was a real talker before his mom died. He was a good one for a story. Sometimes we had to tell him that some of his tales were just like telling lies, but then she died and he stopped talking altogether."

"How odd."

"I know. I keep thinking he might start talking any day."

"No, I mean how odd that he told tall tales."

"Couldn't break him of it."

"Because these pictures come straight from the heart."

"Is that right? How can you tell?"

"Because a child doesn't know how to draw a lie. And besides, most of them don't even try. They're usually too caught up with the actual process of drawing to even bother.

It's not like words, the way people get caught lying all the time, don't you think, Mr. Boyce?''

"Probably so.'' But Chet said this with the clear and deeply unpleasant sense that he'd been the one caught in a lie, that something in that folder had betrayed him, something that Davy had drawn and that she now knew.

At one-thirty Ethan poked his head in her office and hummed the theme from "The Twilight Zone.''

Celia looked up and smiled. "Who's that in honor of?''

"Who do you think?''

She waved him in. "Shut the door.''

He closed it, tiptoed over to her desk and stage whispered, "What's going on?''

"Oh, stop that,'' she replied in a normal voice. "I just didn't want to talk with the door open. Did you see him?''

"Who?''

"Mr. Boyce. Isn't that why you were humming?''

"No, that was in honor of our boss. Why, was Boyce here?''

"He left just a few minutes ago. He wanted to talk about Davy.''

"What did you tell him?''

"As little as possible. He's really weird. I told him I'd have Davy's evaluation done by Monday and we could talk about it then. Then I got him out the door as fast as I could. Why, what's up with you?''

"I got a new one for you.''

"A new what?''

Ethan used both hands to peel down his lower lip. "What do you think?''

She laughed hard. It felt great to laugh, especially at Tony's expense. "You really are a terrible influence, but God, is that an annoying habit or what?''

"You mean you don't like it when he flashes his gums at you twenty times a day? Come on, he's Tony da Lip. Personally, I find it very attractive right after he eats when he's got these little chunks—''

Celia put up her hands. "Stop it, please, that's so gross.''

"So what kind of plans do you have for the weekend?''

He moved aside some pictures and propped his hip on the front of her desk.

"Oh, the same-old, same-old," she trilled. "Tonight the President and the First Lady are dropping by for a look at life in rural America, and then tomorrow the Duchess of York said she needs to see me. Personal problems of some kind. Seems the queen is becoming a bit of a bore." Celia affected a British accent for this last, which Ethan picked up on.

"That's what I so love about Bentman, the social scene is simply exquisite."

"It does set one's head to spinning. Actually"—Celia slumped her shoulders—"Jack has to go up to Trout River for two days, so it's just going to be me, Pluto, and the birds and the bees."

"A regular 'Wild Kingdom' up there, isn't it?"

"A little less wild all the time. They've been cutting the last of the old growth, and now we've got some sicko shepherd with about a hundred of his closest friends tearing the hell out of the biggest meadow."

"Sounds like the President will feel right at home."

"I wish he really could see it," Celia said with feeling.

"It wouldn't make any difference, Miss G."

"No, I know. I'm going to try to ignore it and get some work done tomorrow, go through Davy's drawings."

"What are they like?"

"The headline?"

"A headline will do."

"Strange, very strange. Look, this is pretty transparent, wouldn't you say?" She reached across her desk and handed Ethan one of Davy's pictures. "It's his KFD."

Ethan studied the Kinetic Family Drawing just a few seconds before agreeing. "That's definitely some serious strangeness."

Davy had drawn a demonic-looking man with a mouthful of huge pointed teeth, splitting a log with a hand shaped like an ax. A stick-figure boy held what appeared, at least at first glance, to be a wedge right above the log. Ethan adjusted his glasses and looked up.

"This is not your basic happy home."

"No, you're right. This looks like your basic domestic nightmare."

"And this is how he draws Batman." She held up the picture she'd taken out of Davy's sketchbook. "See the dark area and the hole?"

Ethan leaned closer. "Right, sure, there it is." He pointed to it.

"He's drawn a whole bunch of them the same way. He's clearly obsessed with the pubic area. By shading it so heavily he's trying to hide something, but by tearing the page over and over he's also expressing some powerful anger." She placed the drawing on her desk and looked out the window. "Not unlike what he does when he bites."

"Meaning?"

She turned back to Ethan. "We've got a kid who refuses to talk, right? But he uses his mouth to express his anger by biting. Now the same boy draws Batman obsessively"—she glanced at the picture—"and each time shades the crotch until it tears, and then he does it over and over again. There's a pattern here."

"So you're going to try to figure it out this weekend."

Celia nodded reluctantly, as if going over Davy's pictures at home wasn't such a good idea anymore. But she didn't have much choice. Mary, the hyperactive girl, was coming in for a session, and if she had any time left she hoped to see Allison for a few minutes before the young aide had to run off and do van duty. Allison had told her that she'd been thinking about going back to school to get her master's, and wanted to talk to Celia about art therapy. Then, if she could squeeze in fifteen or twenty minutes, Celia planned to review one of Harold's new drawings. The schizophrenic boy needed all the attention she could give him. Oh, and Tony, he also wanted to see her before the end of the day. Her afternoon was booked, and then some.

"And Jack's going away?"

Another nod from Celia, this one clearly weary.

"Pleasant dreams, Miss G."

"Thank you, Mr. T. Nice of you to plant such pleasant thoughts."

"Do you want some company?" Ethan was smiling but

she could tell he wasn't joking around, not this time; and when he reached for her hand and kissed her wrist, Celia's suspicions turned to certainty.

"I don't think we should be doing this."

But even as she spoke she grew complicitous, for she didn't retreat, and she used the word "we," as if to confirm that the conspiracy of desire had been hatched in her heart as well as his. That simple word also revealed to Celia how much she needed to be touched by someone eager to touch her.

He must have known this too because he never answered with words. Instead, his lips moved from one finger to the next, softly, without hurry, until all five of them had turned moist, chilling slightly, pleasantly, in the air.

He guided her around the desk and she followed his lead, never feeling the floor, only the effervescence that enveloped her. When they kissed her mouth fell open from the weight of pure want, and when his hands settled on the small of her back she pressed closer to his hips. She felt the length of him in spite of his pants, and as her hand filled with his warmth, Tony's voice filled the room.

Their embrace broke with the raw surprise of a tree limb snapping in an ice storm. They both stared at the door. Mercifully, it remained shut. Tony once more called impatiently to Barbara in the reception area. Celia breathed, and her stomach started to settle; but still she cursed her weakness and stupidity. At *work,* she scolded herself.

"I locked the door," Ethan whispered.

"It doesn't matter. I shouldn't be doing this." She backed up a foot, then another. "And what about Holly?"

Ethan gazed at the space that now lay between them.

"She's up in Portland with her mom."

"I guess you guys are having problems again." Celia retreated to her chair, the better to put distance between them.

"That suggests we occasionally don't have problems." He placed his hands on her desk and leaned forward imploringly.

Celia shook her head. "I can't, Ethan, I just can't."

His tone lightened. "I really could keep you company up there in the woods."

"No, Ethan, I mean it." She stared at a pile of folders, so

she could only guess at the effect of her words. When he turned to leave she did chance a look up, and then watched him walk to the door. She wished her sight had remained steadfast, for her eyes now studied his slacks, the creases and folds, rises and shadows; and her body stirred again with delight.

Maybe I'm not so sure. As he exited she started to call him, but stopped before her voice could unveil her desire. No, Cel, no. You're married. *For better, for worse.*

Damn, damn, damn, damn, damn.

32

Celia spotted Tony walking down to his office and picked up her pace. She was already a few minutes late. Allison had peppered her with two pages of questions about art-therapy curriculum—the girl certainly came prepared—and then started in about which schools she should consider. Before either of them knew it, the "children's day" had ended. Allison had rushed out to do van duty, and Celia had hurriedly thrown together her notes and files for the meeting with Tony. She'd had to dig Davy's folder out of the drawer where she'd stashed it after her talk with Mr. Boyce. She'd worried that he might walk right back into her office. He'd done it once; who's to say he wouldn't do it again?

She had alerted Barbara to what had happened, and the receptionist had been horrified that anything so "unseemly"—her word—had taken place on her watch. Celia assured her it wasn't that big a deal, but Barbara had remonstrated to the contrary and then stared at the front door as if to fix her internal radar on the Center's perimeter forever.

Celia had a number of issues she wanted to bring up with Tony, including her confrontation with Mr. Boyce over the snake. She'd intended to tell him yesterday, but after Davy bit Mrs. Tucker the morning had swirled into a series of distractions that had culminated in Ethan's sarcastic suggestion to Tony that they requisition a rack. At that point Celia decided to avoid her supervisor for the rest of the day. But she could not avoid this meeting. It had come at his request, and he looked right up when she paused at the door.

"Come in. Go ahead and close it, please."

Close it? Something was up. She swung the heavy oak door shut, and Tony gestured toward the lone chair that he kept parked at an angle in front of his desk.

"Have a seat."

Celia didn't care for its odd positioning. It left her looking at him over her right shoulder, or twisting her entire body. Though hesitant to rearrange anything in so fastidious an office, she leaned the chair onto its rear legs, squared it with the desk, and sat down. Tony winced as if he'd been struck.

Celia opened Davy's file but before she could say a word he leaned forward.

"Let me tell you about a concern of mine."

He spoke slowly and sternly, and with such grave expression that she rushed to interrupt him, sensing that if she let him continue he would leave her with little to say.

"First, I really want to show you these."

She slid Davy's Batman picture across the desk. Tony did not move his hands from their resting position, so the paper curled and bowed against his fingers before he consented to look down.

"This is what's starting to bother me," Celia said. "Remember his first picture was supposed to be of a person, but instead of drawing a boy like himself, which most boys do, he drew a woman?"

When Tony didn't acknowledge her question she quickly went on.

"Well, anyway, that was strange. But the way he's drawing Batman makes me really uncomfortable. Every one of these was torn at the crotch from all the heavy shading he put in."

Tony picked up the drawing, looked at the hole, and lowered the paper back down to his desk.

"Has it occurred to you," he asked dryly, "that maybe he's just modest?"

Celia's shoulders drooped, and she forced herself to take a deep breath.

"I doubt it. From what I've seen, children do this when they've been sexually abused. They're trying to hide something they're really ashamed of. I don't think we can rule that out as a possibility."

"What, with Mr. Boyce?" Tony rolled his eyes. He *actually* rolled them. Celia could not believe this, but before she could respond, he added,

"It might well be a simple case of a boy feeling a little awkward about his sexuality, and if you ask his stepfather about it without any more 'evidence' "—he raised and wiggled the index and middle fingers of both hands—"than some silly little pictures, you could be upsetting him and the boy for no reason at all."

Silly little pictures. Celia swallowed hard.

"I already did," she said without a hint of apology.

"You already did what?"

"I already asked him about it."

"Please tell me you're kidding." Tony glared at her. She said nothing. "You're not, are you?"

She shook her head.

"That was a big mistake."

"What if I'm right?"

"What if you are? It was something that happened. Unless you can prove it, and this"—he flicked the Batman drawing as he might a fly—"is hardly proof, then all you've done is put him on alert—"

"Or made him watch his step."

"Please stop interrupting me. And you've also put him on guard. A lot of kids claim to be abused, a lot of adults say they were when they were kids, and now a lot of parents are accusing their exes of it. It's a very trendy accusation."

"Look, I know there are bad cases out there. We all know that, but this isn't some witch hunt. It's one kid, the way it usually happens. It's not like Davy's saying a bunch of people in a church forced him to have an orgy on the altar."

"Actually, he's not *saying* anything."

"No, he's not *talking*, but I think he's *saying* plenty."

"You *think*, but you don't *know*. And if you don't have the proof, all you do is stir up a lot of ill feeling toward us. Our job is to get *this* kid"—Tony stabbed Davy's picture with his finger—"to stop biting people, start talking again, and get him back to school. Those are the kinds of results that count. Let's keep it simple, Celia. Simple. And never ever ask a parent if he's abusing his kid if that kid hasn't specifically told you so."

Celia stood up unsteadily and reached across the desk for Davy's drawing. She heard anger in the way air moved

sharply into and out of her lungs, and felt it in the dizziness
that ruled her for a moment.

She held up the picture, noticed it shaking. "I know I
haven't had a chance to totally analyze his work yet, I'll get
to that this weekend, but I can assure you that this isn't unusual. Every one of his Batman drawings comes out the same
way. Every one of them."

"You told me." Tony sounded bored.

She tried mightily to ignore his smug expression. "I know
it's not like finding the stains on the underwear, but I think
he is trying to tell us something, and we should be listening
to him." She found it a strain to speak in such a well-
modulated voice when she wanted most of all to scream at
him. She resisted the impulse. "Davy draws. That's how he
talks. His father has his own way of letting you know what
he wants."

Without sitting down, Celia told how Mr. Boyce had
threatened her with the snake and then started to cut off its
head.

"Are you sure he wasn't just trying to help you?"

She wondered if Tony was deliberately trying to antago-
nize her. She slipped Davy's drawing back into the file and
tried to still her trembling hand.

"No, he wasn't trying to help me."

"Then why didn't you call the sheriff, if you were so sure
he was threatening you?"

"Tony," she said with exasperation as she sat back down,
"what was I supposed to do? Report that he'd tried to butcher
a snake with a knife? Do you really think they would have
done anything?"

"Maybe not." He shrugged. "Look, this ties right into
what I wanted to talk to you about. Maybe you shouldn't be
working with Davy. I think you're getting too wrapped up in
this case and losing your objectivity. Frankly, I'm also losing
confidence in your ability to work with the boy. And after
this run-in it's clear you're not the best person to work with
his stepfather either. I'm not saying the whole thing was your
fault—I don't know, I wasn't there—but I can't have my staff
running around and getting into confrontations like that outside the Center."

Celia's hands fell to her lap, almost spilling the folder and drawings onto the floor. Where the hell should she begin? *Losing confidence in my ability to work with the boy? Not saying the snake was my fault? Running around and getting into confrontations?* Jesus! She realized that every one of his statements was meant to wound her, and that she'd have to triage her concerns.

"I think I'm working very effectively with Davy. He's drawing! He's not responding to anyone else. He sits staring off into space most of the day until he gets into my office. Then he works, and when he goes home he keeps drawing. I think that's significant progress. Furthermore, if you take me off this case, Mr. Boyce accomplishes exactly what he set out to do."

"First of all, this is not some contest of the wills. If I determine that it's in the best interest of the boy to do another type of therapy, something with more rewards and punishments built in, then Mr. Boyce can view it any way he wants. I found it wholly inappropriate, as you might have gathered, that after Davy bit Mrs. Tucker you had him draw a picture of where he felt safest."

"What do you think I should have done?"

"He likes to draw, right?"

"Yes, he does, very much."

"Anything but drawing then. Make him sit in containment by himself for an hour or two. Let him know there's a price to be paid for his bad behavior. But don't reward him."

"We're not talking about a child with mild behavior problems here, we're talking about a boy with long-term disturbances that may have been caused by serious abuse. He's not even talking, for God's sakes."

"Please don't get emotional on me," Tony said with evident distaste. "I'm not going to debate this now. I'll tell you what. I'll think about it over the weekend. I don't like having to take this case from you—"

Like hell—

"—but it's getting a lot more complicated than it needs to be."

She stood up to leave, paused, then reached back into the folder.

"I think," she said in little more than a whisper, "that you should look at this. It's Davy's idea of what he would look like if he were a rosebush."

She laid down Davy's drawing, a nightmarish vision in black of a bush that appeared to be all thorns and barren, brittle branches. Davy had managed only two flowers, and both looked dark and menacing. A black fence with pointy metallic posts surrounded the rosebush. They resembled the bars of a medieval prison. She knew better than to consider this a trump card, and knew too that it was unlikely to convince Tony of the value of art therapy; but she hoped that maybe, just *maybe,* he'd begin to understand that Davy was a boy far too deeply troubled to respond favorably to a one-dimensional behavioral approach.

"Nothing"—she shook her head—"is simple with this boy."

33

Jack strolled up to Ruth's desk and told her she could leave early. "It's Friday, go on. Helen and I can take care of things. Enjoy the weekend."

He'd tried to make it sound casual, the boss exercising his prerogative to be kind, but he could see her suspicion in the way she glanced first at Helen and then at him. She might just as well have wiggled her finger in his face and said, I know all about you two. Recognizing this made Jack realize that she was due for a raise. He'd tell her how much he appreciated the "discretion" she showed in *every* aspect of her work, and he'd make sure to point out that you just can't keep a job in this business without it. Ruth was smart, she'd get the message.

Hush money. No, he corrected himself, not really. Insurance. Most people paid good money to insure their homes, cars, boats, businesses. A fine tradition. He would pay Ruth merely to insure his privacy.

Of course then he'd have to give Helen a raise too, but that could get a little sticky because he was already paying her more than he paid Ruth, who had a lot more experience. Maybe he could convince Helen to stay at her current salary for a while. Fat chance. Helen, he had come to see, was good at making her demands known. It was her idea to send Ruth home early, her idea to have a picnic in the vault, and it was her idea to put the champagne on ice in a cooler to "celebrate our weekend together." All of which left Jack more than a trifle nervous. One of these days Celia would stop by the agency and find it all locked up. Then she would discover that her keys no longer worked and wonder what the hell was going on. But he'd finally brought in the locksmith because he couldn't enjoy himself when he was worrying all the time about his wife walking in on them. And naturally there were Celia's feelings to consider too.

But after this weekend his worries would be over. He'd already told Helen that he wanted their affair to slow down, though her preparations at the moment did not suggest that she was taking him all that seriously. He could hear her in the vault spreading out the comforter and popping open the champagne. He hoped she didn't spill any of the bubbly. He'd hate for it to start smelling like a saloon back there. He was afraid it already smelled like a bordello.

"Jack?"

He looked back and saw her peeking around the corner. "Yes."

"Are we alone?"

"We are now."

"And we're all locked up?"

"Yup."

"Is there anybody out front on the sidewalk?"

"Nope, but why—"

"All right!" Helen burst out butt-naked and started a rude dance that involved several violent thrusts of her groin in Jack's general direction.

He panicked because anybody walking by—hell, anybody driving by—could see this—this *bawdy* display. Not exactly the staid image he wanted for his insurance agency.

Helen bopped up to him, her ample breasts swaying and bouncing and slapping her chest to a beat only she could hear. As she gyrated she reached out and started to undo his tie.

"Are you kidding! Not here, for Christ's sakes!"

He hustled her back to the vault, pausing only long enough to make sure they hadn't been seen. No telling because a car had indeed driven by. He could only hope the occupants hadn't noticed anything amiss at The Griswold Insurance Agency because this . . . well, this was as good as the grist gets for a small-town gossip mill.

"Champagne?" Helen held up two full glasses that she had waiting for them in their "love nest," as she had started referring to the vault with all of the agency's most important records. He dearly hoped she would not slip up and use that term during office hours, as in "While you're back there,

Ruth, would you check in the love nest for the fire-insurance records?'' Jack lost water weight just thinking of a mishap of that magnitude.

He grabbed the glass of champagne and slugged it down. ''Thanks.'' Actually, he needed a belt of something stiffer to calm his greatly frazzled nerves. He still couldn't believe she'd danced naked in the front office and tried to disrobe him in full view of the policy-buying public. Was she on drugs? Maybe he should have made weekly urine tests part of the job requirement.

Helen drained her glass and refilled it. Jack did likewise. What the hell.

She took his tie and used it to perform a number of obscene tricks involving a fair amount of tension against certain of her body parts. He reminded himself to get it dry-cleaned ASAP. Either that or burn it.

Then she slipped his belt from his middle-aged girth, buckled it around her own waist and used it as a hula hoop. Now *this* Jack could appreciate. Wow. His member responded to this latest provocation but clearly not to her satisfaction for she yanked off his briefs, took a deep swallow of champagne, and placed him in her fizzy mouth.

Within moments Jack's perspective on Helen changed notably, and he no longer saw madness in her actions but a distinct poetic grace. Yes, even the public dancing, those wild pelvic thrusts, now appeared to have been nothing less than inspired.

He stripped off his shirt in the midst of her ministrations and stood there until his legs started to shake. She looked up smiling despite the obstruction and drew him down to her. He lay on his back and she straddled him. The smell of sex filled the air, the slightly sour scent they both found so persuasive, and she guided him to her opening. He began to fill her inch by inch. For a moment—no more than a twitch in time—they were still. And then she squeezed, and he began to move.

34

By the time Celia left the Center, the rest of the staff had cleared out for the weekend. The only other car that remained in the parking area was Tony's new Toyota. She was still smarting from her meeting with him, and glad that her work-week had officially ended. Sure, she'd have to study Davy's pictures and prepare an evaluation by Monday, and she was on call if any of the clients had an emergency, but at least she wouldn't have to deal with "Tony da Lip," as Ethan had dubbed him, or with Ethan either, for that matter.

They'd always flirted a little, but they'd never kissed, and certainly neither of them had ever suggested an assignation before. But even as Celia unlocked her car and considered what had happened, she took pleasure in the memory of Ethan's hands on the small of her back, the gently persuasive pressure of his fingers and the ready willingness of her body; indeed, the *neediness* she'd known the instant she'd been touched. And she'd liked his kiss too, open and eager, as hers had been.

Her excitement had surprised her, and when she'd reached down she'd found Ethan erect and ready. When was the last time Jack had been aroused that easily? No, she chastised herself, when was the last time *you* were? *That's* the question. The painful answer, she knew, could be measured only in years. She didn't want to think how many. But the more she brooded over her dalliance with Ethan the more she began to realize that simple lust hadn't been the sole force driving her into his embrace. Hadn't she found herself gazing at him just two days ago in containment, deciding that he'd make a terrific father? Maybe, she thought, your hormones really do start to bubble when the need to breed asserts itself. If Jack's reluctant, find someone who isn't. Or maybe, she reconsid-

ered, you're just skimming the surface of sociobiology to jus-
tify what you did, making excuses while you make a travesty
of trust. But that judgment seemed way too harsh, even to
Celia's Catholic side, and as she fired up the engine she
thought about what she'd told Tony less than an hour ago:
nothing is simple. Well, she repeated, nothing is. Not Davy.
Not desire.

She felt oddly grateful to "da Lip" for his inadvertent
intervention. His loud call to Barbara had stopped them from
going any further, and now that she found herself once removed from the romance of the moment she could see the
wisdom of restraint. Plus, it just seemed so tacky. In the office, no less.

She backed up and started to pull away when she spotted
Davy burrowed into the bushes near the play area. The sight
of him made her brake suddenly and stall the Honda. He sat
with his head down below his knees, as if hiding his face
could hide the rest of him. She restarted the car and pulled
back into her spot.

Who the devil was on van duty today? She started parading
the Center's personnel through a mental checklist when she
remembered Allison rushing out of her office after their meeting. She'd been running late. Doesn't matter. This is inex-
cusable. You don't leave behind a child. The drivers don't
know. Half the time the district sends over a new one.

Davy didn't look up as she approached, so she called his
name softly and shook the bush lightly, which spooked him
enough that he jumped into the open.

"Easy, Davy, it's just me. What are you doing out here?
School's over."

He knew that but he didn't want to go home. That's why
he snuck away when the teacher's helper wasn't there. If he
went home there'd be nothing but Chet till Monday, and he
wanted to stay here. He could live here and draw all the time.
They had a kitchen and bathroom, it wasn't anything like a
regular school, and he could sleep on the floor. They had a
carpet, a nice clean carpet, not like that linoleum at home
with the dark stains. And he didn't need a bed. He didn't
have a real one anyway, just some old cot. He'd be plenty
warm on the carpet, or on the couch in the living room. It

looked like a house too. Someone *should* be living here. He could take care of it when they left. Keep it clean. He knew how. Chet made him do it a lot. He'd figured out how to get in too. He'd seen the window in the basement that was cracked. He'd bust it right open, but he'd fix it too. He would. Someday.

He could have been there the whole weekend. Chet never would have found him. Maybe Mrs. Griswold would have stayed with him. Just for an afternoon, the two of them. They could have watched TV, or she could have read him a book. His mother used to read books to him. He'd sit right next to her so there was no space between them at all and he could feel her body and look at the pages with her, the funny pictures. Dr. Seuss. She'd make her voice change and pull him closer, and sometimes he sat on her lap. Where'd she go?

Davy concentrated on this so hard he held his breath. If he could just remember he could find her and they could run away together and he'd never have to be with Chet again. But he couldn't remember where she was, only that she used to read to him. But that made him happy. Till today he hadn't remembered that at all.

Mrs. Griswold opened her car door and asked him to put on his seat belt, but he had trouble with it. Chet's truck didn't have them. He didn't believe in them. He said so. He didn't believe in a lot of things. Davy liked the way Mrs. Griswold leaned over him and snapped the buckle closed. She smelled good. Then she shut the door and started to come around to her side.

As Celia rounded the front of her car she saw Tony walking down the front steps. She knew she'd better tell him, so she looked at the boy through the windshield and held up her finger. "One minute," she mouthed.

She intercepted Tony on the walkway. He was moving at a brisk pace and grimaced when Celia flagged him down.

"Sorry, but Davy missed the van. I found him hiding in the bushes."

"He missed the what?"

Celia didn't care for his overly dramatic response, and had all she could do to keep from saying, You heard me.

"It's not that big a deal. I can—"

''*Who* was on van duty? That's what I want to know.''

Why was his first impulse to blame someone? Was it a male thing? Then, wincing inwardly, she recalled having had a similar response just before coming up with Allison's name.

''I don't know,'' she lied, hoping for Allison's sake that by the time Monday rolled around Tony would have calmed down or forgotten the incident entirely.

''It wasn't you, was it?''

''No,'' she said curtly.

''Ethan?''

''No, Ethan did it yesterday.''

''Ethan,'' he repeated like a curse, and then said no more. While he stood there, apparently trying to think of *someone* to blame, Celia said she'd be glad to give the boy a ride home, an option Tony sharply tried to dismiss.

''You can't expect me to endorse that suggestion after what I just told you.''

''Then I guess you can do it,'' she snapped. Lowering her voice so Davy wouldn't hear, she added, ''I've got plenty to do around here without running a bus service.''

In truth, she welcomed giving Davy a ride home and was banking on Tony's refusal to be inconvenienced.

''No.'' He studied his watch. ''I can't.'' He looked over and saw Davy in her car, and that appeared to be all the excuse he needed. ''He's already with you. Just take him. But minimize your interaction with him. Take him home and drop him off and *leave*.''

''Fine,'' she agreed crisply, though she had no intention of following his directive.

Tony walked away.

After settling into the car seat, Celia turned to Davy. ''You're going to have to help me find your place, okay? I don't know that area real well.''

She actually had a good idea of where he lived. Center rules required everyone to know how to find the clients' homes. New drivers often needed help with directions, and in an emergency the staff couldn't afford to waste time trying to locate an address. Barbara kept a continually updated map in her desk. Celia had asked for Davy's assistance because she wanted to use every opportunity to develop communication with him.

He looked at her.

"You can just point, but I really do need your help. I hope you don't mind doing a little shopping with me. I've got to make a stop on the way home."

After her kissing affair with Ethan, she decided to put together a romantic dinner for Jack. Catholic guilt. God, would she ever outgrow it? She had her doubts. So she'd serve up some penance along with a breast of chicken, though the former was easier to find in Bentman than the latter. Blame it on Andy. He owned the town's only market, a small, stubbornly ugly food store that squatted like a dirty old hen by the side of the road, an appalling old box of a building slapped together out of local timber during Bentman's big boom in the early fifties.

She herded Davy through the door, plastered with promotional stickers for cigarettes, chew, and "specials" on twelve-packs of Bud, and immediately noticed the filth on the floor, the grit ground into the linoleum by decades of boots and shoes dragging in the dust and mud of the Oregon mountains. Dirt and grime had settled on the shelves too, and turned into a gooey kind of glop that made the cans and bottles stick just a little when she picked them up.

She tried to get in and out quickly, as much for Davy's sake as her own, but this always proved impossible. The aisles were narrow and crowded with rickety displays, and the shelves rose to within inches of the ceiling. She often had to ask Andy to reach up and grab an item for her, and then bide her time while the bald, burly man moved with the speed of a house plant.

If she encountered another customer she'd have to edge along the canyonlike aisles to squeeze by, but the shelves had all kinds of crap hanging from them: cheap little plastic toys, flyswatters, mousetraps, special sponges and doohickies of all types, the kind of junky items that really enjoyed gravity, that dropped to the floor as soon as she brushed against them, and fell again when she tried to hang them back up.

She eyed a package of chicken breasts that did not appear too abused by their internment at Andy's. After sniffing them carefully she decided they would do, then moved on to the produce counter, where she picked out some healthy-looking green beans. Andy had just taken delivery on a crate of local mushrooms, so she bagged a pound of them for a sauce that would go nicely with the beans.

There, she said to herself, with a bottle of wine and the sorbet in the freezer, we'll be set. A candlelight dinner on the deck.

She found Davy ogling the candy shelves just below the cash register, so she told him he could help himself to one item. He immediately snatched up a bag of Gummy Bears, then held them tightly in his fist as if she might change her mind.

He loved Gummy Bears. His mother used to buy them for him all the time. He especially liked the red ones, but all the colors were good. They didn't disappear when you put them in your mouth. You could make them last and last if you wanted to. He could make a bag last all day. She used to joke with him about that, called him a squirrel 'cause he was always saving them up. But if you were smart that's what you did. Make them last. After his daddy died he knew for sure that you had to save up the good times too 'cause otherwise they'd go away before you knew it. And then his mom left and there was nothing left to save, nothing he wanted to keep, and just remembering her was so hard to do. Like her reading to him. He didn't remember that till today. But there had to be more. Had to be. But maybe no matter how hard he tried he could have her only a little bit at a time. And then he thought that maybe his mom was like the Gummy Bears, and he should go real slow. He could think about this one thing, like her reading to him, until the memory melted away completely, and then he could think of another. Maybe he could make her last forever this way. And each time would be sweet as candy. He put the Gummy Bears in his pocket where they'd be safe.

Celia escaped without letting Andy bog her down in one of his interminable diatribes against environmentalists, whom he blamed for the decline of the local economy in general and for his own misfortunes in particular. He'd even been nice enough to give Davy a peppermint, which the boy jammed into the pocket with the Gummy Bears.

As she turned south on the highway, she asked, "This way?" to see if he'd help her. When he nodded she offered a cheerful, "Okay, we're on our way."

The sun hovered just over the mountains to the west, and she guessed they had another hour or so of daylight. Tomorrow night she'd have to set back the clocks an hour, which reminded her to check with Tony to see what Halloween activities he'd planned for the Center. Most of the children loved to dress up as witches or goblins or monsters. Lets their darker sides flourish in a socially acceptable manner, she thought. She glanced at Davy, and it occurred to her that some adults she'd met recently might benefit from this as well.

"What are you going to be for Halloween?"

Davy looked at her but didn't seem to understand the question.

"Have you thought about it? Do you want to be a ghost or a pumpkin, or a—"

Batman. He didn't hear what else she said because he wanted to be Batman, that's all. But he knew he'd never get to wear that cool mask. There'd be no trick-or-treating with Chet. He hadn't said so, but Davy knew. Not like with his real dad, taking him around from house to house and waiting by the curb and then asking him what he got.

Last year Davy had run down the steps of a scary old house with a paper skeleton on the door and showed his father a big Hershey bar. The old man who lived there had said, "Boo," and tossed it into his bag. His dad had said, "That's a good one, Davy. We got to remember this place next year."

But there was no next year. There was Chet.

Celia didn't expect Davy to tell her what he wanted to be for Halloween, but she kept talking to him as she would to any other child. She was genuinely curious, though, to know what he'd be if he had the chance. And then it hit her. What had be been drawing?

"I'll bet you'll be . . ." She made a long pause to get his attention, and succeeded; Davy stared at her intently. ". . . Batman."

When his eyes widened, she knew she'd nailed it.

How'd she know? Davy wondered. It was like she could hear what he was thinking. Maybe she could hear other things too, just like he was talking, so he pictured his dad to see if she'd say, "Your dad." But she didn't.

"I'll bet you'll be a great Batman."

Davy knew he would be too. If he had a real costume he could climb walls just like Batman, and he'd be strong and real fast and Chet would never catch him, and if he did he'd beat him up so he couldn't move anymore.

Celia passed Broken Creek Road and the way to her house, and had a fleeting thought about the shepherd, the kind of costume he might wear; then told herself that next weekend a lot of people would pay good money to try to look as scary as he did every day. Few, of course, would succeed.

"This way?" she tested Davy as she approached a cross-street. He shook his head. "But you'll let me know, right?" He nodded.

A couple of minutes later he pointed left, and Celia slowed to study the forest on the other side of the road. She spotted a two-track that looked like an old logging road, pretty much what she'd seen on the map at the Center.

"Here?"

Davy nodded again.

She drove down the narrow path bordered on both sides by spindly firs that blocked much of the dying light. If she hadn't thought she was almost there she would have switched on her headlights, but she worried that she'd forget to turn them off—she had a bad habit of doing that—and she sure didn't want to get stuck out here.

After about a quarter of a mile Davy pointed again, this time to the right, and she spied a trailer set back a good hundred feet or so off the road. It looked like Chet had tried to hide it back in there. She wondered if he was poaching space on private land. Not that she cared.

She decided to park just off the logging road. Ruts and small logs littered the area closer to the trailer, and she doubted her car had enough ground clearance to pull all the way up. She did turn the Honda around so it pointed back toward the highway.

Davy immediately unsnapped his seat belt, jumped out
with his knapsack, and waved good-bye.

"No, wait, Davy. I'm coming with you."

She'd seen no sign of Mr. Boyce's truck, no sign of him
either; and she couldn't very well leave a seven-year-old by
himself, not in good conscience. So she guessed she'd be here
for the duration. If Chet didn't get back soon, her plans for
a romantic dinner, not to mention some easy-serve penance,
would be dashed.

When he heard her call to him, Davy stopped walking
away. He wanted her to stay, he really did, but he didn't want
her to either. He just knew Chet wouldn't like her being there,
and then what would happen? He worried about this as they
headed to the trailer.

He searched under the lone step and found the key. He
fumbled with the lock for a few seconds before opening the
door, and then hit a switch that lit up a bare bulb screwed
into a socket in the ceiling.

As she stepped in behind him, Celia saw a small couch
with a faded blue Mexican blanket off to the right. Another
old blanket, olive-green, hung behind it and closed off that
end of the trailer.

To the left she saw a small table and two chairs. Behind
them stood a two-burner range, sink, cabinets, and a closed
door, which she assumed led to the trailer's only bedroom.

A TV and VCR huddled on the floor in the middle of what
might have passed for the living room. A modest woodstove
crowded the inches that remained.

Tight, very tight, she thought. She needed just three steps
to reach the kitchen table where she let her eyes skim over a
couple of envelopes. So he gets mail. Or got it at one time.
An Idaho address. Becker, Idaho. She made a mental note of
this.

Davy turned on the TV and worked the VCR with a remote. A Batman movie came on.

"Are you hungry?" Celia hadn't seen him eat any of his
candy yet, which had surprised her. She also wanted to know
what Mr. Boyce kept in his refrigerator. Not much. A few
cans of Coors, a big green plastic bottle of Mountain Dew, a

jar of Skippy, a tub of margarine, and the last of a loaf of white bread. And some milk.

Davy wished she hadn't done that. Chet didn't like people nosing around. That's what he called it. "You nosing around?" he'd said to those hikers last summer when they were in Idaho. "You better leave." And they did. Real fast. Plus seeing Mrs. Griswold by the sink made Davy feel all sick inside and study the floor, the dark stains that Chet made him scrub. Mrs. Griswold was starting to make him think too much about his mom. First, back at the store, and now. He didn't want to think about his mom anymore. It didn't feel good like when he remembered her reading to him, or giving him Gummy Bears. It felt bad. He didn't know why. It just did. He wished Mrs. Griswold would move away from there.

"How about a peanut-butter sandwich?"

He shook his head and looked at the screen. Move. *Move.*

Celia walked past Davy and pulled aside the olive blanket that shut off the space behind the couch. She found herself staring at Davy's cot, along with an assortment of clothing strewn across the floor and spilling out of a yellow laundry basket. She eyed a pair of undershorts on the cot and moved closer for a better look. The olive blanket fell closed behind her. The *Batman* movie formed a wall of sound as she picked up the briefs and studied them for stains. Nothing. Maybe they were clean. She looked at the blanket hanging from the ceiling and tried to hazard whether she could pull off a top-to-bottom search of the trailer. You'll hear him if he pulls up, she assured herself. Go for it.

She systematically examined every article of Davy's clothing, from the T-shirts and socks she picked up off the floor to the rest of his limited wardrobe, which had been stuffed into the plastic basket. She determined from the smell of detergent that they'd just been laundered.

As she pulled back the blanket on the cot to check the sheets she thought she heard a door open. She stood unmoving and scanned the room in a growing panic. She spotted one of Davy's sweaters and seized it. She was on the verge of walking back out and saying, "Here's one, Davy," when Batman spoke and she understood that she'd been listening to the movie.

She returned to studying the sheets but found nothing unusual, a few cloudy stains that were old and could have been
anything. Frustrated, she pulled the blanket back up to the
pillow and tapped her foot twice, impatient with her lack of
progress. Then, as she stood there, she had the awful image
of Mr. Boyce abusing Davy and knew he'd never do it on a
small cot. No, that's true, she said to herself in a coolly professional voice; but the boy might still be bleeding when he
got back here. That's assuming he got to sleep in his own
bed. And that Mr. Boyce made him bleed.

She thought uneasily about the door on the other end of
the trailer. It probably opened to Mr. Boyce's bedroom. She'd
have to search in there. No way around it.

She pushed aside the hanging blanket and saw that Davy
had pulled his sketchbook and pencils out of his knapsack,
though it didn't appear that he'd started to draw yet.

She walked past him, staying as alert as she could to all
the sounds that surrounded her, the night noises coming from
outside these metal walls, and the racket that blasted out of
that plastic box that he watched so insatiably. To double-
check that they were alone she held open the curtain on the
lone window in the living area. The sky had darkened, so she
could see very little. But Mr. Boyce's truck was not out there.
She felt confident of this. He's not around, she told herself,
relax.

She reached for the handle of the door she believed opened
to his bedroom. The metal knob turned but the door wouldn't
budge when she pulled on it. Now that's odd. She told herself
to try pushing on it, but the resistance was just as great. Now
she tightened her grip and gave the handle a good hard tug,
and the door did move, bowing a half inch or so from the
handle, but no farther. She let go and a dull noise sounded
from behind it.

Oh God. She jumped back. The thought suddenly struck
her that Mr. Boyce could have been in there the whole time,
and that he'd been holding the handle from the inside, silently
refusing her entry. Just because you can't see his truck . . .
Her fear flooded over her and she backed up another step, but
she never took her eyes off that handle.

She listened as hard as she could. There had been that one

sound, no more, like a shoe scuffing the floor. Had she actually heard something? Yes, you sure as hell did. There was no imagining that. But it could have been the door. Now she tried to remember if she'd heard it at the exact moment she let go of the handle, but she could not piece together the sequence. The handle, pulling on it, letting go, the sound, all of it jumbled together in her memory.

Should she knock, ask if he's back there? See if there's a bathroom? She actually could use one right now. Would he believe her?

But why would he be hiding? That doesn't make sense. He's nothing if not aggressive. Remember how he just barged into your office? And this is his turf. Get a grip, kiddo! He's not back there. The door's just locked.

She turned around and found Davy moving his head from side to side, as if warning her to stay away. Decisively, she spun back around and pounded on the door.

"Mr. Boyce, are you in there? Is there a bathroom I could use?"

No answer. Only the Joker laughing wickedly in the background.

She stole a final glance at the handle and turned to Davy. She smiled at him, far more brightly than she felt; but his eyes returned once more to the TV. He probably comes home and does this every day. She remembered that she had some children's books in the back of her car. Long ago she'd learned the value of always keeping them with her. You never knew when you'd have to entertain kids.

"How would you like me to read to you?"

He nodded. He'd like that. But he also wanted her to leave. He still had that stiff feeling in his stomach, like it was all stuck together but could break apart at any time and make him sick.

She said she'd be right back.

Whew, Celia exhaled softly as she stepped out into the night. For a tiny place it sure had a lot of bad vibes. She couldn't wait to go home, though she truly dreaded seeing Mr. Boyce. She sought comfort in the idea that he wouldn't dare do anything too outrageous in front of Davy.

She made her way carefully over the ruts and forest debris.

She popped open the hatch and took out a couple of books. She'd start with the story of the three little pigs from the wolf's point of view. It was funny and might even make Davy laugh. That would be a first. But just as she closed the hatch, headlights turned off the highway and crawled into the darkness. She waited, believing it was Mr. Boyce, and shaded her eyes.

But the pickup rolled right past her. Two men with a full rifle rack. They waved at her, and she waved back. She had just started over to the trailer when her bladder reminded her of how badly she needed to go. She didn't think she could put it off much longer. She looked around, edged behind one of the skinny firs, and roughed it.

When she stepped up into the trailer she saw that Davy had finally opened the Gummy Bears. They sat on the floor beside him.

"Do you mind if we turn off *Batman* while we read?"

He shook his head vehemently and clutched the remote to his chest.

Okay, thought Celia, I'm competing with a one-hundred-million-dollar movie for his attention. Wonder who'll win. But as she started to read Davy pocketed his candy and joined her on the couch, and by the time the wolf was explaining that the first little pig was the stupidest creature he'd ever met ("Can you believe it? I mean who in their right mind would build a house out of straw?") Davy had rested his head against her arm, which she happily wrapped around his shoulders. He snuggled right up to her, and she hugged him gently.

She read on until the wolf arrived at the third house. That's when she nudged Davy and said, "The wolf called this little piggie 'the brains of the family' because he used bricks."

She thought she detected a smile on his face. In any case, she laughed herself; and then they both heard a vehicle rolling up to the trailer.

Davy pushed her arm away and rushed down to his spot on the floor. The boy's fear infected Celia too, and she had to tell herself to take a breath. You've got no reason to be afraid.

A door closed. Just one. Seconds later the trailer door opened and Mr. Boyce walked in.

Celia already had closed the book and gathered up the second one.

"Hi, Mr. Boyce. I—"

"Is that your car out there?"

No greeting, no surprise over her presence.

"Yes, I wasn't sure I could get any closer without getting stuck, so I just left it out there."

"Not smart. All kinds of people drive through here. They'll strip it clean in no time."

Celia thanked him for the advice, but thought he sounded more menacing than helpful.

"I wasn't planning on staying long. I just didn't want to leave Davy by himself."

He walked over to the kitchen table and looked at the mail, then at her.

"What happened to the bus?"

"He missed it."

"You missed it?" He glared at Davy, and the boy looked away. Celia could have kicked herself for not lying but she'd always tried to make it clear to her clients that she would not team up with them against their parents.

"It's not a big deal. I kind of live out this way. Well, you know . . ." But she stopped right there because she instantly regretted bringing up the specter of the snake.

Chet didn't catch her comment, or chose to ignore it. "I'm usually here when he gets back," he stated bluntly.

Celia nodded. "I guess I'll be on my way then." She turned to Davy. "I'll finish reading the story to you on Monday. How's that sound? Unless"—she turned to Mr. Boyce— "you'd like to. I could loan it to you. It's really pretty funny. It's about—"

But he was already waving off her suggestion as if it were of no interest whatsoever. An awkward moment followed.

"Okay, Monday then, Davy. I'll see you."

He didn't lift his eyes from the TV.

"Good-bye, Mr. Boyce."

He remained as silent as his stepson, and when Celia brushed past his intimidating stillness she felt her heart hanging motionless in the widening chasm of her chest. She tried to close the door casually behind her, then walked at an ever increasing pace to her car. She stumbled over a rut and dropped her keys, and had to feel around on the ground for an eternity of seconds before she found them. She hurried on, unlocked the Honda with great relief, but still couldn't take a relaxed breath until she turned onto the highway.

Their house looked cozy and safe as she parked, nestled among half a dozen full-skirted firs. She saw it as Mr. Boyce would, or anyone just scraping by, and knew that she and Jack would appear affluent in their eyes, much as they appeared poor to hers.

She left the bag of groceries on the deck and dragged the redwood picnic table to the west side of the house so they'd catch the stars hanging over the valley. With a white tablecloth she thought it would look quite elegant, especially with the candles burning in the darkness. She hesitated over the idea of an open flame in these tinderbox conditions, but assured herself that it wouldn't be a problem as long as they were careful. She'd get out the wine bucket too. She stepped back and saw how the stainless steel would bead with condensation, and imagined too the growing warmth of the evening as she and Jack unwound beneath the moon and stars.

Maybe selling the place was a bad idea. Maybe it's just as well that she'd never brought it up with Jack. Sure, they had to put up with a creep like the shepherd, but eventually he would leave; and in all probability so would Mr. Boyce and Davy. That prospect stopped her short, the startling sense of loss she felt over the possibility that the boy would be taken from Bentman, that all his stepfather had to do was hitch up that trailer and by Monday they could be in another town, or even another state. As silly as it seemed to her, the first thought Celia had was that he wouldn't get to hear the end of the story she'd been reading him. She wanted to see him laugh. She wanted to see him laugh so hard that he'd forget all about his troubles and just be a kid.

She cringed when she remembered how Mr. Boyce had brushed off her attempt to lend him the book. All the boy wants—Christ, all he needs—is some healthy attention, but she knew he'd never get it from that man.

Celia stood on the deck in the darkness and saw Davy far

away, in a new town struggling all over again in a new school, and her eyes dampened. She tried not to cry, but couldn't hold back. The job was just so goddamn depressing at times. She looked down at the lights of the valley, blazing through her tears, and thought of Davy in that dingy trailer all alone with Mr. Boyce. Her sadness quickly turned to anger, and she asked herself what he'd done to make that kid so afraid. I mean, what do you have to do to make a kid so scared that he crawls onto a dirty floor so you can't see him being read to? Come on, she goaded the darkness, what do you have to do to make a kid that scared? Her fingers clenched her sides, and her whole body tensed. That fucker. She shook her fists at the night. That *fucker!* What did you do to him?

She took a deep breath and wiped away her tears. She leaned against the picnic table and considered how much worse off Davy would be if Mr. Boyce did take him away from Bentman. What kind of life could the boy possibly have? He's already so traumatized he doesn't even talk. There would be more school problems, a future of dead-end jobs, if he could get any, if there were any left, and then a family of his own where the whole cycle of abuse could repeat itself.

But she reminded herself that she had a more immediate problem—Tony. Right now he was more likely to take Davy away from her than Mr. Boyce. The irony pained her, but she knew that at least with Tony she could fight back. She'd start by getting the evaluation done this weekend. On Monday she'd present her findings and make her case for keeping Davy under her care. If Tony insisted on another type of therapy, she could always remind him that the district had specifically asked for her help with Davy. She had a good relationship with the superintendent and his staff, and she knew she had some fans over there. A few chits, too. So you don't have to put up with his bullshit. You're too goddamn nice. Kick his butt. Ethan's right. He's a jerk.

She unlocked the door and stepped around Pluto to put the groceries on the kitchen counter. He followed her from the mud room and rubbed against her leg until she scratched his ear and made him purr.

As she pulled the green beans out of the bag she noticed the answering-machine light and hit the ''play'' button. When she heard Jack telling her again to go ahead and start dinner without him, she flipped him off and cursed so loudly that Pluto scampered away in fright.

In a fit of anger she picked up the phone and called the agency. No answer. Of course, she groaned, it's after hours. But they did have a system to get around this, so she called back, let it ring twice, hung up, and called again. Still no answer. She slammed down the phone. What's with him? She'd never known him to work this hard. Twelve- to fourteen-hour days? This has got to stop.

She tossed the chicken into the refrigerator and settled for a plate of green beans topped with a bottled peanut-and-garlic sauce that plopped most unromantically onto her plate. The mushrooms, the wine, the moon and the stars, they'd all have to wait. Maybe by Sunday she'd cool down enough to want to cook again.

She nodded off watching a sitcom and remained asleep until the door creaked open.

"Is that you?" she called out groggily, never dreaming it was anyone but Jack.

He walked over to the couch where she lay and kissed her forehead. She opened her eyes, saw his familiar form, and clicked off the TV.

"Where were you?" She felt drugged with fatigue, and sounded it too. "I tried calling. I was going to fix us a nice dinner because you're leaving. What the hell is going on, Jack?"

"Was that you? I thought I heard the phone but I was working back in the vault. Didn't you get my message?" He sat down beside her.

"Of course, but I don't care. That sucks, calling me up at the last minute like that. I'd planned dinner on the deck. Candlelight, wine." She rubbed her eyes. "What time is it?"

He glanced at his watch. "A little after ten."

"How little?"

"Twenty after."

"That's pretty late to be working, Jack." Her sleepy eyes stared at him. When he didn't respond she shook her head and told him she was going to bed.

She straggled off to the bathroom, leaving Jack on the couch. The warmth of her body rose from the cushions, and he knew without question that this weekend would be the last time he'd cheat on her. He just couldn't do double duty in bed anymore. And he did love her. Truly. And she sure sounded suspicious. Angry, too.

She wandered back up with a quizzical expression and stared at his lap, which made him acutely uncomfortable. He stole a look down, but no, nothing appeared out of order, no revealing stains, just his hands hanging out on his thighs.

"What is it, hon? Something wrong?" He'd worked hard to steady his nervous voice.

"Your ring, where is it?"

"My . . . my what?" he said as if she'd spoken Swahili. Panic rocked his system as he looked down again, more obviously this time, and saw the pale stripe where his wedding band used to be.

"Your ring. I thought something was weird but it didn't hit me till I started washing my hands. It's your ring. You're not wearing it. How come?"

He tried to take heart in her tone: not *too* accusatory.

"No, that's true." He sighed regretfully. "The feeder in the copier jammed, so I took it off so it wouldn't get scuffed up. I must have forgotten it. I'm sure it's right where I left it. Sorry," he added sheepishly.

She nodded, her eyes still heavy with sleep.

"You want me to run by tomorrow and pick it up for you?"

He remembered with another bolt of panic that Helen's rings had been resting right next to his. She might have forgotten hers too. Of course with the new locks Celia would never get in, but that would beg a whole series of other questions. "No, I'll swing by and get it on my way out of town."

"All right. Good night."

She walked away without kissing him, then turned around and came back. "I just want you to know that if you ever stop wearing that wedding ring, you're going to have to find someone to put up with it because I won't."

Jack definitely heard a new tone to his wife's voice, and

it made him feel cornered, exposed. He searched for something to say as she stood there looking at him, but the best he could come up with rang hollow even to his ears.

"Don't worry, hon. I'm proud to be your husband."

35

A goddamn golden morning, that's what it was. Chet threw open the door of his pickup and jumped out. He looked back toward the county road. All the branches had filled in and he couldn't see past them. Good, he was in his nest all secret and hidden, a crow's nest to watch her house. The right moment would come and he would know it.

I didn't want to leave Davy all alone.

No, I'll bet you didn't, not when you could snoop around my place like you've been snooping around my boy all week. Chet could have spit in her face. She'd been close enough. Right there in his trailer. She'd been there the whole time, looking around, seeing the mail. She must have. What else?

She deserved his attention, and now she would get it. She'd made Davy draw those pictures, and she knew, she sure as hell did. She as much as told him so yesterday. First, trying not to say much—*I'll have the evaluation done by Monday, Mr. Boyce*—and then talking about how a kid can't draw a lie, but people get caught in talking lies all the time. *Don't they, Mr. Boyce?* Like she couldn't resist poking him, her voice like some goddamn needle. And then finally saying it:

Just one thing, Mr. Boyce. Has the boy been abused, Mr. Boyce?

She knew. *She knew!*

Hell if he didn't know something too. A picture's worth a thousand words, and he had a picture as clear as a nail to the juicy end of a hammer: Mrs. Griswold going for the door, like his wife had done too. Except he had grabbed her and told Davy to watch. He did too, like a good boy, a real good boy.

But Mrs. Griswold had brushed right past him, used his name like he was nothing.

Good-bye, Mr. Boyce.

That's what she said. That's what she *said!* His voice crackled in his head like sparks in a woodstove, and then he heard his answer like a cool liquid bathing his brain.

Good-bye, Mrs. Griswold. Good-bye.

First a whisper breezing through his body, then a scream, GOOD-BYE, MRS. GRISWOLD. GOOD-BYE. But every syllable silent to the world outside his skin.

The boy's still drawing like a goddamn machine that never quits, sitting in the cab drawing on that fucking pad she gave him, like he drew that picture she didn't want me to see. I saw the look on her face when I took it, like I'd pulled down her pants or something. *Where he feels safest.* A bunch of guns and a prison. That's what I saw. But she saw a lot more.

Oh yeah, she knows.

He leaned back into the cab and grabbed his Thermos, poured out a mouthful of coffee. He'd also packed some sandwiches, and the kid had his pop. "We're going to be there awhile, Davy," he'd told him back at the trailer, "so bring something you can play with *in the truck.*" He'd wanted to make it clear as clear can be that this was no goddamn picnic they were going on. So what did the kid do? Brought that pad she gave him, and there he was drawing, drawing, drawing. Let him, he warned himself. No harm in it now. Not after today.

He screwed the top on the Thermos and tossed it back in the cab. He walked around to the front bumper where he could see both cars, the new pickup with the sign for the insurance agency on the side, and her old piece-of-shit Jap car. The sun had already risen high enough to make him squint and it wasn't even eight-thirty yet.

He watched another half hour before anything stirred. It was her, letting out the cat. He still couldn't believe they didn't have a dog. Even a little yippie dog could cause all kinds of problems, and here they were out in the middle of nowhere with all this land and no dog to keep an eye on it. And no guns! They *are* living on Mars.

He liked the way she looked in her nightgown, kind of sleepy and stupid standing there watching the cat while he watched her. Chet wondered who might be watching him and turned around, and sure enough that kid's eyes were drilling holes in the back of his head. As soon as he caught him, though, the boy got busy drawing again.

What the hell is he up to? He slapped the hood louder than he should have and walked over to the passenger side. Davy's hand froze with the pencil tip an inch or so above the paper. Chet spotted the wings, the mask, and leaned close to his ear.

"You draw all the goddamn pictures you want, but she's never going to see them. She's through looking at your pictures, you got that?"

No answer. He'd rather draw Batman for her all day long than say one word to him, and that infuriated Chet, made him feel slighted by a kid who owed him a lot. Owed him his *life* when it came right down to it because He could take it anytime He wanted to. He had a mind to reach in right now and grab the pad and tear it the fuck up, snap those pencils to pieces. But he *controlled* himself. Let him draw. They're just pictures now.

He heard the distant sound of a door opening and looked up to see Mr. Griswold walking out of the house with his briefcase *and* a suitcase. "What do you know about that."

Then Chet understood that both of them might be leaving, and he saw his plans turn to dust. But a moment later she appeared, still in her gown, holding a coffee cup and talking to her husband. Good girl, he whispered, you just stay put.

He clamped a hand on Davy's shoulder. The boy shrank away but Chet paid it no mind. His eyes were on Mrs. Griswold. "You know something, Davy, a man once said that luck is a funny thing. No matter how much you got, it always runs out. He was a wise one."

Mr. Griswold climbed in the cab, and Mrs. Griswold waved to him from the deck.

Oh yeah, Chet nodded, he's definitely going on a trip, saving his life and he doesn't even know it.

Mr. Griswold suddenly climbed back out and walked over to his wife. He took her hand.

Sure, go ahead. Chet nodded some more. It'll be the last time you ever do it.

He kissed her and turned away. Chet wondered what Mr. Griswold Agency would think when he remembered the last time he did that. That's if he could remember. He'd probably blubber. He looked like a blubberer, but a lucky one at that. He must live right or something. He gets to go on a trip, she gets to die. And I get to use the blade.

He'd planned on taking along his gun. You can't manage two of them without one. You need it till you get them all cozy and wired up, but even then it can . . . *spoil* the experience. Not that he would have ever used it given the choice. He never had. A gun was cowardly, for people who lacked the courage to cut, to feel the moist heat steaming off their skin, first as sweat, then as blood. But now she'd be alone, no dogs, no husband . . . no guns. A prize waiting to be taken, a sweetness waiting to be tasted.

He watched Mrs. Griswold standing on the deck as her husband drove off, like she missed him already. She didn't even know how much. But she would, she would.

The pickup rolled down the driveway, mostly hidden by the row of young firs and a fair amount of brush, then turned onto the county road. No more than fifteen seconds later Chet heard it drive by. And then it was gone. And she was alone.

Meant to be. Truly, truly meant to be.

Mrs. Griswold walked back in the house. Chet cracked his knuckles and stretched his arms wide, open to the day, the sun, every reward and possibility.

He rubbed the boy's short hair. "You know, Davy," he said in a surprisingly soft voice, "when the cat's away, the mice will play."

36

The Bear Haus catered to the summertime tourists who spilled over from Mount Bentman State Park, and apparently also to the lovers who arranged their trysts at this rustic inn. Jack had never even noticed the large log building nestled in the woods well off the highway, but after making love last night in the vault Helen had lain beside him, rubbed his chest, and said she'd spent some very romantic weekends there.

Though dearly interested, Jack had refrained from asking with whom, how recently, or whether she'd had a blood test since then. Instead, he'd replied airily, "Really."

"Yes," she cooed as she nipped his shoulder, "and it was with Ralph, in case you're wondering."

"No, not at all."

But now, as he lugged their bags to the inn, his worries assumed a new cast, to wit, that he would run into someone he knew. He fully expected to find Ruth with her suspicious gaze, moonlighting as a desk clerk when he walked in the front door. Even more reason, he decided, to give her a raise. But much to his relief an old man rose from a stuffed chair and greeted them.

Helen might have sensed Jack's unease because as he lumbered to the room with their bags she told him to relax. "Honey, if we see anyone from Bentman it's probably because they're doing the same thing we're doing."

But Jack owned an insurance agency and therefore was accustomed to much better odds than those afforded by the word "probably."

Helen unlocked the door to a room with a stunning view of Mount Bentman, but that was all that he found impressive about their accommodations. As he rested the suitcases inside the door, she stepped down into the recessed living room and parodied a game-show model by throwing out her arms and smiling at a bear's head mounted on the far wall. Its tongue hung out of the side of its mouth at a peculiar angle and its eyes held a curious gaze. In short, it possessed the vacant look of a voyeur mindlessly strumming himself to ecstasy.

"Don't you just love it!"

Before Jack could reply Helen pirouetted over to the sunken hot tub that took up most of the floor space. She danced along its perimeter and shook her hips, ushering back uncomfortable memories of last night's naked rumba in the front office.

"*And* . . . check this out!"

She hurried over to a red-rock fireplace more than capable of dwarfing the four-foot logs stacked neatly to the side. "We can have a romantic little fire to warm us up."

Actually, it looked large enough to melt the polar ice cap. Hardly what he had in mind, given the unseasonably high temperatures.

"Don't you think it's a little warm for that?"

She pointed to an equally imposing wall-mounted air-conditioning unit.

"You can have the best of both worlds when you stay at the Bear Haus."

"Well, how about that."

Jack didn't want to bust her balloon but the Bear Haus struck him as a bit . . . *excessive*. The sofa and chair were made out of logs, ditto the footstool, end tables, bed and bar. Then there was the . . . well, hell, he didn't know what to call it. Art? Every wall had become a gallery for old saw blades of various sizes and shapes on which forest scenes had been painted in lurid colors above the vicious-looking teeth, a means no doubt of memorializing the pastoral peace they had so rudely put to rest.

He was relieved when Helen suggested they go for a hike. He'd feared she'd want to start up the hot tub, the fireplace, the air conditioner, and make love under the bear's horny gaze. He figured after last night's vigorous lovemaking he'd be good for no more than one round of it today on this, his final weekend of infidelity. From now on it's going to be

different, he vowed silently. It *will,* he said again as if trying
to convince himself.

They padded down a path from the back of the inn to the
trailhead. To Jack's relief they encountered no one, much less
a familiar face. Helen took the lead along the narrow needle-
strewn track, and Jack watched her move with girlish enthusiasm in her freshly pressed khaki shorts. Her legs lacked
Celia's sculpted definition but he found them amply appealing
nonetheless. Now that they'd escaped the oppressive confines
of the Bear Haus, his ardor returned.

"Let's go this way," she said cheerfully as they approached a fork in the trail.

He noted with dismay that the trail marker said it was six
miles to the campground near Mount Bentman's modest peak.
He wasn't up for that kind of punishment and—*bless* her—
neither was Helen as it turned out.

She slowed down as the path widened, and Jack moved
up beside her. They'd been out only fifteen minutes but already he felt winded. She didn't appear to notice. As soon as
he took her hand she started a running commentary on the
trees and ferns and other vegetation, surprising him with the
breadth of her knowledge. She identified numerous species of
moss; berry bushes, which had been stripped clean ("The
bears," she explained casually. The *what!* he said to himself);
and of course the trees that towered over them from both sides
of the trail. Even Jack could tell a pine from a fir, but she
amazed him with her knowledge of deciduous trees as well.

"Isn't it beautiful?" She gestured to the surrounding forest. "I love this time of year. There's something so special
about it. Some things start to die but other things come to
life." She finished on a suggestive note and squeezed his buns
gently.

Despite this bit of encouragement, Jack hiked along feeling
extraordinarily stupid. "How did you learn all this stuff?"

"My daddy." She smiled. "He was a park ranger here."

"Is he still?" Jack tried unsuccessfully to hide his bald
panic. The very idea of running into Helen's father proved
acutely uncomfortable. ("Nice to meet you. Yes, that's right,
I'm Helen's forty-five-year-old . . . *friend.*")

"No, silly. Do you think I'd bring you here if he was

around? Do you have any idea how much he spent on my wedding? He'd kill me if he ever found out. No, he's retired now."

After this they hiked in silence until Helen stopped and jerked his hand.

"Do you see those leaves?" She pointed to a large leafy tree that Jack couldn't have identified if his life depended on it. "Aren't those the most incredible colors?"

"Yeah, sure," he panted.

"That red is a chemical called anthocyanin. It's in the leaves all the time, even when they're green. It's like the leaves have to start dying before all that red can come out. It's just like . . . it's just like blood!"

"Wow"—Jack caught his breath—"you have quite an imagination."

She turned to him and smiled. "I do, and you haven't even seen the half of it yet. Come on, Buster Brown." She tugged on his arm. "I've got *lots* to show *you*."

37

The day was slipping away far too quickly. Celia had planned to go hiking a lot earlier but she'd cleaned the house and treated herself to a leisurely lunch, and then made the mistake of switching on the TV, which had sucked her into a special on young gymnasts. She watched them bouncing and jumping, flipping and twirling, and before she knew it, three-thirty had rolled around. It was so easy to get lazy after a busy week. But that's it, she promised herself, you're going to get moving.

She exchanged her athletic shoes for hiking boots, and locked the door behind her. She took a deep breath and noticed that the acrid smell of the forest fires hadn't faded completely. It still nipped her nose, and a slight taste of smoke remained in the hazy air.

But she smiled as she walked to the edge of the deck. The orchards had all changed color, and the reds and yellows danced on the vast stage below her. The sun, however, now floated dimly over the mountains to the west, and she realized she'd better get started before it slipped from the sky completely. Of course, if she ran late it wouldn't be the first time she hiked home in the dark.

She planned to cut through the meadow just west of the house and then south into the forest that ran along the ridge. She guessed she still felt a little spooked about the incident with Mr. Boyce because she had no desire to take the deer and elk trails on the other side of the county road; she'd rather stay closer to home. But as she jumped down from the deck she remembered turning off the road yesterday afternoon and seeing the broken sign. It was as if it had been hanging in the corner of her eye just waiting to come into focus: our name, only half of it. Is that right?

She stood by the deck clearly puzzled. She actually put her hand on top of her head as though to hold on to her thoughts. Is that right? she asked herself again. She recalled coming up the road and turning into the driveway. No, that's right. It wasn't there. Half of it *was* missing. She found this curious, but hardly alarming.

She started down the driveway and heard the crunch-crunch-crunch of her boots on the gravel, loud in the afternoon hush while all of the forest around her remained quiet and peaceful.

I'm all alone, she thought, and this heightened her good mood even more. Finally, after a week filled with hassles she could do what *she* wanted to do. In fact, she was feeling so good that she started skipping down the driveway. It's true that she felt a little silly and childish, but she also felt free to do as she pleased so she didn't stop whipping up dust until she reached the fence post. That's when she saw the sign. Indeed, it had been split in half recently—she could tell by the unweathered seam of broken wood—and when she looked down she spotted the other half lying by her feet.

I'll be damned. Maybe a bear or a deer knocked it down. Some kind of animal. And she'd heard about the cougars and coyotes, how they'd started stalking people, even stealing babies out of backyards; but she was sure a lot of those stories were gross exaggerations, the rural versions of those urban legends that had crocodiles roaming the New York City sewer system.

She looked closely at the sign. Probably a gust of wind; we've got enough of it up here. Some of the trees even leaned leeward, listing over the land like the masts of big ships.

She walked back up the drive and dropped the broken piece of sign into the burn barrel by the wood shed. They had recently bought four cords of red fir for the woodstove and stacked it neatly inside the open-faced enclosure. Jack had left the small ax he used to chop kindling lying on the ground where it would go to rust if it ever rained. She picked it up and thought, he's so careless, as she sank its narrow edge into one of the logs. The fir was dry and the ax was sharp, and it cut deeply into the wood.

She returned to her point of departure by the edge of the

meadow and worked her way down to a trail. It meandered to her left in a southerly direction for about half a mile. She passed a patch of orange poppies and saw that their petals already had closed for the day.

The trail wandered into a dense forest canopied with Douglas fir and thick-barked ponderosa pine. Minutes later it skirted a large hole that had formed when another giant had toppled over. As she inched past the rotting trunk she saw a meadow up ahead and remembered how welcome she'd always found it. She hurried to its perimeter. From here she could look back and see the forest clearly, which hadn't been possible when she'd been deep in its shadows. That's right, she joked to herself, you *can* see the forest for the trees. She laughed at how funny that old expression sounded, and then gazed across the meadow at a pine that must have been at least a hundred years old. It rose above its brethren and stood heavy with brown cones and bushy green boughs. Its simple beauty filled her with wonder, and a restfulness flooded her with a rare sense of well-being. The moment lasted as few pleasures do, and she felt a powerful worthiness, as if the land had spoken to her in a strange and lovely language, and she had been silent enough to understand it.

She saw a familiar boulder in the middle of the meadow, and climbed it as she had many times before. She found her footing at the top, and though no more than six feet off the ground she felt like a hawk that had caught an updraft from the valley and hovered patiently for prey.

From this heady vantage point she surveyed the wild grasses that surrounded her, and imagined the field mice, insects, gophers and moles, the vast invisible web of life that stretched out for acres on all sides of her. She closed her eyes to the sun and let it linger on her face, and knew that even Indian summer could not last forever. She felt the rays settle on her chest where her dark top drew them in, as if to store away the wealth that winter would soon squander.

She opened her eyes and decided to take off her clothes. She wanted to lie in the meadow and feel the sun on all of her body. She looked around again to reassure herself of privacy, and climbed down. But as she stepped off the boulder she noticed how the shadows of the forest now stretched closer to her; darkness was coming, and she had so little time. She abandoned the idea of sunbathing, and instead looked to the light that still thrived above the trees.

"Stay," she whispered to the day, and with that wistful plea came a song she'd first heard at a college concert:

"Won't you stay, just a little bit longer . . ."

Those lyrics brought a rush of distant memories, and a sadness that washed away the happiness she'd known only moments ago, for she saw in the lengthening shadows of all these trees the inescapable passage of all good times.

38

Chet waited until she paused by the meadow's edge, then snapped the branch in two. She turned around and searched the trees and shadows. He had all he could do to keep from laughing. She'd never find him. This is good, this is real good. She's not standing up on that rock anymore looking so goddamn high and mighty, now is she? She's down here with the rest of us. Look at her. Who the fuck does she think she is?

He tossed the branch onto the ground. Two pieces. Was just one. He liked breaking them. They snapped just like necks.

He kept his distance but moved along as she stepped back onto the trail. Within minutes he climbed to a rise about a hundred feet above Mrs. Griswold. Everything sloped toward her and the valley floor. He figured if he found a rock big enough he could roll it all the way down, maybe take her with it. But that's not what he wanted, not by a long shot.

He could see her real good. Keeping track wouldn't be any kind of problem. Watching was fun. It wasn't any fun if you didn't get to play with them, get them good and scared. They all got scared. Sometimes they got so scared they even tried to play dead. But you don't *play* dead. You're either dead or you're not dead. It's like people saying they're "half dead." Bullshit. There's no such thing as being half dead. None of this in-between shit. You're either up and alive or you're down and dead. No ifs, ands, or buts about it. Of course, if they wanted to *play* dead, fine. Then he'd play, too. While they were playing with him, he'd be playing with them. He'd talk to himself. Why not? It was a game. He'd say things to make them think he was scared, that he'd gone too far. He'd sound panicky, like he was thinking of leaving. But it was a *tease,* and like any good tease he'd string it out for as long as he could. He knew that for them—tied up, messed up— each of those minutes went on forever. It was as if he could feel the emptiness in the air all around them, those hollow motes of hope as big as the sky, and that slim promise of survival he loved to break.

He'd keep a close eye on them while they played possum. But they always gave off some sign of life, and when he grew good and tired of waiting he'd use his razor to carve out the raw truth. That's when they'd stop their goddamn lying and start screaming.

You don't *play* dead.

He watched her and figured she'd have to hike back the same way she came. He'd scouted around and hadn't seen any other trails, so he sat on a log and waited. Got all the time in the world, nothing but time.

"Time, time, time is on my side, yes it is . . ."

A song from his teens. Mick Jagger. He was an evil one. Not a man, not a girl, an *in-betweener.* Like her with that little-boy's butt, and that priest that showed up after the old man left. Running around in a robe just like a girl, talking about my misdirected youth. Misdirected. He was the one that was misdirected. Miss this and Miss that.

Father Jim, plump and sweet, old and tired, had tried so hard to teach Chet about the Church. That was the year he'd been an altar boy, and they'd had lots of long talks in the rectory about Jesus and God and the Virgin Mary. Talk, talk, talk, that's all he did. But it was Chet who ended up telling Father Jim about good sin and bad sin.

No, no, the father had argued, there's only bad sin. But Chet knew better, knew that if you were God you made all the decisions about sin, and if you made all the decisions about sin, then you could make some sin good and some sin bad. Simple. He'd explained this to Father Jim over and over again but he wouldn't listen. Stubborn. He'd just sit there shaking his head until one day Chet told him he could prove everything he was saying.

"Prove it? Now how you going to prove it, Chester?" He always called him Chester even though Chet had asked him not to.

Chet had the most powerful urge to show Father Jim *exactly* what he meant, but he couldn't do it to a priest, not in the rectory. So he'd forced himself to sit there beneath the wooden crucifix and shrug his shoulders like he was stupid; and Father Jim had patted him on the back and told him not to feel bad, that questions about God had confounded great minds for centuries.

Chet managed to remain silent only because he knew that his most cherished secret would one day make him equal to the universe itself, to that great black ball of life and death folding and unfolding into eternity.

That day came a few years later when he met Susan Edwards in a trailer park outside Lincoln, Nebraska. A single mom with six-year-old Ritchie. She worked a warehouse job. No family nearby, no friends to speak of either, no one to miss her; and no one ever did, near as Chet could tell. As soon as he cut into her he confirmed his deepest belief, that murder made him immortal, and death made him God. The experience of crushing to death that gray pigeon when he was a kid paled when he silenced Susan's last struggling breath. This was a person, and then she was no more. He watched the blood race down her chest and knew that she would always be his. And in time so would her boy.

He'd kept her trailer, slept in it still, and met other Susans and their sons. He learned that nothing was easier than finding a lonely mom trying to raise a little boy all by herself. Spit twice in a crowd and you were bound to come up aces. Spend time with them and you found the twin rewards of murder nesting deep inside their home, for the mother gave you her blood, and the boy was the gift she'd borne.

But now he'd run right into the most interesting challenge he'd ever known, a woman foolish enough to think she could figure *him* out. He smiled because he knew that she wasn't even smart enough to figure herself out. Look at her, she doesn't even know if she's a man or a girl. Boy's hair, tiny ass, nothing on top. Who *does* she think she is?

There she goes, hurrying down that trail, looking back. He waved. He knew she couldn't see him. He liked to play with them. But he wouldn't play for long. Play time was over. He could feel it in his guts.

But even so he picked up another branch and snapped it in two just to see her jump. Goddamn, she did too. He laughed, and had a hard time keeping it down. This is going to be fun, making her jump, jumP, juMP, jUMP, JUMP— higher, higheR, highER, higHER, hiGHER, hIGHER, HIGHER . . . till she couldn't jump at all.

39

Davy stopped drawing and hugged the pad to his chest. It was starting to get dark. He didn't like to be alone in the dark but he didn't want to be with Chet either. He wanted his mother. He wanted her to come right now and get in the truck and drive away so they'd never have to see Chet again. Davy stared at the shadows, hoping she'd be there, but she wasn't. Then he had to look away because the darkness scared him.

He'd been sitting there since Chet left, except for when he had to go in the weeds. But he'd hurried because he didn't want Chet catching him because he'd want to help, and Davy didn't want his help. He just wanted him to go away and never come back.

He looked at his pad. He'd been working all day on Batman, but he didn't like any of the pictures. They were no good. Stupid, that's what they were. He'd balled up each one and thrown it on the floor, and now he kicked them around and stomped on them, and the paper made that angry noise like when you crushed it, like it's fighting back but can't, not really.

Maybe before it got really dark he could finish this one and get it right. He almost had it done and thought the wings looked good, and the rest of it too. It was the dark parts, he'd been messing them up for days, ever since he started. They took a long time, especially where Batman's legs and stomach came together. That's where it had to be black. It wasn't right if it wasn't *black*.

He bore down on the pencil and made it darker and darker. It got so thick that it started to shine. Davy felt sure he was going to get it right for the first time. It *would* be perfect. He kept moving the pencil back and forth, back and forth, over and over again, and it got blacker and blacker, shinier and shinier, and then . . . the pencil tore a hole in the paper, gouged right through it just like all the other times.

Davy felt sick. He crumpled up the paper and threw it on the floor where it landed on top of dozens of others, each with a hole where he'd tried so hard to make it perfect, where he'd tried so hard to make it black.

40

Chet was furious with himself, as angry as he'd ever been. He'd let her slip back to the house. Hell, he didn't even know she was back till she put the damn lights on. Near as he could figure, she had hiked down toward the valley and looped back around.

Okay, Mrs. Griswold, round one, it's yours. But that's it. He stood in the trees and stared at the door, then the window above the bed, knowing that now he was going to have to go in after her. So be it. He knew the layout, and he'd certainly seen enough of her to know she wouldn't be a problem once he got inside.

He stepped back when she cracked the door to let out the cat. What a useless goddamn pet. It jumped off the deck, and he thought about killing it. Something else for Mr. Griswold Agency to look for in all the ashes, the bones of a cat.

But Chet felt no urgency about the animal, and when he looked for it again its black form had disappeared into the night without making a sound. He did admire the cat's stealth. It reminded him of the speed and suddenness of his own attack, the way he could seize and silence a woman in a matter of seconds. He loved to feel the shock that came alive in his hands, the delicious way muscles tense, skin stiffens, bones shake.

His mouth moistened and his crotch stirred. He would enter the house . . . and then they would be alone. The police called it home invasion, and that's how he preferred to think of it too—invading. He was an . . . *invader*. He liked to invade and take the last thing they'd ever give up, the very last thing. They'd fight like hell for it. They just didn't know when to quit. He'd always have to tell them, "Give up, this isn't getting you anywhere."

He heard his voice, his wise counsel, the way he'd always tried to reason with them, but then reminded himself that it was better to save your goddamn breath. They never listened. Never.

41

Celia rinsed the salad spinner and rested it on the dish rack. She checked the stove clock and saw that it was already past eight. She'd procrastinated with Davy's drawings, no question about it. Maybe it was simple avoidance. Throughout the week she'd seen some disturbing elements in his pictures. Hardly surprising, given his stepfather. He'd certainly turned out to be a strange one. Back on Monday morning he seemed so concerned and interested, but by the time he picked Davy up at noon he'd become sullen. The next time she saw him was late Wednesday when he'd scared her with the snake, and then yesterday he was downright cagey: pushing and probing, asking questions and holding back; and insinuating that Davy was a liar and that his birth father was responsible for whatever signs of abuse she'd found, saying that he might have "got to the boy." What an odd way to put it, she thought, though hardly unusual. Still, it did suggest that sex with a child was somehow a prize you received after you'd cleared a series of obstacles. Of course Davy might have been traumatized by his real father, and Celia knew she would have considered this more seriously if Mr. Boyce hadn't wanted to have it both ways: if he hadn't blamed Davy's father and Davy too. But what she found most revealing was that he hadn't expressed much concern over the real possibility that his stepson had been hurt. Only that defensiveness, tossing around blame like seeds, hoping desperately that one of them would take root. Sorry, Mr. Boyce, not with me.

But as she walked back to the bathroom she again worried that his suspicions of her would make him flee with the boy. Christ, it's not like they have any ties to anyone. Wait a second, she corrected herself, that's not true. Davy definitely has responded to me. He's still keeping a flat affect with everyone else at work, but I'm making headway with him. She recalled that not only had he drawn for her, but he'd nodded and pointed on their way to his trailer yesterday, and then snuggled beside her on the couch. If she could persuade Tony to let her keep working with Davy, she was sure that one of these days he'd start talking too. She wondered for a moment what he'd say, what his first words would be.

No, Davy has ties here. It's his stepfather who seems so rootless.

She turned on the tap and closed the drain. Now it was time to listen to the only language the boy had shown a willingness to use. She placed Davy's drawings and file on a simple wooden tray that fit across the tub, then added a scratch pad and pen to her portable desk. She liked to work while she soaked.

Despite her misgivings about Davy's pictures, she found it fascinating to study the lines in a drawing to see how they shaped a whole, how the themes written in the language of form related to one another and composed the larger story of an individual life.

She straightened up, saw the window shade, and quickly pulled it down. Most of the time it seemed silly to do this—no one else lived on the ridge—but whenever Jack traveled she felt a little less safe, so little that in the past she had hardly paid it any mind. But tonight was different. An uneasiness had crept over her as she'd hiked out of the meadow. She'd heard branches snapping at least twice, but hadn't been able to spot any animals. Or people. The fear she'd felt had prompted her to take a different trail back home. She felt more comfortable now, in no small part because she'd closed the shades and locked the doors, the common-sense things anybody would do.

She took off her bra and scratched her sides and shoulders where the straps had been itching her all day. What a relief. She struggled to get her snug jeans past her slim hips, and finally had to sit on the toilet seat to pull them all the way off. Into the hamper. Her socks and panties soon followed, along with her top and bra.

She relieved herself, then stepped into the tub and sank

into the warm water, taking a moment to relax before starting to work.

Chet crouched on the deck right below the bathroom window. It was open an about an inch, and he'd heard the *pssssss* of that hot stream and that horrible tinkling too; and then that goddamn toilet paper, the sound of it unrolling and . . . and what she *did* with it.

Now he listened to the water sloshing up against the sides of the tub as she settled in, so close . . . so close he could almost . . . *touch* her. He could even see the panicky look she'd give him if he walked in right now, and he heard the rank horror that would darken her voice:

What are you doing here, Mr. Boyce!

Mr.BoyceMr.BoyceMr.BoyceMr.Boyce.

She'd be curled up in the corner of the tub trying to hide her nakedness, shaking or shouting or both. But not for long, not the shouting.

He wiped his palms on his .pants, then looked up at the stars and moon. The night started to drain like an open wound.

42

Celia opened Davy's file and pulled out his first assignment, the pencil sketch of a person. As she had pointed out to Tony earlier in the week, Davy's decision to draw a woman was highly unusual. Boys almost always drew boys, and girls drew girls. When she first looked over the picture she'd been reluctant to attribute great significance to this. Besides, other compelling elements competed for her attention: the absence of a nose, for instance, which strongly indicated a lack of emotional release for the boy; the distinct disconnection between the head and neck that she'd often seen in the artwork of clients who feared their bodies, for whatever reasons; the large feet, a feature that sometimes showed up in portraits by children who felt trapped; and of course the single line that Davy had penciled in for a mouth, which made the woman in this picture appear no more willing to speak than the boy who had drawn her.

But even as the week progressed and Davy had produced other work, Celia's thoughts kept returning to his original decision to draw a woman. This transparent gender confusion made sense only if the boy was questioning his own sexual identity, if he *felt* like a woman; and she knew Davy would feel like a woman if he'd been forced to act like one. Suspicions that had been forming all week, greatly underscored by the Batman drawings, now began to harden, along with a sense of dread. Celia had worked with dozens of sexually abused children, and had never been spared the unpleasant jolt that accompanied the stark recognition of pain. Her revulsion was only exacerbated by her understanding of just how difficult it would be for most of them to stitch their lives back together. It had taken her years to recover from the beatings she had suffered, and at times she would still come across remnants of her tattered childhood that needed mending.

She put aside Davy's first drawing and tried to do the same with her own troubled feelings. The time had come to examine his second picture of a woman, the one he'd rendered when she asked him to draw the "opposite sex," a term she'd had to explain to him. He had duplicated his first effort in virtually every detail, but filled more of the page. The longer lines and larger dimensions indicated to Celia that he had started to relax with his art, giving breadth to his portrait as he began to breathe easier. Even after a decade of study she was still amazed by the enthusiasm that most children eventually brought to their artwork, and it was true in almost every culture around the world. A child would fill pages, given the opportunity. Art brought out the innocence in even the most hardened children, and art therapy revealed the brutal truths hidden in the undergrowth of their fears. Celia saw the first hints of this in Davy's gender confusion, and in the way he'd drawn the woman's features. Subtle signs of distress. Nothing terribly obvious yet. Nothing like the holes in the Batman pictures.

She moved on to his House, Tree, Person Drawing. Weird, she thought, very weird.

The House, Tree, Person Drawing had become a standard technique among most art therapists. The house stood for an individual's family, the tree for his sense of purpose, and the person was how he viewed himself. Celia quickly realized that Davy's was one of the strangest examples she had ever seen.

First of all, his sky held a sun as well as a large dark cloud that spilled a smudgy, harsh-looking rain. She saw nothing nurturing in the cloud with its filthy rain, nor did she see how any sustenance could be derived from the sun. It resembled a fried egg with misshapen borders and an oblong yoke, the kind of sun that can't provide warmth; for a boy, she thought, who can't conceive of any.

She chewed on the tip of her pen and looked away for a moment, and as she did, something shifted deep inside, as if an old emotion had fallen off a shelf and landed a little lower in her stomach. She knew why this happened, and every time she worked with an abused child the realization grew stronger: though trained as an academic and blessed with the refined tools of the intellect, Celia remained an abused child herself. The years were not mileposts on a highway taking her farther from her childhood home, they were merely markers along the never-ending path of a memory that never dulled and certainly never died. When she looked at a picture she saw more than a client's loneliness, terror, or absence of love, she felt some of their anguish too. And when her own arms and legs and stomach grew leaden as she worked, she knew it was the added weight of her own childhood that she carried. So Davy's fight had become her fight. She couldn't help this. Despite years of therapy, professional distance had been closed to her by painful personal experience. It made her work tougher but it also made her very good at her job. Anger and outrage had turned her into a relentless investigator. Her tenacity already had led to four criminal convictions under Oregon's rape and sodomy laws. Three of the men had done time. Not much, but some. The fourth, a local middle school teacher, committed suicide the day after he'd received a two-year sentence.

She studied the house in Davy's House, Tree, Person Drawing, a square box with a triangle on top for a roof. Not at all unusual for most children, but Davy lived in a trailer. Celia quickly concluded that the picture illustrated the boy's sense of dislocation, and perhaps a desire to be in any house but the one he had to call home. Yet even this drawing contained powerful clues. For starters, it did not have a path leading to the front door, and even more revealing to Celia was the fact that the front door did not have a handle. Entering this house would be difficult, and no one, she believed, would learn its secrets easily.

Next, she checked the windows. He'd drawn one on each side of the door, and divided them with crossbars as boys generally do. This was different from girls, who typically included curtains that were parted in the middle and pulled to the sides. But unlike most boys, Davy had drawn so many crossbars that he'd created the appearance of a prison cell, which is probably how he feels about his house, she thought. That's the pits. But then she suddenly grew irritated because as she studied Davy's drawing she realized that she also felt like a prisoner of fear. In her own home, her own bathroom, no less. She looked at the window shade and felt a tremendous desire to tug on it and send it spinning back up so she could see the stars and the milky glow of the full moon. That's one of the reasons we live up here, so we can have all that.

The bottom of the shade dangled right above her, about an inch from the base of the window. It formed a narrow strip of darkness that teased her with the wide-open possibilities of the night sky. But she never reached for the shade. Not even the allure of the heavens could overcome the caution that guided her now.

43

Chet was pressed against the wall looking up at that one-inch opening in the bottom of the bathroom window. He couldn't take his eyes off it, the way it beckoned him, welcomed him, said, She's waiting for you, Chet. She's waiting.

He loved the power of seeing them . . . *naked* . . . when they didn't want you to see them, when they'd grab a towel, a goddamn rag if that's all they had, and hold it against themselves. Hiding when there's no place to hide.

Let me see you.

When they shook their heads he'd hold the razor high above him with both hands, the sacred host with its single edge, and he would feel the power invested in Him through our Lord Jesus Christ, amen.

The *naked* truth.

Dominus vobiscum.

Yes, He was God, getting to see what He wants when He wants.

Chet put his hands on the bottom of the window frame and started to move out of his crouch. He'd have to breathe softly or she'd hear his excitement. The goddamn window was open just enough to give him away . . . or get him inside.

No, you're just going to look. That's all. Go in later, when she's asleep. But his words formed weak links in the chain of restraint.

He heard scratching noises from inside the window. A moment later something splashed in the water and she said, "Oh shit." He liked it when they talked like that. Sometimes he'd make them do it.

He'd whisper in their ears, anything, anything that came to mind, though some things always came to mind, and he'd make them say it:

"I'm dirty."

"I'm dirty."

"Whisper, goddamn it."

And they'd whisper, you bet.

"Faster."

They'd whisper so fast they'd shake and run out of breath, so furiously they wouldn't hear him when he told them to stop. That's when he'd have to shut them up. He did, too, so they couldn't say anything at all.

He raised himself up and a board creaked under his feet. He fucking froze. Nothing. Silence, the kind that sucks the goddamn life out of you. Two, three minutes of deep, dead silence. Then a meow. The goddamn cat again. She said something to it, but he couldn't make out the words.

He moved up the wall until his eyes were even with the opening at the bottom of the shade. He took another breath as quietly as he could. The air entered him in shifts, as if his lungs were cranking open. Slowly, he stood up a few more inches and angled his head so he could look right down at her. It had taken him long minutes of quiet careful maneuvering to get into this position, and now his rage threatened to rip him apart because she'd surprised him yet again. She had some kind of *board* hiding her body, and she had a *paper* in one hand and was petting the goddamn cat with the other; and she was turned away so he couldn't see a thing. All that for *nothing*. He could feel his crotch and mostly he felt *nothing*. Like he saw *nothing*. Goddamn her to hell. *Nothing Nothing Nothing*.

He stared at her brown hair, short like a boy's, and her small head. Everything about her was small, and he knew she'd be easy.

But then he saw something that made him duck—the reflection of his eyes in the mirror on the bathroom door. They had been plainly visible, as dark and present as the night.

44

Celia started chewing on the end of the ballpoint again as she studied the only window Davy had drawn in the triangular roof. He'd shaded it so much it was black. More secrets, she thought, especially with all this crosshatching. He'd covered the roof with it.

She put her pen down just long enough to scratch her left shoulder, and it rolled off the tray into the tub.

"Oh shit."

She fished it out and dried it with the end of a towel hanging from the rack. When it still wrote cleanly, she felt like rejoicing. She hated having to get out of a tub once she'd settled in.

The deck creaked but the sound barely penetrated her consciousness. A second or so later she thought idly of Pluto and figured he must be out on the deck. She made a few notes in Davy's file.

She looked once more at the house in the House, Tree, Person Drawing and noticed that Davy had not included a chimney. No sign of warmth, she thought. Well, that's certainly consistent with everything else I've seen. She made note of this as well.

She returned to the picture and noticed for the first time that the clouds with the dirty rain hovered above the house. She hadn't made this connection till now. How'd I miss that? It darkened her suspicions of Davy's home life even more. It also caused her to take a second look at the tree, and that's when she saw that he'd positioned it right under the fried egg sun. Of course. Look at it. The tree—Davy's sense of purpose—was a horrid evergreen with spindly branches all sloping sharply downward. It came to a peak pointy enough to

serve as a weapon. Celia bit down on the end of her pen
again. Burnout, she decided, this kid is toast.

Not a single living creature perched on those dead-looking
limbs. This appalled her. When healthy children drew trees
they often included birds, bees, bunnies, puppies, all kinds of
animals and insects—appropriate or not—because they
wanted to fill their make-believe world with as much love,
laughter, warmth, and concern as their own childhood. But
Davy's tree appeared as lifeless and dry as tinder.

She made more notes, and then examined the person in
the drawing. She viewed this as a self-portrait. What she
found most striking and disheartening was that Davy presented himself as a stick figure—the only one she'd seen so
far. Worse still, he'd drawn his stick-figure self without feet,
hands, ears, nose, or pupils; and he'd formed its mouth with
a single twisted slash.

"Jesus," she whispered. She shook her head but kept her
eyes trained on the stick-figure boy. He was Davy devoid of
flesh, of life, Davy as nothing but bones connected with little
more feeling than the dots on a coloring-book page, the ones
that eventually form the outline of a featureless face.

When she started to write, the words came feverishly: "No
feet, wants to flee; no hands, has no power; no ears, cannot
hear or doesn't want to; no nose, cannot express emotions;
no eye detail, doesn't see his world; mouth distorted, closed,
cannot (will not?) talk. Stick figure looking away from house
and tree. Definitely wants out. Fear everywhere."

Pluto slipped in through the unlatched bathroom door and
meowed. Celia looked up and managed a smile despite the
depressing material on her makeshift desk. She put her pen
down and rubbed his soft fur. She needed to connect with
something alive, warm, and caring in its own peculiar way.

"You are such a gorgeous little guy."

She did think he was a great-looking cat, one eye, scars
and all. She scratched his ear, and that's when it dawned on
her that Pluto could not have made the noise out on the deck
a few moments ago. He was a big cat, but not big enough to
make a board creak. What's more, he'd been inside the house,
and they didn't have a cat door. Jack wouldn't hear of it. For
Pluto to get in or out, either the door to the living room or

the one in the mud room had to be opened. She stilled her hand and tried to remember if she'd locked up. Her fear was quite simple: Pluto had come in the house when someone opened one of the doors. She looked up and caught movement in the mirror. She did a double take and it was gone, but she could have sworn she'd seen something. Eyes? In the window? Now she saw only that narrow strip of darkness. Had Jack come home from Trout River, opened the door, and let Pluto in? That would be strange.

"Jack?" she called out, hoping he *had* come home but knowing better. "Jack? Are you back already?" She made an effort to sound casual, but her fear would not let her.

She almost panicked as she tried to recall whether she'd let Pluto in the house. Yes, you did. Remember? You let him out, then you let him in. That's right, she said softly. But then another fear gripped her: What made that noise?

She studied the window again. There was only that band of darkness, but she realized it was wide enough to let someone look in. Maybe someone had been. That possibility terrified her, and she wrapped her arms across her breasts as she concentrated on what she'd seen in the mirror. She wanted to remember nothing, but she could have sworn that for a split second a pair of eyes had been looking back at her. Dark eyes. Or had she seen something that wasn't there, like Harold with those horrible beetles? This possibility also scared her, that her fears had so overwhelmed her mind that even the world of appearances had begun to assume its most frightful forms.

Then she noticed that the window, like the shade, had not been closed all the way. "Oh no," she said to herself. Just those two words—"Oh no"—cinched as tightly as a packsaddle. She sat there for at least another thirty seconds before urging her arms and legs to move. Just push the tray forward, stand up, and lock it. Simple. But it wasn't simple, she was too scared to move.

Several minutes of absolute stillness passed. Her arms pressed against her chest. She no longer looked at Davy's drawings but at the window with its inch of darkness opening out into the night. The bathwater cooled, and the air draped her with a velvety chill. She saw goose bumps on her skin.

Yes, that's right, you're cold. Now shut the window.

She slid the tray forward as quietly as she could and raised herself into a crouch. She had a wall of fear to climb as she stood up, and when she reached the bottom of the window she paused for a moment to peek. She couldn't see much because of the shade. Her legs straightened and she lifted it aside. It was still very difficult to see because of the bathroom light shining behind her, but then suddenly a strained-looking face appeared no more than an inch or two away. Her heart thumped so loudly it echoed in her chest, and she lost her breath as she ducked. She saw it move too, and she hugged the cold tile wall before realizing that it was her own reflection in the glass that had frightened her so.

Her breathing slowly steadied, and she stood back up.

Celia, close the window.

But she was so tense when she reached up that her arms moved slowly, as though unfreezing by degrees. She also felt water trickling down her thighs, drips as cold as the metal frame of the window itself. She slid it into place.

The lock, turn it.

She did this too, nice and tight. Then she pulled the shade all the way down. She wanted no more of the night, not the stars, the moon, and certainly not the darkness.

45

Davy felt his stomach rumble, heard it too, like a bear. He worried about bears, especially in the dark, roaming around hungry, looking for something to eat, something like Davy. He was hungry, too. He'd had one of the peanut-butter sandwiches before it got dark but he wanted more. Some warm milk, like his mom used to make for him late at night, heating it up in a saucepan and stirring it around till it steamed. Then she'd pour it in a glass and he'd drink it while she watched. Sometimes she'd play with his hair too, her fingers lifting it up and letting it go. That was before Chet took him to the barber. On the way he told him he'd be getting a buzz cut. "It's easy, you don't even have to comb it, and I *like* the way it feels." He must 'cause he was always touching it. But not like his mom. He hated the way Chet touched him, always at night. That's when he'd do it to him.

Davy wanted to open the car door just enough for the light to come on, but Chet had told him about draining the battery. *It better start when I want it to.* So he sat in the dark and heard the night noises and hugged his pad and felt bad about Batman. He wondered if he'd ever get it right. All those holes in the paper. He moved his foot back and forth and heard the pictures that he'd messed up shifting around. They sounded like a pile of dead leaves. Then he stopped and it was still, still as air. Again he heard the night noises. It could have been a bird, that's all, not a bear. But it could have been something else. He shuddered and closed his eyes tightly, scared that something really would reach in and grab him. Something like Chet.

46

Celia yawned and curled up on the couch in the living room with the last of Davy's efforts, his Kinetic Family Drawing in color, which he'd done completely in red. Well, not quite completely, she corrected herself as she pulled it out of the folder. Under the bright table lamp she'd detected faint pencil lines above an otherwise boldly colored drawing. More shading, she thought right away. But why so light?

She moved the KFD directly under the lamp, and saw that the pencil lines formed an odd shape; and then as she studied it she recognized the crude form of an angel. It appeared to float above the red stick figure of a boy. She could just make out the wings extending from the body, no arms but definitely wings; and legs protruding from the bottom of a gown, which lent the figure a distinctly feminine cast. His mother, thought Celia, that's got to be his mother.

But what Davy had not drawn proved most arresting of all: the angel had no head. The wings rose to the shoulders but the shoulders rose to nothing. No neck, eyes, ears, nose, nor mouth. No face.

There are no accidents in art, Celia reminded herself. Davy's omission of a head said as much, if not more, than all the details he'd included. Perhaps his mother's face had been too painful to contemplate. But why? Why would the face itself be such a source of pain?

Celia looked up at the ceiling and tried to puzzle out what she could not see.

Put it in context, she advised herself. You've got to do that first. She lowered her eyes to the drawing, pausing long enough to glance at the shades drawn over all the windows in the living room. She noticed strips of darkness along the edges, the night peeking in as it had in the bathroom. She stared at the window closest to her, and after reassuring herself that nothing was amiss—*No, nothing at all*—she returned to Davy's picture, which was a striking study in contrast: those barely visible pencil lines, and the rich red he'd used everywhere else.

Colors were tricky. They were linked closely to feelings, but Celia was reluctant in any evaluation to ascribe meaning to them quickly. Common wisdom, for example, saw red as an angry color—the color of blood and rage; but red was also Santa's color and the color of Valentines Day. No simple formula existed for analyzing a child's color choices. A girl might grab a green crayon or felt-tipped marker because it was easiest to reach, or a brown one for the same reason. But Celia doubted that Davy's choice of red was an accident. Color was all in the context, and the context, she was beginning to see, was not simply abusive, but brutal.

The KFD was supposed to show Davy and his family in an activity. Most children drew scenes of picnics, gardening, or families playing games. Even deeply disturbed kids generally managed to suggest a degree or two of normalcy in a picture like this one. It was as though they felt they had to. Not Davy.

The horizontal drawing featured an outsized Mr. Boyce on the left side. He appeared to be on the verge of splitting a log in the center of the page, and the stick figure of Davy held what looked like a wedge just above the log. A pile of wood lay behind the boy and to the right. The headless angel hovered above him.

She concentrated on Davy's drawing of his stepfather first. He had made him look like a monster, and she noted how much this contrasted with her first impression of Mr. Boyce as a handsome man with distinct features. But Davy had exaggerated his stepfather's size and made him appear as big as Frankenstein. His nose loomed as two huge nostrils, which she recognized as the perspective Davy would have looking up at him. She picked up the pen and wrote in the boy's file that the large appearance of the nostrils strongly suggested that Davy feared the emotion Mr. Boyce expressed around him. This was Celia's analytical side. Her emotions provided a simple and more direct verdict: Boyce was a beast.

The boy hadn't ignored his stepfather's dark eyes either. Even on paper they looked monstrous; and he'd drawn him with massive feet, legs, and arms; boxy shoulders; a thick neck; and, most grotesque of all, a hand shaped like an axe.

A big belt buckle drew attention to Mr. Boyce's crotch in the picture much as he intended to—consciously or not—in real life. She remembered the way its oval shape pressed against his narrow waist, the bronzed relief of a horse bucking right over his belly button.

Just below the buckle Davy had colored in his stepfather's lower abdomen. The shading extended down to the tops of his legs. Celia realized that the boy had put a great deal of effort into covering up Mr. Boyce's genital area, and she knew she didn't need a degree in art therapy to reach an obvious and sickening conclusion.

But she hesitated before picking up her pen because the longer she studied the picture the more aware she became of other damning elements. The hand shaped like an axe, for instance, was aimed at the wedge, which the stick-figure boy held over the log. The wedge, Celia saw with a shock, resembled a penis. No question about it. Not *even* a stretch. And the stick figure with his twisted mouth and missing features looked as scared as he had in the earlier picture.

But she still couldn't take her eyes off of Davy's drawing long enough to write up her notes because one alarming image led to another. She mulled over the pile of logs on the right side of the drawing for a couple of minutes before understanding that this might well be Davy's way of saying the abuse would go on. *Abuse*? A queasy feeling muddied her stomach, and she thought, abuse? Abuse? Call a spade a spade, it's *rape!*

And then as she sat there studying the drawing, her anger building, she suddenly understood the chilling reason why Davy had used so much red: it was the devil's color. Of course, that's it! Davy saw himself in hell with his stepfather, his mother rising above them, free only in death. Celia looked for the angel's feet but found that Davy hadn't included them. That made sense too. In the earlier drawings of women he'd included big feet, which had indicated to her that he'd felt weighted down. But this angel was on the move, rising from the hell below. But what had been so horrible for his mother, so harrowing that she remained headless in the boy's otherwise vivid imagination? What could possibly . . .

The answer that came to Celia stilled all her other thoughts and made her search the shadows in the room. Murder. Maybe Boyce had killed her, committed an act so terrifying that Davy could not render it. Or maybe he could not even remember what had happened and had blocked out all but her absence. If that was the case, then the boy's memory might return slowly, painfully, perhaps even faintly at first, like an angel barely visible, faceless but not forgotten. Celia studied the empty space above the wings, and nodded to herself. The boy who had spoken without words might have drawn an important clue without lines.

Now she did pick up her pen and try to write, but succeeded with only the basics: "Graphic indicators of sexual abuse. Check with state and local authorities to see if stepfather has criminal record. Check death certificate for mother—Becker, Idaho. Alert Services to Children and Families."

There, she'd finished, but the hand that held the pen still shook and she could barely read what she'd written. That's okay, she didn't have to read her notes. She'd read Davy's drawings, and they all spelled out a simple plea for help. She would make sure he got it too. She'd nail that bastard Boyce, send him to prison and set the boy free. At best Boyce was an abuser, and he might also be something far worse.

She closed the file and placed it on the table, then checked the clock. Late. Too late to call Tony tonight, for all the good it would do; but tomorrow morning he'd hear from her, Sunday or not. And he'd get on the line to the state or she'd do it herself, protocol be damned.

She stood up, yawned deeply, and felt her exhaustion. A shiver of fear too. She double-checked the locks on the doors, dragged herself into the bathroom to brush her teeth, and never once looked at the shade, the window, or the world outside.

47

They'd hiked, hit the hot tub, polished off a bottle of wine, and made love. And now, as Helen prepared herself in the bathroom for yet another round of sex, Jack lay in the log bed next to the log wall staring at the log door, and felt pathetically incapable—despite his sylvan surroundings—of producing even the flimsiest of woodies.

Helen had dismissed his concerns with a flick of the wrist and the promise of "greater delights to come." He could have done without the pun. Actually, he could have done without Helen but he knew this was a situation entirely of his own doing.

He heard the rustling in the bathroom and wondered what she had in mind now.

When she opened the door a few minutes later she wore a gauzy white gown that flared fetchingly from her waist to mid-thigh. Jack had to admit that the backlighting from the bathroom did turn her formidable figure into an enchanting silhouette.

"I'll be with you in just a sec, sweetheart."

A moment ago he would have taken that as a threat, but he found himself mesmerized by the sight of Helen carefully and seductively putting on lipstick.

He stirred, and a sting issued from where she'd rubbed him raw just a couple of hours ago. But the discomfort faded as his excitement grew.

He looked down and witnessed the yeasty effect of her appearance in the tent pole poking up the covers. Amazing. At that moment he decided she was indeed a miracle worker, an Annie Sullivan of sex.

He touched himself, as if to confirm the Lazarus between his legs, and watched Helen place the lipstick on a bureau

and move to the end of the bed. She lifted the covers with a
flourish and disappeared. The mattress creaked as she began
to kiss the inside of his knees. Her hands soon swirled up
over his thighs, and as her lips closed around him Jack felt
all of his reservations dissolving like mints in his mouth.

When he grew fully erect she lifted her gown and straddled
him. He entered her gratefully.

His pulse quickened as he offered his thrusts, and though
spent, though clearly pushing beyond the broad limits of simple desire, he made love to her.

He rolled her over, found a rhythm and gloried in it. He
perspired and dripped his salty excess onto her face and chest.
His entire body turned slick from exertion, and Helen's did
too. They squirmed and slipped and slapped against each
other, a wet heaving bundle of tremulous flesh. His ample
stomach spilled over hers as he tried to come, to feel his great
pleasure at last. Ten minutes, fifteen. Twenty. His muscles
burned—arms, shoulders, back—as he pressed repeatedly
into her. His buttocks shook and his belly rolled, but still the
shiny carrot of climax eluded him. He reached for it, chased
it, and always it remained just out of reach, a teasing spectacle
of doubt. And then the first hints, the first brutal hints of
impotence.

Oh Jesus, not *that!* He moved even more vigorously, but
for naught, and grew mortified at the prospect of flopping out
of her a defeated man. He tried to conjure up every erotic
moment he'd ever known with Helen, but no memory moved
him. And then he thought of Celia, a summer afternoon a few
years ago out on the deck. She'd been wearing shorts and a
halter top when she suddenly stood up and took them off.

"What are you doing?" he'd asked.

"I'm going to sunbathe."

She'd lain on her stomach on a towel in the bright sun,
and he'd sat beside her and slowly caressed her pale cheeks.
His hand had moved to her upper thighs, and without a word
from either one of them she'd parted her legs. His fingers slid
easily over her opening.

Within minutes her back arched and those pale cheeks rose
as she pressed against his hand. Her breath sounded quick
and hard in the stillness, and when she came she cried out

his name. He'd quickly mounted her from behind, as hard as he'd ever been.

He stiffened again and pounded at Helen with renewed confidence. The fickleness of his passion stunned him even as he felt the cunning strength of every muscle freeze in the first flash of climax. And then he knew their staggering release, the way they poured the blue balance of all eternity into a single spasm of time.

He lay on top of Helen spent and panting, happy and dumb and wildly accomplished. Three times in twenty-four hours. A regular world-beater. But now that he'd come, he thought only of leaving.

48

Celia snuggled beneath the covers, but could not stop thinking about how unsettling her evening had been. It had started at dusk with those weird noises on the hike back to the house, and ended after midnight with Davy's most disturbing picture. She'd handled some tough cases but Davy's looked like the grimmest yet. Abuse, maybe even murder. Come morning she'd report Boyce, which might mean going head-to-head with Tony. She sure didn't welcome that prospect. So much for her weekend. She wished she could put aside all of her anxiety and let her tiredness take over. She even tried to tell herself that everything would work out okay. You'll see. Just relax.

And so she did. She fell into a sleep so deep that it spared her all the troubles that had bedeviled her day. She was at rest with the timeless dreamless passage of night and never heard the footsteps stealing across the deck, or the stealthy hands moving up the wall until they reached the window right above her bed.

Chet bit down on the razor. He loved the taste of the metal, the familiar flavor that whipped up his sweetest memories. A blade was a thing of true beauty, like taking a thousand pins—just the very tip of each one, the part that sinks into skin like it's born to be there—and sealing them all together into a single straight line. That was a blade. And the most beautiful thing about a blade was the way it sliced the whole world into two—winners and losers. None of this in-between shit. And she was a loser. She sure as hell was. He'd known that when he first laid eyes on her. Standing there all snugged up in her tight little jeans with her little-boy's haircut.

Who's she think she is?

And now she's lying on the bed, inches away. It wouldn't be long now. He smiled and his lower lip peeled open. The razor nested right above it, a steady steely presence making its way into the night. Maybe he would kiss her first, bless her with the blood of her very own lips, joined in the beginning as they would be in the end.

He studied the layers he'd have to get through. First, the screen. Then the window itself. And finally, the curtain. It hung lifelessly, a light color, maybe even white, but that could have been the moon's doing. It was a full son of a bitch tonight, and he paused long enough to thank the moon for thinking of him.

He took the razor out of his mouth and ran it swiftly down the left side of the screen. He was a man who knew his tools, his product, his trade. It made a zinging noise, but soft. That was the thing about razors, and Chet knew this to be true: they made everything they touched seem soft, especially skin. You thought you knew a lot about skin, you thought it was soft, but you had no idea how soft skin was till you put a razor against it and pressed down just the slightest little bit. Soft, soft, soft, that's what it was.

He thought he heard her stir, and listened closely. He had to. It was do-or-die time. If she moved quickly, it meant she'd found him out, and he'd have to tear through that window before she tried to get away. That's when it got messy, searching the house, dragging their sorry ass out of a closet or bathroom, or finding them on the goddamn phone dialing and dialing and having to take it away 'cause it might be one of those cell phones, but otherwise he'd laugh 'cause he'd already ripped the hell out of the phone box. It was always the first thing he did. A good warm-up, popping it open and cutting all those wires. But there they'd be dialing away until they finally got the message, and he'd tell them "Put it down," and sure enough they'd do just like he said, like they'd never planned to use it in the first place. He'd never had one that didn't. It's like they knew it was all over, and you know what? They were right. It was all over.

The stirring sound faded. He didn't think she was awake. Not so much as a peep from the other side of the curtain. But just as he lifted the razor to make another cut he heard an odd noise. Something moved, then it didn't. Now what the fuck was that? He reached a cautious finger through the screen, and then another and another until he had his whole hand inside it. He touched the glass and slid his hand up until he could feel the top part of the aluminum frame. He hated wooden windows, the kind you had to wrestle with. This one crawled right along its tracks. Smooth as smooth can be. Pure fucking magic. Open sesame. Now he could reach right in and grab her at any time.

He parted the curtain for his first glimpse. The effort forced him to turn to the side, and he was looking down the length of his arm when he spotted that black cat on the bed. Goddamn, he hated cats. What's with that fucking eye? Where's the other one? That single pupil stared back at him in the moonlight, and he had a powerful urge to pluck it out.

Kill the cat. Kill the cat. Words kept repeating themselves, sending him a message. He listened. He always listened.

He watched the cat watching him, and tried to stare down that filthy little creature but it wouldn't look away. Like it's got my goddamn number or something. Chet would not be stared down, but that cat would not back off. He tried like hell to put hate in his eyes, and he might have succeeded because lo and behold, the cat started making noises like it was a deep fryer popping and hissing and spitting out its oily anger.

Chet was not pleased, not one little bit, because the last thing he wanted was for Mrs. Griswold to wake up. He finally forced himself to look away, but vowed to get even. He peeked at her. She lay there as still as the night, and the cat quieted down.

But just as he was about to make another vertical cut, Celia turned onto her back. He heard this and hurried to take another look. He was damn well ready to rip right through that screen if need be. He saw her face and understood that she had shifted positions. The cat made a soft brushing noise. Chet peered at it. He couldn't tell what the hell it was doing. Celia moved again, and he almost jumped on her. But it was just her hand. She rested it on the cat, and he stopped himself at the very last second.

When he heard her breathing nice and steady, he slowly

withdrew his arm and sliced open the right side. Zing, smooth as can be, a razor making things right with the world.

Again, Celia moved her hand but continued to sleep. Then, as he cut open the bottom of the screen, the unusual sound brought her fully awake.

She held her breath and opened her eyes slowly. She saw the shadow behind the curtain. The dark figure reached up to the top of the window, and she heard that sound again— zzziinng. That's a knife, she thought. Or a razor? She wanted to run, she wanted to flee. She couldn't move. She was frozen, a block of ice melting madly on the bed. Perspiration ran down her face and neck, cold beads on clammy skin, and a snapping sound penetrated the room. An opening in time appeared when nothing happened—silence hovered above the bed, and silence huddled beneath the covers—and then she heard an explosion of noise as he tore through the window.

The weight of him tumbled onto the mattress, and Celia felt the hard bones of his arms and legs striking her. The curtain rod landed inches from her head, and his hands raced all over her body—everywhere at once—pulling, lifting, pushing. She screamed and flailed and tried to get away but she was trapped by his weight and the blankets that bundled her. Pluto screeched, as though crushed, and Celia tried to sit up. Before she could rise more than a few inches Chet grabbed the screen he'd cut out and used both hands to force it down onto her face, a fist on either side of her cheeks. He pressed it so hard against her nose and mouth she couldn't move, and her eyes were pinned shut. The mesh burned like a brand, as if a hot little bit of meanness throbbed in every one of those wires. She tried to push him off, but couldn't. She did manage to turn her head to the side, away from him, which enraged Chet. He weighted the screen like he was doing a pushup, and the mesh flattened her ear and stretched tight as steel across her cheek. He saw her skin ooze up through the screen's tiny holes. It was like seeing her through nylons or panty hose. He liked it when they wore that shit over their face. Yeah, do it, he'd tell them, and they would. His cock was hard, goddamn it was hard, like it was trying to fuck its way right out of his pants.

"You're hurting me," Celia slurred. He'd squeezed her

lips into the shape of a fish mouth, and she could hardly talk at all. She couldn't see him either.

Hurting you? You think I'm hurting you *now?* Derision riddled his thoughts, and there was the corrosive inflection of cruelty when he repeated her words to himself. Fuck you, Mrs. Griswold, this is *nothing.*

"Shut . . . the . . . fuck . . . up."

When he spoke she knew it was Boyce. The voice, body size too, and a familiar odor, piney and sour. That's when she knew he'd been in the house on the day of the snake, when she drank that glass of water by the sink and noticed the unusual smell. Now it steamed off his skin and filled her nose again, an awful presence that stained the air, pillaged the room, and took her prisoner. She felt a warm drip on her cheek, then another. He was sweating on her, and breathing loudly, the snorting, snuffling sounds of a man who's working harder than he's used to . . . or who's excited. She thought of the knife, or razor, and stiffened. Jesus, don't cut me. For several seconds her fear fused with his breathing, and that's all she heard—his hot gamy breath above her—and that's all she thought about—the knife, the razor. And then her fear returned to those fragile words: Don't cut me.

He had her good and scared. He could tell by the way she lay there like she'd melt into the mattress if she could. The covers were down around her belly and she had on some kind of nightgown. No matter. Not for long. He pressed the screen down on her face with one hand while he used the other to work his belt buckle loose. The buttons on his fly pulled apart easily, and he reached into his jeans. He had to root around to get ahold of his cock, and then he had to suck in his stomach to make enough room for it. But it popped right out, hard as fucking bath pipe, and it felt good in his hand. He saw it in the moonlight, the tip all wet and shiny and loaded like a goddamn gun.

Celia had heard the belt buckle clank like a chain and the impatient sound of him searching around in his pants. Then the rustling had stopped, and now she knew what he planned to do.

Oh God.

She rolled over quickly, as she had at the Center when

clients had tackled her. She caught a glimpse of his startled face through the mesh and tried to press her advantage; but he recovered immediately, grabbed the back of her shoulders, and forced her down to the bed. He frightened her by how easily he did this. He was even stronger than he looked. She now lay on her stomach with her face pressed into Jack's pillow. She could smell her husband, his hair. It was a relief not to smell Boyce.

Chet pulled down the covers and saw that her nightgown fell to her knees. He took out his razor. Goddamn.

His cock was thick, and glossy threads of semen dripped from the tip, shiny filaments alive in the silvery light. His hand trembled as he scooped up a strand and brought it to rest on the sparkling surface of the blade. He raised it with great care to his waiting tongue. Even so, as he licked off the semen he nicked himself, and a red blossom splashed on his penis. He looked down, then closed his eyes to savor the salty blood and silky seed mixing in his mouth, so viscous and so pure. He knew that even minutes from now the braided aftertaste would remain a constant and pleasant reminder. Now he was ready for her. He had served himself the sacrament of semen, and had received the blessings of blood: He was the altar boy now God in the dark house of the Lord.

Dominus vobiscum.

Et cum spiritu tuo.

"Don't move," he whispered as if there might have been someone else in the bedroom, "and I won't hurt you."

He believed that too, that he wouldn't hurt her. Each of those moments had their own kind of truth, and each of them would prove to be false, for that would be then and this was now.

She felt both of his hands on her back, the right one curled, as if it might be holding something—the knife, or razor? Her thoughts kept lurching back to that staggering fear: Don't cut me.

He circled around Celia on his knees, took one hand off her back and pulled up her nightgown, then stared at her skin. He felt like a jeweler with a gemstone, something raw and wonderful waiting to be cut, a man who can see every little detail in what he's about to handle, the preciousness and precariousness of his venture, who knows that nothing can be rushed because one little upset, just one little slip of the wrist could turn all of his efforts to dust.

He had a sudden urge to cup the milky perfection of those cheeks, to fill his palms as he kissed that dark circle with his lips and tongue. He put his razor back in his pocket and held them dearly, the plump rectitude alive in his hands, and he spread them until she was as open as a field.

Celia felt her skin stretch and the invasion of cool air from the window—the stark utter nakedness of the night—and then she knew his hot breath. His lips and tongue followed, and she gripped the blanket tightly. She lay with her buttocks clenched like angry fists and listened to the loud wet sounds he made without the slightest hint of self-consciousness. Moments later his teeth began to nibble her, and she slowly became aware of the way his lips were peeled back and pressed against her skin. That sensation remained—even in the midst of all this—unnerving, unnatural, and undeniably insistent. He paused and his breath no longer felt hot, but chilling, passing over the moist remains like a fog. He kneeled back and used both hands to yank down his pants. The belt buckle clanked again, and she threw herself to the side, almost off the bed.

He grabbed her gown just below the armpit and jerked it so hard the sleeve tore open. He rolled her onto her back and saw the look on her face. He knew what she was going to do before she did. He was so sure of this he put his hand over her mouth as the noise started to come out. He'd have to gag her. Hammers worked best. Jam the head of it in her mouth and duct-tape it shut. He smiled when he remembered how the handle stuck out, and he smiled again when he heard her try to scream. Try all you want. Try-try-try. He felt his hand crushing her lips; and then he felt something else, something so completely painful that all he could do was gasp.

Celia was biting him. Her teeth were grinding through a chunk of his hand right below his thumb. She was biting down so hard she could feel his skin pressing against her gums.

He yelled an obscenity and tried to pull his hand free.

Good-good, her thoughts howled as his skin began to tear.

She bit down even more. He pushed her head to the side and held it at arm's length. Celia became vaguely aware of blood seeping into her mouth and starting to run down her throat. He tried to punch her face, but landed only one ineffective blow before she reached up and protected herself. She ground her teeth deeper and deeper into his palm until her mouth all but filled with his pulpy flesh. Her jaw ached from the fury of her bite, as if there were hollow spots under every tooth, throbbing little pockets of pain. And he tasted horrible, like the tough salty rind of some horrible stinking fruit; but she wouldn't let go, she couldn't. She'd eat him alive if she had to.

He had never known anything like this—sheer fucking agony. She'd bitten through to bone—he was sure of it—and when he tried smashing her head up and down, the pain was so intense he thought he'd pass out. He wanted to rip out her fucking eyes, do something—anything—that would hurt her forever, but he couldn't do a fucking thing because first he had to get his goddamn hand out of her goddamn mouth.

The trickle in Celia's throat grew thicker and thicker until she couldn't keep herself from gagging. The first cough freed his hand. It flew from her mouth and rage filled his face. She coughed again and kicked wildly at him, caught him in the chest and heard a loud grunt as she lunged for the bathroom. She had just clambered to her feet when he grabbed her leg with his bloody hand. It slipped from her knee to her ankle, and for one surging moment she thought he'd lost his grip; but then he yanked her leg and she fell facedown on the floor. He came tumbling off the bed, but held on. With her free leg she kicked at him frantically—mule kicks—but he never let go. He was like some large animal too dumb and driven to consider its pain.

He lay there while she struggled, the two of them linked in the moonlight by his grip. She clawed at the carpet to try to get away. He let her struggle. She wasn't going anywhere, and he needed time to regroup. His thoughts were a swamp. It wasn't supposed to be like this. It never had been. Jesus fuck, his hand throbbed.

Less than a minute later Celia stopped kicking. She had to catch her breath, she couldn't help it; and that's when he seized her other foot and started pulling her toward him. She was sliding backward on her belly. She dug her fingernails into the carpet and felt them bend and break. She heard him grunting and that carpet noise too, the dull hideous scratching when the knap peels open, like rows of wheat in a windstorm.

He let go of her left ankle and clamped down on her calf. He repeated this to her right leg. He was *crawling* up her body, and she shook uncontrollably. She felt his hand—wet, bloody, sticky—by her nightgown. He reached up under the hem, and she screamed, ''No,'' and tried to kick again; but he was kneeling on her feet and calves and crushing them with his weight. He grabbed her left buttock so hard the muscle burned with pain, and she tried to buck him off. He tore at her gown and her head snapped up off the floor as the neckline caught around her throat. Celia choked and gasped for air; and her head twitched violently when he yanked on the fabric, like a horseman trying to control his mount.

Ride 'em, cowboy. You gonna buck like a bronc, I'm gonna ride you like one. Chet loved the way her head whipped around, and he really liked those choking sounds. He kept the pressure on while he slid his right knee up between her legs. Then he threw the gown up over her head and heard her face hit the carpet.

This time she didn't scream. She hadn't the strength. She coughed twice and closed her eyes. Her arms trembled, and her legs twitched like the limbs of a lab animal suffering a slow dissection.

He could see her defeat before he touched her, and when he grabbed her hips to lift them, she was limp. But so was he. The struggle had cost him his erection. No matter. He wasn't worried. He'd get hard; he always got hard. He took out his razor and looked at all that creamy whiteness she kept hidden away. Already, he felt himself rising, the blood that rules, that rushes down and lifts him up. He poised right above her secret circle, and watched as more of that silky semen spread its web. He was sure his cock was like one of those flowers on a nature show where they speed up the film till it looks like the petals are reaching out to fuck the sun. He was just like that, growing larger and larger until it touched her crack. He got so excited he squeezed his muscles and made it bob up and down, over and over. Each time it rose it slapped his belly and an arc of semen flew loose, and each time it fell it struck her bottom and dampened her rigid flesh.

Celia had stayed still for what seemed like hours. He had spread her thighs open with his knee, and she had felt him growing in the dim light. There had been the brush of flesh against the inside of her leg, and the way the wet tip had come to rest on the warm space between her cheeks, like some animal finding its perch. Then he had started this . . . this *insane* game with his member. It smacked her over and over and made a dull wet sound.

It stopped moving as suddenly as it began. He let it rest there, in that place he preferred. His hands spread her cheeks open, and he started to press forward. She knew what he wanted and knew, too, that he'd tear his way in to get it. A horror deep and primitive overcame her, a fear much greater than herself, and she rammed back into him. His penis bent painfully before it sprang aside, and he reeled slightly as she rolled over and started kicking fiercely. She pulled her gown off her face and felt bone beating against bone—her heels, shins, and knees hitting those hard undaunted places on him— but she barely noticed the bruising contact. She pumped her legs madly and got lucky: her left foot struck him squarely on the throat, and she heard a harsh wheezing sound. His hands retreated, and she saw his chin drop to his chest. But she saw very little else because she was scrambling across the carpet and staggering to her feet. She made it to the bathroom and lashed at the door to try to shut it. It slammed with a shout—though whether from herself or the walls she could not tell—and then she fumbled away precious seconds trying to get it locked. She succeeded, but the lock wasn't much— a spring mechanism built into the handle itself—and she had no faith that it would hold.

49

Jack sat on the side of the bed and stared glumly at the floor. He'd promised Celia he'd call, so he called, but it didn't even ring, just a recording saying the phone was out of order. That didn't make any sense. They'd lived up there six years and they'd never had any problems with the phone.

Helen cuddled up to him and ran her fingernails down his back. He found her touch so irritating that she might just as well have been running them across a blackboard.

"Please stop." He shrugged her hand away.

"What's the matter?" she taunted. "She's not home and you're all worried?"

"No, it's not—"

"She's a big girl. Maybe she's having some fun of her own."

He turned around and offered Helen a pained look.

"I don't think so."

"That's probably what Ralph would say right now if someone asked him, and look at me, just full of your joy juice."

She lifted the sheet and exposed herself.

Jack turned away. "That's not it. I'm getting a recording saying the phone's out of order." He picked up the receiver. "I'm calling the operator."

Helen sat up and watched him with a bemused expression.

"Yes, operator, could you check 427-8053? That's right, Bentman."

He cupped the mouthpiece.

"I've got to know if something's wrong."

"You know what I think? I think you're feeling guilty now that you've had your fun."

He held up his hand to shush Helen and spoke to the operator.

"When can you get someone out there? No sooner? Okay, thanks."

He put the receiver down and massaged his brow. Helen squeezed his thigh.

"I've got a plan to take your mind off the old homestead."

He stood up and took a step away from the bed.

"No, please, let me think."

"Sure, sweetheart, go ahead, but don't think too much because the night's just begun."

She slid her hand up the back of his legs, and he jumped as if he'd been goosed. "Stop that!" He turned to face her. "I'm going back. Sorry."

"What!" She sat up.

"We've lived up there without any problems, and now we've got some jackass shepherd who's been making threats, and all of a sudden the phone stops working." He started to pace. "I'm telling you it doesn't feel right."

"So you're going to drive all the way back because of some stupid shepherd?"

He was already pulling on his shorts and pants. "You make it sound like a trip to the North Pole. It's only forty minutes, faster if I hurry."

Helen covered her breasts with the sheet. "I don't know if I'm going to be able to get away again anytime soon."

"I'm sorry." Actually, he was elated to hear this. "But I'd never be able to forgive myself if something was wrong up there."

"There's nothing wrong at your house, Jack, but there's definitely something wrong up there." She pointed to his head.

"What do you mean?" he said as if he had no interest whatsoever in her answer.

"You never really wanted to come here in the first place, and now you're using any excuse to leave."

"It's *not* an excuse." He recoiled when he heard the pleading tone in his voice. "I really want to make sure she's okay."

"See you Monday," Helen said curtly as she lay down and turned her back to him.

"Fine," Jack snapped. He grabbed his suitcase and rushed out the door, never pausing, not even once, over the woman—or the safety of the world—he was leaving behind.

50

Celia leaned against the full-length mirror hanging from the door and listened to Chet struggling to breathe. She felt no victory, only a penetrating sense of his revenge:

You hurt me, so I'll hurt you.

It was written all over him, in everything he had done and in everything he would do. She knew this as she knew the panic of this never-ending night.

But once more she'd found refuge, however slight, in a bathroom. As a child it had been the one place in the house where she could free herself from her mother's frightening outbursts, though she hadn't been permitted to lock the door.

"No, you may *not*," she'd told Celia. "If I want to come in and see what you're up to, I better not find that door locked. You hear me?"

But curiously, she hadn't come in. Oh, like any warder she'd jiggle the handle as she walked by, but even that stopped after a couple of weeks. Perhaps the prerogative alone had been enough to satisfy her.

Celia had always scheduled her solitude with care, preferring the afternoons to the mornings and evenings when her two sisters and mother busied themselves with the toilet and vanity. And if the rental had a second, less desirable, bathroom, she'd make certain to use it.

She would sit on the commode cover and read for thirty, forty minutes at a time, escaping the censorious comments of her mother; or worse, her cruelly inquisitive ones: "You think you're learning something I don't know? Don't kid yourself, dearie, there's nothing in those books of yours I haven't seen before. Nothing. What's this? What are you reading now?"

Celia would hand over the book dutifully, she wouldn't have dreamed of doing otherwise, and her mother would glance at the cover, maybe read a sentence or two from whatever page she had opened to.

"Good God, not another one of your ballerina stories. Don't you ever get tired of this crap?" She'd thrust the book back into Celia's hands. "Go ahead, finish it. Just don't go getting any ideas. You're already a little prima donna."

Celia lost herself in the childhoods of other girls, the ones who came to life page after page and who appeared far more inventive than she, for they always found a way out of their difficulties while Celia remained trapped year after year.

But as she grew older and her tastes in literature changed, she discovered ever more complex stories about grown-up women. In many of their troubled tales she found striking similarities to her own life; and for this she was grateful, to find reassurance and kindness in the company of strangers.

The bathroom had once been her sanctuary, inviolate and benign. Now it held her prisoner and thundered in silence.

With her legs still shaking, she searched for the light switch and flipped it on. The overhead made her squint, and she felt an almost blinding pain in her frontal lobes. She stood still until the pain began to fade, then turned around and faced the room, careful the entire time to keep her body pressed against the door. The coolness of the mirror came to life on her shoulder where her gown had been torn.

The shade over the tub window snagged her attention, and she thought about how he could break the glass and climb in after her. She remembered throwing the lock, but thought little of its protection now.

Her hands hung by her sides, and she reached back with her fingertips to touch the door, as if to steady what could shake and shudder and suddenly split apart. She sensed him slouching toward her, and she listened carefully for those rough choking sounds that had escaped his throat after she'd kicked him.

Nothing. He was quiet now. Was he still there, or had he slipped outside to find the window? She looked back at it. No face stared in. Not yet. She turned just enough to place her ear against the mirrored door when another chilling thought announced its rude arrival: he might also be listening, his horrible face a mere inch or so away. Nothing but the door separated them, and she knew it was piteously thin. It was a door, not a barricade, and what was a door? An illusion, a silly belief that you could close yourself off, that you and you alone could define what was yours. This was a lie, had always been a lie, and now stood as an invitation to mortal violation. There was no private domain. There was only invasion: first of space, then of self.

She heard him moving, a rumbling, low and relentless. His assault had just begun. He would not stop until he'd destroyed and defiled everything she had ever honored. Celia knew this as glass knows stone in the moment that explodes between them.

She swallowed with difficulty. Her throat did not want to work. She felt rigid, but not like rock, like ceramics—clay sculptures of club-footed creatures that stand for ages in dark corners and shatter to pieces in the frazzle of a single moment. The room turned small and suffocating. She'd locked the door, she'd locked the window, and now as she leaned stiffly against the mirror she realized that the very fear she had known earlier in the evening had come to pass: She had become a prisoner in her own bathroom, much as Davy was a prisoner in his own home. The saint for whom she'd been named—Saint Cecilia, the patron saint of music—had been sentenced to die in a bathroom for refusing to deny her faith. But she escaped, Celia reminded herself, she got away. Only to die—that's *right*—at the point of a sword.

Celia knew she *would* die before she'd let this man, this beast, take her in hand one more time.

Chet's jeans were down around his knees, and he almost tripped before he could pull them back up. His throat still hurt like hell, but nothing had been broken near as he could tell. He was breathing okay. The first minute or so after she kicked him it hurt so bad he thought he was going to choke to death, like there were metal bands down there cutting off his air. For awhile he'd actually stopped thinking about her. But his throat didn't feel so bad anymore, and even his hand had stopped throbbing. Best of all, she's in there, the fucking bathroom, and she sure as shit isn't going anywhere. He smiled when he realized this.

He switched on her bureau lamp and found her underwear drawer right away, the one filled with panties and bras in mostly pale colors, peach, baby blue, yellow, and some of them in that nude color too. And pink, like the pair he'd ripped apart. He remembered how good it felt to tear them to pieces. She had a whole drawerful of them. Underthings to cover her up and underthings to hold her up. But she sure as fuck doesn't need this.

He pinched a pink bra between his thumb and index finger, as if it might dirty him, and lifted it out of the drawer.

Goddamn . . . she doesn't *need* this.

He threw it on the ground and kicked it. Then he reached in and grabbed a fistful of panties and pressed them to his face. He took a deep breath. They felt soft and satiny and smelled of laundry soap, just like the pair he'd held up to his mouth a few days ago and moistened with his breath. He searched his hand. *This* pair. He dropped the others to the floor and held her pale underpants up to the light. He could see right through them. They ask for it. They really do. He threw it down with all the others and stomped them with his heel. They made him want to rip the gown right off her back. Make her stand naked in the night.

Celia thought she heard him open a drawer, but she couldn't be sure. She listened to a sudden flurry of movement. Yes, he's in there. Nevertheless, she glanced at the window. She feared he was everywhere.

He jiggled the handle, and she felt his brutal presence in the door. The lock held. She had been terrified it would spring open as soon as he touched it, like a tarantula that jumps into the air the moment it's approached. She was tempted to hold the handle—to try to steady it from her side—but her hands shook so badly she was afraid she'd pop the lock. And if she held it she'd be touching him too, for she would feel his madness through the metal, the hard cut of his darkest intentions.

The door now vibrated violently as he tried to wrench it open, and it took all of Celia's concentration to keep leaning against the jouncing mirror. He tried repeatedly to force his way in, but the handle held and the lock did not fail.

She thought of fleeing, of climbing through the window herself, but could not take the first step. She thought of fighting him, but knew she couldn't do that either. What Celia understood was neither flight nor fight, but the moment that hung eternally between them, that refused to relinquish either of its two terrifying options; that produced paralysis, frozen seconds that ticked off forever.

She was learning about fright, the way it could bite into the hardest bone and fill every hollow spot of hope with dread, with horror, with mortal resignation.

Bam!

She leaped away from the door. Her whole body shook. She looked down and saw the pointy tip of his boot sticking through the mirror just inches from where she'd been standing, no more than a foot and a half above the floor. Jesus.

Bam!

He kicked again, and the mirror crashed to the floor in a coruscating explosion. She stared at the pile of glistening shards and felt as though she were in someone else's bathroom living someone else's life. Nothing was right, everything was wrong. She looked up and saw the rectangular outline where the mirror had hung . . . and more of his boot sticking through the door.

She forced herself to step onto the broken glass and lean against the naked wood. The sickness in her stomach clotted. The door shook. It was hollow-core, cheap. It would never hold. Neither would she. That's what she believed—the weakness in the wood reflected a weakness in herself—that even as it splintered and broke apart, she too would fall from the fury of his attack.

She had just turned her head to scan the room for something—anything—when he grabbed her leg. She screamed and looked down and saw that he had stuck his hand through the hole he'd kicked in the door and was dragging her to the opening. His fingers were digging into the bones right above her knee and leaving red trails on her from the bite. She beat him with her fists but he did not let go. His grip only tightened. The pain was excruciating.

In seconds he had worked his hand all the way around to the back of her leg and turned her toward the door. His grip felt like a steel clamp, and he used enormous force to start pulling her knee through the hole. With terror, she saw that he was trying to drag her entire body through it. Splinters tore into her skin, and her torso was forced against the door, which shook without pause from his efforts. She tried to push away, but failed. It was horrifying to feel his hands and know that his raw hate and rank animal heat were little more than an inch away, and that all that stood between them was this flimsy hollow barrier, these two thin layers of wood and glue and screws. The hinges screamed—as if they might sheer off at any second—and the handle banged repeatedly into her hipbone. It was as though the mirrorless door had come to life like the blank face of evil, a vicious vibrating extension of him that shuddered with the grisly power of his every exertion.

He clawed at her and dragged her knee deeper and deeper into the hole, and then—with her leg bent at a sharp angle—she felt something so unbearably painful that it stunned her breath and rendered her lungs silent. He'd slashed her knee-cap with a blade, a deep metallic probe of bone. And again. The sudden pain shocked the urine right out of her system, but Celia was only dimly aware of the warm currents that ran down her legs. She was dying the horrible death she had always feared and could no longer think. She knew only an animal-like awareness of extinction and survival, and the savage gap that lay between them.

She beat the door with her fists and screamed and yanked on her leg with a fear she had never before known, and managed to break free of his slippery grasp.

She backed up over the broken glass and fixed her eyes on that hole like a child who has seen an apparition and knows the ghostly presence is real, ravenous, and ready to devour her. She looked down at her knee, drawn to it as a body is always drawn in a time of death—not to its life—but to its wounds, to the rough seepage that seals its fate.

Her kneecap was crimson with a wash of blood. It ran down her leg and puddled on both sides of her bare foot. She wiped it with her hand and revealed the cross, the two lines he had carved into her flesh. Their intersection was centered, the cuts almost even in length. She felt marked, stained and scarred with a demon's stigmata.

She looked up and saw his hand hanging there. Strangely, he had not pulled his arm back through the hole after she'd broken away from him. It was as if he didn't know fear. He pointed to her; and when he spoke it was spooky, as if his finger were actually talking and not the man himself hunkered down behind the door.

"I'm coming in. You hear me?"

Celia found herself nodding at the finger.

"You open this door and let me in and I won't hurt you. Or we can do it the hard way."

Celia was still nodding.

"You scared? There's no reason to be scared. I'm not angry. I've had dog bites worse than this."

He stopped pointing, and opened his hand. His palm was red, and she saw a dark purple color where her teeth had ripped apart the base of his thumb. He turned his hand over, and after a second's delay a flap of spongy flesh, held only by a hinge of skin, fell loose and dangled in the air. He made it jiggle; and Celia thought she'd be sick, not from the mutilation but from the strict memory of the bite itself, of lying on her back and having to fight like an animal to survive, only to find herself here, bleeding and wet and wounded, and faced with the thick chunk of tissue that had filled her mouth and made her gag. She could taste him still. He shook it again. Her stomach lurched.

"See, that's not so bad. So tell me, what's it going to be?"

Chet sounded pretty relaxed, and for good reason: he was enjoying himself immensely. He figured that no matter what happened, everything would work out just fine for him. One way or another, he'd have her. Nobody does this to me—he jiggled his hand again and felt the weight of the loose skin— and walks away. He knew that biting cut both ways.

You bite me and I'll bite you.

Celia stared at the wound. Once more, his hand just hung from the opening in the door, and for a full ten seconds it looked lazy and bloody and bored.

"Okay, don't say I didn't warn you."

He started to reach up and feel for the handle. That's when she heard Pluto, the same painful cry her cat had made when she'd accidentally stepped on its paw. But this was no accident, no accident at all.

Boyce withdrew his arm quickly, like a bloody animal burrowing into its hole. She heard a scuffling sound and a gut-wrenching scream from her cat. A hacking and gurgling. And then silence. Seconds later she watched as he stuffed Pluto through the hole. He had to shove the cat's hind end in first, and he held him by the back of his neck. He'd slit Pluto's throat from ear to ear. The fur on his chest was soaked with blood. He'd also gouged out his one eye, and the gaping socket cried a red stream that ran down his shiny nose and spattered the broken glass. She saw her cat's fractured reflection in the zigzag pieces of mirror on the floor. Insanely, Boyce started bouncing Pluto up and down on his rear paws, as if he were trying to make the dead cat dance.

Maybe he was. She heard him humming the same maniacal tune over and over. It was all of madness, the sounds mixing with the night, demanding attention even as she stared at the gory spectacle: Pluto's eyeless head rising and falling, its limp legs touching down on the glass, its matted fur dripping bright red spots all over the broken mirror, its belly sagging and front paws sticking straight out in the stiff-armed pose of Frankenstein.

Chet hummed to himself. He heard his little ditty clearly in his mind and had no idea that it had passed from his lips. When he knew for certain that she'd been listening, he stopped and shook his head. He didn't *want* to share it with her; it was a private pleasure, and now she knew. She would pay for this too.

He dropped Pluto's body onto the glass, and withdrew his arm. A moment later he reached back in and flipped the cat's eyeball at Celia. It struck her nightgown just above the waist and fell to the tile, making a distinctly moist sound, like a wad of wet toilet paper. She gripped her belly, bent over, and fought her nausea. When she looked up, still shaking, his arm once more hung from the hole in the door. Fresh red streaks ran from his fingers up to his elbow. A paralyzing fear left her almost breathless: He'll rape me with his fist. She lived this terror so single-mindedly that she didn't notice Pluto for several seconds.

Her cat hissed softly, trembled, and started to stand. She was shocked he was still alive. The eyeless creature tottered on his front paws and dripped more blood onto the bed of broken glass. His head turned in Celia's direction—she was sure it did—before swinging down and to the side like a drunk's. Pluto raised one rear leg before slipping on the slick surface and finally collapsing.

"Where do you think you're going?"

Boyce's hand clamped around Pluto's neck.

"No!" Celia screamed. "Leave him alone."

He picked up her cat and slammed him back down. A noise escaped Pluto's mouth, and Celia cried out when she heard it. Boyce gloried in her reaction and beat her cat savagely against the shattered mirror until the broken pieces scattered across the tile. He pounded Pluto into the floor with so much force that Celia heard the cat's bones breaking from several feet away. When Boyce had finished, he flipped Pluto's body toward her. It landed like a bag of marbles. Red bubbles trilled from its black lips.

Boyce lay on the floor outside the door and stared at her through the hole. Then he reached out and picked up a piece of glass. He flicked it at her and watched her jump. That's right, jump, goddamn it, JUMP. Another piece. And another. Like he'd flicked matches at that ugly retard when he was a kid, all the way home from school. Watching her cry until finally he'd taken the whole fucking pack and lit them all at once and pushed them into her frizzy fucking hair and listened to it sizzle. He could still smell her burning. It smelled great.

He pulled his arm out of the hole, but kept looking in. Celia could make out only the roughest circle of his face, but his grin was apparent in the crinkling of skin around his eyes and in the slightly upraised movement of his sharp-edged nose, as if these two senses—along with all the others—were slow-dancing with death.

She touched her wet face and realized she was weeping. She wanted to ball herself up and never see or hear anything again. If she could have climbed into life's womb, she would have done so and never looked back. She was starting to go numb.

Boyce's features disappeared, and his hand came through the hole and reached for the handle, stretching and straining and gaining inches with his efforts. His fingers were almost upon it when she saw the veins in his arm and remembered how the serious suicides did it: they sliced themselves open the long way. They were usually the older kids who had been shuffled from one foster home to another, the thirteen- and fourteen-year-olds who were already homeless, who found a flop for a week or two before they were forced to move on— the children who wanted no part of life and were trying to end it as quickly as they could.

She ripped open the cabinet door right below the sink and searched frantically for the razor blade they'd used to scrape paint off the bathroom window just two weeks ago. She found it lying off to the side and picked it up carefully.

She studied Boyce's arm. It looked like sculpted stone with ropy veins that rose like ridge lines on a topographical map.

She held out the razor nervously. She was standing close to him but not close enough. Come on, she urged herself, do it. Do it. Do it before he kills you. Do it before he does it to you.

She trained her eyes on a big purple vein that ran along the outer part of his forearm. That's where she would start the cut—close to his wrist—and where she would end it— down by his elbow. She would open him up with one long slice, and then hack his arm as he pulled it away.

She stepped over Pluto's body and moved within inches of Boyce's hand. She lifted the razor, swallowed, and almost choked on her dry throat. It felt as if she'd inhaled a corn husk, and as she worked her mouth to try to find some moisture his arm suddenly straightened and his hand brushed her gown. He immediately lunged for her, and she jumped back and slipped on the bloody tile, dropping the razor as she reached for the edge of the vanity to keep from falling. He quickly withdrew his arm and kicked the door again, widening the hole. She backed up all the way to the tub and stepped into it as his arm snaked through the opening. Her feet burned, and she saw her red footprints on the floor, the yellow water too. The tub felt slippery, and the blood looked especially bright on the shiny white surface.

She raised the window shade and looked at the latch, the same one she'd fastened hours earlier.

He's coming in. I've got to get out.

Her thoughts were that simple. She looked back at the door and saw that his hand had disappeared.

Bam!

Now the hole was huge, the size of a dog door.

Jesus, can he get through that? Celia tore at the latch but failed to open it.

"Where... do... you... think... you're... going?" The same words he'd used with her cat, but slower this time, and grim, like her mother when she was angry. He peered through the hole, and she could see his entire face, no longer handsome but horrifying. His dark eyes held her as he started to laugh.

He's crazy, she thought. *Out of his fucking mind.*

But Celia was swirling around her own form of madness, the prairie fire of fear that filled her with terror for she now knew her greatest nightmare: not that he would kill her but that he would drive her insane. Already she sensed a hard truth: a mean understanding of mutilation as the underbelly of everything.

She wept over this and fought to see the world as it really was, and she succeeded at this intimidating task, though her only reward was reality and this proved terrifying too: his eyes, the hole in the door, the broken bloody mirror, her cat crumpled like an old rug, the red streaks on the tile, the yellowish puddle, and the razor blade she had dropped.

"Hey, what's that?" He had spotted the razor and pointed to it. "Were you going to cut me?" Chet stared at it. He remembered how his arm had been hanging out there with no protection, none. *And she was going to cut me. Fair is fair, she'll find out.*

He reached down and twirled it around his fingers as a magician will a coin, sliding it over his knuckles until it felt as smooth as oil. He paused only briefly to test the sparkle of its edge, and then resumed the rolling motion as he talked.

"I'm going to have to cut you up, you know that, right? I mean, fair is fair."

Celia didn't say a word. She watched the way he kept moving the razor around. It was a mean trick. He stopped suddenly and held it pinched between his thumb and index finger, like a tiny tomahawk, with that single sharp vertical edge facing her.

"I'm going to scalp you." He laughed. "What do you think of that?"

Celia kept her silence.

"I don't hear you saying anything now, Mrs. Griswold, but I'll bet you had plenty to say about Davy's pictures, didn't you? You thought you had it all figured out, didn't you?"

She could not hide the tremor in her voice: "You do things to him, you touch him, don't you?" She nodded heavily, almost uncontrollably, and noticed that her whole body was shaking terribly.

"I don't do anything the boy doesn't like."

"You're a liar!" she screamed, and her fists pounded the air in front of her. "You lie to him, to me, you lie to yourself."

Chet's voice never changed pitch, never grew angry. "I'm going to make you a promise right now, Mrs. Griswold. You want to know what that promise is?"

She stared at his hand as he continued to toy with the razor.

"I promise that you'll never see the light of day, and that by the time I'm through with you, you won't want to. Now *that's* a promise, Mrs. Griswold . . . and I always keep my promises."

His hand moved quickly to the door knob. His kicks had enlarged the hole, and now he had no trouble reaching the handle. Desperately, she tried to open the window latch. Her hands shook badly and slipped, and her shoulder fell against the glass. She looked back and saw him turning the knob. She wasn't going to make it. There's a point in most murders when the victims know it's over, when they understand that they can continue to struggle but they can't continue to survive. This was Celia's moment. She knew he was coming in, and when the door lock sprang open she no longer had any possible doubt.

She stabbed at the window latch convulsively with the heel of her hand, but with no real hope of escape. It surprised her when it gave way. In a single frenzied moment she slid the window up, punched out the screen, and hoisted herself onto the sill. She heard sounds a few feet behind her—the sweep of broken glass, her dead cat kicked out of the way—as she hurled herself headfirst toward the deck.

He might have grabbed her foot as she fell out the window, she couldn't be sure. She rolled across the redwood and fell to the ground. Nausea flooded her entire body as she hoisted herself up and raced madly down the driveway on unstable legs. Crunching sounds from the gravel shadowed her every step, and at any moment she expected him to drag her down from behind; but the noises came from her own bloodied feet. She realized this only after she'd run halfway to the county road and stopped. She had to. She could no longer choke down the vomit surging through her system. She spilled her stomach onto the dry vegetation and tried mightily not to gag. As she leaned over, drool dripping from her lips, she saw the lights in the living room go on. Her hand shook as she wiped her mouth, and so did the branch when she moved it aside for a better look. Boyce's head passed by the kitchen window; he appeared to be searching for something.

She noticed again how badly her legs shook. The soles of her feet had been tortured by the glass and now by the gravel. A sharp pain throbbed in her right heel, and she held it up in the moonlight to examine it closely. A bloody sliver of glass protruded from the very back, and she eased out the two-inch length slowly, suffering the sharp pain in silence. She knew she couldn't run any farther. The wounds in her feet she might be able to bear, but the agony in her knee only worsened as she stood there.

She spotted the flashlight beam as he opened the front door. It moved back and forth, and she figured he'd found the one they kept on the kitchen counter. He didn't seem to know which way she'd fled, and she tried hard to quiet her heavy breathing.

Chet couldn't see her, but this didn't bother him as much as smashing his head against the window frame when he'd tried to grab her goddamn foot. He'd slipped on the floor—

fucking blood—and he figured that little miscue had cost him at least half a pint. She'd got his hand and now his goddamn head. He wiped his brow and saw that he was still bleeding. That's the way it was with head wounds, they bled a lot. He knew about these things. Bashing himself like that had also cost him a few precious seconds, and then he'd made another mistake by not watching to see exactly which way she ran. It was just like the fuckup he'd made when she was out walking around in the goddamn woods. He was taking too much for granted, and he cursed himself roundly. But he'd found her quick enough then, and he figured to do the same thing again. He knew for a fact that she didn't have a prayer, not out there, not by herself.

"Time, time, time is on my side . . ."

He moved the flashlight back and forth and followed the beam carefully. He saw lots of trees and lots of scrub. That's okay, he told himself, because sooner or later I'll see her. Don't worry, Mrs. Griswold. I'm coming. You can't hide forever.

"Time, time, time, is on my side, yes it is . . ."

51

Jack roared down the highway at ninety miles an hour. He glanced at the speedometer and pressed even harder on the accelerator. Straight stretch, no problem. Besides, he reassured himself, the moon's got the whole world lit up like a power plant.

He'd scanned the radio for company, but the only station he'd found—other than Bentman's KLOG, never an option—was playing a Saturday night "oldies" show. He loathed them, but he listened. He loathed them because certain songs could play in his head for days, like the ditty he'd just heard:

"B-I-N-G-O, B-I-N-G-O, B-I-N-G-O, and Bingo was his name-O!"

But he listened because even the most insipid songs could bring back memories of his youth that even a young lover could not compete with.

Then there were the songs that left him empty with ache, that he could barely endure but never turned off, like "Heart and Soul." Every time he heard it he remembered his sister as a gangly eleven-year-old plinking out the notes on an old upright piano. She passed away three years ago from breast cancer, and Jack still mourned the loss.

Other songs made him think of Celia, the early years, and he longed for those times too, before he started cheating on her. The marriage had never been the same after that, not for him. He'd wanted it to be, but it never was. You can't reclaim the virginity of your passion. He'd read that in a self-help book back in Chicago and had been condemned to remember it always.

He snapped out of his sad reveries when he heard that a "big hit" by Burt Bacharach was coming up. He'd always liked his music, especially the one that goes, *"Raindrops keep falling on my head . . ."*

But first there was a commercial for chewing gum, then another for shampoo. And another . . . and another. He leaned back, saw that he'd topped ninety-five, and looked for the turnoff for Bentman. Any minute now. He would hug Celia as soon as he walked in the door, no matter how late it was, and he would love her as he never had before. They *would* have children, a family, a life. He could not amend the past but they could have a new beginning.

He glanced once more at the dash and saw that he was approaching one hundred. Better slow down. But something else caught his eye, and he looked back at his left hand, which held the steering wheel, and saw that his wedding ring was missing.

"Goddamn it!" He pounded the wheel so hard it vibrated. After picking up the ring at the office on the way out of town, he'd left it behind at the Bear Haus. Jesus! He eased up on the gas and debated whether to go back. The turnoff for Bentman appeared up ahead on his right. He really wanted everything to be perfect with Celia, and she would notice the missing ring. She sure did last night. And then he'd have to lie again. He was sick of lying to her.

He could always go back and get it. It wasn't as if she was expecting him to walk in the door anytime soon. But another hour and a half of driving? In the middle of the night? The pickup slowed to fifty-five as he tried to decide: Home . . . or back to Helen?

52

Celia was still shaking as she ducked behind the young fir trees that lined the driveway. She watched the monster on the deck as all prey watch the creatures that stalk them, and slowly understood that more than their respective positions had changed: In the bathroom she had been trapped like an animal, now she would be hunted like one.

But long ago she'd learned about hate, how to keep *more* than an arm's reach away from its grip. She'd spent years skulking around her mother's house, slipping into corners, closets, slipping out, listening intently for her mother's footsteps on the stairs, on the carpet, and learning to read their mood as one reads the clouds for the disposition of the sky. All of this came into focus as she stood bent and bleeding on the long dirt driveway, for she wondered if the battering she'd suffered as a child had made tonight inevitable, had hung an invisible sign on her back that said, *"Go ahead, hit me, beat me, fuck me, kill me."*

Maybe it had been so from the start. Maybe her father had indeed raped her mother and left that pathetic woman stewing in his sweat and semen. Conceived in violence, destined for murder. Celia saw the abysmal symmetry and shuddered because it suddenly made perfect, perverse sense. If there was such a thing as fate, then she would die tonight. Raped, beaten, murdered. She understood the truth of this even as the air cooled her skin, the blood clotted her wounds, even as that flashlight carved up the darkness. But she also knew that more than anything she wanted to live, and that she had to think clearly.

She figured that from where he stood Boyce could see the two obvious directions in which she could have fled: down the driveway—the path she had chosen—or toward the woodshed to the right of the house. That's where she and Jack had stacked the red fir, and where, she remembered, the small ax for kindling lay buried in a log. For several seconds she wished she'd run to the weapon. She even imagined using it on him, but she knew better than to believe in her revenge. The ax would never have yielded to her anger, for that would have meant closing in on him, gripping the handle tightly, and driving the sharp edge into his skull; and she knew she couldn't do that. All she wanted was to get away from him. She was so thankful that she'd retreated from the house that she performed a ritual she hadn't thought about in twenty years: she blessed herself with the sign of the cross. Her gesture was so reflexive that she didn't realize what she was doing until she had done it. All those Saturdays in the confessional—*Bless me, Father, for I have sinned*—and all those Sundays at communion—*In the name of the Father, the Son, and the Holy Ghost*—had made their presence known.

Through the thick tangle of trees she saw the beam moving, scanning, and knew without question that it was better to flee than to fight.

She decided that if he did walk toward the woodshed, she would start hiking to town on an old logging road about a quarter of a mile away, the first of many dirt roads back in the hills and forests to the north of their house. It was terribly overgrown, crowded along both sides by dense vegetation, and the drought had parched much of it, but if she remembered correctly the trees and bushes would be thick enough to hide her. A huge pine marked the point where she could find her way onto the road. She doubted it had been driven in years, and wasn't entirely sure she could find her way to town once she entered its labyrinth. But that should be easy, she told herself. Just keep going downhill. Everything flows to town—the rivers, streams, even the roads. They must. Right?

But what if he comes this way? She posed this question as she eyed the distant flashlight. Then what? She didn't have a ready answer. The very thought of him walking toward her almost froze her with fear. Maybe the logging road anyway. If I can disappear onto it before he gets to me. But she had serious doubts: her feet had been shredded by the broken mirror, and her knee throbbed. She touched the deep gashes and realized they'd always be there, hard ridges of scar tissue in the shape of a cross. You should be so lucky, she said to herself. And she knew this was true: the cuts on her knee would mean little if she could survive, nothing more than small scars in a life that now knew much bigger ones.

She tried flexing her leg but shooting pains made her stop almost immediately. She kept it straight and tried weighting it. There, that's better. At least I can move. But can you run? She considered this question for no more than an instant before knowing that she could not.

Yet she remembered running from the house, and realized that only the anesthesia of fear had made this possible. Better to drag her leg into darkness than ever to know that kind of terror again.

But you're getting ahead of yourself, she thought. Let's see what happens. Just wait and see.

She didn't have to wait long.

The flashlight bobbed as he stepped off the deck. She heard a loud hissing sound, almost a whistle. Then another, and another. Finally a fourth before she understood that he'd slashed the tires on her car.

He took a few steps and stopped. She held her breath. "The woodshed," she whispered to herself, "go to the woodshed." The flashlight moved back and forth as if he couldn't decide, and then he started down the driveway. Oh Jesus. She took three limping steps and knew she'd never make it to the logging road. Now that he was walking toward her, it seemed miles away. And he'll hear me. She saw how her bum leg would drag on the gravel as it had here in the brush.

She looked around, painfully aware of the spot of light growing larger and larger, shifting from side to side as he searched, and searched, and searched. For her. She could almost hear his footsteps. She didn't know what to do. Her head twisted everywhere at once, and that's when she spotted it no more than fifteen feet away. It sat in the moonlight like a dark lesion in the earth.

No, she shook her head. No way. I can't.

But the flashlight now threw a bright beam. She saw it penetrating the night, peering here and peering there, pausing as he stared at a branch or behind a tree, and continuing on. She imagined the light shining on herself in another minute or two. His footsteps became clearer. He was closing in. When she could delay no more—when it might have been too late already—she limped through the moon shadows, lifted the heavy wooden cover, and slipped quietly into the tank.

53

When Celia closed the cover, a thin slice of moonlight penetrated the tank just enough to let her see the dark surface of the water, which appeared flat, unruffled by the lumpy dead rats they'd discovered two weeks ago. She found the water surprisingly cold considering how warm the days had been, and she shivered as she pumped her arms and legs to stay afloat. She also felt uneasy and exposed when her gown drifted up around her bottom.

She listened constantly for him, but mostly she was so relieved to have found a hiding place that it was only after she'd been in the tank a minute or two that she wondered how she'd get out. She'd had to let go of the housing to slide in, and now she wished they'd been patient enough to fill the tank all the way up.

She was thinking about this when a claw brushed her ankle. She jerked her foot away so fast that a piercing pain shot through her knee. Then a tail slithered like an eel across her instep, and she took a sharp breath—the rats! Oh Jesus, they're here, the *rats!*

She was afraid to move, but had to tread water. And her knee hurt. God, did it hurt. Seconds later her big toe struck a bloated body. The fur gave under the impact, and she touched bone, the hard parts that had not rotted. She moaned—she could not help herself. Another rat slid across her bottom like a snake and settled against the crack of her behind. She squeezed her buttocks together and turned in the water. She felt its snout bump against her hip. As she pushed it away, its hard little head struck her elbow and she shuddered. They're attacking me. They're *attacking* me! She remembered how horrible those creatures looked floating in the water, their bloated bodies, tiny teeth, and long naked tails, hairless stringy things that trailed through all the dark dirty places where they lived and ate and dribbled their waste in sour little bundles.

No, they're *not* attacking you. They're not. They're dead. She ordered herself to breathe. *Breathe*. She used the same techniques she'd taught the children at the Center: I am breathing in. I am breathing out. Breathing in. Breathing out. In. Out. But she couldn't stop thinking of the rats. They were down there. All of them. Somewhere. Waiting, waiting, waiting. Waiting for her.

And he was waiting too. Out there. She saw his face, the way he'd looked at her through the hole in the door, how he reached for the razor she'd dropped and twirled it around his fingertips, then held the blade straight up so she couldn't help but see its sharp shiny edge: the cruel manner of a man who knows how to play with panic.

She heard his footsteps and listened intently as they grew louder, though they weren't very loud at all, a *crunch-crunch-crunch* that told her he was still walking down the driveway. She caught a blink of the flashlight beam in the corner of the tank, but it disappeared and the moon's milky rays returned.

Celia heard his footsteps grow softer, and she breathed more easily. Her chest had been as tight as baling wire. She had just begun to worry about the rats again when he called out her name:

"Mrs. Gris*woooold*."

He sounded as if he was really enjoying himself. She guessed he was at least forty or fifty feet away, somewhere down near the entrance to their property. His voice turned even more playful now:

"Come out, come out, wherever you are."

Celia shook her head and continued to tread water, but her legs slowed from the effort. They felt weighted, and her knee still ached as if it were filled with venom. The real possibility of drowning stabbed at her through all this darkness and all this fear.

But she wouldn't let him do that to her. Fuck him. *Fuck* him!

It was bad enough that he'd forced her into this filth but she'd be damned if she'd let him kill her. There had to be a way out of here. She pictured the tank in daylight. The last time she'd been out here was that Sunday two weeks ago when she'd tried to seduce Jack. She remembered how he'd rebuffed her when she peeled down her shorts to show him her sexy new panties. She'd been so ready, ovulating—she'd taken her temperature for months, seen it dip and seen it rise and kept the charts just as she was supposed to—and he'd been no more interested in her than the beautiful young men of the Portland Gay Men's Chorus. Last weekend she practically had to drag him into bed, and for what? One of the clumsiest sessions they'd ever had. His half-baked hard-on flopped out of her twice before he finally managed to come. What an ordeal. He'd worked so hard and for so long that she'd honestly feared he'd have a heart attack. He'd been in what she privately dubbed his "major concentration mode," no longer kissing and caressing her but gripping her buttocks like life preservers and straining like a man more apt to give birth himself than to deliver a spoonful of semen. She wondered what went through his head at times like that. Did he even think about her, or was it a kind of masturbation, with her body providing little more than the lubricant (and scant amounts of that by the time he was through)?

And then, as she treaded that dark dirty water, a staggering possibility struck her: she *might* be pregnant. Jack had, after all, climaxed; and she'd been careful to lie on her back for a full hour, determined to soak up every bit of that hard-earned seed. No period yet, either.

Pregnant? *Jesus!*

That possibility flooded her with renewed determination. At this time in her life she wanted nothing more than to be a mom, and she could be well on her way; but if that bastard out there got his hands on her she'd never even have the chance to find out.

"No way, no way," she repeated breathlessly as she pumped her legs. She recalled what Renata had said at the workshop on protecting yourself. She'd told them to avoid retreating whenever possible, and then she'd wanted to know how many of them skied. Most of them had raised their hands, including Celia. Renata had said that dealing with angry clients was just like hitting the steeps: you had to stay forward and attack the mountain. "You've got to take control." She'd said that two or three times. Also, "Work with whatever you've got," and "Get in their face."

Okay, okay, thought Celia, chilled and tired, but what do I have to work with in here? And how the hell am I going to get in his face?

She shook in frustration, and listened as Boyce began to retrace his steps. Again the *crunch-crunch-crunch* as he drew nearer. Again, her legs treaded water that felt thicker and thicker. The rats had floated away, maybe from her efforts, but she was growing colder and weaker by the moment. She recalled that hypothermia made you stupid before it killed you—drained blood from your brain just as fear did—and she worried that she would make some simple-minded mistake that would reveal her hiding place.

Her hands searched the slick plastic wall for something to hold on to; her leaden legs needed a rest. But she couldn't find purchase anywhere. She tried to reach up to the housing, but it was at least a foot beyond her outstretched hand, and as her arm came down she slipped under the water for the first time. She had to fight back to the surface and found herself desperately short of breath and gasping for air. Maybe that's why it took her a full second to feel the dead weight of the filthy beast draped over her head, and the naked tail brushing against her lips.

She ripped the rat off her head, felt its spongy sodden body in her hand, and threw it to the side. She heard it splat against the wall like a wet towel as she gasped again and gulped a mouthful of the foul water. She spat it out, and coughed and gagged with revulsion. Then she worried about *him*, had he heard her? She listened to his footsteps, louder now. Keep pumping your legs, she urged herself, keep pumping. *Don't give up.* You can hike for miles, you can do this. She was counseling herself and paying strict attention to the lazy way he had of walking when she saw herself standing by the tank with Jack, before she'd made her overture, talking about whether it could get clogged up. Of course, the intake line. It's back there. She looked over her shoulder. Somewhere.

Slowly, reluctantly, with the sure knowledge that her legs could not last forever no matter how much she willed them to, Celia made her way around the tank. She dreaded running into the rats and didn't want to touch anything in that foul darkness down below, that bottomless well of water where she hoped the beasts were buried. Her stomach muscles and buttocks were balled into knots, clenched like fists against all that was cold, dark, and dead. She moved slowly, as if through a swamp. She heard him walking by on the driveway, cocky, she thought, like he's king of the roost; and as she listened to him draw closer she got angrier.

She guessed she was near the intake line, reached out, and found the heavy rubber tube. She also found a spider web. She tried to shake it off, couldn't, and plunged her hand into the water.

She grabbed on to a clear spot, and finally rested. What a relief. Now she could wait him out. Her body followed the lead of her arm and drifted toward the line. But as she drew closer she had to endure a new horror when her legs parted a jellied mass of fur. In the midst of this she also felt something sharp, and knew with a sickening dread that these were the claws scraping her skin as the rat bodies swirled up around her. Dozens of claws, dozens of tails, dozens of dead rats eddying around her legs and bottom and belly and breasts.

She choked down her terror and squeezed the intake line to keep from screaming. She had all she could do to bear her silence, and then she heard it. A squeak-squeak. Again, squeak-squeak. Slowly she turned her head to the side and looked right into the beady eyes of a live rat crouched on a brace for the intake line. A sliver of reflected moonlight revealed its whiskers twitching no more than six inches from her face. Suddenly it rose up on its hind legs, bared its horrible teeth, and clawed at the air between them. Celia gasped audibly and pushed away, and that's when she noticed that Chet had stopped moving.

54

Jack drove up the winding road to the ridge. Yes, he would go home, and if Celia asked him about the ring he would lie to her one more time. But a white lie. He'd tell her that on the way out of town he'd forgotten to stop by the office to pick it up. She'd believe him. Sure she would. She was always giving people the benefit of the doubt. God knows, it had worked in his favor more than once. Then he'd hope like hell that Helen would be considerate enough to return the damn thing when she came to work on Monday. She was, after all, still an employee.

He reached the ridge and started south, marveling over the beauty of the clear night sky and full moon. He knew the road well and once more pressed hard on the gas pedal. He took the curves like a pro, whipping up curtains of dust with each quick turn of the wheel. He whizzed by the stumps that only a week ago stood as proud ancient pines, and sped toward the meadow. Here he was coming home *earlier* than expected. Why, in mere minutes he would hold his wife in his arms and know the comforts of home. He couldn't wait to see the look on her face. These warm, happy thoughts left him so distracted that he didn't see the lamb until it was too late. He slammed on the brakes but heard a distinct thump as he skidded to a stop. Then a pathetic bleating overpowered a song by Jim Croce as a plume of dust drifted over the truck.

He turned off the radio and sat there grimacing, about to get out and inspect the damage (he figured the fender might be banged up pretty bad) when he saw sheep looming through the billowing cloud. The entire flock had risen from the meadow and started wandering over to the truck, their long lugubrious faces staring vacantly at him. Up ahead the moonlight also revealed a man stepping out of the shadows. He quickly joined the woolly procession. This had to be the odd-ball shepherd Celia had told him about. Jack reached for his wallet, figuring on making a quick on-the-spot settlement. How much could a lamb cost, assuming it was a total loss? It *sounds* like it. The creature's constant—and *murderous*—bleating was beginning to get on his nerves.

He hoped the shepherd didn't prove overly sentimental about animals. That could drive up the cost of this little mishap. Jack saw that he had five twenties, a ten, and some singles. More than enough, unless the shepherd tried to get greedy. Just let him. He knew how to handle injured parties who tried to press their luck. He had long experience with *those* kinds of people. You just had to set limits, *firm* limits.

When he finished counting his money he saw that the shepherd had made his way past the flock and now stood in front of the pickup staring at the injured lamb. Jack could see him clearly in the headlights, a strange-looking man with a big fuzzy beard and lots of hair. Actually, a *grotesque*-looking man. Jack changed his opinion the moment the shepherd turned his eyes on him, and if he knew anything about human nature—and as an insurance salesman he prided himself on having a keen sense about people—the shepherd was not a happy man. Jack had seen the same expression on the faces of certain policyholders when they picked up their claim checks and learned for the first time what "pro-rated" *really* meant.

As the shepherd started walking up to the cab, Jack's urge to dicker with him vanished just like that. Poof, it was gone. Now his only urge was to peel right out of there, but the flock blocked his way, and even if they didn't it would mean running over the lamb. Of course, that *would* put an end to its incessant bleating.

He decided after seeing the shepherd's grim face that he wouldn't even get out of the truck. He'd crack the window an inch or two, and see how it went. Celia had said he was a weird one. No sense taking chances.

He glanced at the door lock, relieved to see it in place, and forced himself to smile at the . . . well . . . *angry*-looking man standing beside the cab.

"Hi," Jack said, managing a perky tone that he hoped would ease the tension.

"What happened?" the shepherd slurred.

Oh great, Jack thought, drunk *and* stupid.

"One of your sheep was wandering around the middle of the road, and I guess I must have hit it. I'm sorry. I didn't mean—"

"You must have been moving faster than a rooster in the henhouse." The shepherd swayed as he spoke.

"No, not at all. It was out in the middle of the road," Jack repeated. "I tried to stop, I did, but it was too late." He felt silly talking through the cracked window and knew it made him look fearful, so he rolled it down. But he regretted this when the shepherd cozied up to the door.

"What the hell you doing up here anyway?" He scratched his beard. "It's the middle of the night."

"What am I doing up here? I *live* here."

"You do?" the shepherd asked keenly.

"Yes, I do," Jack insisted, mistaking the shepherd's interest for awe. "I've got a place up the road a couple miles from here. With some acreage," he added with noticeable self-regard.

The shepherd nodded. "You also got yourself a little lady that drives a little car?" He leaned his head right in the window, and the cab filled with the stench of cheap wine and rotting teeth.

Even as he willed himself to be still, to be silent, Jack felt himself nodding and realized he'd been had.

"So you're the one"—the shepherd poked Jack's shoulder—"that took little Bucky to the pound."

"Little Bucky?"

"Yeah, you are. You're the one all right." He rested his hand on the back of Jack's neck. His grip felt as dry and rough as the inside of a peanut shell. "It's a funny thing, ain't it?"

"How's that?" Jack said nervously.

"How you do one dumb thing and it makes you do another."

"What do you mean?" Jack figured as long as he could keep him talking the shepherd wouldn't do anything with that goddamn hand. He tried to shrug it off gently, but failed.

"You go and take little Bucky to the pound for no good reason and get him killed, just like that." He snapped his fingers, a sound as hollow as the hole in Jack's stomach. "And me? I don't have no one watching my sheep at night." His hand returned to Jack's neck, grasping it even harder. "So one of the little ones goes wandering off and you run him over with your damn truck." He looked toward the front of the pickup where the lamb continued to bleat piteously. "You know what's gonna happen now, don't you?"

"I think so. I pay you?"

"Yeah, that's right," the shepherd said with sudden anger. "You pay."

55

This time the light in the corner of the tank did not disappear. It remained steady, a star that never blinks on a night that never ends. Celia listened intently as the *crunch-crunch-crunch* of gravel turned into a softer, much more menacing sound: the crackle of boots crushing dry grass. Then the wooden cover opened, and he pointed the flashlight right at her. After so much darkness, she had to look away.

He threw what appeared to be a heavy sack into the tank. It made a big splash, and several seconds passed before she could make out Pluto's body floating in front of her.

"When the cat's away, the mice will play."

Chet started laughing. He was damn near giddy. This was as good as it gets. Finding her here was a goddamn gift or something.

He could just make out her gown drifting up around her body, but not much else. Fucking water is *dark*. That's okay, she's not going anywhere. Helpless, that's what she is. No more of this running around, no more misbehaving on me.

He shook his head reproachfully, which she saw in the haloing light. But when he spoke he tried to make a joke about her bathing for him.

"Nice of you," he added.

She didn't respond.

"I guess I could leave you in there, but that wouldn't be any fun." Chet was wild with joy. He'd never known a woman to be so completely at his mercy. This was as good as it gets.

She treaded water and the dead rats swirled around her body, their fur as slimy as egg whites. She cringed. He saw this.

"Pretty cold down there?"

Again, she did not respond. She watched Pluto drifting away and felt a sudden need to hold her cat. But she shouldn't show weakness. Not now, not here, not with him. She had to take control . . . *somehow* . . . and give this man everything he'd earned. *Everything*.

"Help me," she pleaded. "Help me out of here."

56

Little Bucky come back and bit you right on the ass, didn't he?''

.The shepherd leered at Jack, who was sitting on the ground in no condition to respond. The first kick had nailed him in the stomach and knocked the wind right out of him. That came *after* the shepherd had dragged him out of the pickup. Other kicks to the back, chest, legs, and head had followed, along with a vicious punch to his jaw that had loosened a molar and finally landed him on his butt about twenty feet from the truck.

Now he hugged his aching ribs, which competed with his aching back for most of his attention. The shepherd staggered sideways as he tried to straighten out what looked like a length of wire he'd pulled from the rear pocket of his filthy jeans.

Christ, that asshole's strong, but Jack could also tell that the shepherd was drunk and definitely had trouble standing up straight. He'd mumbled something about tying him up, which no doubt explained whatever he was doing with that wire. But Jack knew he would resist this to the death because he had no intention of letting this scummy shepherd wire his hands and feet together so he could slowly torture him over some dead dog and a stupid lamb. At least the woolly critter had finally shut up. Thank God. Maybe it was dead too. They're just animals, for Christ's sakes. But Jack could see there would be no reasoning with Mr. Personality.

The shepherd lurched forward, and Jack flinched.

"Put your hands behind your back." Or words to that effect. The alcohol had tangled up his tongue.

Sweet Jesus, here we go. Jack's entire body washed with adrenaline because this . . . *this* he would not do.

"Why?" His voice cracked and he sounded as if he was whining. He hated himself for this.

"Why?" The shepherd repeated Jack's question with considerably more force, despite his drunken state. " 'Cause I want you that way. Hands back here. Come on, come on."

Incredibly, he gestured impatiently at Jack, like a tired cop about to cuff some miscreant. He even prodded him with his foot. Jack wanted to snap it right off his leg.

The shepherd moved behind him, and when Jack felt him reach for his hands he twisted around, lunged for his legs, and managed to tackle him. He flushed with the sudden victory of seeing the stunned shepherd on his back. Now he pounded him like a man possessed. He saw his opportunity and drove his fist right into the shepherd's crotch. With the sweetest satisfaction he'd ever known he crushed that soft sack with his knuckles. When the shepherd's eyes blew open and he grabbed himself and moaned, Jack could have done a war dance. He had just learned that nothing numbed pain faster than hurting . . . *really* hurting the person who had hurt you.

He spotted a rock the size of a honeydew melon and considered smashing the shepherd's skull, but mostly he just wanted to get out of there. He ran back to the pickup where he found the sheep still crowding around the injured lamb.

"Get out of my way," he growled. He felt exhilarated, as alive as he'd ever been, and wasn't about to be stopped by some sheep.

"I said, *out* of my way!"

But the sheep would not cooperate with Jack in his moment of glory. They just stood there dumbly. He climbed in the truck, slammed the door, and hit the horn. They didn't so much as blink.

He considered driving off the road to weave his way around them, but that would take him back toward the shepherd. Not a pleasant prospect despite Jack's pumped-up condition.

Before he could think this through, the shepherd climbed to his feet. Holy shit. Jack dropped the transmission into four-wheel drive and slammed the accelerator to the floor. He bounced over the much-abused lamb, and hit or ran over at least a dozen more sheep before he plowed his way through the flock. Despite the carnage he was impressed with the pickup's ability to surmount these considerable obstacles, and took no little pride in his own skill as he made his way over the last of them.

With a clear road ahead, he raised his fist in victory. *Mano á mano*, and he'd won. *Yes!* He felt more courageous, more in control of his life than ever before, and never heard the tortured bleating that rose in his dusty wake.

57

Celia treaded water right below Chet, still waiting for him to help her out of the tank. Her legs couldn't keep this up much longer. He'd been strangely silent for two or three minutes. Another mood swing? As if it would make much difference: he only went from bad to worse. More than anything she worried that he had become suspicious.

"You sure you want me to?" he finally said. She had no idea what she was asking for. Or maybe she did. Maybe she *wanted* it. Some do. "Ask and ye shall receive." Father Jim always said that with a smile.

She moved her head up and down emphatically. "Yes, please."

"I should keep you in there for what you did to me." He nodded as if deep in thought, and the flashlight bobbed. Then he turned it on her, but couldn't see much. He would, though. Her little-boy butt. Naked. He'd stare and stare and stare.

Celia said nothing. Her jaw was tight; the rats were all stirred up, brushing against her body.

"You hurt me," he said petulantly.

She looked up again, blinded by the beam, and managed to apologize. She tried to sound contrite, and might have succeeded.

"You mean that?" This truly pleased Chet. When they started saying they were sorry, they were finished. And they did, almost all of them sooner or later. And then they'd say it over and over again. Even with a mouth plug—"Oom er-ee." Sometimes he'd make them say it, and they would. God-damn right they would. "Again," he'd whisper, and they'd try just as hard as they could, not that it made a fuck's worth of difference. And here she was saying it already. He wondered what she'd say later, when she was really sorry.

He leaned over the edge of the tank. Celia saw the tips of his western boots backlit above her. "Yes, now help me, please."

But something startled Chet, and he backed up. "What the hell was that?"

Celia didn't know what he was talking about. Then the sound of a vehicle reached down into the tank.

"The sheriff's patrol! Thank God. You'd better—"

"That's not the sheriff's patrol. There's no goddamn sheriff's patrol out here." He stared at the lights on the county road, he could just make them out through the trees. "Your goddamn husband?"

"What?"

He hurried to the other side of the tank, grabbed the handle for the cover, and slammed it shut. Once more Celia found herself in the dark water listening to his footsteps, but this time they were in retreat.

58

Jack glimpsed the house lights all the way out to the county road. That surprised him. Celia rarely stayed up this late. He figured it must be a hell of a good movie. Or a real page turner. But even that wouldn't account for all those lights. *Maybe whatever it is has her all freaked out.*

He pulled up alongside the Honda and rushed in the house. He wanted to surprise her and tell her all about beating up the shepherd. He knew it was juvenile, but he couldn't help himself.

He didn't find her in the living room, and the TV wasn't on.

"Celia? Celia, you back there, hon? I'm home."

Silence. *Hmmm, now that's funny.*

"Hon, are you okay?" No answer. *Maybe she nodded off reading.*

A hissing punctuated the air outside but Jack didn't notice because he'd just walked into the bedroom and switched on the light. Before him lay the clear evidence of a violent struggle: the blood on the bed, the window screen and curtains, and the sheets and covers on the floor. Then he saw the light in the bathroom and the gaping hole in the door, which hung halfway open.

"Celia?" His voice sounded much softer now, and a pleading tone appeared when he repeated her name. "Celia?"

He inched his way toward the bathroom, peering into every shadow, looking over his shoulder, trying to look everywhere at once.

When he stood just three feet from the battered door, he spotted the broken mirror and the blood puddled on the tile floor. *Jesus, is that hers?* A tremor started in his legs, and he squeezed both hands into fists to try to choke off his fear. In the horror of his imaginings his wife lay slumped and bleeding against a wall, a terror immediately compounded by a trickle of watery blood that squiggled like mercury across a square of tile.

Slowly, he pushed open the door. It creaked. He had never heard it do that before, and he stopped. He didn't want to go any farther, but he couldn't walk away, not if he wanted to live with himself. She might need his help. But—and this was his greatest fear—whoever did this to her might be in the bathroom waiting to do the same thing to him.

He had never felt more defenseless than he did as he took his next step. He had to will his feet to move, and still he couldn't see past the open door.

He filled his lungs. One more step, and another. Now that he'd left the door behind he found that he could not turn to his left. Instead, he stared resolutely ahead. He knew this was foolhardy, knew that he must, he simply *must* turn his eyes to whatever awaited him; but this proved more difficult than forcing himself into the bathroom because now he would see exactly what had happened here . . . and what might happen to him.

Or would he? His eyes crawled to their corners, but he spied no one ready to spring at him. As he turned for a better look he heard a sudden movement. He jumped and scanned the room in a brutal heart-thumping panic before seeing the bottom of the window shade shaking. It had unraveled an inch or two. That's all it was, he promised himself. That's all.

The window itself was wide open, and a blood smear drew his attention to the bottom part of the frame. He forced his eyes down even farther to the tub and saw the red footprints. Small footprints, not a man's, and he knew with a sickening dread they were Celia's. Oh Jesus. Crude violations, savage intimations. He felt every one of his tightly packed fears break loose from his bones, percolate in his blood, and push through his pores. Cold sweat streamed from under his arms.

Celia, he said to himself, too frightened now to speak her name aloud.

Nothing answered but the same eerie silence. He took a step back and his shoe crushed something squishy. It felt . . . *horrible* . . . like a body part. He swallowed, looked down, and lifted his foot. A grotesque, gelatinous oval the size of a child's navel stared back at him. With a stomach-churning shudder he looked around the bathroom and thought frantically, where's the cat? But he did not see Pluto, only blood and broken mirror, one splashed on the other; and then he returned to the mashed oval and could no longer avoid knowing that he'd just stepped on the cat's only eyeball.

He trembled as he quietly scraped the jellied remains off his shoe. Then he crept back into the bedroom, listening uneasily to the restless sounds of the floorboards.

He felt the emptiness of the room, the utter lack of life, but feared what he could not see, the madness that might be hiding in the armoire, the closet, or just outside the bedroom door because whoever *did* this to her . . . could do this to him. Always that same terror returned. But he sucked in another deep breath and told himself that two could play this game, and he found some courage in remembering how he'd vanquished the shepherd.

He entered the hallway. Light from the bedroom threw long shadows along its entire length, including the outline of a man. Even though he knew it was his own shadow, the appearance of another human form gave Jack a monstrous chill.

He had to walk right by the hall closet, dark behind the louvered doors that opened and closed like an accordion.

If he hit the switch on the wall, it would turn on the lightbulb in the closet and he'd see if someone had hidden inside. But that would undoubtably force the hand of the intruder, and if he could make it to the kitchen he could help himself to the knives.

So he eased past the doors and didn't take his eyes off them for even a second. He turned away only when he reached the living room. High above him the blades of the Casablanca fan rotated, and when he chanced to look up he saw shadows swiftly orbiting the room like dark creatures that fly only at night.

He turned to his right, then quickly left, his ears pricked for even the slightest sound. That's when he finally heard Celia, far away, barely audible. He did manage to make out his name and something about a killer. He wondered if she meant the shepherd. Maybe the son of a bitch had been returning from his drunken pleasures when he ran into him. That made sense to Jack, and he greeted this possibility with relief because if the shepherd had done this . . . well, he had already taken care of him. We're not likely to hear from that asshole again anytime soon, now are we? He nodded to himself, for despite his fears the memory of his victory—*mano á mano*—pleased him as much as ever. And if the shepherd had hurt Celia, then what he'd done to the shepherd would seem even more heroic to her.

He did not call back to his wife. He stepped softly into the kitchen and withdrew a knife with a foot-long blade from the butcher-block stand. He turned it edge to edge to catch the light, and admired its possibilities. Now he felt truly armed. He looked for the flashlight but discovered it missing. He wondered if Celia had taken it. Or the shepherd?

He picked up the phone hoping against all hope that a dial tone would greet him and he could call 911. But the line was as silent as the house.

Celia gripped the intake line with a straight arm to keep herself as far as possible from the rat still huddling on the brace. She kept her other arm wrapped tightly across her chest, and her legs sealed together to try to bundle herself against the mass of cold slimy carcasses pressing against her body.

She had to marshal all of her will to listen for Jack. She feared she wouldn't hear if he moved within shouting distance. But only the cicadas called out to the night, and after no hint of her husband for several minutes she figured he must have entered the house. But he wouldn't be there for long, not after he saw the bedroom and bath, and the blood. Good God, be careful, Jack. *And get me out of here.*

If he didn't come, if Boyce attacked him, cut him, paralyzed him, killed him . . . her fears escalated until she reached the grisly understanding that she might have to save herself. Climb out of here? She stared at the rat on the brace, its snout and whiskers moving once more, as if keen to this delicious new possibility, and doubted she could ever bring herself to grab its gristly body and drown it. Yes, she told herself, you can, you must. No, she thought, no way, not in a million years. I'll wait. He'll come. But then she wondered if "he" would be Boyce. Her hand choked the intake line, and she again resolved to climb out. It'll bite you and rip at you with its claws, but you'll grab it and hold it under for as long as it takes.

But she'd give Jack a few more minutes. She'd count off the seconds and steel herself for the rat. She couldn't wait forever, not with Boyce out there. She had to move. She had to do *something*.

She tried to shore up her nerves by reminding herself that many years ago she had made an escape; and at the time the threats she faced were no less daunting, the stakes no less high.

Her mother's beatings had never paused for more than a week or two, and at twice Celia's weight and with half a foot more in height she had ample bulk to bully her youngest daughter. On the morning of Celia's eighteenth birthday she used it to punish her for failing to appreciate properly the card she'd given her.

"I don't know why I even bother," she'd said in a frighteningly calm voice as she pulled the belt off the hook in the linen closet. "No matter what I do for you, it's never good enough, is it?"

Celia *had* thanked her, but when her mother advanced with the belt she didn't attempt to reply or protest. She'd learned years ago that her mother's rage never listened to reason. As the first blow came she curled up into the fetal position and tried to protect herself, but the belt buckle still caught her on the left eyebrow, and could just as easily have taken out the eye. After an eternal minute of feeling it crack against her arms and head and body, her mother tossed it aside and beat her with her fists, tearing at Celia's hands to get to her face. Her fury spent, she returned the belt to the hook, picked up her purse as if nothing had happened, and slammed the door. Celia climbed up off the floor, dragged herself onto the couch, and peeked out from behind the curtain. When her mother disappeared down the block, Celia called a taxi. The gift she'd longed for was now within reach.

She packed frantically, a suitcase and knapsack, then sailed into the bathroom to grab her toiletries and toothbrush. She caught her reflection and groaned. Her face had been bruised, and a thin stream of blood ran down from the corner of her eyebrow. She washed the cut and put on a Band-Aid, but had no time for makeup.

She left her bags in the bedroom, lest her mother return suddenly, and moved back to the curtain in time to spot the gleaming yellow cab inching down the street, the driver studying addresses. Her heart jumped as she raced to the door. And then she froze. She was about to defy her mother as she never had before. That was the word she'd always used: "How dare you *defy* me!" Celia stared at the handle, the bolt lock, and urged herself on.

But seconds passed before she could force herself to open the door. The driver had just braked in front of the house and hit his horn.

"I'm here!" Celia screamed so loudly that a neighbor with a bag of groceries turned around and stared. Celia worried that she might try to stop her, then remembered that her mother had no friends, only enemies, real and imagined. Celia waved, and the woman, though clearly puzzled, raised a hesitant hand before rallying up her steps.

"I'm coming, just a second," Celia shouted to the driver. She ran to the bedroom and breathlessly grabbed her suitcase and knapsack.

On her way out she placed her house key on the end table, then closed the door softly, as if to leave the past as undisturbed as possible.

She hurried with her bags to the curb. Tensely she shoved them into the backseat, sure that during those few moments of distraction her mother's powerful hand would grab her from behind and her cold voice would ring out: "Where do you think you're going, dearie?"

But only the driver had spoken: "Looks like you went a few rounds."

Celia glanced nervously at the house. "The train station, please."

The "please" had always been the touch that she recalled most clearly. She'd been old enough to leave home legally, had planned her departure for years, yet remained so intimidated by her mother that even with the cabbie she spoke it less out of politeness than as a plea.

Please, like Oliver Twist with his empty bowl: "Please, sir, I want some more . . ." All the please please please that crucified childhoods the world over with their desperately muffled hope and their clearly defined despair. She'd said "please" plenty to her mother, for all the good it had done.

The driver didn't say another word. He flipped on the meter and pulled away. Celia didn't dare a final glance. She leaned against her bags and trained her eyes straight ahead as the dimes and dollars started to click away.

As soon as she found a seat on the commuter train she huddled over her compact, studied the mirror, and began to doctor her face with makeup as she had so many times before. She peeled off the Band-Aid, saw the blood crusted on her eyebrow, and darkened it with mascara. Her hands shook terribly, and even as she snapped the compact shut she knew she'd done a lousy job.

She'd plotted her route carefully and planned to get off at Penn Station, then travel west to Chicago. She had saved $378 from waiting tables all summer at a steamy crab house down by the docks. Six, seven days a week of putting on Pan-Cake to hide the bruises on her neck, back, face, and arms; and then touching them up as the night wore on and perspiration washed away her attempts to cover up her injuries; learning that a customer's inquiring gaze usually meant a black-and-blue mark had poked through the makeup.

That's all she fled Long Island with, a cut eyebrow, a suitcase half-full of clothes, a knapsack, and the memories. She would discover that after the bruises faded and the clothes wore out, the memories remained so indelible that it was as if she'd been tattooed with the bloodstains of her childhood.

She hadn't relaxed until she'd boarded the Amtrak, stashed her suitcase in the overhead bin, and taken a seat by the window where she could turn away from her fellow passengers. That's when she began to believe that her mother had not tracked her, and that she had indeed set herself free. She stared out the window as Manhattan rolled away, the river too, and felt tears of relief dampening her cheeks and spilling onto her skirt. She tried to brush them away but they'd already formed a dark bloom on the burgundy fabric. Her nose clouded, and when she checked her knapsack for a tissue she noticed the conductor standing in the aisle.

"Are you okay, young lady?" he said softly. He was older, black with a puffy white mustache.

"I'm sorry," she stuttered, careful to keep her head down so she wouldn't reveal much of her poorly made-up face; unaware that her reflection in the window already had given her away. "I know it's in here."

"Don't worry about your ticket none. Here." He leaned over and gave her a freshly pressed white handkerchief.

She nodded her thanks.

"You traveling alone?"

"Yes." Her voice had become barely a whisper.

"You leaving whoever did that to you?"

Again she nodded.

"You're going to be okay now, you hear me? You go on to where you're going and don't go back. You'll be okay. Chicago's a good town, lots of nice folks. You'll see. Now take your time with that ticket. Don't worry yourself about it. It's a long trip."

She swallowed hard, and as she wiped her eyes thought that perhaps his kindness had marked her anew, and that the path she had chosen really would lead to a better life, the kind some women had known since birth, where you were less wary than welcomed, less leery than loved.

She'd left home twenty years ago last month, and had spent ten of them with Jack. She found herself crying, then screamed his name so hard that her entire body shook.

Jack heard her again, calling his name, and a few seconds later she repeated something about a killer. But you're still alive, he told himself, and if you survived him—whoever he is—I will too. Of course, if she'd been tangling with the shepherd he could understand why she'd feel that he was a killer. But he's definitely not, Jack thought dismissively, and he looked forward to assuring her of this.

He hurried out of the house, tracking her distant voice. It sounded as if it came from behind the wall of firs that lined the driveway. He stopped and studied the shadows that greeted every turn of his eye, but it was damned difficult to see into all that darkness. If he was going to find her quickly, he had to risk calling out to her.

"Celia, I'm here, where are you?"

As soon as he said this he knew he'd revealed his location, so he spun around quickly, holding the knife in front of him like a real street fighter. But no one challenged him. And he told himself that no one would, not if they were smart.

"I'm in the tank," she screamed.

The *what?*

"Be careful. There's a guy out there with a *razor!*"

A razor? He glanced at his foot-long blade. Good luck, buddy. Cocky, but still cautious, he walked toward the firs and tried to look past them.

"Don't worry about me. I'm coming."

He pushed aside a branch, and saw more trees and bushes and the wooden tank cover reflecting the moonlight. He wondered how the hell she had ended up in there, of all places. Christ, couldn't she have picked a better spot?

As he stepped past the firs the branches scraped against him and rustled back into place. He paused as they settled, and looked around carefully. Now he realized that a man could be hiding in any of a dozen places: in the shadows, crouched behind a tree, behind the thick vegetation, anywhere. Jesus. But standing so close to the firs cut off his view of the driveway and made him feel just as vulnerable, so he forced himself forward.

He'd covered about half the distance to the tank when he heard the twangy snap of a twig. He froze. What the hell was that? He looked around but saw only those shadows. He pivoted his right foot softly from side to side, then his left. No, he hadn't stepped on anything. But he *had* heard it. He was sure of it. He kept the knife in front of him but the glinting metal proved less persuasive now.

Still, he remained ready to strike as he moved ever closer to the tank, always looking from side to side and glancing back behind him. In this fear-driven manner he made his gains.

When he drew within three feet of the tank another twig

snapped, and now Jack did jump, and he sucked in a mouthful of air that sounded sharp in the stillness.

"Jack, be careful. He's out there."

"It's okay, hon. It's okay."

He reached toward his wife's voice, felt the edge of the cover, and tried to lift it, but couldn't. He realized he was standing near the hinge where the resistance was greatest, so he inched toward the middle. While still facing the shadows and keeping his knife hand free, he lifted the cover without once looking in. When he'd raised it high enough he heaved it like a shot put and it thundered open against the far side.

"Jack, thank God."

But still he didn't look down until he'd studied every tree and shadow that surrounded him. Then and only then did he dare a glance at his wife's pained face. He took heart in the fact that all the noise he'd just made hadn't attracted anyone to leap from the darkness. Maybe they won't, or maybe— hell, it was *likely*—they were gone.

He finally looked at Celia. "Are you hurt?"

"Yes! Get me out of here. Quick. Someone's out—"

"The shepherd?" Jack interrupted with great hope. "Because I just beat him up."

"No, not him," Celia replied frantically. "Davy's step-father. Get me out of—"

"Davy who?"

"Forget it! Just," she sputtered, "just get me out of here."

"Okay, okay, here." Jack kneeled and stretched out his free hand. She was a couple of feet away and appeared to have trouble moving through the water. He looked back over his shoulder but only the night looked back.

"Hurry," he urged.

"I am," she said grimly, "but there are ra—"

She stopped in mid-sentence and her eyes shot past him. As he turned around she screamed, "Watch out," but it was already too late. A powerful arm wrapped around his chest, and a short sharp blade pressed against his neck.

"Drop it, asshole."

Jack hesitated even though he didn't have the knife in a useful position. He'd been weighting the hand that held it while he reached for Celia, and now the man with the blade was leaning on him so forcefully that Jack could hardly move his fingers.

"Now!" Chet hissed.

"I'm trying."

Jack released the handle by scraping his knuckles against the hard dry earth. Chet kicked the knife away.

"Good boy," he whispered in Jack's ear.

Chet held the razor firmly against his neck and watched that big vein throb like the skin of a drum all stretched tight and just beating away for all it's worth. He saw it thumping in the moonlight, and remembered how he'd seen a vein just like it two weeks ago, the boy's mother, who knew she was going to die, begging him to let the kid leave. "He doesn't need to see this," that's what she'd said. But she was all wrong. He *did* need to see it, and so does Mrs. Griswold.

"Please don't hurt him."

There she is, begging already. We got a long night of this ahead.

"I'll do anything you want, just don't hurt him. Please."

Anything? But you're going to do anything I want anyway. You got to do better than that, Mrs. Griswold. He shook his head over her foolishness and pressed the blade harder against her husband's neck. The big asshole started to squirm. He moved his lips closer to Jack's ear. "You're not cut yet. I just nicked you, so quit moving or my hand could slip."

The body stilled, and Chet smelled the sweat steaming off him. Then he saw the blood rise up along the edge of the blade. But that's nothing, not the gusher. That's just a little skin stepping aside. He could almost hear this guy thinking, What am I gonna do? What am I gonna do? And praying too. Oh, you bet. Jesus, save me, save me. That's right, saying his prayers like a good little boy. Praying for life and saying you're sorry when you're about to die. Eternal life. But I'm the only one around here that makes anything eternal. That's right, Me. I cut you, you die forever and ever. Nothing, not even your goddamn God can change that. I let you live, I give you life. I'm your God, not him in heaven, but Me.

Chet's hips began to twitch, and the words that fevered his thoughts now passed from his lips, still so close to Jack's ear that his breath registered with every urgent word:

"Say I'm your God."

"What?"

Chet pressed the blade closer. Only the vein's thin membrane stood between life and death.

"Say it, say I'm your God."

"You're my God.

"Mean it!"

"You're my God!" Jack cried out.

"Forever and ever."

"Forever and ever!"

"Amen."

"Amen!"

The razor moved, a brief, horrifying probe deep into his neck, a sharp stinging sensation, and Jack heard Celia scream and knew from her terror and the burst of warmth and wetness on his chest that his life had been taken.

The powerful arm let him go. He grabbed his neck as a booted foot pushed him into the tank. He fell into the cold darkness, bleeding now deep in the water, fighting for air even as he gripped his neck hard enough to choke himself, trying desperately to stanch the wound, to cauterize it with his will; but his heart beat on dumbly, pumping pumping pumping away every moment he might have known.

He filled with the fear you can know only once. He reached for Celia, touched her hand and held it. He prayed that he would never let her go.

But his life passed from him, and his body rolled over. As he turned limp, she stiffened. Her legs and hands stopped moving, and she sank beneath the surface. She struggled for air, and when she came back up she looked at her husband but no movement betrayed his death, only the ripples that ruffled the water by his head, the blood pulsing rhythmically from his neck.

She looked up at Boyce, still standing there, watching like a man at peace in his domain as he calmly returned the razor to his shirt pocket.

She'd seen how he reveled in the kill, took his time, teased Jack, and then murdered him. She thought of dying too, of sinking one final time and not fighting back, of drowning herself rather than letting him take her life as he surely would.

But a hatred as deep and cold as the water poisoned her every thought, and she knew she must live, if only to kill.

He swayed slightly, hand on his hips.

"You still want my help, or am I going to have to drag you out of there?"

"Yes," she sobbed softly, "please help me."

59

Chet braced his left foot against the wooden housing, bent over, and offered his hand. It took more will than Celia knew she had to reach up and grab it. She tried not to shudder as his dry calluses pressed roughly into her soft shriveled skin.

He attempted to pull her up, and she struggled to help, but her shoulder felt as if it was coming out of its socket.

"No, stop," she shouted. "That hurts."

That hurts? He let go of her and watched her slip back into the tank. For a second or two she disappeared. Then he saw one of her hands moving as she resurfaced. Pretty deep, he thought.

When her head bobbed back up, he put the flashlight down and told her to give him her other hand.

"I can't. It hurts."

"Serves you." The spitefulness slipped out like a mouse from a floorboard.

"Look, I'm really sorry."

Chet smiled, but his voice remained gruff. "Let's just get you out of there. Here, like this." He locked his grip around her wrist. "You do the same to me," he ordered. Now they were linked tightly together.

"On three, okay?"

"Okay," she agreed.

"One, two, three."

He pulled and she pulled, and Celia came up out of the tank. Her shoulder hurt as she caught the housing with one foot and then the other, but not so bad as before; and the cold water had dulled the ache in her knee.

They were both breathing hard, and Celia was shivering too. He bent over and picked up the flashlight that had been spending its beam on the ground. He held it on her. She could tell he was staring at the dark spot where her gown clung to her pubic hair, and at her rigid nipples.

"That's the containment tank." It was a slip of the tongue. She didn't catch it and neither did he. Celia noticed a big bruise on his forehead.

"Who cares? Get moving! Back to the house." He kept the light on her. He wanted to watch her march all the way, see the little boy's rump move around. His crotch began tightening again.

"It's for fighting fires. With the drought we try to keep it pretty full. You never know." She started to weep. "It's horrible down there."

"Shut up!" Sound travels, though to what he couldn't imagine. Just get her back to the house, close the door, plug up her goddamn mouth and she can make all the fucking noise she wants. He knew she'd try. Goddamn, they all tried, mostly begging—"Stop, stop, stop" (amph, amph, amph, with the mouth plug)—even the ones doing it to themselves. But it was their decision—"Do it, or I'll do it for you"— and goddamn if they didn't too, just take that fucking razor and cut themselves right up. They liked it too. But he always had to finish the job. They never liked it that much.

"Let's go!"

"It's full of rats!" she cried.

"Rats?"

"It's *crawling* with them!"

He pointed the flashlight into the tank. He hated rats, hated them. The worst goddamn things in all creation. Just seeing them made him sick, made him want to puke. He stared at the tank. "I don't see any." And he didn't want to see any either. Only thing he saw was that goddamn cat and her goddamn husband. There aren't any goddamn rats in there. "Let's get mov—"

"It's *full* of them," she repeated.

"Full?" He took another look at the dark pool as Celia started to scream.

What the hell . . . He turned around in alarm and saw her eyes—huge, like the others' eyes when he was finishing them off. Big eyes popping right out of her head; and then he saw some kind of dark thing in her hand. He felt it too—the claws, the goddamn *claws*. Jesus . . .

Celia was shoving a dead rat right into his face. She saw his surprise, his fear, and this drove her on. He tried to fend her off and dropped the flashlight. She pressed the rat against his nose and mouth and ground its claws harder and harder into his skin. He reeled and swung wildly at her, but she gripped the rat tightly and kept it in his face; and that's when she felt it too, not just the spongy slimy fur, but the hard bony body itself, and the tail jammed against her forearm until he fell backward into the tank.

He made a loud splash. She dropped the fat soggy beast and wiped her hands on her gown. Chet surfaced, and Celia got a good look at his wet features. In a rage, she picked the rat back up and hurled it at him. It struck his head, and the dark rodent clung to him like mud to a wall. He grabbed at the creature to pull it off—and he succeeded—but not before she saw the tail hanging over his face and shaking, as if the rat were feeding in the nest of his hair.

He pushed it away and fought for air as he churned water violently in his heavy boots. Boyce didn't look like a man who would die easily. Already he was moving toward the intake line where he'd found her. She had seen insanity in his eyes. She'd seen it before—in him, in others—and now she felt it in the air between them, as tangible as that tank, as real as those rats. His body jerked crazily, and he kept pushing at something underwater. He looked back at her.

"I'm going to kill you." Then he turned away and struggled over to the intake line. When he caught hold of it he shook his head, as if he felt sorry for her.

60

Celia's first impulse was to slam down the tank cover, but it didn't have a lock and she was sure he was strong enough to crawl out from underneath it.

He's going to get out.

Those words echoed in her thoughts for several seconds before she considered running. Try it, maybe you can. But the moment she started to bend her knee even a little, the sharp pain returned.

As Chet shimmied up the intake line the rat on the brace squeaked in his face. He never hesitated before smashing it against the wall with his fist. The rat plopped into the water, dead. Chet hauled himself up another foot and paused, perhaps to catch his breath, possibly to catch her eye. His were large and as dark as ever.

"I mean it. I'm going to kill you." He had the strength for this, for one more threat. He hugged the intake line tightly with his left arm as he reached for his breast pocket. He unsnapped a pearl button and pulled out the razor. "You're dead." He put it between his teeth as he had done when he was outside her bedroom window, and started inching back up the line.

She spotted the knife that Jack had taken from the kitchen. It was lying on the ground near the flashlight. She picked it up, and though she'd used it hundreds of times before, it now felt foreign to her. She gripped it as a weapon and thought of stabbing Boyce as he tried to climb out. She even saw the way his hands would grab on to the housing, and how she could drive the long blade right down through his flesh and pin him to the wood.

But she halted before she ever got started. No, even that wouldn't stop him, for she could also see how he'd yank the blade away and turn it on her. No, she couldn't do that.

She stood unmoving, her stomach muscles knotted, her arms tense, her legs as unsteady as her breath.

Do something. Do *something*.

Her eyes raced around the small wooden shelter until she spied the fire hose that she and Jack had stacked two weeks ago. She forced herself into action. She pulled out the heavy copper nozzle and reached for the rope that started the motor. It had a small black rubber grip like a lawn mower's, and she yanked on it. But the engine didn't turn over.

The choke, she thought, the choke. She picked up the flashlight and searched wildly until she found the yellow knob. She turned it and pulled the rope again. Nothing.

Shit.

Chet grunted, and Celia looked up. One of his hands clutched the top of the housing.

Jesus God. She yanked on the rope again. Nothing. Come on, *come on*, she urged.

Maybe . . . it's . . . not . . . going . . . to . . . start. She heard her mother's icy inflection and thought it might be true. When was the last time we ran this thing?

She saw him rising like a reptile and tried again. Nothing. Her arms ached. Her body kept shaking. Her hands felt weak. Again: *putt*. It sounded once and then no more. Again, crying: *putt*. Again: *putt-putt*. Each time the rope recoiled as though rebuking her.

She screamed in frustration and fear, pulled, and heard the engine start up. Thank God.

Abruptly, it stopped.

She thought he said something. Or was he grunting? She couldn't be sure. He was staring back at her, and his lips were moving. He was still biting down on that razor, it glinted between his gums in the moonlight. He was definitely saying something but she could not hear him. She did see that he had both hands on the housing and was starting to hoist himself up.

"Dead meat." Chet kept repeating those words to himself—"dead meat, dead meat"—because that's what she was. Every time he said the word "meat" he could feel his lips touching the razor between them. That felt good, like he was already kissing her good-bye with the blade.

He had an elbow out of the tank and was trying to lift a knee onto the housing. She was seized by panic; it seeped through every pore and made her whole body slippery with terror.

"Jesus, Jesus." She wrapped the rope around her wrist, felt it pressed as tightly against her skin as his calloused hand had been minutes before, and pulled once more. The engine offered its anemic *putt-putt*, and roared to life.

She grabbed the nozzle and remembered the choke. She reached down and turned it off as two hundred feet of fire hose started pulsing with pressurized water. She stepped toward the tank and waited . . . and waited . . . and waited . . . for the water.

He just about had that knee up on the housing when the hose came fully to life. It flailed like a snake tossed onto a fire, and when the water burst from the nozzle it was all Celia could do to hang on. But she did.

She aimed the powerful stream at his back and flattened him against the side of the tank. The water hit him like a prizefighter's fist that never lets up. His leg surrendered first, banging against the side of the tank until it fell into the water again. Celia went to work on the elbow up on the housing, and in seconds forced it back down as well. He held on, though, like a man hanging from a bridge.

She worried that he might hang on forever. She thought of the little red gas can, and remembered that when they'd worked on the tank they hadn't checked it. She had been about to pick it up to see if it was full when Jack discovered the rats.

I *could* run out.

While gripping the hose tightly, she reached for the can, picked it up, and felt its dreadful lightness. I *will* run out.

That realization scared her almost senseless.

In seconds, she figured out what she had to do. She kept the stream on him and started to drag the heavy hose carefully around the perimeter. Too carefully.

Hurry up.

When she was standing right over him, she pointed the

nozzle at the top of his head and lowered herself down until the tip of it was only a foot or so from her target. Water exploded off his pale scalp, and the spray almost blinded her. But she held the cold metal tightly and watched his arms straighten under all that pressure. The hand she'd bitten was the first to start to give.

"Die, fucker, die," was her only thought. "Die, fucker, die," an obscene mantra that she chanted over and over. She wanted to force him down with the rats forever.

She watched him slip from one set of knuckles to the next, and the next, until he held on with only the tips of his fingers.

Die, fucker, die. Diefuckerdie. She longed to see his hands slip away completely, and she concentrated on this to the exclusion of every other possibility; and there were many of them, even now. Celia's focus was so narrow that she saw very little: the part in his hair shifting spastically under the pressure of the water, the coronas of spray lit up by the flashlight lying on the ground, and those fingertips clinging with simian strength to their last bit of life.

When he started to reach up, she scarcely believed he could do this. No, she thought, you can't, you *can't.* "No!" she screamed, but still his hand rose slowly, defying her words with yet another drumbeat of threat. It was the one she'd bitten, and she saw the white spongy skin flapping from the force of all that ricocheting water. He was reaching for her, and when she finally pulled away from his grasping claw she stumbled and landed on her side. The stream bent one of the fir trees along the driveway, and Celia felt the hose trying to rip right out of her hands. She fumbled with it before hugging it tightly to her chest. She looked back and saw that he was pulling himself out of the tank. He had a knee up on the housing, and his head and chest were rising. A new wave of horror threatened to overwhelm her.

She struggled to her knees. The still wildly pulsating hose throbbed in her hand, as if it were about to rip free; and when she saw him starting to stand she was tempted to drop it and try to flee. She had weakened, and it was all she could do to hold the nozzle. She aimed again. The stream moved in an arc that caught and stunned him. But the arc passed, and so did another precious second before Celia could re-aim. He stumbled forward as she wrestled with the hose. He had traveled about four feet when the flow found its target. It hit him in the chest and lifted him right off the ground. He looked like a man taking a shotgun blast: His arms were spread out in front of him, as though holding desperately to an invisible rail; his trunk was bent inward from the force of the water; and his legs were apart as he flipped backward into the tank.

Celia inched toward the wide dark hole. She saw him treading water as she had been not so long ago. He was in the middle of the tank, several feet from the intake line and close to Jack's body. She pointed the nozzle at Boyce's head and forced him under. Every time he started to come back up, she drove him back down again. For a minute or two his arms flailed as he fought his way to the surface, but soon there was only his inky outline rising and falling to the rhythm of the hose. The tank water roiled in the milky moonlight. It churned and seethed and slapped the black walls, and then she saw the rats. The tank was thick with them. They bubbled up around the two lifeless bodies. It was as though Celia had whipped up all the dead that had ever died there. She tried to drive the rats down too, but there were so many of them that as soon as she hit one, another would rise to the surface.

She was still gripping the nozzle tightly when the gas ran out. The engine died as it had come to life with a few *putt-putts*.

The last of the water dribbled out. She heard the *plop-plop-plop* of the final drops, and the muffled noise when one of them fell onto matted fur, or hair. The broad night fell quiet. She tried to get a good look at him but the moon had moved above her and the nighttime shadows were shifting, chasing the darkness they held so dear.

She walked around the tank and picked up the flashlight lying on the ground. It was still on, though its beam had grown weak and yellowish, and its reach could have been measured in inches.

A chill wind ruffled the pines, and the air felt icy against her wet skin. She staggered as quickly as she could back to the house. He had left the door open, and she never stopped to close it. She reached for the phone. Weeping with relief, she dialed 911. Nothing, no ring, no busy signal, nothing.

The phone was dead.

61

Celia gripped the edge of the kitchen sink and breathed rapidly. She tried to calm herself. "He's dead," she kept repeating, he's dead. You killed him. But nothing had ever been certain in her life, except that uncertainty would prevail.

"How would you girls like to go to Disneyland?"

Her mother smiled broadly as she stood by the table in the small kitchen, and her daughters looked up and yelped in anticipation. "Yes, Mommie, yes. Oh, please."

Disneyland. Celia could hardly believe it. She'd seen the Magic Kingdom on TV but it was like Never-Never Land, not a place that she could actually go to. To think that she would! Mickey Mouse and Donald Duck, Snow White and the Seven Dwarfs, and all those fireworks and the parade down Main Street. And the Teacup Ride, spinning around and around, getting dizzier and dizzier. She tingled with anticipation.

"Well, so would I, but we're not." Her mother's smile vanished and her voice grew loud. "You think I like working all the time? Don't you think I'd like a vacation for once in my life? Don't you think I'd like to have some fun?"

She turned back to the sink, and her three girls sat in the horror-struck silence. A moan soon rose from one of them. Celia wasn't sure which one, maybe all three of them had moaned. Her mother whipped around with the wooden spoon. "Who said that?" She hovered above the table, the foot-long spoon waving in the air. "Who said that?" she demanded. "Tell me right now or all three of you will get it."

And then the panicky finger-pointing began, along with Celia's sense that you could count on no one, not your mom, your sisters, not even yourself; because while Marion and Sharon had pointed at her, she had been pointing at them.

Celia grabbed a glass and turned on the faucet. She gulped the water and exhaled. *Jesus, I've got to get out of here.* She slammed the glass down so hard it shattered. She barely noticed.

The car, where are the keys? Then she remembered that he'd slashed the tires—on both cars. Jack had told her never to drive on a flat tire.

So what? her inner voice raged, and she yanked her shoulder bag off the breakfast bar. The keys jingled when she picked them up, and as she hurried to the door she also heard the invasion of night noises: the rustle of the pines; the distant clicking of the engine cooling; and the cicadas, their belly membranes beating madly.

She climbed into her Honda and checked the locks and windows on all four doors. The motor started with only a little reluctance, and she hit the high beam. The transmission slipped smoothly into drive.

WUMP, WUMP, WUMP.

The flat tires flopped against the ground. She didn't care, she didn't care if she drove on bare steel as long as she made it to Bentman alive.

WUMP, WUMP, WUMP.

She drove as fast as she dared, which wasn't very fast at all. With two good legs she could have beaten the Honda in a race. It just plodded along.

WUMP, WUMP, WUMP.

But driving was a lot safer than trying to walk or run, and less painful too. She was glad her car had an automatic transmission. When she had eased herself into the front seat, her knee had ached severely. She couldn't imagine using a clutch pedal.

She drove toward the county road with a gritty urgency, gripping the steering wheel tightly as she passed the tank off to her left.

WUMP, WUMP, WUMP.

She watched the ruts in the road and listened to her small car strain. The soft sounds of rubber turned sharper, and she guessed that one of the tires had just slipped off the wheel. No matter, keep going. She felt protected in her car, and wanted nothing of the world outside. The night was a pestilence that had crawled out from under the sky.

In this wobbly manner she drove down the driveway to the entrance to their property. That's where the Honda high-centered. The ruts were too deep for a car without tires. She gunned the engine, but the wheels spun uselessly. Her neck muscles tensed, and the pain slinked down her spine.

Shut off the lights.

She did this quickly. And then she turned off the engine too. She didn't want to make any more noise than was necessary.

Don't just sit there.

But the idea of unlocking the door felt horrible. Go out there? For what? Her car now blocked the driveway, and even if she *did* get out and walk back for Jack's truck, she couldn't go anywhere. She shook her head. No way, I'm not touching that lock. But she also knew it could be days before someone came up here, and it could be him.

No, not *him*, she promised herself. It can't be him. He's *dead*.

But she saw him anyway, bashing her window, reaching in, dragging her out of the car, beating her senseless. She saw all this in the theater of her fears, big screens, one for every wall.

So with a swallow, a breath, and a stomach-clenching move, she opened the door.

62

Celia tried hopping on her right leg, the good one, but after all she'd been through she didn't have the strength to do this for more than a minute, so she weighted her bad knee as little as possible and dragged her foot along the gravel road. It worked, in a fashion. And it hurt, a lot.

In a couple of miles she'd be at the shepherd's campground. She'd have to sneak by that creep. Jack had said something about a fight, so it would be best to avoid him. Jack . . . she saw his body floating facedown in the tank and realized that she'd just thought of him as a living, breathing man. But he's not, he's not. She felt such a breathless absence of emotion that it shocked her; but she'd had no time to grieve, and still had so far to go. She looked down the darkened road and forced herself into the present. The shepherd, you were thinking about him. He's up by the meadow, but once you get past him it's all downhill to Bentman. She figured it might take all night to get to town but at this point she didn't care, as long as she got there in one piece. And who knows, come morning she might run into one of the loggers. They always seemed friendly enough.

She took two more steps before she heard a rustle in the forest off to her left. Faint, barely audible, but something—or someone—had definitely moved back in there. She stiffened and thought of the twigs snapping at dusk by the meadow; but this noise sounded different, more like the crackling of a fire as it starts to build. It grew louder still, and Celia was seized with the certainty that it was Boyce.

He's alive.

No, he's not, she reassured herself. He's with the rats. But reassurances counted for little on a night like this. She tried to hurry and swore quietly at her pain. Her movements were excruciating, and she felt herself slowing down even as the thrashing forest sounds closed in. She knew she'd never out-run whatever it was and decided her only hope was to hide. She looked ahead, searching for the towering pine that marked the intersection with the overgrown logging road. She'd use the plan she came up with just before she climbed into the tank, when Boyce had begun walking down the drive-way with the flashlight. She could burrow into the brush and eventually take the logging road to town.

She limped and listened and looked everywhere for that tree. Maybe it's not there, maybe they cut it down. She wasn't sure of anything anymore and stumbled along for another eternal minute before she saw it rising above dozens of others. It loomed up ahead on her left just as she had remembered.

The crackling in the forest drew closer and closer, like a fog that sweeps along the currents of the land, and she heard a horrible snorting and knew it was him. She choked down her fear and tried one more time to run but her sliced-up knee made her want to scream, and that's when she realized it was her own hot breath that stalked her so.

Before turning by the big tree she looked over her shoulder. She saw nothing but moonlight on the county road. Maybe it's not him. But the comfort of this thought did not stop her from rushing headlong into the branches and bramble. She pushed them aside, plunged forward, and smashed her swollen knee into the corner of an open tailgate.

She almost fainted. She tried to swallow her sobs and all but crumpled to the ground. For at least ten seconds she could do nothing but absorb more pain than she'd ever known. She hunched over and held her arms and face close to her battered knee, as though embracing it gently might ease the agony. It didn't. She wept silently.

When the pain lessened she hauled herself along the sides of the truck bed to the door. It groaned loudly when she opened it, and the dome light turned the cab into a beacon. The moment was also charged with a revelation: Davy was rubbing his eyes and waking up. Seeing him confused Celia, but not enough to slow her down. She was, in fact, a good deal more distracted by the dome light, the pain raging in her knee, and the question of the key: Is it here? She found it in the ignition, and the truck started right up. She closed the door, and the darkness returned.

For the briefest division of time she considered backing out to the county road, but shivered at the prospect of rolling toward the very sounds she'd been running from all night. She knew right then that she'd take the logging road. The rivers, the streams, these old roads, they all flowed to Bentman. Right?

She searched wildly for the gearshift. Her right hand swept over the floor before she realized that the shift lever stuck out from the steering column. She had never driven a truck this old and had to guess at the transmission pattern. The clutch pedal tortured her wounded leg when she pressed down on it, and as she eased it out they bucked backward and stalled. She had guessed wrong.

"Shit."

She turned the ignition key again and tried pulling the shifter toward her and down. When she let out the clutch the truck moved forward, and the pain in her knee lessened slightly.

The lights, the lights. Branches raked the sides of the cab as they drove through darkness. Twice the truck bounced over fallen logs as she grappled with knobs all over the dash. The headlights came on as the radio blasted, "KLOG, where every day is Earth Day." She shut it off. The pickup listed to the driver's side as they rolled over a rotting stump, but up ahead Celia could see that the dirt road widened enough to avoid most of these obstacles.

Davy looked at her, and she reached across and patted his leg. She didn't know what to say to him, so she didn't say anything at all.

She checked her rearview mirror and saw nothing behind them but the night. Her only thoughts were on making it to the sheriff's office in Bentman.

63

Celia negotiated the dark logging road with great care, avoiding the forest debris wherever she could, bouncing along as she scanned the cab nervously and checked on Davy. He was sitting bolt upright, as if he shared her horror. An eerie greenish light fell across the boy's face; and she found the source in the instrument panel, which glowed brightly, as if the dash had been dabbed with radium. She noticed the gas gauge, an eighth of a tank; enough, she thought, to get them to town.

Every few seconds she also studied the rearview mirror, convinced that Boyce's dark eyes would soon stare back at her; but the mirror revealed only the flat nothingness of the night, and she drove on. Still, the uneasiness persisted. It felt like a cold breath on the back of her neck, a ghostly presence that drifted along on the fog of fear, and she turned around fully, no longer trusting the mirror to give life to the world. See, he's not there, she comforted herself. Thank God. She turned her attention back to the road, and relaxed her neck by rolling her head. And that's when she saw him break out from behind a bush no more than twenty feet away. He glared at her, drenched with water and rigid with rage.

Celia jammed on the brakes, understood immediately that this was a mistake, and tried to run him over. But the distance was too short, and she couldn't get the old truck to accelerate quickly enough. As the pickup neared him Boyce stepped neatly to the driver's side and jumped onto the running board. She watched him grab for the door handle, and saw that she'd neglected to lock the cab. She pounded down the button and felt her heart totter on the edge of shock.

Chet pressed his face close to the glass. His mouth moved but she could not hear him. Her hands choked the steering

wheel as he threw himself onto the hood and stared at her.
He beat the windshield with his fist, and she had to move
from side to side to see past him.

He climbed onto the top of the truck, forcing her to look
through the smears he left behind with his wet boots. She
heard his body scraping against the metal inches from her
head, and then he pounded the roof so viciously she could
feel it vibrating right above her.

A thump shook the pickup as he jumped into the bed. Now
she did see his dark eyes staring at her in the rearview mirror,
and despite clear evidence to the contrary she believed he'd
been there from the very beginning. He pressed both hands
against the glass, and she had to struggle to keep from hy-
perventilating.

Davy turned around in his seat and recoiled visibly at the
sight of his stepfather. Celia checked his door lock, saw it
sticking up, and in the ungodly glow of the cab reached across
him and pounded it down.

She also had enough presence of mind to turn the boy back
around to spare him the bizarre sight of his stepfather, but it
was too late. Davy had seen him, and he had seen that look
on his face. Davy was terrified.

Never before.

Chet spit out more of that rat water and tried to catch his
breath. His throat burned. So did his nose.

Never again.

He coughed and fought off a stomach spasm. She'd forced
water down his nasal passages and into his gut. Rat-fucking
water. She'd held him down for almost two minutes at one
point, and he'd felt those foul rotting bodies whirl around
him, tails and teeth and claws. Her goddamn husband too.
Worst of all, she'd made him play dead, and he loathed her
for that, for reversing their roles, for making him act like
some goddamned girl.

You don't play dead.

But he had, goddamn right he had. Because of her. She'd
done that to him. But there was one big difference, one huge
fucking difference, and he savored this knowledge even now:
He would've made damn sure she was dead, picked up the
biggest goddamn rocks he could find and caved her fucking

skull in; but she had walked away. Big difference, the difference between life and death.

His and hers.

Never again.

He repeated these words to himself like a penitent in a pew, and when his lips no longer moved he watched her drive and nodded his head. The forest was his. He knew it well. He'd bushwhacked through acres of brush and trees, and now was eager to ride.

Deeper. Deeper.

Simple thoughts—no more sentences for him. Simple words—breaking loose like blood clots—here, there, and everywhere.

Celia's eyes captured the mirror briefly. Boyce kneeled so close and the window was so thin. Old glass, as old as the truck. She trembled at the possibility of it breaking, and imagined his fingers reaching around her neck. She scooted so far forward that her body pressed against the steering wheel as she drove. Don't stop, she told herself, whatever you do, don't stop.

The forest thickened on both sides of the logging road, and it towered above them. She longed for the valley floor, its level roads and stable lives. She tried to will them there. *Down,* she insisted, to the town, people. She wanted no more of the ridge.

But they didn't descend. They began to climb a hill, and she had to press harder and harder on the accelerator. She looked at the gas gauge again and was aghast to see that the needle had dropped to almost empty. She swore silently. She had an impulse to roll the truck and send Boyce flying, crush his body with the weight of all this metal.

She tried in her terror to weigh the risks. Old truck—no seat belts. No way to protect him. Her eyes flashed at the boy. And what if it starts on fire? What if we're trapped inside? What if the son of a bitch survives? Celia was plagued by "what ifs" and abandoned any thought of rolling the truck.

She turned and saw his face still staring at her from behind the glass. He hadn't moved an inch in all that time. How much time? she wondered. Five minutes? Fifteen? She hadn't a clue.

They drove through a clear-cut ravine. Stumps rose along both sides of the truck, startling her with their brutal appearance: *All this life, all this death.*

And then the road began to narrow as they reentered the woods. Once again branches smacked the fenders and windshield. She saw the suffocating density of trees and roots and felt clammy perspiration reappear on her body as a cold mist. She also saw how the road was likely to end: as a wedge pounded into the heart of the forest, with the truck squeezed into its very tip. She heard limbs snapping against the cab, horrible popping sounds that rattled her nerves as much as the entangling forest rattled the truck. It looked as if the trees had legs, and as she drove forward they marched beside her in tighter and tighter formations.

The logging road faded quickly into two ghostly tracks. Open up, open up, open up, she begged. She wanted nothing so much as she wanted the ceiling of this forest to yield to the brilliant cathedral of night: the stars, the heavens, the neat blazing orderliness of the universe above.

But the ceiling never lifted. It remained shut, sealed as firmly as a coffin lid. Not even the cloak of moonlight could warm the dark limbs that enveloped them.

They bounced over the rotting remains of fallen trees, and branches bashed the truck repeatedly. The cab shook as if it were about to fall apart.

A fat limb struck the windshield and revealed a tightly spun web of cracks. It was as though they had been there forever, sleeping peacefully in the glass until awakened by this blow. Dozens of jagged angry arms reached out from the milky center. Celia thought if she could focus on a single piece she might make out where they were going, but focusing proved difficult and she drove on almost blindly. She tried looking through a long slim section just above the dashboard and managed to see the closing ranks of all these trees. The wedge—she shook her head—the wedge was choking them to death.

In seconds the trail disappeared entirely. The dense forest soaked up their headlights and left them in darkness. She looked out the side window and saw the shadowy crush of trees. They horrified her. The forest she had loved was betraying her at last, turning to final blackness. She felt its long arms reaching out, taking hold of her, slowing her down.

Boyce shifted his weight. She felt his motion, looked back, and saw that he had become a lumbering shadow. They now traveled at a speed at which most people walked. The truck jumped over another log. Within seconds she would see that it marked a boundary for all of them, from where they'd been to where they were going. Celia felt the truck slowing even more. She heard the front and side windows battered and scraped by branches and bushes she couldn't even see. The sounds were frightening: scratching that grew louder and louder, as if the forest were a gigantic black cat tearing at the cab with its claws, and they were its prey huddling inside. The pickup ground to a halt.

She stomped down on the gas pedal. The engine screamed. The tires spun. The truck shuddered, and Celia felt her anguish like a whip. Here in the deepest darkness, where life teemed with tentacles of trunks and vine and branch and bough, she would die. She ground the ball of her foot into the accelerator, and her leg froze in this position. She heard a loud clump—one of the tires caught something solid—and they were propelled forward.

The truck rolled onto what might have been road. Celia saw moonlight again and thought they had come, finally, to the open night of Bentman. She peered through the cracked windshield as the truck slammed to a stop. Her chest hit the steering wheel, and she reached for Davy to check his forward motion. She saved him from the dash and yanked him back onto the seat. When she looked at the boy, stumps appeared in the window behind him, thousands of them stretching over an endless hillside, each one rising as a tombstone in a vast cemetery. The logging road ended here, in this place of graves and rotting roots and severed tree trunks that poked the eyes out of the night with a cool gray indifference. This was what had stopped them, the final remains of a giant clear-cut. They paused at its very threshold.

The rear window exploded. Glass rained on them, and Celia instinctively covered Davy's head with her hands. She turned and saw Boyce standing above them in the bed with a large, heavy-looking object in his hands. He pulled violently on a rope. His chain saw roared.

Celia shoved Davy down to the seat and worked the column shifter. She popped the clutch, and the pickup bounced in place before the tires grabbed the earth and started steaming backward.

Boyce teetered with the weight in his hands. He overcompensated for the reverse thrust of the truck and stumbled forward. Celia saw the steel edge—blurred by the screaming chain—lunging toward them. She slid down in the seat and once more pinned the gas pedal to the floor. Boyce missed his target and struck the roof with his saw. Brilliant sparks exploded off the metal surface, and the smell of burning oil tainted the air. He recovered, reared back, and rammed the long vibrating blade into the cab. He grazed Celia's ear before burying the steel tip in the dash. The saw shut off automatically.

A breath later the rear of the wildly careering truck crumpled as it struck a huge pine. The sudden stop slammed Celia's and Davy's heads into the back of the bench seat and hurled Boyce into the thick trunk. She had backed into the forest.

Celia looked at the dark figure sitting in the bed of the pickup. No glass separated them any longer. She saw how easily he could come forward, reach in, and grab her. She wanted to flee, but had to force aside branches and tree limbs just to open the door. The dome light lit up the truck, and now she could see Boyce leaning back against the thick tree that had stopped them.

He grabbed the side of the bed and tried to climb to his feet. She searched the ground for a broken branch—anything—to use as a club, but Boyce collapsed of his own accord, obviously injured.

Thank God.

A peculiar noise arose from the cab, and when she turned around she saw Davy reaching under the broken chain saw and smacking the seat on the driver's side.

She couldn't see anything and didn't understand why the boy continued to do this. His stepfather moaned, and she looked back at him. This shift in her attention caused Davy to pound the seat even harder, as if frustrated, and then she heard something that stunned her.

"Guuun." He repeated this tortured syllable: "Guuun." It was the first word he'd ever spoken to her.

She saw him pointing to the floor of the cab, where he'd pulled a handgun out from under the seat.

She looked at the gun and glanced at Boyce. He hadn't moved. She reached in and picked up the revolver. Blood dripped from her ear, and she became aware for the first time that it had been cut. Her ear hurt, but nothing like the pain she'd known earlier tonight, and even now it could not compete with the throbbing in her knee.

She held the revolver firmly as she approached the back of the pickup. She pushed aside branches where she could, stepped over others, and slowly limped until she was even with the rear tire. Boyce sat with his head leaning slightly forward. He was about four feet away.

Her whole body came alive with the prospect of killing him. A true tingling raced up and down her spine, an almost euphoric sense that permeated her thoughts and made her oddly joyful. She wondered if all killers experienced this feeling. Maybe, she thought, that's why they kill.

She pointed the gun right at his head. His eyes turned away, and she followed their path. Davy was looking back at them through the broken rear window.

She realized she was on the verge of executing Boyce right in front of his stepson. She hesitated.

Kill him anyway. Go ahead. Do it.

The impulse was strong and sudden, as clear as the sound of the truck idling. She smelled lead fumes rising from the exhaust pipe.

Her hands shook. The weight of the gun made insistent demands on her tired arms. She knew that if she intended to shoot him she must do it now. He looked back at her as if in this moment he knew his doom.

"You son of a bitch," she whispered. And then she repeated herself, louder, "You son of a bitch."

The passenger door opened against a bush and both of them saw Davy slide out of the other side of the truck. His stepfather spoke to him in a harsh voice.

"Get over here. Now."

"No, don't," Celia said firmly. "Get back inside."

"I mean it. Get the fuck over here."

Celia knew in the primacy of that moment, in the sound of his words, that Boyce could have no plans but to use Davy, to take him as a shield, a hostage to her conscience. He was banking on her not shooting him, and on the boy doing what he'd been told. Davy was indeed moving toward the back of the truck.

"Go back," Celia begged, but she knew he would obey this man as he always had done. When Davy's steps took him within a few feet of Boyce, she steadied the gun, aimed right at his head, and pulled the trigger. In the horror before the blast she heard the metallic sound that gun lovers treasure: the hammer cranking back to the point of no return.

But there was no explosion, no smoke, and no skull splitting wide; and she sickened when she learned the truth: the gun was not loaded.

Boyce started to crawl toward her.

It's over. It's over. Her own petrified thoughts defeated her more than Boyce. The hand that now held the gun turned weak and shook almost uncontrollably. When she squeezed the trigger again it was the last vestige of survival at work, the instinct that wins out against all others, that twitches after thought gives way to fear, and hope to its own dismissal.

The metal resounded hollowly, and he started to laugh. His amusement grew louder and more grotesque.

She saw him drawing closer and prayed for a bullet as she squeezed again and again.

Clack, clack, the empty chamber sounded until her finger went soft against the trigger. A flickering silence followed, an inexplicable time lag before the discharge. The shot was so loud—so sudden—and so unexpected that it tore through her not with hope, but with the fear that in her despair she'd let the gun settle on herself, on the boy, on anything but her target.

But it did not matter where Celia's gun pointed because it was the boy's weapon that had spoken. He stood there holding it straight out with both hands, a stance he might have borrowed from television, the movies, or even from his stepfather. Smoke rose from the barrel, and through its quickly thinning pale Celia saw Davy squinting.

Boyce's body collapsed to the metal bed.

"Pow-pow, you're dead," the boy whispered in the hush that followed.

64

Celia nervously placed the tips of her fingers on Boyce's neck. His skin felt bumpy and filthy, and she pulled her hand away before checking his pulse. The bullet had killed him. She had no doubts. His open eyes stared lifelessly at the treetops, and a stillness blanketed his body. She did not need to touch him to know he was dead. And this time she was right.

Davy's arm hung by his side, the pistol pointing downward. He was an elective mute who had struggled to speak, a victim and a witness who had used a gun to pronounce a strict and final sentence.

He'd been scared, and Celia thought he'd probably taken his cue from all the charming killers who stalked the screen, and all the real ones who stalked the land. She looked at him. He's just a kid. A kid with a gun. She reached across his stepfather's body and took it from him. The handle felt warm. She laid it on the bed of the truck and put hers aside as well. She hugged him and began to cry, and as the tears streamed down her face she felt his arms encircle her back, as though to comfort her.

She grieved for Davy then, for a boy who had survived the worst the world could offer. Freed from his stepfather, yes, but all alone now. A killer too, a kid killer. She could see the headlines—she'd seen them before—and knew the courts would have their way with him. This shooting would become the highlight of his record, the sum total of who he was, and always cast a doubt—no matter how small, no matter how unfair—on the little boy in her arms. It would make the world wary of him, and he'd be shuffled from foster home to foster home, another lowly deuce in this wild game of chance, a throwaway kid in a throwaway culture. Another quiet crime against humanity.

She saw the gun lying there and decided at once to reduce his odds. She would not make him begin his new life with such a burden.

"They don't need to know this," she said.

Davy watched her pick up the gun and wipe the handle with her torn gown until no print could have survived. She held it in both hands and pressed her fingers against the wood and metal until her claim to the killing was clear. Then she laid it back down.

"I shot him, not you. Okay? That's our little secret."

He didn't say anything, and he didn't nod, but he knew about secrets and could keep one more.

Celia took his hand. She found it warm and wonderful to hold. She had been hard enough to survive; now she wanted to be soft enough to make it worth her while.

Slowly, painfully she led him through the branches and bushes to the cab.

"Hop in."

She edged her way along the front fender to the driver's side. The engine was still idling, and the headlights still peered at the clear-cut. As she pulled forward the first light of day appeared, and the stumps glimmered like ghosts. She had to back up several times to get the truck pointed toward the forest for their return trip. Before they got underway she stepped out of the cab, found a dead pine bough, and knocked out most of the windshield so she could see.

They bounced as they started to roll over the trampled brush, and Celia heard a thud as Boyce's body fell from the bed. She never slowed down but she did glance in the rear-view mirror and saw his corpse lying by a stump. The sheriff could drag his body away. Or the coyotes.

She made it all the way back to the county road before they ran out of gas. She and Davy walked the rest of the way home. It wasn't far, and morning had come to the ridge.

65

The county courthouse stood just three blocks from where Celia now lived but she drove her old Honda anyway. The weather looked rainy, and her knee still ached if she tried to walk for more than a few minutes.

"You'll be fine in time," the orthopedist at Cascade Memorial had told her, though she doubted his glib prognosis. Maybe her knee would heal completely, but that was the easy part. She thought matters of her heart would remain unsettled for years, maybe forever.

Three weeks ago she had buried Jack in a cemetery that overlooked the Bentman River. Since his death she felt as hollow and fragile as a reed. She missed her husband and coped as well as she could. One day at a time, right? That's what she told herself daily.

The children at the Center had been sweet, lots of handmade cards and heartfelt condolences. Harold Matley, the schizophrenic boy, had put his arms around her at lunch and held her much as she had once held him. What goes around comes around, she thought at the time. Later, in the privacy of her office, she cried when she remembered Harold's kindness. She cried easily these days.

"Jack, Jack, Jack," she said softly as she braked at a crosswalk for an elderly woman. Celia found herself saying his name a lot. It only made her sadder and she knew she should stop, but couldn't. She missed him terribly. They'd had their problems, and toward the end she'd even wondered if their marriage would work out. She still wondered, and this was the loss she felt most keenly, the undetermined future that would never be known, the loose ends of both their lives.

The entire staff from the Center had come to the funeral. So had the two women who worked in Jack's agency, Helen and Ruth. Helen had been quite emotional and awkward with Celia. Moreover, she chose that moment to press Jack's wedding band into her hand before turning away. That had shocked Celia. The night before the murder Jack had said he'd left it by the copier, but she and Ruth had searched every inch of that office. She'd wanted to bury Jack with his ring on. And here was Helen handing it over and acting as if *she* were the bereaved widow. Her behavior made Celia question if something had been going on between the two of them; and these doubts gnawed at the memories of her marriage and stained them with suspicion.

Before they'd left the cemetery Tony had lumbered up to say he was sorry. Celia assumed he meant about Jack's death, but then he'd gone on to say, "I just had no idea what we were dealing—"

She had put up her hand to stop him. "Not now, please." She didn't want to think about Boyce any more than she had to, though she knew his horrifying presence would haunt her forever.

Tony had mumbled an apology and walked away.

Ethan had overheard this exchange and sidled up to Celia. "I guess old Sasquatch put his foot in his mouth. God, that must have hurt, they don't call them Bigfoot for nothing."

A silly remark, and at times past she probably would have laughed. But not here, not now. She let him hug her, and then she left the cemetery alone.

She returned to the Center the day after the service. She could have taken time off but didn't want Davy to feel abandoned. She'd worked with him every day, including weekends. Tony had agreed to this readily. She'd also started seeing a therapist in Portland to deal with her own problems.

Last week Ethan had walked her out to her car, just like old times, and told her that he and Holly had split up.

Celia had rested her briefcase on the hood of the Honda and looked him in the eye. "Is it for sure this time?"

He nodded solemnly, and she placed her hand on his sleeve.

"I'm sorry to hear that, I really am."

"Thanks, but I didn't bring it up to get your sympathy."

"No, I know that, but I'm going to need some time, a lot

of time. I'm just not ready to get into anything right now."

He told her she could have all the time she wanted.

She'd listed their house and land with a local real estate office. The agent was a young woman who had been uneasy with her and looked away when she ventured that a sale would not come quickly. Celia understood: the violence, the deaths, the now unspoken forces that had driven her from the ridge would drive away others as well.

She told the agent to do what she could. The Griswold Agency also went up on the block. That was about the same time the shepherd burst through the door and demanded to see Jack. Ruth positioned herself at the counter and used her formidable presence to insist that he calm down. Then she explained that Mr. Griswold had passed away.

"Passed away. You mean dead?"

"That's right. There was a big story in the paper about—"

"I don't get no damn paper!" He slapped the counter. "Took me a long time to find him, and now he's dead. I got a claim against him too."

Despite his rough manner, and body odor that grew stronger as he stood there, Ruth offered to help him.

"Is it your car, your home?"

"No, it's my sheep."

"Your sheep?"

"Yeah, my damn sheep! Thirteen of them. My dog, too. He killed him just as sure as I'm here."

The shepherd's voice softened when he told her about little Bucky and the pound, but he bristled as soon as he started to explain how Jack had plowed his pickup right through the flock.

This struck a chord with Ruth, who recalled that Celia had mentioned just the other day that she'd dropped Jack's truck off at Marty's Body Shop to get some work done on the front bumper. She said she planned to sell it.

"Let me see what I can do, okay?" Ruth tried to smile and hold her breath at the same time.

"I want something done, and fast. Oregon's too damn crazy. I'm going back to California."

"Can you come see us tomorrow?"

The shepherd promised he'd stop by, and shortly after they opened the following day he walked through the door. Ruth handed him a generous check that Celia had authorized over the phone. He snatched it up and stared at it for several seconds.

"I thank you. This is fair, even if it don't bring back little Bucky."

Ruth tried to appear sympathetic as she backed away from the counter and fanned the air.

"Sir, Mrs. Griswold, she's the wife of the late owner, she had us make some calls to make sure there's enough money to replace the sheep and buy two prize Border collies."

He glanced at the check. "Yeah, I can see that, and that's just what I'm going to do. You tell her that." He turned to the door, then looked back. "She's a little lady, ain't she?"

"Compared to me she is, but that's not saying much." Ruth laughed, and the shepherd left smiling.

Ruth and Helen ran the agency while half a dozen potential buyers looked it over. Celia hoped it would sell quickly. She had no interest in running the business, and she didn't need the income; Jack had insured himself for two million dollars. But she did plan to stay in Bentman, at least for a while. She had fought for her own life, and now would fight for Davy's.

She had rented a room in a large Victorian in town. The two women who owned it—older, longtime companions—treated her well; and Celia felt safer there, though she doubted she'd ever feel truly safe again. Naturally, if her plans worked out she'd want to find a house of her own. A small one would do nicely as long as it had a yard.

She parked her boxy little car and limped up the courthouse steps. A sheriff's deputy was walking out and held the door for her. He smiled and asked how she was doing. She nodded and said fine. She had done and said that many times since the night Jack was murdered.

"You still up on the ridge?"

Celia shook her head. "I moved to town. Why, Jim, you want to buy my place?"

The deputy chuckled. "No, thanks, I think I'll take a pass."

"That's what they all say."

She asked if he'd seen Judge Walters this morning.

"Just a few minutes ago, heading down to his chambers."

The warmth of the old building felt good as she stepped inside. Indian summer had ended, and so far November had been cold and wet. As it should be, she thought. The Portland paper said the drought was over, and that the long rainy season had begun.

Juvenile Court Judge Harry Walters had scheduled Davy Boyce's hearing for ten o'clock. Celia had given herself extra time because she was determined to talk to the judge beforehand. It was nine-thirty when she knocked on his door. A long moment passed before he opened it.

"Harry, I wondered if I could speak to you for a minute or two."

Judge Walters paused before inviting her in.

Harry Walters bore a slight resemblance to Celia. Like her, he was short, willowy, and graceful in the manner of athletes blessed with a low center of gravity. She'd heard he was a long-distance runner and raced in the marathon up in Portland every summer. Good training, she thought, for trying to solve the endless problems of troubled children.

Celia claimed one of the two leather chairs in front of Walters's desk. A bronze scale of justice perched on the corner to her right. She noticed the blindfold and the extended arm.

Judge Walters pulled out his swivel chair as Celia glanced around the room. Though she'd known him for years, she'd never been in here. Dark paneling covered the walls, and the light that drifted through the closed window painted the room gray, like the day, the sky, her mood.

"So, Celia, how are you doing?"

She didn't answer his polite question. Instead, she fixed him with with a direct look that concealed her apprehension.

"I want Davy."

"Boyce?" The very sound of disbelief.

She nodded, and Judge Walters, relaxed and gracious only seconds ago, now glared at her.

"Celia, I can't believe you're doing this. You know I can't talk to you about the case unless everyone's present—the lawyers, the juvenile court counselor . . ." His eyes cut sharply to the door, as if to reassure himself that it was still closed. "I could be disbarred for even meeting with you like this. I had no idea that's what you wanted. I know what you've been through, but that's—"

"No, you *don't* know what I've been through!" Celia shot out of her chair and leaned forward. "And you don't know what Davy had to go through with Boyce, but I do, and that's the point." She pounded his desk hard enough to rattle the scales of justice. "I know what he went through because for one night I had to go through it too. And if anyone's earned some extra consideration it's that kid whose life you're going to be deciding on out there."

She snapped her fingers at the door but never looked away from Walters, who stared at the phone to his right. Celia feared that he'd call for a sheriff's deputy to have her removed. But then he asked her to sit down and lower her voice, and she took this as her cue to continue. She spoke quickly.

"Harry, he's talking to me. He's not talking to anyone else, and he *needs* someone to talk to. That's critical. Otherwise it's like his mind is in a prison except for the hour or two a day when we get to work together. The rest of the time he's locked up, and this is one kid you don't want to lock up. That's all he knew with Boyce. If he doesn't get full-time care he could spend the rest of his life in courtrooms. He doesn't deserve that. He deserves a good life, and I can give him that."

The springs sounded in Walters's chair as he rose. "I know he's responding to you, there's no question about that." He walked over to the window and stared at the street. It had started to rain. Fat drops splattered against the glass. Celia heard tires on the wet pavement, their sibilance and the silence that followed.

"Harry," she said softly as she joined him, "more than anything he needs love, and I've got that." Her voice broke, and she turned away as the tears came, tears of rage, tears of sorrow, too, and tears for the man Davy might become if he didn't get the help he needed soon.

Walters placed a hesitant hand on her shoulder, and Celia pinched the bridge of her nose and wiped her eyes.

"He sure didn't get any love from Boyce," she added in a husky voice.

"No, he sure didn't." The judge's hand dropped from her jacket, and then traveled to his chin as if he didn't know what to do with it.

"And the Kentsons can't do that much for him." Celia had met Davy's foster parents: fiftyish, good-hearted, but not especially bright or competent. She thought Walters must know all this too. She stood with her back to the window while he reclaimed his seat.

"They're good people," Walters said without much feeling, and Celia allowed that this was true.

Walters started to say something, then paused. She watched him study his appointment book before eyeing her carefully.

"This conversation *is* off the record, right?"

"Absolutely." She returned to her chair and sat down.

"All right, just so you know, I've looked at the staff reports and I do think Davy would be better off with you."

Celia released a deep breath. "I can't tell you how happy I am to hear—"

"Not so fast. It's not that simple. If we grant you custody we're probably going to have serious problems with some of the reporters who covered this case. It could put the court in a very awkward position. You must know that."

She nodded. The killer of the stepfather taking custody of the son, that's what worried Walters because that's how the world would see it. Celia blamed only herself. She had lied to protect the boy, and now was trapped by the kindness of her deception.

"Celia, those tabloid shows would be chasing Davy down the street again. I can't expose him to that. Once was more than enough."

She didn't need any convincing on this point either. She'd been appalled by the attention generated by the Boyce case, and the headlines—in print and on TV—that had followed. All that bizarre activity had terrified Davy, but she thought they could wait out the most irksome reporters because they also seemed to have the shortest attention span. She mentioned this to Walters.

"But if we play the waiting game, that means I can't grant you custody for a while."

"I know," she said glumly, "but if it keeps Davy from having to go through all of that craziness again, then it's worth it. Give it a few weeks, give it a month or two, if you have to. The reporters will forget about us. Something else will get their juices going. What's Bentman to them anyway? Some dying timber town, that's all. Then give me custody, do it on a trial basis if you have to."

Judge Walters thrummed his appointment book, then flipped the pages forward. He studied his calendar.

"I've got him down for a review in January. We could do something about giving you custody then."

Celia reached across his desk and shook his hand.

"Harry, you're a good man."

"But a lousy judge. I shouldn't be doing this."

"I think you're a great judge."

"My colleagues will have my hide if word ever gets out."

"Don't worry, it won't."

At two minutes to ten Celia walked into the courtroom. She spotted Davy sitting at a table with his attorney, the young woman Judge Walters had assigned to him. A long black braid ran down the middle of her back. Davy's hair looked very short next to hers. Yesterday at recess he complained about his crew cut, and Celia had rubbed his head and said that he could have any kind of haircut he wanted.

"That's your choice."

Davy beamed when he heard those words, and reached up nervously to feel his hair.

Now he turned around slowly. She thought he might be looking for her. She had told him she'd be there. She vowed always to be there for him.

When their eyes met, she smiled. So did he. And then she said a quiet prayer. For Davy. For herself. And for the baby she nursed within.